Praise for *London,*

'A VERY special book . . . It's gorgeous,
real, believable and BEAUTIFUL'
Marian Keyes

'Witty, well-paced and wonderfully entertaining,
with a heroine you really root for'
Daily Mail

'Funny, smart and gorgeously romantic . . . The perfect
read to make you smile on the rainiest of days'
Katy Birchall

'We adored this beautiful, nostalgic love story'
Fabulous

'The sort of book that sweeps you off your feet and
wins your heart with laughter, tears and the whole
cavalcade of city life . . . An unforgettable love story'
Jane Casey

'Such a glorious treat'
Harriet Evans

'Wonderful. An epic, enduring love story that is so
funny, tender and warm. I love everything about it'
Cressida McLaughlin

Sarra Manning has been a voracious reader for over forty years and a prolific author and journalist for twenty-five.

Her eight novels, which have been translated into fifteen languages include *Unsticky*, *You Don't Have to Say You Love Me*, *The House of Secrets* and her latest, *Rescue Me*, published in 2021. Sarra has also written over fifteen YA novels, and light-hearted romantic comedies under a pseudonym.

She started her writing career on *Melody Maker* and *Just Seventeen*, has been editor of *ElleGirl* and *What to Wear* and has also contributed to the *Guardian*, *ELLE*, *Grazia*, *Stylist*, *Fabulous*, *Stella*, *You Magazine*, *Harper's Bazaar* and is currently the Literary Editor of *Red* magazine.

Sarra has also been a Costa Book Awards judge and has been nominated for various writing awards herself.

She lives in London surrounded by piles and piles of books.

London with
Love

SARRA MANNING

HODDER

First published in Great Britain in 2022 by Hodder & Stoughton
An Hachette UK company

This paperback edition published in 2023

1

A CIP catalogue record for this title is available from the British Library

Paperback ISBN 978 1 529 33663 4
eBook ISBN 978 1 529 33662 7

Typeset in Plantin Light by Hewer Text UK Ltd, Edinburgh
Printed and bound in Great Britain by Clays Ltd, Elcograf S.p.A.

Hodder & Stoughton policy is to use papers that are natural, renewable
and recyclable products and made from wood grown in sustainable
forests. The logging and manufacturing processes are expected to
conform to the environmental regulations of the country of origin.

Hodder & Stoughton Ltd
Carmelite House
50 Victoria Embankment
London EC4Y 0DZ

www.hodder.co.uk

Dedicated to the late, great Sarah Hughes who knew a thing or two about growing up in the suburbs while dreaming of the city's mean streets. You are very much missed.

'The streets of London have their map, but our passions are uncharted. What are you going to meet if you turn this corner?'
Virginia Woolf

PART ONE

1986

I

September 9th, 1986
High Barnet Station

High Barnet was the end of the line. The end of the Northern Line. Though actually it felt like the beginning of nowhere. It wasn't even *in* London.

Jen, trudging up the steep slope from High Barnet station, prided herself on being a Londoner. It was an intrinsic part of who she was, like having blue eyes and not eating any vegetables except tomato and cucumber. Though her dad said that tomatoes were actually a fruit and her mum said that cucumbers were mostly water and had very little nutritional value and maybe she could just *try* a courgette, which was a bit like a cucumber and a valuable source of vitamin C and potassium. To which, Jen countered that if she needed vitamin C, she'd eat an orange. (Being argumentative was also an intrinsic part of who she was.)

When it came to being a Londoner, although Jen liked to think that she was a child of the mean streets of the inner city and the grimy alleys of Soho, the sad truth was that she lived in an outer London suburb. Mill Hill. It did have a London postcode, but the little 1930s semi where Jen lived with her mother and father and her hell-spawnish twin brothers was practically on the last street in London before London became Hertfordshire.

And while she might have gone to school in London, she'd actually chosen to do her A levels at Barnet College. In

Hertfordshire. But Jen had decided that she wasn't going to let that define her.

During the summer holidays, Jen had decided a lot of things and they all centred on her becoming someone new.

For instance, she'd stopped being Jennifer and become Jen. *Jen.*

There was something uncompromising yet mysterious about Jen. Those stark three letters could contain multitudes (or at least Jen hoped that they might).

There had been seven Jennifers in her year at school, but they'd all been called Jenny whether they liked it or not. She'd been Jenny R to most of her classmates and Jenny the Ginge to the gang of girls who'd done their best to ensure that if your schooldays really were the best days of your life, then Jen was due a refund. Besides, she wasn't even ginger. Her hair was auburn. Dark auburn. The same dark auburn as beechnuts or even conkers, but that wasn't the sort of subtle distinction you could point out when five girls were dogging your footsteps along corridors that reeked of disinfectant and boiled meat, chanting your name as you stood shivering behind a towel in the changing rooms and cornering you at the bus-stop.

No wonder Jen had read up everything she could on rheumatoid arthritis and had managed to convince the head of PE that her knees were crumbling and instead of netball or rounders, her time could be put to better use in the school library with an improving book.

That was all in the past. School was a memory. A series of unpleasant incidents Jen had already started to refashion and reframe into a handful of amusing stories that masked all the pain and loneliness of her early adolescence.

Now Jen could be the person she'd tried on at weekends and within the walls of her tiny box bedroom in that little mock Tudor house where daily life was punctuated by the steady roar of the motorway at the bottom of the garden and beyond the motorway, the railway lines.

Jen had moulded her new self from every book that she'd ever loved, from *Ballet Shoes* to *The Bell Jar*, and all the songs she listened to on the John Peel show on a tinny transistor radio under the covers. But new Jen had only been fully realised a few short days ago after a shopping trip, funded by the money she'd saved from babysitting and a summer holiday job in a photocopying shop in Edgware. There'd also been a one-off clothing allowance from her parents, who knew they'd lucked out in the genetic lottery with their eldest child and only daughter. Yes, Jen was argumentative and from an alarmingly young age had specialised in flouncing out of rooms, stomping up the stairs, and slamming her bedroom door but that was the worst of it. She tolerated her younger brothers, Martin and Tim, she'd come in from school and after doing her homework, would make a start on cooking (a vegetable-free) dinner and as she'd failed to make any real or meaningful friendships at school, she rarely went out. Without any pernicious peer pressure, Jen had never drunk alcohol, smoked or hung around with boys in parks and railway stations. Or got pregnant by one of those boys.

So there'd been only mild dissent from her mother at what Jen considered an essential college wardrobe. A prized pair of Levi's 501s, turned up twice to show to better advantage her new eight-hole, black Dr Martens boots, two stripy T-shirts, a collection of garish patterned skirts and dresses from charity shops, which her grandmother had taken up for her so they came to that sweet spot between the knee and mid-thigh. There was also a huge baggy Aran cardigan purloined from her dad's wardrobe along with the Crombie coat he'd worn when he was a teenager. Completing the transformation was a full collection of Seventeen make-up from Boots (no more using the Marks & Sparks palettes that she got every Christmas) along with the usual back to school kit: pencils, pens, notebooks and folders.

Jen was wearing her DMs, Levi's and a Smiths T-shirt with the cardigan today and lightly perspiring as she walked past a chip shop, past the Courthouse, past a newsagent's. Early September was too warm for a very hairy, very heavy wool cardigan but Jen had wanted to make a great first impression. Because today truly was the first day of the rest of her life. School was behind her. Ahead of Jen was the freeform, organic life of college. There were no timetables, nobody taking the register or shouting at you for running down the corridors.

It was a whole new beginning. Or it was meant to be, except an hour later, as the A level English literature class gathered in a first-floor room in the main college building, Jen felt like she might just as well be invisible. No one seemed to notice her at all, even though she'd purposely placed a copy of *Bonjour Tristesse* in the original French on the table in front of her. She'd found it in a charity shop in Paddington and though she'd got a B for her French O level, she was struggling to make much sense of *les travailles de Cecile*. But what was the point of pretending to read *Bonjour Tristesse* in French if no one was there to see Jen do it and think to themselves, *Oh my God, that girl is so mysterious, so fascinating, so cool? I must become friends with her immediately*.

Unlike school with its old-fashioned desks with inkwells and lift-up lids arranged in serried rows, the tables and chairs were arranged in a haphazard horseshoe with their tutor (no teachers here) at the front. There were twenty students, two to a table – Jen was sharing hers with Miguel, a strapping, biracial boy with an easy, drawly American accent, who had angled his chair away from hers so he could trade insults with his friends at the next table.

Jen kept her eyes down and focussed on the other book she'd brought with her, a copy of *Longman English Series: Poetry 1900 to 1975*. In the orientation pack that had been posted out, they'd been instructed to choose a poem from the anthology that spoke directly to them.

Jen rested her chin on her hand as she listened to most people rattle through the rhymes and rhythms of John Betjemen's verse. 'A Subaltern's Love Song' was proving particularly popular. One boy, Rob, a raw-boned, sultry-lipped youth with a quiff, insisted on reading 'This Be The Verse' by Philip Larkin even though it wasn't one of their set poems 'because they've fucked me up, my mum and dad.'

Jen's hands twisted anxiously under the table as a pretty girl across the room read out 'The Fire Sermon' from T.S. Eliot's *The Waste Land* in a breathless, compelling voice suggesting she was probably part of the Theatre Studies gang – the gang that Jen felt a particular affinity with, though she'd rather have rectal surgery without an anaesthetic than stand on a stage proclaiming.

'Jen? What have you got for us?'

It was Jen's turn to scrape back her chair and stand up in front of nineteen utterly disinterested students and the long-suffering gaze of Mary. Mary was their twenty-something tutor who had a nice line in flowy, flowery dresses, had already overshared about her boyfriend and was just the kind of quasi authority figure that Jen could really respect.

'I'm going to read "Lady Lazarus" by Sylvia Plath.' In her head Jen could orate with the best of them; outside of her head she just wanted to get through the poem as quickly as possible in a sub-audible monotone. Especially when Mary pressed her lips tight like she was trying to flatten the smile, which matched the glint in her eyes. As if every year, there was a bookish girl who didn't mix well with others and had decided that Sylvia Plath spoke to her and only to her. As if Jen wasn't special at all.

But still 'Lady Lazarus' was Jen's favourite poem from her favourite poet and as she read, spitting out words like feathers, her voice grew louder and clearer, throbbing with the emotion of not just the poem written by a woman who was so wronged and beaten down that she'd take her own life a few months after writing it, but of all the emotion and energy it took just to be a sixteen-year-old girl. Also, Jen had red hair and, like, Sylvia Plath, she too cut a tragic figure.

There was silence for seven seconds (because Jen counted them in her head) and then Mary said, 'Very nice,' and pursed her lips as if she was hiding another smile. Jen collapsed into her chair then tried to collapse in on herself, hunching over the desk, all her weight resting on her elbows, her face mostly obscured by her hands.

Jen didn't eat men like air, not at all. Also, why would you even want to? But she did capture a strand of her hair between her fingers, so she could chew on it, a nervous habit that she still hadn't grown out of.

There was just one more poem to be read aloud, by some-one called . . .

'Nick?' Mary queried. 'You weren't at orientation last week.'

'I wasn't,' Nick agreed.

Jen had been so busy worrying about reading out loud and hunching in on herself and sucking her hair that she hadn't even noticed him. But now he was all she could see. Like every other person in the room had ceased to exist. They were just filler. Background noise.

Nick was tall and skinny, lanky arms folded, long legs stretched out in front of him. He was wearing a leather jacket, a proper leather jacket, like James Dean was wearing on a post-card which Jen had stuck to her bedroom wall, tight jeans and pointy-toed boots. His dark hair was long enough that he could push it back from his face with his fingers, to reveal cheekbones like geometry as Lloyd Cole sung in 'Perfect Skin.' He had a beauty spot above his mouth, on the right. Just one brief but all-encompassing glance was enough for Jen to know that she wanted to press her lips against it until the end of time.

Jen looked away, face aflame, not that anyone was staring at her; they were all staring at him. Nick. Because he was equal parts beauty and danger and because he was arguing with Mary, even though she was a figure of quasi authority.

'What if a poem didn't speak directly to me?' he demanded, holding the book up to his ear, like it was a shell and he wanted to hear the sound of the sea.

'Well, then I'd say that you're not trying hard enough,' Mary said. Jen felt slightly vindicated that she was pursing her lips again, as if this too – a beautiful, bolshy boy arguing about the set text – was something she had to put up with every year. Maybe she played student bingo with the other lecturers during lunch. *Yes, I had Sylvia Plath girl, five points to me.* 'What about some Louis MacNeice? One day, years from now, you'll appreciate what a work of . . .'

'But it isn't years from now.' Nick put the book down and reached from under the desk to lift up a ghetto blaster. 'There's other kinds of poetry. I'm going to plug this in, yeah?'

He didn't wait for Mary's reply, an amused 'knock yourself out,' but got up and looked around for the nearest socket. It was right behind Jen, who forced herself not to turn around even though the rest of the class didn't have any problem with swivelling around, craning their necks to unabashedly stare as Nick crouched down to plug in his equipment.

Jen couldn't even begin to imagine what might speak to this boy's soul. Maybe something by Allen Ginsberg? No! He was more of a Rimbaud type. Or Baudelaire might be his thing. In which case, why couldn't he just read it out loud like the rest of them?

There was a decisive clunk as he pressed down the play button. A crackle and hiss, a tambourine tapping out a beat, familiar, delicate chords that Jen knew so well, then a woman singing in a strong Germanic accent. 'I'll Be Your Mirror.' Third song on the second side of *The Velvet Underground & Nico*. It was a love song. A song about someone seeing all the things that you hid away from the world and loving them, loving you . . .

Jen turned round in her chair to see Nick still crouched down, marking the beat on his knee, his hair obscuring most of his face, and Jen sighed a little. He looked up, as if that tiny gust of expelled air had reached him, dark eyes locking on to Jen's face, and she couldn't look away until Miguel sitting next to her shifted position and thumped his elbow on the edge of the table.

Miguel swore, the song finished, Nick raised his eyebrows at Jen in what seemed like a challenge and the moment was gone.

Jen wished it had never started.

'That's it for today. I want you to write me two pages on your chosen poem by Thursday,' Mary said, as people gathered up papers and pens and shoved books in bags. 'Rob, Nick, that would be two pages on a poem from your set poetry book.'

Jen scuttled for the door, then for the safety of the girls' loos. It was busy in the gap between lessons but it emptied out quickly enough so she could stare at herself in the mirror. She'd been experimenting with a green correction stick to tone down the red in her complexion but she could never blend it in properly so she always had a faintly bilious tinge to her face.

Nothing that some powder wouldn't fix. Jen dabbed at her cheeks with the whitest powder Boots had to offer but still her ruddy moonface stared back at her. She added more eyeliner, more mascara, still not sure of what effect she wanted to achieve, only knowing that she hadn't achieved it yet.

As she carefully applied Miners frosted lilac lipstick, the door opened and the girl who'd read from *The Waste Land* walked in. Or rather she caught sight of Jen and paused as if Jen's presence in the loos, at the mirror, was something she hadn't expected. Then she nodded at Jen, who waited for her to go into the cubicle then ran the cold tap so neither of them would be embarrassed.

Jen planned to leave immediately but she was delayed by a smudged streak of mascara and a voice from the cubicle. 'So . . . what did you think of all that?'

It seemed wrong to be starting a conversation while you were having a wee. Whenever Jen went Up West with her grandmother, she was always shouting to Jen from the next cubicle in John Lewis and it was always mortifying.

'Think of what?' Jen asked, over the sound of the toilet being flushed.

'That boy. Nick.' The door was unlocked and opened and the girl caught Jen's eyes in the mirror again. 'So pretentious. What was that song anyway?'

' "I'll Be Your Mirror." It's by The Velvet Underground. It's on the album with the banana on the cover,' Jen explained.

The girl shook her head like that simply couldn't be true. She was elfin thin in black and white stripy top, black 501s and black monkey boots. Her glossy black hair was pulled back in a swingy ponytail and her deep brown eyes didn't need massive amounts of mascara and liner to make them huge and doe-like; they did that all on their own.

'Never heard of them,' she said dismissively of the band that all the other bands interviewed in *NME* always name-checked. Jen had expected them to be noisy, dense and without any proper tunes, but when she'd risked dropping a five-pound birthday record token on that album with the banana on the cover, she'd found eleven songs that spoke directly to her soul. Or maybe only ten on account of the fact that one of the songs was called 'Heroin' and she was firmly in the just say no camp. 'I'll ask Rob. Rob's really into music. He says that he never misses the John Peel show.'

I listen to John Peel! Jen's subconscious screamed. Jen just nodded.

'So, you never said what you thought of him? Of Nick?' the girl prompted. She had an eager look on her face as if Jen's opinion would clarify everything.

Jen thought back to him brushing behind her chair. The slight displacement of air. How she couldn't look at him, but had been so painfully aware of him. Already she'd memorised the exact placement of that tiny, devastating beauty spot on his upper lip, the curve of his cheekbones, how his fringe obscured his eyes but when he'd swept his hair back, she wanted to drown in their depths.

'He's not for me,' she blurted out because it was the truth. He looked older than the rest of them and while Jen understood and recognised Rob's scrubbed good looks and the semiotics of his quiff and Smiths T-shirt, Nick put the fear of God into her. 'Boys like that. They're not . . . I don't think . . .'

'Pretentious?' the other girl persevered, but it wasn't just pretentious, though actually playing a Velvet Underground poem in an English literature A level class instead of reading out a sonnet by Siegfried Sassoon was the very definition of pretentiousness.

It wasn't even that Nick was out of her league.

It was his carelessness, his casualness, callousness. Boys like that would hurt you. Jen didn't have any experience of boys like that; she didn't have any experience of boys at all.

But she had plenty of experience of people who didn't care what other people thought of them. The girls at school who'd made the last five years of her life low key terrible. Sue, from across the road, who said what was on her mind, even though what was on her mind was usually unsubstantiated gossip about the other people who lived on their little stretch of suburban street. Her grandfather, Stan, who said the most devastating things without ever thinking about the damage they wrought. When Jen had been five and parading about a Southend beach in her first bikini, Stan had said that she looked like a right little porker and hadn't backed down even when Jen cried, even when his own wife and daughter had stood up to him for once. Rarely did anyone stand up to Stan; life was easier that way. But to this day, whenever Jen tried something on for the first time and stared at herself in the mirror, she always asked herself if she looked like a right little porker in it. Sadly, the answer to her jaundiced eye was usually yes.

So, Jen knew a thing or two about careless people and how they could hurt you, which was why she'd already decided to stay out of Nick's line of fire.

'He's just not someone I would ever be friends with,' she said firmly.

'Me too!' The girl gave Jen a good, hard look, frowning slightly as her gaze came to rest on the frosted lilac lipstick. Then she nodded. 'I'm Priya. You can hang out with us. Come on!'

Jen picked up her black canvas haversack adorned with badges and hefted it over her shoulder, while Priya held the door open for her with an air of impatience as if usually someone was holding the door open for *her*.

'Who's us?' Jen asked.

Us was Priya, Rob and George, a lesser version of Rob, still with the quiff and the Smiths band T-shirt but pudgier yet weedier, a smile on his broad open face as he pulled out the chair next to him in the college canteen.

'Your three favourite Smiths songs?' he asked eagerly, catching sight of the badges on Jen's bag as she sat down.

It was everything that Jen had dreamed college might be as she and George debated their favourite Smiths songs and why *The Queen Is Dead* was a better album than *Meat Is Murder*. Rob had given Jen a tight, not altogether friendly, smile when she first sat down but soon he joined in. Only Priya was quiet though Jen kept trying to pull her into the conversation.

'So, new friend, what's your name?' Rob asked, when it was time for Jen's French A level class while the three of them planned to hang out in the canteen for a while longer.

'I'm Jen,' she said firmly, as if no other versions of herself had ever existed.

*

And just like that, Jen had friends. What she hadn't achieved in five years at secondary school, she'd managed to master in one morning at college.

During free periods, she and Priya would go to Boots on the high street to try out eyeshadows on the backs of their hands or to the tiny little Topshop, even though they had the same clothes in there, week in and week out. Otherwise, they'd sit in the canteen and Priya would provide a running commentary on everyone in their eyeline. Who she liked, which was a very short list – basically all the Foundation Art students and a very select few of her fellow Theatre Studies extroverts.

Then she'd move on to who she didn't like, which was a much longer list. All the students 'who are too thick to do A levels'. That included the girls who were studying Tourism & Travel or Hair & Beauty, with their Sun-In and their stone-washed jeans. And the boys, who were studying Electrical Engineering and Plumbing, and were really rowdy and always having big, shouty not-quite-pretend fights.

Mostly, Priya wanted to talk about Rob. What he was wearing that day. What he'd said to her that day. How he'd looked while he was saying it. The long and detailed subtext to what he was saying. 'It's not like I fancy him. His big thick lips, they're all rubbery.'

Rob didn't have rubbery lips. He had perfectly ordinary lips. But Jen wasn't going to point that out, because even to Jen, who'd never been kissed, never been anything with a boy, it was pretty clear that actually Priya did fancy him.

When Jen wasn't with Priya, she was with George. There were eight or nine charity shops on Barnet High Street and they visited them all at least once every two days. They'd pop into Our Price on the corner, to be condescended to by the guys who worked in there. Then they'd visit Harum Records at the other end of the high street; the staff were friendlier and they had a box of old seven inch singles, which were reduced to 60p.

Finally, they'd settle in the café across the road from the college, to sit upstairs with a scone and a cup of coffee each. Jen didn't like coffee but now she was sixteen, it was imperative that she learned to drink something hot that wasn't hot chocolate.

'Every time you take a sip you look like you want to cry,' George would always note. Trying to encourage her tastes to something older and more sophisticated had to be worth spending 65p on a cup of bitter bilgewater and forcing it down. It took Jen's mind off George who used these café chats as an excuse to talk about Priya. About how beautiful she was and how lustrous and shiny her hair was and were her parents strict because he wasn't being racist but Indian parents tended to be quite strict and maybe Priya wasn't allowed boyfriends, but if she were allowed boyfriends then did Jen think there might be a chance that the boyfriend could be George?

'Has she said anything to you?' he'd ask hopefully.

Jen would take another sip of coffee, screw her face up at the taste, and shake her head. 'We don't really talk about boys. Unless it's to bitch about the Electrical Engineering students.'

Rob's name was never mentioned, but on some level, George had to know he wasn't the one Priya wanted. He *had* to.

Some days Rob even joined them on their charity shop/record shop trawl. 'Haven't you read that?' he'd ask incredulously when Jen triumphantly plucked a copy of a book from the carousel in the North London Hospice shop. No matter whether it was *Tender is the Night* or *Valley of the Dolls*. 'Wow!'

'Yeah, actually I preferred their earlier stuff,' he'd say without fail when George would spend some of his hard-earned weekend job money (he worked in the hospital canteen and spent most of his time being made fun of by the older women on his shift) on a new single that he'd heard on the John Peel show the night before. 'That single isn't bad. But it's just, you know, quite pedestrian.'

The four of them even had their own preferred table in the college canteen, along the wall next to where the Foundation Art students congregated but not so close that it looked like they were obsessed with them. Although maybe the four of them were a little bit obsessed with them because the art students were older and cooler and if there were art students who weren't that cool, then Jen never noticed them. She only noticed the girls who wore paint-stained boiler suits, patterned scarfs tied around their back-combed hair. And the boys! With their leather jackets and long fingers clutching high tar cigarettes.

The art students all looked a lot like Nick – so Jen wasn't surprised when she saw him hanging out with them. Priya had done some not-at-all-discreet digging and had discovered that Nick had done the first year of A levels at the local boys' school then crashed out after spectacularly failing his summer exams. Now he was forced to repeat the whole year again with people younger than him, people whom he didn't acknowledge with so much of a flicker on his impassive face.

Most days Jen cycled to college, which took twenty-four minutes exactly. Then she'd wedge and lock her bike into the rack, which was situated next to the entrance of the art block, right at the back of campus. Separated from the main college building by a small grass square, as the weather grew colder, damp autumn seeping in, there were very few students loung-ing on the lawn. Most mornings, Jen saw Nick huddled with a couple of other boys on the stone wall that edged the grass, as they had one last cigarette before classes began. Nick held his cigarette between his thumb and forefinger, like he was used to having to quickly conceal it if someone spotted him. Not that anyone cared. You were even allowed to smoke in the canteen.

Jen would act as if she didn't care either. When she'd real-ised that she'd be spending the next two years in the same English A level class as Nick Levene, she was relieved that she was already clear in her mind that, like peas and pastel colours, Nick was not for her. He wasn't someone she would ever speak to. She'd make do with gazing at him from a distance. Jen didn't mind having crushes that would never amount to anything. On the contrary, she was entirely comfortable with the bittersweet pangs of unrequited love for boys she'd never even spoken to. So, if her face was bright red in the mornings when she hurried past him and his art boy buddies, it was simply because she'd just cycled four and a half miles and hadn't had time to apply her green colour corrector concealer. That was all.

2

December 12th, 1986
Brixton Station

College life hummed along in a pleasurable way. Jen liked the subjects she was studying for A level. She liked that she had friends that she actually hung out with after college and even on the weekends, when she wasn't babysitting. She liked her life and she particularly liked not having a permanent knot of dread lodged in her stomach as she had done when she'd been at school.

Yes, everything was just fine. Until The Smiths announced that they were playing Brixton Academy.

There had been military campaigns which had taken less planning than going to see The Smiths at Brixton Academy. After much debate, George and Rob were entrusted to go to Brixton to buy the tickets the day they went on sale. Jen and Priya then spent long hours planning what they would wear, finally settling on a slightly fancier version of what they normally wore: flowery dresses with black tights and DMs. That was as dressed up as they got, as anyone would get.

On the actual day of the gig, Friday the twelfth of December, in the year of our Lord nineteen hundred and eighty-six, tattoo the date over her heart, Jen and George planned to get to the venue early, queue until the doors opened and then run to the front, (saving a spot for Priya and Rob who were too in awe of their Theatre Studies tutor to skive) and stay there no matter what. 'At the end of the gig we might even be able to get up on stage,' George mused as they left college at lunch-time. It was the first time either of them had ever bunked off but they'd decided that missing one History lesson would have no lasting impact on their results when they took their A levels eighteen months later.

On the tube, they talked about the gig. What songs they might play. If there might be new songs. If it was true that Johnny Marr had damaged his wonderful, god-given, guitar-genius hands in a recent car crash and might not play at all. George did try to talk about Priya at one point, but Jen shut that down pretty quickly. Only the day before when she'd given Priya her overnight bag (Priya's dad was picking them up after the gig and Jen would stay the night at Priya's) so Jen could be hands-free for the gig, Priya had launched into a long monologue about how George was 'really getting on my nerves. He keeps staring at me. I'm not being big-headed, Jen, but he's not in my league.'

'Yeah, I get that,' Jen had said noncommittally because if that was how she felt, then it was up to Priya to tell George. Jen wasn't going to be the messenger. Nothing good ever happened to the messenger.

So as soon as George started with the Priya-worship, Jen nudged him extra hard and pointed down the other end of the tube carriage. 'Isn't that one of the Jesus & Mary Chain?'

George's head swivelled a full one hundred and eighty degrees, eyes gleaming. Then he gave a disappointed sigh. 'No. I think it's someone who really, really likes the Jesus & Mary Chain.'

They got to Brixton just before 2 p.m., on high alert to any danger, as they exited the tube station. They were in South London for one thing and South London might just as well have been a foreign country. Plus, they'd had riots in Brixton the year before so they were both wary that there might be people on the verge of rioting at 2 p.m. on a winter's afternoon, Molotov cocktails held aloft, that sort of thing. There weren't. Just the usual collection of people you'd see on any London high street. Old women shuffling along with shopping trolleys. Two men on a fruit and veg stall shouting, 'Six oranges for a pound! Lovely apples! Come and get your tomatoes!' A gaggle of boys in school uniform pushing and shoving at each other.

As well as possible riots, George had been worried that he wouldn't remember where the Academy was, but it was literally in front of their eyes. He wanted to start queuing right away but Jen persuaded him that the queue wasn't that long and the doors didn't open for ages and then they'd have another long wait. They went to Wimpy for something to eat, though George warned Jen not to drink anything because then she'd need the loo.

'It's different for boys,' George explained as he watched with narrowed eyes as Jen sipped the orange juice that was accompanying her hamburger (no ketchup, no pickle, no lettuce) and fries. 'We're like camels. We can hold it for hours.'

For someone who'd whinged about having something to eat first, George munched his way through an entire Wimpy Grill, then a Brown Derby, all washed down with gallons of Coke.

Then, even though she didn't need to, Jen went to the loo while George tutted impatiently and looked at his watch because he obviously didn't have a grandmother to teach him about the benefits of an insurance wee.

Finally, they joined the queue that snaked around the side of the Academy. George tried to do a headcount of the people in front who would ruin their plans to stake their place right in front of the stage. Jen shivered because she wasn't wearing a coat – her mother would kill her – just her nicest flowery dress and a black cardigan, which was no match or barrier against the chill December winds. There were two boys next in line who'd travelled down from Newcastle and Jen listened as they chatted to George, though the conversation mostly consisted of them taking turns to shout out a band's name, the more obscure the better, and then waiting to see what the reaction would be. None of them wanted to be caught liking a band that wasn't cool so they usually decided that most bands were awful. Apart from The Smiths.

'I bet you're only here because you fancy Morrissey,' one of the Newcastle boys sneered at Jen who waited for George to jump in and defend her; he didn't and then the boys went back to their interminable conversation about the cover for 'What Difference Does It Make?'. Jen couldn't wait for the doors to open so she and George could lose them. She was half tempted to lose George too.

Over an hour later, a ragged cheer went up and the queue started to move. They inched closer, ever closer, to the entrance then it was a mad rush of showing their tickets, being patted down by a security guard (ugh!) for any recording equipment then George took hold of Jen's hand and she forgot that she was angry with him and they ran through the foyer, through the doors and into a still almost empty auditorium. A mad fifty yard dash for the stage. They didn't get right to the front, but were second from the front. Jen clasped her hands together and jumped up and down because she was close enough that if the crowd shifted, she'd be right in Morrissey's eyeline. Close enough that she could stretch out her hand and maybe he'd pull her up onto the stage . . .

In half an hour, the hall quickly filled up so it was a sea of blurred figures behind them. The floor sloped downwards and as Jen kept looking out for Priya and Rob, she could see that there were people at the bar at the back of the room, people gathered together in clumps by the door, and above them in the balcony people were sitting down.

'What's the point of going to see a band if you're going to sit down? You might just as well let someone who really appreciates them have the ticket,' she said crossly.

'I bet those people are really, really old,' George added scathingly and Jen forgot that she was still a little bit mad at him as they bonded about how sad it was that anyone over thirty would go to a gig when they were clearly far too decrepit to enjoy it.

'Clinging to the last vestiges of youth,' Jen sniffed, as the music stopped and the lights dimmed and she thought her heart was going to leap out of her chest. George gripped her hand really tightly but let go as a band came on who were very definitely not the Smiths.

'Pete Shelley. He was in the Buzzcocks,' George told Jen, like she didn't already know that and she was back to being a little mad at him again.

When the crowd surged forwards, it was all Jen could do to stay upright. She'd never been right down the front before at such a large gig. In fact, it was a secret she'd take to the grave, but the only other gig she'd been to was Duran Duran at Wembley Arena with her mum and they'd been stuck in the rafters.

Eventually she figured out how to move with the crowd and when they played 'Ever Fallen In Love' Jen found herself singing along with gusto. There was something freeing about being one tiny part of a huge whole; they had a commonality, a shared purpose, so that it felt as if she really and truly belonged for maybe the first time in her life. It wasn't The Smiths, not yet, but it was almost perfect until George bellowed in her ear.

'God, I really need a wee!'

Jen was unmoved. 'You're just going to have to hold it in.'

George managed to tie a knot in it for the rest of the set but when Pete Shelley and his band left the stage and an impatient roar rose up, he shook his head unhappily. 'I have to go. Save my place!'

'How am I meant to do that? And where are Priya and Rob?' But George had already been swallowed up like he'd never even existed.

But Jen wasn't on her own because they were all there together. They all loved the same thing: the same four people and the music they made.

The crowd waited. Jen was wedged against the wall of bodies in front of her and hemmed in from behind too. She could feel excitement rising from the soles of her DMs sticking to the tacky floor to the top of her head, the ends of her hair already soaked with sweat.

Still they waited. Screaming in anticipation as the roadies carried instruments onto the stage, taped setlists to the floor, adjusted the height of the mic stand.

Just when Jen was starting to think that it would never happen, the lights dimmed again and 'Take Me Back To Dear Old Blighty' the old music hall song repurposed as the intro for *The Queen Is Dead* gently plink-plonked through the PA. Jen's blood itched in her veins because suddenly *they* were there.

Mike Joyce crashed his drums and they began to play and Jen couldn't even hear the song over the rushing in her head and the roar of the audience until Morrissey with a black cardigan wrapped around him started to sing.

Instead of being a solid mass of bodies, the crowd suddenly separated and Jen was knocked sideways again and again, as her prized spot was snatched away by boys. Not even boys. But men, burly men, arms and legs akimbo, thrashing and falling as they turned the front of the stage into a moshpit. More and more of them materialised, launching themselves through the crowd. Jen got an elbow to her head; someone twice her size slammed into her ribs and she quickly became desperate to get out of there.

She hadn't even noticed that there were hardly any girls down the front, just a mass of testosterone and XY chromosomes. As she frantically tried to twist her body this way and that and wriggle through almost imperceptible gaps that opened up in the seething mass, Jen was startlingly aware that she was a girl. Painfully too, as a hand clamped down on her breast hard enough to make her gasp, hard enough that it would leave a bruise and she could only free herself by digging her nails into the phantom hand until she was free.

Jen managed to shift a few steps further back until she was caught in another pocket of mayhem and flailing limbs. Someone's drink hit her shoulder and someone's hand was suddenly between her legs. She looked up into a laughing leering face and stamped on his foot so that he let her go and pushed her so hard that she rocked back.

She desperately tried to stay on her feet. If she went down, she'd never get up again. Not with any of her bones still intact. She couldn't understand how an hour ago they'd all been one, together, and now she was in the middle of a brutal battle. She slid on the lager-slicked floor, clutching at people to stop herself from pitching further forwards until there was yet another hand on her.

'Are you trying to move back?' someone shouted in Jen's ear.

'Yes!' she yelled and they took her hand, leaning over her like a human shield and guiding Jen backwards, stumbling up the sloped floor until there were people no longer behaving like the barbarian hordes but watching the band, moving to the music, singing along. Having a whale of a time. Jen kind of hated them.

'Are you all right?' asked her rescuer. Sweat was stinging her eyes. Jen wiped at them futilely with a sweaty hand. She was, at this point, 90 per cent sweat as she realised she'd just been saved from a bloody, untimely death by Nick Levene.

'I know you.' Her voice was so hoarse she could hardly form words. 'From college.'

'Oh, it's you,' he said, pushing back his hair to peer into her sodden, ruddy face. 'So, really, are you all right?'

'I'm fine,' Jen assured him, nodding her head so that the soaked ends of her hair slapped wetly against her cheeks. At least it wasn't possible for her to get any redder. 'Thanks. Sorry. You're missing everything.'

She was missing everything too. She'd spent the last month dreaming about this hour and a half, where she'd be in the same room, breathing the same air as her idols. None of this was what she'd imagined. She also imagined that Nick would leave now that she was no longer at risk of death by moshpit but he stayed standing next to Jen as the band played on.

Despite the horrific experience she'd just endured, when they launched into 'There Is a Light That Never Goes Out' Jen was so caught up in the emotion of the song, of the call to what was basically a joint suicide pact that she could hardly bear it.

She glanced sideways at Nick. He glanced back at her, so for one moment, they shared something real and meaningful and perfect. He nodded his head in acknowledgment that he'd felt it too then turned his gaze back to the stage and for the rest of the set, they weren't two strangers who took English A level together twice a week; they were together.

The Smiths left the stage after a triumphant, tribalistic

'Panic' and Nick turned to Jen again. 'Are you getting the tube home?' he shouted over the frenzied applause.

Jen was still caught up in the spell, so it took a while to adjust to the thought of the world outside with its tube stations and long journeys home and friends that you'd got separated from.

'I'm getting a lift,' she shouted back, looking about as if Priya might emerge from the throng. She didn't and before Jen could even wonder at where she might be, The Smiths were back for a rousing rendition of 'The Queen Is Dead', the guitar a discordant wall of sound, Morrissey brandishing a placard that said, 'Two Light Ales Please'.

Nick looked at Jen and she looked at him looking at her. 'Shall we?' he asked, holding out his hand and even though she was covered in bruises and her ankle was throbbing and she'd wake up the next morning with a black eye, she let him pull her back into the crowd so they could dance. Like they were waltzing on *Come Dancing*. He twirled her, she spun him; at one point they danced cheek to cheek and sang along, their voices loud, her throat sore until the music crashed to a halt, Morrissey whipped off his T-shirt and Jen stilled in Nick's arms. He let go of her instantly and suddenly it was awkward.

'You should go and find your lift,' he said, but this still wasn't over.

The band were back *yet again*. Jen and Nick stood side by side for 'William It Was Really Nothing', arms touching for the final, *final* song, 'Hand In Glove'.

Johnny Marr bent over his guitar to wring out the last notes as Morrissey picked up the mic stand like he was about to hurl it into the crowd. He didn't and then he too was gone. The Smiths were gone. Never to return.

The lights blazed on.

Jen blinked like a mole above ground for the first time. People pushed past on their way to the exit but she and Nick stood there for another minute, still trapped in a spell from the music, the strange half hour that had brought them together . . .

'Right, I need to get my stuff out of the cloakroom,' he said and without another word, not even a nod, he turned and walked away.

. . . and now they were apart.

Jen's feet were stuck to the floor. She prised them free and squelched to the door that led to the foyer. She was still covered in a fine film of sweat, her thin dress clinging damply. She'd tied her black cardigan around her waist but it was long gone and her whole body hurt. Like the time her grandfather Stan had sneered in the face of a best before date and insisted that the peach yoghurt that had been in the fridge since God was a boy was perfectly fine and Jen needed to stop being such a fusspot. She'd spent the next twenty-four hours puking and her ribs had felt as if someone had taken sandpaper to them. Much the same way that they were feeling now.

Jen limped into the Baltic wastes of the foyer. She did one sweep of the perimeter but she couldn't find Priya or Rob or George and even though she'd sweated out pretty much all the water content of her body, she needed a wee, which involved a long queue for the ladies.

Small waves of panic were eddying through her aching limbs because Priya was her ticket out of there. She couldn't wait to get back to Priya's huge house in Winchmore Hill, where warm clothes and central heating awaited, along with everything Jen needed for a sleepover. Except it was an overnight. Sleepovers were for kids.

All Jen had was her travelcard, a small purse with hardly any cash in it and her front door keys, all stuffed into the money belt from her old school uniform, which her mother had insisted she wear under her dress. At the time, Jen had protested that she could take a little bag with her but that would inevitably have gone the same way as her cardigan. She felt like phoning Jackie to tell her that but really so she could hear her mum's voice. Then Jen would probably cry and confess that she couldn't find the others and she was alone in South London where there had been actual riots the year before.

It was such a tempting thought, though it was gone ten and her mum was usually tucked up, lights out, at 9.30. Jen even looked around the lobby for a payphone and that was when she saw the three of them standing to the side. Frozen in a little tableau, which didn't need subtitles. Priya was biting her lip, arms folded, Rob looked triumphant, unashamed, with his arm round her waist and George's head hung heavy. Then he took off his glasses so he could wipe his eyes.

Jen took a step towards them, mouth still forming the words, 'I've been looking for you everywhere!' but she wasn't moving forward, mainly because someone had their fingers clamped round her wrist.

'I'd stay well out of it if I were you,' Nick said, his voice low and urgent. But this time Jen didn't need rescuing.

'They're my friends.'

'Maybe not,' he smiled without humour. 'Nothing like a messy love triangle to break up the old gang.'

Jen turned away and stumbled towards George. He was the one who needed her right now. He looked stunned, as if little cartoon stars should be circling around his head. 'What's going on?' Jen asked though it was pretty obvious what was going on.

'You said that you were going to tell George,' Priya said, her huge eyes had never looked more doe-like. 'You promised that you'd say something.'

'I never promised that,' Jen said and Priya gasped as if she couldn't believe it.

'Why would you lie about it?' Rob piped up and for someone who always had an opinion on what everyone else should have been listening to or reading, he was playing this very low-key. 'Priya said that you'd have a friendly word with George.'

At the mention of his name, George threw Jen a wounded look like a baby bird that had just fallen from the nest and wasn't sure if she was going to pop him back or grind him underfoot. 'You had a hundred opportunities to tell me,' he said, which was true because there had to have been at least a hundred times when he was banging on about Priya.

'This has nothing to do with me,' Jen insisted, putting her hands on her hips for extra bolshy emphasis. 'I didn't say anything to George because I was never told to.'

'But I specifically asked you if Priya was interested in me . . .' George reminded Jen, which was true but it was also true that Jen had always quickly changed the subject because she didn't want to get involved and the subject was boring.

'I suppose this is because you thought you had a chance with Rob.' Priya sniffed as if the tears weren't far away. 'That would have been really convenient. Me with George, you with Rob . . .'

'Except I absolutely don't fancy you,' Rob said, each word a death knell for Jen's self-worth, even though she absolutely didn't fancy him either. 'And wow! You kept that quiet.'

'It was obvious,' Priya said when the only obvious thing was that she was a bitch. What was that word Mary used to describe someone with unscrupulous cunning and dishonesty like Iago in *Othello*? Machiavellian. She was a Machiavellian bitch. But a Machiavellian bitch who was meant to be giving Jen a lift back to her house for the night.

'Look, I think there are a lot of ... everyone is very confused and maybe we should sort this out tomorrow. Or even better, on Monday,' Jen said reasonably even as she wanted to choke on the injustice of it all. 'Also, I don't fancy you, Rob. We're just friends like me and George are just friends, right, George?'

Jen gave George a friendly punch on the arm but he reared back like she'd right-ended him on his BCG scar. 'Fuck off, Jen!' he spluttered. George was always so bumbling and polite that Jen had never even heard him even say the f-word and it was horrible to hear it now, especially when it was aimed at her.

George staggered off, weaving unsteadily through the fast dispersing crowds like he was drunk even though he'd told Jen that once he'd drunk half a pint of shandy then had to go to bed for the rest of the day to sleep off a ferocious headache.

'Yeah! Fuck off, Jen,' Priya said and finally Jen understood. It was much easier to assign Jen the role of villain than for Priya to admit that she'd toyed with George's affections when all the time, she was after Rob.

'Actually, we should both fuck off,' a voice said from behind Jen because apparently Nick Levene had been standing there this whole time so he could bear witness to Jen's total humiliation and a lot of slanderous accusations being thrown her way. 'If Priya isn't going to give you a lift home ...'

'I would rather die,' Priya exclaimed, which made Rob gave her a wary look but he deserved everything that was coming to him.

'We're going to miss the last tube, if we don't hurry,' Nick said and he made a gesture with his hands, ushering Jen towards the doors.

'We'd better get a move on then,' Jen said, like she was well used to catching the last tube home when in reality this was the latest she'd ever been out. And then without waiting to see if Nick was coming with her, she walked away, body already hunched over in expectation of the gusts of icy wind that rose up to greet her. At least if she ended up with hypothermia she wouldn't have to go to college on Monday.

3

December 12th, 1986
Edgware Station

'I can't work out which one of them you're in love with? Rob or Priya or your devastated friend with the glasses?' Nick asked when he caught up with Jen.

She pushed back the bedraggled hair from her face so he'd get the unexpurgated version of her best glare. 'I'm not in love with any of them. They're my friends.'

'Looks like you're going to have to find some new friends then.' Nick had been much nicer when he was saving Jen from being trampled underfoot. She couldn't believe that this was the same boy who'd waltzed with her an hour ago. Now, like everyone else, he was behaving like a dick and so Jen allowed herself to hate him. Silently. Seethingly.

She hated him all the way to the tube station, all the way down the escalator and onto the tube. But he didn't take the hint, just sat next to her, long legs stretched out as Jen stared at the reflection of the two of them in the dark windows of the train.

She looked awful. Her hair was limp, damp and frizzy, downcast face pudding-like. Jen's only consolation was that, for once, she was quite wan instead of glowing like a Belisha beacon.

So much for new Jen. And her new life and her new friends. New Jen was just a thinly-veiled disguise for old Jenny the Ginge.

'You cold?' Nick nudged her with his elbow because he didn't realise that her shiver was actually a shudder of despair. Though actually she was cold. In fact, she was freezing. He dumped a pile of white cotton in her lap. 'You can wear this, but try not to get it too sweaty.'

'This' was a Smiths T-shirt, with the dark green *Queen Is Dead* cover printed on it. She gratefully pulled it on with a sound from the back of her throat that was *thank you but I'm still hating you*.

Even though smoking had been banned on the tube a couple of years before, Nick pulled out a crumpled box of Marlboro cigarettes from one of the inside pockets of his leather jacket. 'Do you want one?'

Jen shook her head. 'I don't. Also, you're not meant to.'

He shrugged. 'Suit yourself.'

Nick was a proper smoker. He had a silver Zippo lighter instead of fumbling with boxes of matches like Rob did when he smoked. Rob held the smoke in his mouth for a count of five but Nick properly inhaled then breathed out with an air of deep satisfaction like smoking was the greatest thing in the world. He obviously had never seen those slides of blackened lungs that Jen had been shown at school by a lady who'd started off lecturing them on the perils of smoking before moving on to the dangers of being sexually active, which consisted of slides of gonorrhoea-infected genitals and a quick precis on the various types of contraception available. 'But none of them are one hundred per cent effective and so the best way not to get pregnant or contract herpes is to simply not have sex.'

Jen really didn't have to worry about the dangers of being sexually active. She couldn't help but sigh. Nick nudged her again. It was starting to get annoying. But also his leg was brushing against hers and he was leaning in close so she was overwhelmed by the smell of cigarettes and leather.

'What?' Jen grunted.

With the hand that was holding his cigarette, he gestured at the Victoria line map above the seats opposite them. 'Where do you need to change? Do you get the Piccadilly Line?'

'You what?' Jen leaned forward and squinted at the stations. 'Northern Line. Euston.'

'High Barnet branch?'

'Edgware,' she said. 'And you?'

'Edgware.' He didn't sound very happy about the prospect of her charming company for much more of the journey home. Not that Jen could blame him. 'Well, Mill Hill, but Mill Hill East station is a bit useless if you live in Mill Hill.'

'I do. Live in Mill Hill,' she admitted. 'But nowhere near Mill Hill East station.'

'Then we need to change here,' Nick said as the train pulled into Euston station.

It wasn't very busy. Only a few stray Smiths fans about as Nick walked decisively down the platform, Jen tagging along a couple of steps behind him like a dutiful concubine. He seemed to know where he was going, which was the Northern Line platform, a High Barnet train showing on the indicator board, followed by an Edgware train seven long minutes after that. They sat down on a bench. Nick lit another cigarette.

'I don't even know what time the last bus goes from Edgware,' Jen wondered aloud.

Nick shot her an exasperated look. 'You're not going to get a bus,' he said witheringly like getting a bus was a really weird thing to want to do.

'The 113. It will drop me at the top of the road. Or nearly at the top. I live off Apex Corner.' Living off Apex Corner, one of the busiest roundabouts in North London and one of the reasons why her mother refused to learn how to drive, indicated that Jen didn't live in the nice bit of Mill Hill.

'Oh, I live off the Broadway.' He named a street full of big detached houses that was round the corner from the doctor's surgery Jen went to. 'Anyway, you can't get a bus. The buses are finished this late.'

'You're joking. That's just ... it doesn't even make any sense.' Jen contemplated the long and painful murder of the faceless and idiotic person at London Transport who thought it was a good idea to make sure that the buses stopped running before the last tube trains had got to their final destinations. 'I swear to god, that when I'm grown up, I'm going to live next door to a tube station.'

'Yeah, right.' It wasn't a sneer but agreement. For a brief moment they were back in sync, simpatico again. 'So ... Priya said that you said I was pretentious.'

'I said what?' Jen shook her head, not just in denial but because she couldn't have heard right. Also ... 'Since when do you have cosy chats with Priya?'

'She loves a cosy chat, does Priya,' Nick revealed. 'Also, she's Ravi's cousin. You know Ravi?'

Everyone knew Ravi. He was a college celebrity: one of the Foundation Art students, who always wore a moss green velvet jacket, and had a coterie of the prettiest second year A level girls who'd sit with him in the canteen or the café across the road and hang off his every word.

'Yeah, I know Ravi and I never said you were pretentious.' Jen was all ready to launch into an impassioned speech about how it was Priya who'd said he was pretentious but there'd already been too much 'I said/No, you said' tonight. And also, she didn't want to remember what she *had* said about Nick. That he wasn't for her. He was beyond Jen's realms. Right now though, as they waited for the last tube out of Euston (which would be a sight as welcome as the last chopper out of Saigon), they were very much of the same realm.

'*You're* pretentious,' Nick said and he definitely didn't mean it as a compliment but Jen couldn't help taking it as one. 'You and your Sylvia Plath poems.'

He was giving her a depth, an edge, which she absolutely didn't have.

'Says the boy who was too fancy to read a poem so he played The Velvet Underground instead,' Jen scoffed.

'You know who The Velvet Underground are?' He didn't bother to hide his surprise.

'Yes of course I do.' Jen waited for him to come out with the usual guff that boys did. That Rob would. About how he preferred their earlier stuff and that she probably didn't appreciate the nuances in their work, but Nick just shrugged.

'Cool,' he said. 'And I'm not pretentious. I'm discerning.'

'And Priya is what Mary would call an "unreliable narrator".'

'You're probably right,' Nick conceded just as the indicator board showed that the Edgware train's arrival was imminent. Jen leaned forward to see a glow lighting up the tunnel, then two ghostly pinpricks of light came into view and the mice on the tracks scurried away to safety.

The train was almost empty. By silent agreement they grabbed one of the pairs of double seats in the centre of the carriage, sitting opposite each other so Nick could sprawl out and Jen could prop her feet up on the seat, like the rebel she really wanted to be.

It was her favourite stretch of tube line. The journey was underground until just before Golders Green when the train would suddenly hurtle into daylight (when it was actually daylight) and take her by surprise every time. It wasn't the most thrilling of scenery to look at – roofs and chimney pots and dilapidated office buildings – but then the train would plunge tunnelwards again after Hendon, only emerging just before Colindale and, rather thrillingly, the Police College. If you were lucky, you might even see some plucky cadets on the assault course, but now it was all darkness as she stared out of the window at her own distorted reflection.

They sat in silence but Jen couldn't think of anything else to say to Nick and she was growing increasingly more concerned about the last leg of the journey.

She could call home and her dad would come and get her. She had no doubt about that, though it would lead to having 'A Talk' and she didn't want to have to explain that she was back to being Old Jenny again. Jenny No-Mates. Her mother always took Jen's disappointments on her own shoulders as if they were a direct result of poor parenting. It was also very close to Christmas and if this strange night ended up in sanctions then Jen didn't want the new hi-fi that she'd ringed in the Argos catalogue to be withheld.

She could walk home. It wasn't *that* far. It would probably take half an hour and it was mostly walking down a big main road, which was well lit enough that no one could drag her down any dark alleys and do something awful to her.

The only other option was to take a minicab and Jen had never done that before and didn't have the money to pay for it. Maybe Nick was getting a cab and she could owe him the fare until next week.

'This is us,' Nick said unnecessarily as the train crawled into Edgware station. Jen was stiff and sore as they hobbled through the deserted station and outside to where there wasn't a single bus to be found. Not one. Nick had already warned her, but now that all hope was gone, Jen realised that she'd still been harbouring just the tiniest amount of hope.

There was a big estate car idling at the kerb, which flashed its lights. Nick held up his hand in greeting because that was obviously his lift. Jen looked around for a payphone.

'I'll see you then,' Jen said. 'Thanks for everything.'

Nick shook his head like she was the most annoying person he'd ever met, though Jen was sure that she wasn't. After all, he'd met Priya too, hadn't he? 'Don't be a twat,' he said gently. 'Of course my dad will give you a lift home.'

Jen didn't make even a token protest but limped over to the car. Nick opened the back door and a blast of warm air hit her.

'Hi. Hello. I'm Jen,' she babbled as she climbed in and almost had a little cry as her bottom was instantly nestled in cushioned leather. 'Thank you so much.'

'This is Jen,' Nick echoed as he sat in the front seat and slammed the door shut. 'I said we'd give her a lift. It's on the way.'

'I live off Apex Corner but you can just drop me off at the slip road past the motorway bridge and I can walk from there. It's only five minutes.'

'Don't be ridiculous.' Nick's dad said sharply. Jen couldn't see him properly just a dimly lit view of his profile but that was sharp too. 'I'll take you to the door. Obviously.'

Classical music was playing, something a bit tinkly yet discordant. It was the only sound in the car. Jen knew for a fact that if her dad had picked her up, even though he'd be wearing his navy blue anorak over his pyjamas, even though he'd be cross with her for waking him up and dragging him out, he'd have wanted to know how her night had been. Had she enjoyed herself? And was she completely mad going out without a coat?

But Nick and his dad didn't say a word to each other and the first person to speak was Jen as they approached Apex Corner and the big glowing Happy Eater sign before the Shell garage where he needed to turn off.

She'd never been so pleased to see her little house come into view and had the door open before the car had even come purring to a halt. 'Thank you. Thank you so much,' she whispered fervently. 'I'm so grateful.'

'That's all right,' Nick's dad finally said as if it wasn't all right and was in fact a major imposition, but she didn't even care because she was home, a minute and a flight of stairs away from her own bed.

'See you Monday, Sylvia,' Nick said, without turning around.

'I thought her name was Jen,' his dad said as Jen closed the car door as quietly as she could.

She expected the car to drive away but it wasn't until she'd hurried up the drive, managed to extricate her key from the money belt, which had chafed something rotten and had the front door open, that she heard it accelerate away.

PART TWO

1988

PART TWO

1938

4

Bank Holiday Monday
August 29th, 1988
Mill Hill East Station

'I don't know why you want to spend your birthday at that fella's house, when you should be spending it with your family,' Grandpa Stan said, as he'd been saying for most of the day.

'It's four in the afternoon. I've spent most of the day with you. I deserve some time off for good behaviour, don't I?' Jen demanded huffily because spending most of the day with her grandfather was torture. Everyone thought so, so she didn't know why her mother and grandmother were giving her a pained look even as Stan's florid face went from red to purple.

'You might be eighteen today but you're not too old to put over my knee for a good wallop,' he choked out. Then he couldn't say anything because he was rooting in the pocket of his zippered cardigan for his 'puffer', the asthma inhaler he'd insisted he didn't need for years until he ended up in casualty and was diagnosed with irreversible scarring of his lungs. But oh no, Stan Hamilton always knew best. 'Think you're better than us because you got some A levels and you're going to university. Well, I'll tell you something for nothing . . .'

He paused for another huff, while Jen stood there rolling her eyes because Stan telling her something for nothing had been a recurring theme ever since she'd got an unconditional offer to study English at Westfield College, an outpost of the University of London just off the Finchley Road. She could still live at home thanks to the 113 bus, which was why Jen had wanted to go to Manchester University instead. But then she'd have rent to pay and money was always tight, even though her mother had gone back to work once the twins had started secondary school.

They hadn't realised that even with the two salaries coming in Jen still qualified for the full maintenance grant, so she'd accepted the offer from Westfield and Stan had been furious about it ever since. He'd have been furious with whatever Jen had decided to do that wasn't a secretarial course.

'No man is going to want some smart-arse girl who thinks it's above her to iron a shirt,' he told Jen now with his second wind. 'You think you're so clever.'

'That's enough, love,' Dorothy, Jen's grandma said as firmly as she dared. 'Quite right that Jen's going to celebrate her birthday with her boyfriend. She's spent far too much time with us oldies, as it is.'

'Not my boyfriend, just a friend who's a boy,' Jen said a little wearily because it didn't matter how many times she said it, the message never seemed to get through.

'I'll see you off,' her mum said, getting up from the dining table.

'He always has to be horrible,' Jen muttered because Stan's hearing was infuriatingly sharp. 'It's my eighteenth birthday. I did all right in my A levels – why can't he be pleased for me?'

Jen knew why. Because her grandfather had led a narrow life full of bad luck and bad judgment for which he blamed everyone but himself. By the same measure, he couldn't bear to see anyone else doing well for themselves. Not even his only granddaughter.

'Tell me about it,' Jackie was saying now. 'Wouldn't let me go to grammar school, even though I passed the eleven-plus.

Then he made me leave school at fifteen to get a job because he said that I was only a girl and I didn't need an education.'

Jen tried not to show her impatience but she'd heard this sad story so many times. Times that had increased exponentially now that she'd achieved the academic accomplishments that had been denied her mother.

'But then if you hadn't left school when you did, you might never have met Dad at the offices of North Thames Gas and then you wouldn't have had me,' Jen pointed out, as she always did at this point in the conversation. 'You'd have deprived the world of *me*! What a tragedy that would have been!'

'Well, I suppose there's that,' Jackie agreed, a faint glimmer of a smile breaking through. 'And your brothers too.'

'Oh, I'm sure the world would have managed just fine without them,' Jen said as they both listened to the high-pitched tones from upstairs where Martin and Tim were playing on the Nintendo and, judging by the sound of a couple of thumps and a pained 'Ow! What did you do that for?,' one of them was losing and not taking it very well.

Jen picked up her bag from the bottom of the stairs – still the same black canvas haversack but now it was tattered and completely obscured by badges – then checked her reflection in the hall mirror. Eighteen didn't look that much different to seventeen even with the new red lipstick from her grandparents: Chanel, to match the bottle of Chanel No. 5 that her parents had bought her.

Jen didn't really like the smell of the perfume but it was *Chanel* and her parents had really tried to step out of their lives and into hers to buy her a present that she'd love.

Now, she frowned as she checked that her hair was perfect. She always backcombed the front section into a quiff then pinned and secured it with a brightly patterned scarf, nicked from Dorothy's huge collection of scarves, which smelt of

Yardley's lavender and camphor balls. Her two flicks of liquid eyeliner were even, Jen decided, then frowned again as she caught Jackie looking at her while she looked at herself.

'What?' Jen asked a little defensively. 'I know you think it's too much make-up but . . .'

'Oh, Jenny, you look so beautiful. You've become a stunning woman,' Jackie said, producing a tissue from her bra so she could dab her eyes with it. 'I can't believe how much you've blossomed in the last two years and you've got such a lovely shape. It's all that cycling.'

'Shut up Mum,' Jen hissed, turning away from the mirror and her distinctly not beautiful reflection. She was always going to be less than other girls. She was even less than her own mother. Jackie's hair was a more vibrant shade of red, her eyes bluer. And then there were all the ways that Jen was much more than Jackie, who was five foot tall and weighed eight stone so that next to her, Jen always felt like a heffalump. 'Don't call me Jenny. And get off me!'

Jackie had her arms tight round Jen so she could plant kisses on her face, not just out of emotion for the special day but because she knew that it would annoy Jen. Borne out by the next words to leave her mouth: 'You *are* beautiful but I still say that someone could have died in that dress. And do you have to wear those big clumpy boots? It's August for Christ's sakes.'

'Not that again.' Jen shrugged out of Jackie's embrace and smoothed down her dress. There was a vintage stall in Camden, which had rails of thirties, forties, fifties and sixties dresses for a fiver each. Jen particularly loved the thirties dresses with their novelty prints; she had a black crepe dress with dancing poodles on it, but this dress, her favourite, was a fifties day dress, in a cheerful royal blue with big white polka dots, short sleeves, a blouse collar and pockets. She sincerely hoped that no one had died in it. 'I'm going.'

'Have a nice time,' Jackie said, delving into her bra again. She treated her bra as an extra pair of pockets; secreting tissues, shopping lists, even the odd Murray mint and, on this occasion, a ten-pound note. 'In case you need to get a cab home.'

'I have birthday money,' Jen protested, but she still took the very crumpled and very warm tenner, her other hand on the door handle as she tried to make her escape.

'You've got your phone card and you've written down the number of the cab company? Not the one on the parade, they're awful, but the one in Hale Lane?'

'Yeeeessssss . . .' Jen let herself be pushed out of the front door. 'Yes. Don't wait up.'

'Don't be too late then,' Jackie called out as Jen hurried down the cracked crazy paving. 'And I don't care if it is your eighteenth birthday, don't drink too much.'

'Love you,' Jen said, raising her hand, which didn't count as any kind of agreement that she wouldn't drink too much.

With Throwing Muses on her Walkman and her DMs striding fast, it wasn't long until Jen was on the doorstep of an imposing Arts and Crafts style detached house. It had gables and interesting angles and stained-glass inserts in its windows. Original fireplaces with pretty tiles inset on either side. Unlike Jen's house with its anaglypta wallpaper painted in Dulux's Hint Of A Tint Barley White, this house's rooms were painted deep, dark colours like mustard and a heavy blue to offset all the original wood panelling on the walls and the herringbone parquet on the floor.

And in this house there was *stuff* everywhere. Instead of having just one painting on the wall (at Jen's a reproduction Canaletto hung above the faux mantelpiece), there were huge smudgy paintings all over the place. In the kitchen, which was so big that it had a settee as well (they called it a sofa), was a huge table with piles of newspapers on every surface. They got *The Times* and the *Guardian* but no one seemed to ever read them, whereas the Richards got the *Daily Express*, even though Jen complained that it was right wing dross. Alan had been reading the *Rupert* cartoon since he was a kid and Jackie loved Jean Rook's column.

At Jen's house they always kept their fruit in the fridge, while here fruit was put in a bowl so that there was always the pervasive scent of bananas past their prime in the air.

Yes, Nick Levene was still in a different realm to her, but even so, Jen was ringing his doorbell then waiting to be granted admittance to his house.

There was also far less parental intervention at Nick's. His father, Jeff, was hardly ever there as he was too busy operating on the ears, noses and throats of North London and when he was, he barely acknowledged Jen's presence. His mother, Susan, said that Jen should call her Susie but when Jen did, 'Susie' looked like she wanted to punch her in the throat. Also, whenever she opened the door to find Jen on the doorstep, as she did now, her face collapsed a little.

'Oh, it's Jennifer. Again,' she said with a gritted smile even though she'd been told many times, many, many times, that it was Jen. Then she just stood there, not exactly blocking Jen's way but not exactly welcoming Jen into her well-appointed home.

'Did you have a good holiday?' Jen asked. Susan and Jeff had just come back from a fortnight in Greece. Nick had been left home alone, as his older twin brother and sister (being the lonely only sibling of twins was something Jen and Nick had in common) had joined a group of old school friends in Tuscany at a villa somebody's aunt owned. The Levenes were the kind of people who always knew someone abroad they could stay with, but anyway they had Jen to thank for the fact that their house hadn't been trashed when, of course, Nick had thrown an impromptu party. As it was, a couple of glasses had been smashed and someone had thrown up in Susan's herbaceous border but it could have been so much worse if Jen hadn't turned away a lairy group of gatecrashers by pretending that she didn't speak a word of English and refusing to let them in.

Much like the way that Susan was still body-blocking Jen. 'Lovely holiday, yes. Thank you,' she added rather grudgingly. 'Paxos is so unspoilt by tourism.'

But weren't Susan and Jeff tourists? Jen took a step forward, 'So . . . is Nick in?'

With a sigh, Susan stood aside. 'He's mouldering away in his room,' she said, like that came as any surprise.

Jen made her way up the stairs, the banister smooth under her fingers, to the second floor (because of course the usual two floors wouldn't be enough), where Nick had his lair. Music leaked out from under the door at the end of the corridor. He always listened out for the doorbell when Jen was expected, not that he could ever stir himself to actually come downstairs and let her in, and had 'Jennifer She Said' by Lloyd Cole and The Commotions cued up for when Jen pushed open the door.

'I've been expecting you.' He always said that too. He was sprawled on his bed and leafing through the new issue of *NME*, the Primitives staring back at Jen from the cover

Jen flung herself down on the sagging leather chesterfield. It was ripped in places and she knew to stick to the right-hand end. The other end had a rogue spring, which had torn more than one of her dresses. 'Glad to see you're making the most of the gorgeous August sunshine,' she said drily because the curtains were closed, though the sun was doing its valiant best to break in through the gaps in the drapes. 'You must be seriously vitamin D deficient.'

'I'll live,' Nick said though he looked practically consumptive. Like a modern-day equivalent of *The Death of Chatterton* as he lay on his side, propping himself up on one elbow so he could watch Jen as she rooted through her bag for menthol cigarettes and a lighter. Another reason why she preferred to come to Nick's rather than make him come to hers. Her parents had no idea that she smoked, because also buried in her bag were extra strength Polos, a can of Impulse (though the Chanel No. 5 would do instead) and if Jackie ever complained that Jen reeked of fags, Jen insisted at great length that it was because everyone else was smoking but her. 'Want one?'

Nick screwed up his face at Jen's packet of Consulate. 'Those aren't proper cigarettes.'

Jen shrugged. 'They're minty fresh.'

There were other, more compelling reasons that Jen preferred running the gauntlet of Susan to hang out in what Nick referred to as his garret, because he was still really pretentious.

Jen's room was tiny. It was more of a boxroom with room for only a couple of boxes, three at the maximum. There was the bed, which took up all of one wall, with just enough space at the end that she could sit on it and use the double aspect windowsill as a desk. Then, on the other wall was a built-in wardrobe and next to that a chest of drawers with her stereo perched on it. Outside on the landing was a set of shelves for her books and records.

Obviously, Jackie and Alan weren't happy about Nick coming round to lounge on their daughter's bed, but there really was nowhere else for him to sit. Jen had to keep the door open, which meant her parents would complain about the noise from her stereo but, as they were always telling Jen, they had to learn to compromise. Then there was Martin and Tim finding every excuse to loiter on the landing and make kissing noises.

But Nick had a huge room with a double bed and his own bathroom. An en-suite! Jen hadn't even stayed in a hotel room with an en-suite before.

His walls were painted black but were mostly obscured by posters: The Smiths. The Velvet Underground. The Rolling Stones. The Jesus and Mary Chain. Jen had so many happy memories of the last nearly two years, which all centred on curling up on the battered leather sofa, while Nick played whatever new record he'd bought that week. *Surfer Rosa, Strangeways Here We Come, Rattlesnakes, Sound Of Confusion, Darklands* and older stuff: *Forever Changes, Kick Out The Jams, The White Album* . . .

Best of all there were no annoying little brothers, no pained demands from the foot of the stairs to turn 'that racket' down and no argy-bargy about keeping the door open.

But even if the door had been kept firmly shut, Jen and Nick wouldn't have been doing anything they shouldn't. Apart from the smoking, and legally, she was old enough to smoke even if her parents didn't approve. Now, she lit up, sucked in, held it for a count of three and blew out. It might be bad for you (although mentholated cigarettes couldn't be *that* bad), but smoking was cool and that was all there was to it.

Nick went back to the *NME* so Jen was free to stare at him. His hair was so long that it was a wonder that he could see through his fringe. He could easily be one of the boys from one of those bands that he loved so much. Even off-duty, he was still wearing a Stooges T-shirt, tight jeans and his pointy-toed boots . . .

'Here you go!' Jen's silent and discreet gazing was interrupted by Nick abruptly sitting up so he could reach behind his pillow then throw something at her, which she failed to catch. 'Happy Birthday!'

'You shouldn't have,' Jen muttered, reaching down to retrieve whatever it was. 'It's no big deal.'

'It's the hugest deal,' Nick insisted, swinging his legs round so he could rummage through the debris on his bedside table. 'Jackie and Alan's little girl has officially become a woman.'

'Piss off,' Jen said, her fingers finally closing around the missile, which had ended up under a knackered old coffee table. All the old furniture in the house eventually found its way up to Nick's room. 'Aw, you made me a mix tape.'

Nick made the best mix tapes. Full of songs from albums that Jen couldn't afford to buy and songs that she'd heard once on John Peel and songs that she didn't know anything about but they quickly became her favourite songs, the soundtrack to her life. All Nick's mix tapes had titles, this one was called 'Jennifer In Blue'; the cover featured an impossibly beautiful woman from the thirties or forties shot in black and white.

'Jennifer Jones, actress,' Nick said, without Jen needing to ask. 'You know I love a conceptual mix tape.'

God, yes, his pretentiousness knew no bounds.

'I also got you a few other bits and bobs,' he said nonchalantly, and Jen smiled coolly, like this was still no big deal.

The other bits and bobs consisted of an old edition of *The Bell Jar*, much older than the copy that Jen had bought a couple of years ago, the font gothic yet stark, the only other adornment a crushed rose. 'Well, that's cheery,' she said brightly. There was also her very own pleasingly chunky Zippo lighter ('so you won't keep nicking mine') and a set of three French school exercise books or 'cahiers' as they said on the front. 'For all the notes you're going to take as a student of English literature,' he said, peering over a pair of imaginary spectacles at Jen.

'I love them,' she said, holding the notebooks to her chest. 'I love everything.'

He hadn't spent a huge amount of money on her. There wasn't even a birthday card. There were no Chanel logos but these gifts showed that Nick understood her better than anyone else in the world. He knew the secret heart of her.

'No one likes a gusher, Jen,' he said mildly, now sorting through the detritus on top of his chest of drawers and grabbing keys, wallet and cigarettes. 'Come on, we should go.'

Nick didn't even bother to say goodbye to Susan or give her a rough approximation of when he might be home. 'We're not talking,' he said to Jen out of the side of his mouth like he didn't really want to get into it, as they walked towards the Broadway.

'Because of the A level results,' Jen said in a voice that was more neutral than Switzerland during the Second World War, but it was still enough to make Nick curl his top lip.

'I didn't want to go to university anyway,' he said as he'd been saying for as long as Jen had known him. 'I'm already a year behind.'

Jen didn't point out that a lot of people now took a gap year (though Alan and Jackie had been both aghast and bewildered at the idea). She also didn't point out that Nick hadn't done one lick of work for his A levels. If he'd put in even the minimum amount of effort, he'd have got C grades but he hadn't even done that.

'So, what are you going to do then?' she asked.

'Got an interview for Tower Records.'

They'd come to the bus stop. Jen craned her neck to see if there was a bus coming then turned back to Nick. 'Working in Tower Records would be cool,' she said, because she always tried to be supportive of Nick's choices even when she didn't agree with them. University was the pinnacle of achievement.

A good education was a foundation for a successful life. It was the one chance everyone had, no matter where they came from, to become something, someone, better. And Nick had had so many more opportunities than Jen. Prep school. Tutors. Public school. Maybe the most annoying thing was that he was really smart, without even trying, whereas Jen had gone to the little primary school at the end of her road then the nearest comprehensive and she'd had to work and work, make endless revision schedules, read so many books to get her three A grade A levels and yet here was Nick determined to throw everything away. 'How much is the staff discount?'

'It doesn't matter how much the staff discount is. Jeff and Susan are packing me off to Essex,' he said, as the 240 nudged its way under the bridge and Jen dug into her bag for her purse.

'Essex? That's a cruel and unusual punishment, isn't it? What's in Essex?'

Nick stuck out his head as the bus approached. 'Apart from a lot of girls in white stilettos and blokes in shell suits with footballer haircuts?'

'Yeah, apart from that?'

The bus pulled in and they got on. It wasn't worth going upstairs for the short ride to the station but Nick said that the downstairs was for pensioners and children so Jen took the stairs, hand clutching her skirt to her. Not that Nick would try to look up it, but still . . .

'They're paying for me to do the NCTJ course at Harlow.' Nick slumped down sideways onto the seat in front of Jen's. 'National Council for the Training of Journalists,' he elaborated further. 'They seem to think that I'm going to work on a local paper.'

He said local paper in the same way that Jen would say sewage farm or kiddy fiddler. 'Grim. Can't see you doing death knocks and writing up school fetes.'

Jen was sure that many words had been said and that this solution had come only after a lot of door-slamming from Susan and nostril-flaring from Jeff. She couldn't help the tiniest shard of resentment that niggled at her because Nick, once again, had had something handed to him on a silver platter. They were *paying* for him to get qualified. If Jen's family had been expected to pay the university tuition fees then there was absolutely no way that she'd be going to university.

'Is there a music journalism module you can do?' she asked. Nick shook his head and slumped even further.

Jen stared out of the window. She always preferred the 240 to the 221, because it went on a scenic route around Mill Hill village before getting to the station. Today, the twee houses and the duck pond weren't the distraction they should be because Nick was in a mood and it was ruining the only day of the year when it was all about her.

'Though you could just be a music journalist now,' Jen persevered though she didn't really know why she was bothering. 'Julie Burchill was sixteen when she started writing for the *NME* and Tony Parsons was only a little bit older than that. Go to a gig, write a review, send it in.'

Nick found the strength to hook his arm over the back of his seat. 'It's not that easy.'

'What could be easier?' Jen was bored with this conversation, but she was never bored of looking at Nick, especially when he was pouting like he was now. She wished that she'd put her sunglasses on so she'd be free to stare longingly without him realising.

'You really think I could?' He rested his chin on his arm so he could stare up at her. 'I know you say my writing's good but you have to say that.'

'I don't have to say that,' Jen insisted because she liked to think that her feelings for Nick were deeply undercover. After all he wasn't her boyfriend; he was just a friend who happened to be a boy. 'You know I tell it like it is. For instance, it's my birthday and you're being a dick.'

Nick doubled down on the pout then sat up. 'You're right, I am being a dick. It *is* your birthday and for the rest of the day I'm going to celebrate you.'

Jen waved a hand in front of her face like he was being ridiculous but also to fan away her blushes. 'Are you still being a dick? It's hard to tell.'

'I'm not very good at sincerity. And I haven't even congratulated you on your amazing A level grades, which you didn't even need because you got an unconditional offer.' Nick grabbed Jen's hand so he could try and wave it, but she pulled away with a wary look. 'God, I'm being genuine. Even Susan was impressed, but mostly she was annoyed. "Jennifer's going to university, is she? What does her father do again? That's right, he works for the Gas Board whereas your father is a top-class surgeon and you got Ds and Es."'

Nick's sour lemon face and voice was a pretty accurate representation of his mother. God, Susan really was a bitch. And now that Nick had celebrated Jen a little, she could afford to be magnanimous, downplay her achievements. 'I might be going to university, but I'll still be living at home, remember? No wild nights in the Student Union bar for me.'

'Well, I'm not exactly giddy about the Harlow nightlife. They've got a couple of decent music venues but I'll be back in London every weekend so we can still hang out,' Nick said casually, as Jen's heart lifted. 'Unless you'll be too busy with your new university friends . . .'

'Hardly,' Jen said with a sniff, as the bus sailed past the big Institute for Medical Research, then The Watchtower, the Jehovah's Witness headquarters, on its descent towards Mill Hill East station. 'Come on! There might be a train waiting.'

Nick uncurled himself from his seat with as much speed as he was capable of. They lurched along the bus and ran down the stairs, twisting to see if they could see the station through the window.

'Oh, yes! There is a train!' In her excitement, Jen pressed the bell three times and bore the wrath of everyone on the lower deck shooting her daggers and the driver shouting, 'All right, all right. Keep your hair on.'

At last, the bus pulled into the stop. Never had the doors opened so slowly. Jen and Nick leapt down from the bus, all ready to dart across the road but had to pause as a 221 nosed in behind the 240 and watch the train slowly, tauntingly, move off without them on it.

'Fuck!'

'So annoying!' Jen scowled. There was nothing to do at Mill Hill East but catch a tube train out of there.

It was a weird one stop outpost of the High Barnet branch of the Northern Line. Instead of going all the way to High Barnet, every fifteen to twenty minutes there'd be a Mill Hill East train that would deviate from the usual route at Finchley Central. If you missed one, then you'd be stuck waiting for a good fifteen minutes, which was why Jen preferred to . . .

'Don't even say it!' Nick told her as they crossed the road.

'This is why I prefer to catch a 113 to Hendon and take the tube from there,' Jen said, undaunted.

'Except it takes ages.'

'Yeah, and this is *much* quicker.'

They both glared at each other in the deserted ticket hall. Nick could pout but when Jen was sulking, there was not a person on God's green earth who could out-sulk her.

Nick didn't even try. Instead, he decided to go for deflection. 'No bad moods on your birthday,' he said in an uncharacteristically jaunty voice. 'Only good times.'

'There are no good times to be had at Mill Hill East,' Jen pointed out, but Nick had his hand stuck in one of the front pockets of his already tight jeans and she had to turn her head away, her cheeks toasty, until he stopped rummaging and held out a pile of coins.

'Come on! It's time for your birthday photo shoot,' he said, grabbing hold of Jen's hand and pulling her towards the photo booth, which was always a fixture at any tube station.

'I look awful in photos,' Jen complained, but Nick was already pushing back the curtain, adjusting the stool and then, her heart thumping harder than it should, he pulled her down so she was sitting on his lap. 'I'll crush you.'

'Literally or metaphorically?' Nick asked with a grin as he wrapped his arm tight around Jen's waist. Her heart pounded even harder, as he leaned forward to feed coins into the slot.

'Both,' she croaked, because she couldn't think of a time when she'd been so physically close to Nick, close enough that she could take great lungfuls of the heady smell of him: leather, cigarettes and Elnett hairspray. Close enough that she could see the tiny little mole just nestled in the secret patch of skin behind his earlobe, which Nick probably didn't even know existed, though Jen had spent a lot of time thinking about kissing it. Though not as much time as she'd thought about kissing the smudgy brown freckle near his mouth, his beauty spot, that marred but also emphasised the perfection of his exquisitely carved lips. Close enough that she could feel the heat of him through the thin cotton of her dress, as he pressed against her.

'Give me your best silly face!' Nick said leaning back to stick out his tongue and Jen had just enough time to screw up her features as the first flash went off. Then she opened her mouth wide in a silent but heartfelt scream for picture two; for picture three she fashioned her hands into claws and hammed it up like a pantomime villain and for the last picture she cast her eyes to the heavens in rapture because Nick had pulled her in even tighter so he could press his lips against her cheek. It was a split second as the flash went off that seemed to last forever though it also seemed to last for no time at all.

'Happy birthday,' he said softly, making no move to let go of her, his mouth still so close to her skin that his breath tickled her ear, his arms tight around her.

Jen blinked and turned her head slightly so they were nose to nose. She couldn't speak. Could hardly breathe. All she had to do was move forward just a fraction, purse her lips and they'd be kissing.

She stared at Nick and he stared back. His dark eyes seemed to be all pupil.

She could do it. She could be braver than she'd ever been and move the three centimetres that would mean she was kissing her friend who was a boy but not her boyfriend.

'Jen?' Nick whispered.

She blinked again. 'What?' she asked in a throaty, raspy sort of voice like she actually inhaled her cigarettes.

'Just . . . just . . .' He closed his eyes, which you'd totally do if you were about to kiss someone, but then he opened them again and he let Jen go so she wobbled alarmingly, without him there to hold her. 'I think I just heard a train pull in and also, I'm not saying you're heavy, but I can't feel my legs anymore.'

'Oh my God!' Jen tipped off Nick's lap so quickly that she almost tripped over her own feet. She wrenched back the curtain to discover that the world was still turning and that a train had indeed pulled in because people were trickling down the stairs from the platform.

She would have shouldered past them, knocking them flying like weeble-wobbles, but Nick called out, 'The photos!'

They'd been gazing at each other for so long that it only took a few more seconds for the machine to finish whirring and whooshing and for the strip of four photos to suddenly appear. Jen grabbed them. She wanted to crush them in her hand while they were still wet so she wouldn't have to see the last picture where she must have the mooniest, drippiest, give-the-game-away-est expression on her face, but she couldn't quite bear to.

She wanted proof that she hadn't imagined it. That Nick really had kissed her. Cheek kisses on her birthday were still kisses.

'Let me see!' Nick tried to take the photos from her, but Jen twisted out of his reach.

'I am not missing another train,' she said, turning to race up the steps and they just had time to collapse in their seats before the doors shut.

Then it was enough to distract Nick with a blow by blow account of Grandpa Stan's best moments from the day, including describing the spaghetti Bolognese which Jen had requested as her birthday meal as 'foreign muck', until Nick completely forgot about the photos and Jen could safely tuck them into her purse, where they were at least out of sight if not yet out of mind.

5

Bank Holiday Monday
August 29th, 1988
Camden Town Station

The sun was still shining when they emerged from Camden Town station; the soft, diffused sunlight of a late August evening.

'We need to stop at the offy,' Nick reminded Jen as they headed up Parkway.

Even though Jen was still discombobulated from those three minutes in the photo booth, she also felt a frisson of delight at the thought of being able to purchase her first legal drink. Even if she had been buying alcohol without incident or confrontation since she was sixteen.

As it was, the man behind the till in the off license didn't pay Jen any attention as she went for her alcoholic drink of choice: a bottle of Strawberry MD 20/20, a sickly sweet but moreish and potent combination of sherry, port and fortified wine. And to hell with it! It *was* her birthday. She grabbed another bottle and went over to Nick who was perusing bottles of red wine like he was a true connoisseur.

'It's not a dinner party and you're not Keith Floyd,' Jen protested. 'Also, do you even have a corkscrew?'

'There's this thing you can do with a shoe to open it,' Nick said vaguely, eyeing up his boots, then Jen's. 'Anyway, don't know how you can drink that bitch piss.'

'That's both sexist and offensive.' Jen clutched her bottles tighter.

'Let's get vodka,' he suggested, heading for the counter where the spirits were kept so they couldn't be pilfered by any passing ne'er do wells.

'I can't drink vodka without a mixer and also, we don't have any glasses.' They went through this same sequence of events every time they were somewhere that sold alcohol.

'Whisky?' Nick wasn't giving up without a fight.

Jen made gagging noises.

'OK, well I guess I'll get some lager then,' he decided, like he always did, and grabbed a six pack of Stella Artois. 'Crisps?'

'Salt and vinegar, please.'

'I'll get those for you as it's your birthday, but I still don't approve of your alcohol choices,' Nick said, jerking his head to indicate that Jen should place her bottles on the counter. 'Maybe now you're eighteen, your palate will get more sophisticated.'

'I wish,' Jen said because her palate was still very immature. The only cheeses she would eat were Edam, Emmental, Gouda and Dairylea, basically cheeses that didn't taste of cheese. The only fish she would eat was a fish finger. And on three separate occasions, Susan had served her hummus and pita bread and on all three of those occasions Jen had heaved at even the thought of getting the mush made from chickpeas anywhere near her mouth. 'Maybe this will be the year I learn to love olives and start drinking gin and tonic.'

It was just as well the party they were going to wasn't the kind of elegant soiree with wait staff swishing about serving gin and tonics and offering little bowls of olives. Nick had once said that in some places they served olives *in* martinis, but he was clearly taking the piss. There were no such culinary hazards when they finally arrived at their destination: a large patch of lawn in Regent's Park, which was nearest to the entrance at the top of Parkway and also had a good view of the giraffe enclosure at London Zoo.

Not that Jen was particularly bothered about spotting any giraffes. Not when the people sprawled on the grass, clutching at cans and bottles, bags of crisps and packets of biscuits scattered like loose change, broke into an enthusiastic round of applause as Jen and Nick walked towards them.

There had to be at least – Jen took a quick headcount – thirty people gathered to celebrate her birthday, despite it being the Monday evening of the August Bank Holiday weekend. Even when Jen had primary school friends, it had been hard to rustle up enough guests for a party. Just another disadvantage of being a late August baby, along with always being the youngest in your class and people assuming you were an uptight perfectionist just because you were a Virgo.

'Happy birthday, Jen! Have you had your first legal drink yet?' someone called out.

There had been fizzy wine at lunch. Asti Spumante, not champagne. Jen had managed half a glass until Stan had said that she was putting him off his food with her sour face and Alan had watered down the rest with lemonade. Not that Jen was going to tell anyone that.

'Just about to,' she said, holding up the flimsy carrier bag so her two bottles of MD clanked together.

'Come and sit with us,' Harry insisted, because she (Harry was short for Harriet) was probably Jen's best friend from college; her best friend who was a girl.

After that fateful Smiths concert and two awful weeks at college where Jen wasn't sure what Priya had said about her but knew it couldn't be anything good, Jen had been approached by Harry and two other Theatre Studies girls, Linzi and Lucy. Linzi and Lucy were generally considered the prettiest girls at college and Harry had bleached platinum hair so the three of them were, like Nick, from another realm.

'We don't believe anything that Priya is saying about you,' had been Harry's opening gambit when they'd tracked Jen down to the tiny Topshop.

Jen had clutched onto a rail of pastel-coloured knitwear for support. 'What has she been saying about me?' she'd asked fearfully.

'That you did everything you could to come between her and Rob . . .'

'I didn't . . . or if I did . . .'

'Obviously, you don't fancy Rob cause he's a dick,' Linzi said, in her very confident, very posh voice. 'There is no way that he's read all those books or listened to all those albums.'

'Unless he's two hundred,' Lucy had added. 'And he isn't. He's sixteen but he thinks he knows everything and Priya isn't a girls' girl even though girls should stick up for each other.'

'So you can absolutely hang out with us, if you want to,' Harriet concluded, giving Jen a quick up and down. Jen had been wearing Alan's old Crombie coat over a crimplene dotty dress from Oxfam with the ubiquitous DMs. 'I mean, you're cool.'

You're cool. It had been said in such an off-hand but matter of fact way as if Jen's coolness just was. That the coolness encompassed not just Jen's outer trappings – the second-hand clothes, the DMs, the eyeliner – but Jen's personality. Her shyness which often came across as standoffishness was considered by these three girls to be the mark of someone who was aloof because she didn't care what other people thought of her.

Anyway, they'd all been friends now for nearly two years because they hadn't been put off by Jen's lack of cool once they got to know her. Priya had dumped Rob or Rob had dumped Priya before Easter (it was hard to know who to believe) and when she came back after the summer holidays, she hung out with a small sub-section of the new intake of Art Foundation girls who'd all gone to private school, had long, flicky hair and went skiing for the spring half term. Meanwhile, Rob started going out with one of the new A level students, a very small girl who gazed at him like he was the snake charmer and she was the snake.

And George? Jen waved at George who was sitting on the other side of the crisps and biscuits birthday picnic spread from her. He'd phoned up to apologise the very next day after The Smiths concert and they'd agreed to forget that he'd ever told her to fuck off. Also, although Jen was sworn to secrecy, George had confided that he was pretty sure he was gay, but was going to wait until he'd got to university to do anything about it.

Turning to the matter in hand, Jen unscrewed the top of the first bottle of 20/20. 'That's it, she's going in!' someone bellowed, as she took a big gulp to loud cheers.

Then there were presents to open: so many little orange Penguin Classics paperbacks, more mix tapes, a Creation Records compilation album, a vintage dress that Jen had been coveting, little pots and jars of make-up and beauty-related lotions and potions.

George had baked an actual cake, smothered it in chocolate buttercream and had even gone to the trouble of bringing eighteen birthday candles with him. Then, even though Jen's friends considered themselves to be the arbiters of cool for North London, maybe even the whole of London, they sang 'Happy Birthday' as the cake was ceremoniously placed in front of Jen on a Woolies carrier bag. (As George had pointed out, the grass in any London park was bound to be soaked in dog wee.)

'Make a wish,' George said, as Jen paused from smoking a cigarette so she could blow out the candles.

Jen made the same heartfelt yet futile wish that she'd made every time a wishing opportunity had presented itself in the last two years or so.

Then she sat back and felt a little sad, just for a moment, until they realised that despite remembering birthday candles, George hadn't brought plates or napkins or a knife. 'Though George shouldn't be expected to remember everything,' Jen said loyally.

Someone had a Swiss Army penknife and they sterilised the most cake-cutting-compliant blade with vodka and everyone who wanted a ragged piece of cake had one.

It didn't sit well with the strawberry wine, but Jen tried not to grimace as she washed down a very large piece of the cake with the last dregs left in her first bottle.

The night came in slowly. It wasn't even eight but they were in the dog-end days of August now and a chill breeze rippled through the park. The sky was fading from the brilliant blue it had been before but there was still some time for Jen to start on her second bottle before the park closed at nine. First, she hurried to the loos with Harry and Linzi because they shut at eight.

'I'm all about pacing myself,' Jen said, as she let Harry and Linzi spritz with the Chanel No. 5. 'I'm not a kid anymore. I can hold my drink.'

'I can think of something else you should hold,' Linzi brayed, with a leer. 'You absolutely have to get snogged tonight, Jen.'

It was like having a glass of cold water flung in her face. 'What? Why? Why do I need to get snogged?'

'Because it's your birthday,' Harry explained patiently, as if a letter detailing all this had been posted out, like Jen had got her National Insurance card just before she turned sixteen. 'You must have your eye on someone.'

'Yes, you must!' Linzi insisted, tucking her arm through Jen's, so she could tug her back to their little birthday party *sur l'herbe*. 'We've never ever heard you talk about who you fancy.'

'That's because I don't fancy anyone,' Jen said. There were lots of boys whom she appreciated aesthetically but she didn't want to kiss them any more than they wanted to kiss her. The only boy she fancied, the only boy she wanted to kiss more than she'd ever wanted anything, was Nick.

'Seriously though, Jen, you should get some practice in before university,' Harry advised her with a frown.

Jen doubted there'd be much opportunity for snogging anyone at university. The Westfield College site was tiny, barely even a campus, and it had only become co-educational in the last twenty-five years. She'd had a lovely interview with a Miss Marple-ish lady don; they'd talked about Jane Austen and Jilly Cooper and she'd been advised to read Virginia Woolf's *A Room Of One's Own* once she'd described her own narrow room and windowsill as desk situation.

'Officially, if we make an offer you'll receive it in writing,' the lovely lady don had said. 'But, unofficially, I look forward to continuing this conversation when I see you next autumn.'

It had been an incredible moment – maybe the first time that her cleverness had been praised, validated. Her parents were proud of her but it was tinged with the what-ifs of what they both might have been if circumstances had been different.

Only Nick saw her cleverness as something indelibly linked to Jen. He always wanted to know what she was reading, what she thought about it, what she thought *he* should read next.

And while Nick was in her life, Jen couldn't imagine wanting to snog any other boy. Not even if Kidderpore Avenue, where Westfield College was located, had foxy boys with tousled hair and devilish smirks lined up on either side and all of them wanted to kiss her.

The sheer thought of it made her smile so Harry nudged Jen hard enough that both of them nearly toppled over. 'I know that smile. You're definitely thinking about having a snog tonight. What about Ollie?'

Ollie was heading to Glasgow School of Art in a few short weeks. He had dirty blond hair and a dirty look in his eyes to match and he would have been perfect except at a party earlier in the summer, when Harry had been in Provence with her parents, a girl had angrily confronted Ollie about giving her friend crabs.

'Not Ollie.' Jen came to a halt again.

The sky was still darkening, deepening, but that only made Lucy's silvery blonde hair stand out all the more. She was sitting with her gazelle-like legs tucked under her and leaning into Nick who was next to her. He was resting on his elbows, *his* long legs stretched out and crossed at the ankle. Their heads, one dark, one fair, were close together and Jen heard Lucy laugh. That was silvery too. A tinkling sound like bells. Not heavy, clanking church bells but something delicate and twinkly. Then Lucy leaned her head against Nick's shoulder and he kissed the top of her head because Lucy was Nick's girlfriend. Not a friend who happened to be a girl.

They were dating. Had been for seven long months. Heads always close together so Nick could say things in a whispery, husky voice and Lucy could laugh like tinkling fucking bells and now they were kissing.

Every time that Jen saw Nick and Lucy kissing, and she'd

seen them kiss *a lot* over the last seven months, she was relieved that she'd never revealed her true feelings to Nick.

Even before Lucy, it was clear that Nick had a type and that type was ... not Jen. He liked languid, ethereal girls (drippy girls, Jen often thought to herself when she was having an uncharitable moment) who draped themselves about and sighed and never had to carefully appraise a dress before they tried it on because everything always fitted their waifish bodies.

Jen wasn't the same sturdy, amorphous 'little porker' she'd been at the start of college. She'd grown taller, slimmer, she had breasts and hips now, though she didn't know what to do with them, except to be faintly embarrassed about their existence. She never wore anything too tight and now tugged the loose bodice of the polka dot dress, because she would still never be anything even approaching waiflike. It was just one of the many reasons why it was better to be Nick's friend and have that friendship be a precious thing, than suffer the disappointment, the crushing humiliation of being turned down, than not having Nick in her life at all.

Jen liked to think of herself as being above suspicion. Never once had she given herself away. No longing looks when she thought that no one else was watching. Never displaying one iota of jealousy when Nick and Lucy started officially seeing each other at the beginning of the year. On the contrary, she'd been an absolute trooper about it, even though she now spent approximately 73 per cent less time with Nick than she used to.

'About time you guys got together,' she'd said with a carefully cultivated wry exasperation when Nick had delivered the world-tilting news on one very grey Tuesday morning. 'What took you so long to realise that you make the perfect couple?'

Of course, Jen had already guessed. She was always attuned to Nick's presence; could pin-point his whereabouts in a crowded room with laser-like accuracy. And last Christmas, wherever Nick was in a crowded room, there Lucy was guaranteed to be, if not next to him, then close by. Unlike Jen, Lucy didn't need to disguise the yearning glances that she'd throw Nick's way, followed up by a flutter of her long eyelashes, a pout of her ridiculously full bottom lip. And the rest was history. A particularly bloody, unpleasant piece of history like the Battle of Culloden or the Spanish Inquisition.

Lucy was meant to have been looking after their stuff but she had eyes only for Nick so Jen was relieved that her bag was still there. She was even more relieved that no one had swiped the second bottle of strawberry wine. She snatched it up, muttered something about mingling, then attached herself to another group and determinedly drunk 75 cls (whatever a cl was) fast enough that if someone from the Guinness Book of World Records had been passing, Jen would have been guaranteed her own entry.

As it was, when it was time to move to a second location because the park closed at nine, Jen was drunk. Not tipsy. Not merry. 'Fucking hammered,' she slurred proudly. 'Paralytic. Drunk as a skunk. Inebriated.'

'Being drunk has done nothing to diminish your word power,' Nick said, and he put his arm around Jen to steer her across the road. It would have been perfect if his other arm hadn't been around Lucy, who was looking at Jen with concern.

'Maybe you should eat something to soak up the alcohol?' she suggested.

'I don't want to soak up the alcohol,' Jen announced to cheers from the art boys. 'I like being drunk.'

She kind of did like being drunk. For once, she wasn't preoccupied with plucking at her clothes so they didn't cling to her body. Or thinking carefully about what she was going to say before she said it. Or not betraying her crush on Nick

– except it wasn't a crush. It was unrequited love and as torturous as anything Jen had read about in her *Longman English Series Poetry* anthology.

When they reached the nearest pub, they spilled out into the huge beer garden, splitting up and spreading out to whichever tables and chairs happened to be free. Jen was pushed down onto a wooden bench, because she was listing to the right and on the verge of toppling over. Then there was a never-ending supply of Malibu and pineapple, her pub drink of choice because it was sweet enough to mask the taste of alcohol.

Soon her tongue felt like a heavy, lumpen thing inside her mouth, but it didn't stop her from talking.

'You're shouting, Jen,' George kept saying but she wasn't. She was just very enthusiastically joining in the discussion of where they were going to go when the pub closed. Maybe to see a band at the Dublin Castle or to a pub on Chalk Farm Road which always had a lock-in.

No one was listening to Jen, and she didn't really have a firm opinion either way. Especially when suddenly her most pressing priority was the urge to be sick.

'I need some fresh air,' she bellowed at Harry.

'We're in a bloody beer garden, there's plenty of fresh air,' Harry pointed out.

'I need fresher air,' Jen insisted and when she wobbled to her feet no one stopped her.

Halfway round the beer garden, in a staggery, stumbly circuit, Jen changed course to crash her way through the pub to the loos, bouncing off people and spilling drinks as she went.

'Sorry! Sorry! Sorry,' she chorused in a sing-song voice that was easily as annoying as spilling someone's drink.

There was a queue for the Ladies but shouting, 'It's my

birthday and I'm about to vom!' meant that Jen could push to the front of the queue and dive for the first available cubicle.

It turned out that she was going to be sick imminently but not immediately. Jen did think about putting her fingers down her throat – Linzi swore by it – but decided instead that it was much nicer to slide to the floor and press her hot face against the cool tiles.

Waiting to be sick in the correct environment for being sick was a sure sign of Jen's new maturity. She lay there for a little while, heard someone say, 'Is she all right in there, do you think?'

Whoever it was obviously thought that Jen was A-OK because they left and then more people came and went and Jen lifted her legs so they were propped up against the opposite wall of the cubicle. She decided that her legs looked very slim from that angle, as the toilets on either side of her flushed in unison and the doors opened.

There was the sound of running water – she really should think about having a wee while she was here – then, 'Has anyone seen Jen?' Linzi asked in her foghorn voice that would be much better suited to a parade ground then a pub toilet in Camden.

'Oh, Jen will be fine. Jen's cool,' replied the breathy voice of Lucy.

'Jen's cool,' Jen mouthed to herself, free to roll her eyes as hard as she could then wished she hadn't because it made her feel dizzy. Or dizzier.

'Jen is cool,' Linzi confirmed. 'But, you know, I never really feel like I know who Jen is.'

'Yeah. You can't really talk to her because she's quite . . . not stuck up, but she's quite closed off. She doesn't like to get deep.'

'Sometimes I wonder if she even likes me,' Linzi said though

Jen did like Linzi but at the same time she had also thought that Linzi wasn't capable of this kind of introspection. 'The only person that she really seems to like is Nick.'

There was a moment of silence so deathly that Jen did actually wonder if she had just died, but no she was still lying on the floor in a pub toilet, suddenly as sober as if she'd drunk nothing but water all night.

'They're just friends,' Lucy said mildly. 'That's what Nick says and I believe him, even though the way she looks at him when she thinks nobody's looking ... you can tell that she fancies him.'

There was another pause and a clattering as if they were delving in make-up bags. Jen wanted to storm out of the cubicle and deny everything but she stayed where she was and wondered if it were possible to actually overdose on sheer mortification.

'But you don't mind her hanging out with Nick,' Linzi said as Jen heard the door open.

'No, because he doesn't fancy her. He said so. He said why would he fancy her when she's not even pretty, that he only started hanging out with her because he felt sorry for her and then I said ...'

Whatever Lucy had or hadn't said in her stupid breathy voice would remain a mystery because the door shut behind them and then Jen curled herself into a little ball and burst into shuddering tears.

6

Bank Holiday Monday
August 29th, 1988
Camden Town Station

There was nothing like sobbing for fifteen minutes straight *and* hearing some hard home truths to ruin your eighteenth birthday. Jen stared at her face in the mirror, the same mirror where Linzi and Lucy had touched up their make-up while they'd casually destroyed her.

Jen *looked* destroyed. Her eyes were so bloodshot and swollen from crying that she could hardly see out of them. The red Chanel lipstick that she'd been so proud of and thought so sophisticated, was just a garish, smeared memory. Her eyeliner and mascara were streaked down her cheeks in grey rivulets. And still she cried.

She stood there and gazed dispassionately at her reflection while she sobbed. Jackie always said that Jen wasn't a pretty crier (apparently she wasn't a pretty anything) and Jen was forced to admit that it was true. Her mouth was a gaping, wet maw, her face scrunched and red. How she looked on the outside was exactly how she felt on the inside.

Ugly. Unwanted. Unlovable.

A friendship, which had been so unexpected and so priceless to Jen was nothing more than Nick feeling sorry for her. *Pitying* her. And though she'd thought her secret was safe as she clutched it tightly to her heart, everyone knew and had been laughing at Jen behind her back.

Oh God.

Nick *knew*.

He'd discussed it with Lucy. Had discussed Jen's lack of prettiness at great length. It wasn't even that she minded – OK, she minded that quite a lot – it was that all those precious hours she'd spent with Nick, all those afternoons in his bedroom listening to records and talking had been a lie. She'd told him things about her family, her past, what she hoped for her future, that she hadn't told anyone, and it hadn't meant anything to him.

She didn't mean anything to him.

Jen was still crying, a hiccupy, breathless crying rather than full-on weeping, when she finally left the toilets. The first person she collided with was George.

'Jen! Everyone's been looking for you . . .' He paused to take in her ruined face. 'Are you all right? Have you been sick?'

'No.' She shook her head and closed her leaking eyes. 'But I'm not all right. I have to go home.' She clutched hold of George's wrist. 'Can you go and find my bag, please?'

'Oh, Jen.' George's round face was creased with concern. 'But what about all your presents?'

Why had anyone even bothered to get her a present when they were all laughing about her behind her back? Talk about a long con. 'I don't want them. I just want to go home.'

'You don't want to say goodbye to everyone?'

'No!' Jen let go of George who instantly grabbed her as she swayed uncertainly on the spot. 'Please, George. I need my bag. I'll wait outside the front. Don't tell anyone. Please.'

'If you're sure . . .' George tailed off as more hiccuppy sobbing prevented Jen from insisting that she'd never been more sure of anything in her life.

She stood outside the pub, right on the very edge of the kerb so she could flee as soon as George reunited her with her bag.

It was dark now, the roads quiet. All Jen could hear was the hammering of her heart and her shuddering breaths. She just wanted not to be here. To be back home so she could shut the front door and feel the walls close in on her. In a comforting way this time.

The pub door opened and Jen glanced behind her to see George with her bag and Nick following him.

'Jen? What's up?' he asked, his voice and face soft like he actually cared for her. 'Have you been sick?'

'I'm fine,' she said tightly, still gulping a little from the tears. She couldn't look at him so turned to George. 'Thanks for getting my bag.'

He passed it over then tried to hand Jen a couple of carrier bags. 'Your presents.'

She pushed them away. 'I don't want them.'

George and Nick shared a look like they'd already had a chat about how to solve a problem like Jen. God knows what else they'd chatted about over the months. Was George in on it too?

'Come on, Jen. Come back inside,' Nick said, reaching out a hand, which glanced off Jen's arm before she reared back.

'Don't touch me!' she bit out and she couldn't stand to be there anymore. To be his adoring little sidekick while all the time he was simply playing her, pitying her, then telling Lucy all about it. 'I'm going home.'

'Don't be a dickhead,' Nick said with a flash of a smile like Jen just needed to be teased out of her bad mood. 'Do you need some chips? Another drink? Some water?'

'I need to never see your face again!' Jen hurled herself into the road, narrowly avoiding being mown down by a black cab, the cabbie winding down his window to tell Jen exactly what he thought of her.

'Are you fucking blind? You need a white stick and a fucking guide dog, love!'

'Jen! What are you doing?' That was George.

'Why are you acting like a crazy person?' And that was Nick, destroyer of worlds.

Jen flung up a hand, middle finger rigid in reply to all three of them and scurried round the corner onto Parkway. She was crying again. Or rather, tears were streaming down her face no matter how much she scrubbed furiously at them with the back of her hand.

Then there was a touch on her shoulder. 'What's going on?'

She shook Nick off. 'Leave me alone.'

'I'm not leaving you on your own in Camden in the middle of the night,' Nick said, keeping up with Jen's half skip/half run pace with insulting ease. 'What's upset you?'

Jen ground to a halt and she was all ready to tell him exactly what had upset her. With hand gestures and post-watershed language. A vituperative, verbatim account of what Lucy had said. But just saying the words out loud, each one of them a death knell for what she'd thought was a genuine friendship even if it had been something more, so much more, on her side, was too painful.

She settled for one dull sentence. 'We're not friends anymore.'

Nick rocked back on his heels. 'What are you talking about?'

'We never were friends. And those people . . .' she gestured in the direction from which they'd come. 'They're not my friends either. It's all just been a huge laugh, hasn't it? I'm not a real person to any of you. I'm just a pathetic loser.'

'What the fuck are you talking about?' Nick asked with an edge of frustration. 'Don't go all Sylvia Plath on me.'

That was meant to be one of their in jokes, if you could have an in joke about a woman so crazed with misery and depression *over a worthless, cheating man* that she killed herself by sticking her head in a gas oven.

When Jen was being moody, Nick called her Sylvia and when Nick was being a pretentious arse (these were both common occurrences), Jen would mockingly call him Lou Reed.

But the only real joke was the one that Nick had shared with Lucy and Jen had been the punchline.

'I'm going home,' she repeated, ignoring Nick as he walked alongside her, keeping her face set and still as he kept asking her what was wrong, until his confusion turned to anger.

'This is ridiculous, Jen, you're being ridiculous,' he spat, as they got to the station. She pulled out her purse and took out her travelcard. 'What the fuck is going on? Has someone said something to piss you off? It must have been a hell of a something.'

'Oh, it was,' Jen assured him, head bobbing up and down like the little nodding dog they had in the back of the family Ford Escort. 'It was really something.'

She stuck her card into the ticket machine, viciously shoved her way through the turnstile and snatched her ticket out of the other end. But despite everything, she couldn't resist one last longing look at him and then Lucy and Harlow could fucking have him.

Nick stood there and stared right back at her, so it was like those minutes in the photo booth at Mill Hill East station, which now felt like they'd happened to someone else someplace else, in another time.

The world slowed down, then melted away and it was just Jen and Nick and the pull between them, which she must have imagined even though it was still tugging at her now.

He mouthed her name, 'Jen,' then lurched forward as a burly goth guy behind him barrelled past to use the turnstile.

The moment was gone. Had probably never even existed. Jen turned away and hurried down the escalator.

'Jen!' She could hear him behind her. 'Jen! What the fuck?'

She increased her speed, pushing at any idiot who was blocking the left-hand side of the escalators, but still Nick's shouts were louder and she was sure the wind that always whistled through the station was his breath on the back of her neck.

The stairs levelled out at the bottom and with a shaky dismount Jen leapt off the escalator, but Nick was right behind her now, a firm grip on her arm as he pulled her away from the bottom of the escalator, firm enough that she couldn't shake him off as he steered her to the left and up against the small portion of wall that separated the passageways that led to the Edgware and one of the southbound platforms.

'Stop. Just stop,' he said as he brought them both to a halt. 'I'm not leaving and you're not leaving either. Not until you tell me what's wrong.'

There was no way that she was saying the words out loud. And yet . . . What if she was wrong? What if she hadn't heard Lucy properly? Even though, despite everything she'd drunk, Jen still had a perfect recall of what Lucy had said.

'Come on, Jen, tell me,' Nick said in that low coaxing tone of his, which had made Jen start smoking and drinking and lying to Jackie and Alan about where she was going and what time she'd be home. When Nick spoke to Jen like that, looked at her with those dark, dark eyes from under his mop of dark, dark hair, she couldn't deny him anything.

'She . . . Lucy said . . . I heard her . . . you're not really my friend. You just feel *sorry* for me,' Jen muttered so Nick had to lean closer to hear her, though this time, his smell of leather and cigarettes and hairspray didn't thrill her, and she didn't want to press her lips to the little mole, that perfect beauty spot . . .

'I'm friends with you because I like you,' Nick said with enough force that Jen wanted to believe it was true. 'That night we saw The Smiths and what happened afterwards, that was a proper bonding experience. Right?'

'Right,' Jen echoed uncertainly.

'And yeah, the Monday afterwards at college, it was obvious that you didn't have anyone to hang out with so I stepped up . . .'

' . . . because you felt sorry for me.' Instead of lurching alarmingly like it had been doing, Jen's stomach sank.

'Maybe I felt sorry for you a little bit but mostly I wanted to hang out with you because I thought you were cool,' Nick said, still leaning close, his eyes boring into Jen's, as if he were daring her not to believe him. 'Jen, you know me well enough to know that I don't do anything unless I want to. I don't do stuff out of the goodness of my heart. I'm an iconoclastic rebel in a leather jacket.'

'You're pretentious, you mean,' Jen said as she was meant to, but it didn't feel like an in joke anymore, rather words she'd learnt by heart and recited whenever Nick fed her the cue.

'This is such a silly thing to get upset about,' he continued smoothly, shifting a little so he wasn't leaning in so close anymore. 'I don't know why Lucy would say that.'

'That's not all she said.' It all came rushing back now that Nick had given her some space. 'She said . . .'

'What did she say?' Nick looked expectant, curious, not at all worried that the information Jen was about to impart could destroy him like it had destroyed Jen. 'Tell me!'

But if he had told Lucy that he'd felt sorry for Jen, he'd just admitted it after all, then he probably had said the other stuff too. 'You don't fancy me because I'm not even pretty.'

'Ah . . .' It was a sigh tinged with regret as his own thoughts about Jen's lack of beauty were parroted back to him. 'We're friends. You're probably my best friend. You know I care about you.'

It was torture to listen. To have those small crumbs thrown in her face. 'Everything's ruined.'

'Don't be a twat, Jen,' Nick said as he always did at least once whenever they hung out. 'Nothing's ruined. Lucy just gets a bit jealous sometimes and maybe I told her what she wanted to hear just so she didn't keep going on about it. You know, so we could keep hanging out without her getting all narky. You and me, we're still cool.'

They were the very opposite of cool. Just like Jen had never once been cool. Not really. You could only fool some of the people some of the time. 'She said . . .'

'Honestly, all this she said business . . .' Nick shook his head, smiled in that sly, smirky way that Jen lived for. 'You're better than this.'

His hand was still on her arm, his touch warm, though Jen was clammy and cold from the crying and the shock. But she was undaunted. She'd come this far; she might as well stagger the last few metres. 'You don't think I'm pretty.'

Nick dropped his gaze for the first time. 'I don't think of you like that. We're mates.'

'But objectively, you don't think I'm pretty,' Jen persisted like a dog with a bone.

'It doesn't matter whether I think you're pretty or not,' Nick said, his voice so quiet now that it was Jen who had to lean in to catch every wounding word.

'Because you don't fancy me!'

'Because I'm going out with Lucy. I fancy Lucy! You know that I do.' Nick let go of Jen so he could fold his arms. 'This is so stupid. Why are you being like this?'

Jen rolled gritty eyes. 'Why do you think I'm being like this?'

'This is what Susan does. Answers a question with a question. It's *so* annoying.'

'But you *do* know why I'm being like this,' Jen said, trying to stand firm even as people brushed past her as they emerged from the passageway that led to the southbound platform. 'You feel sorry for me. You don't think I'm pretty. You don't fancy me and to make matters worse, you've discussed all those things with Lucy, including . . . you also talked about . . .'

'No, we didn't talk about anything else,' Nick said quickly, too quickly. 'That about covers it and I know that maybe I shouldn't . . .'

'You talked about . . . you *know* . . .' She just couldn't get the words out. They were so incriminating. So secret. Or that was what Jen had thought.

'What do I know?' Nick asked and just the way he'd lowered his voice again, had closed the gap between them was enough for Jen to know that he already knew.

'You know that I fancy you.' Saying it out loud wasn't cathartic or liberating. It was fucking horrible. Jen put her hands up to cover her cheeks. She wasn't cold and clammy anymore but burning from the heat of a thousand suns. But Nick was taking her hands away from her face so he could hold them down by her sides, his fingers threaded through hers. 'That's what Lucy said.'

Jen stared at a fixed point on the opposite wall, to the left, the Edgware platform that would take her away from all of this.

'Look at me, Jen.'

She shook her head. 'No, I won't.'

'Is it true? Do you fancy me?' he asked, closer now than he'd been before so even though the wind swept through this no-man's land between escalators and platforms, Jen could feel the heat coming off his body. 'Have you always fancied me?'

'Don't do this to me,' she croaked because she might have fancied him, had always fancied him, but she'd kept it a secret because she'd always known that Nick would use it against her. She'd thought he'd reject her, but it turned out there were worse things than being rejected. Much worse things, like Nick toying with her, teasing her, touching her like she really was pretty and that she fancied him and he fancied her and there was no Lucy ... 'I already feel like shit and you're just making everything worse.'

Jen yanked her hands free and ducked out from where she was practically pinned to the wall.

'Don't be like this, Jen,' he said, and she paused because there was still a tiny hopeful part of her that wanted him to make all of this better. 'I'd much rather have you as my friend than anything else.'

She recoiled like he'd spat in her face. 'But we are not friends. We can never be friends. Not after this.'

'All right! OK! Yes, I knew that you fancied me,' Nick ground out like Jen had forced the words from him, and in a way she supposed she had. 'But I go with girls like Lucy because ... you're just ... you're just ...'

It was his turn to flounder and Jen's turn to snap impatiently. 'I'm just *what?*'

'You're just too much like *this*!' Nick threw up his hands to demonstrate just how much of *this* Jen was. 'Nothing is easy with you. You're just too intense. You read too much into things. And it would have been easy to lead you on, but I never did, Jen, because I liked you too much.'

'No, you just talked about me with Lucy who's talked about it to Linzi and probably Harry and *everybody*,' Jen hissed. Her face was on fire. 'I bet they're talking about it right now. About what a fucking loser I am!'

'You're not a loser,' Nick insisted and Jen didn't know why

he was sticking around. It wasn't his usual MO. When things got difficult, he was the first one to bail.

'I am. I'm a total loser and I'm going home.' Jen finally realised that she could end this awful night and this awful scene by simply moving her feet and walking away. 'Have a nice life.'

'You're being a dick,' Nick called out and she probably was, but Jen didn't care; she'd stew about it tomorrow. Right now she was hurling herself along the fifty metres or so that would get her the hell out of there.

She'd almost reached the Edgware platform when there was a hand on her arm again and Jen was about to pull free *again*, when his words made her freeze.

'Just for the record, I do think you're pretty. If I didn't, then I wouldn't do *this*,' Nick said, his voice breathless as if he'd had to run after her.

And then he turned her round. And then he kissed her.

Nick was kissing her.

His mouth was on hers. His lips on hers. His tongue in her mouth. It was forceful. It was very wet. It was not at all how she'd imagined it.

Her first kiss. It wasn't meant to be like this.

Above the roaring in her ears, Jen could hear the slow rumble of a train as it pulled into the platform. She wrenched her head to the side to make it stop and shoved Nick hard enough that he stumbled backwards.

'Jen! Wait! For fuck's sake! Just stop . . .'

Jen didn't just stop; she was in forward motion, head down as she fought her way past the people streaming off the train.

'Jen!'

She jumped onto the train just in time.

'Stand clear of the doors, please.'

Nick was still a couple of crucial metres away from the platform, but he was close enough to hear Jen as she shouted, 'I hate you and I never ever want to see you again!'

For once, her timing was perfect. The doors shut on her last intake of breath and Nick made it onto the platform just in time to see the train slowly pull away, his face stark, then blurred, then gone.

PART THREE

1992

7

Thursday, February 20th, 1992
Mile End Station

Jennifer was gently eased out of sleep by a light but insistent tugging at her foot, accompanied by an annoying chant of, 'Get up! Get up! Get up, you lazy tart.'

She peeled open one eye, which was sticky with last night's make-up. 'Don't call me lazy,' she groused. 'I didn't get in until after three, I had to wait ages for a night bus.'

'Noted. Also noted that I shouldn't call you lazy but it's all right to call you a tart.' Kirsty smiled down at her and tugged at Jennifer's foot a little harder.

Jennifer yanked herself free and turned over, wriggling to get comfortable again on the lumpy pillow and scratchy sheets, which her parents had bought from BHS when she'd left home three years before. Dorothy, her grandmother, had said that BHS might be cheaper but it was always better to pay a little extra for the quality and go to Marks & Sparks instead. Jennifer thought about that every night when she thumped the wafer-thin pillow to give it some shape. She thumped it now. 'Go away. It's too early.'

'You made me promise to get you up and out of bed before I left for my tutorial group. It's already gone ten,' Kirsty announced, which were the magic words to have Jennifer flinging off the equally lumpy and thin duvet and swing her legs out of bed.

'Why didn't you say?' she demanded, grimacing as her feet

made contact with the sticky lino that covered most of the floor in their flat above a butcher's on the Mile End Road. You had to go through the kitchen to get to the bathroom, which was just one more inconvenience in a home full of many, many inconveniences. Like the insulation tape around the windows in winter because they didn't have double glazing or central heating. Or the incoming calls only telephone. Or the gas cooker that was so ancient that it didn't have gas rings but gas vents which ignited with a ferocity that could singe your eyelashes if you weren't careful. Or the fact that Gary Andrews, the butcher from the shop downstairs (or 'Babyface Andrews, the bastard butcher from the basement' as Jennifer and Kirsty called him), had been given a key by their landlord so he could collect the envelopes of cash they left out on the first Monday of every month. Gary would let himself in at all times, which was a good reason not to wander about for too long in a state of undress.

But the rent was only sixty quid a week and it was a brisk five-minute walk to campus and an even quicker walk to the tube station. All her life Jennifer had dreamed of living near a tube station and now her dreams had come true (Oxford Circus was only twenty minutes away!) so she couldn't really complain, although Jackie had cried the first time she'd seen the flat. And Stan had said that he'd dragged himself out of the East End by his bootstraps and now his granddaughter had dragged herself back there to live in a rat-infested shithole. (There *were* rats, but they never ventured up to the first floor, preferring to congregate at night on the pavements outside when the shops and fast food joints on the Mile End Road put their rubbish out.)

By the time Jennifer emerged from the bathroom, as squeaky clean as the rudimentary facilities would allow, Kirsty was heading out of the door. 'Are you working tonight?'

'I am not,' Jennifer said gratefully.

'Want to rent a video and get disgustingly drunk while we barely watch it?'

'Always.'

'Always!' Kirsty grinned and then she was gone, door slamming behind her, feet stomping down the stairs.

It was 10.30 and Jennifer was due at work in an hour. She hadn't had time to do laundry, but she had clean pants, she'd only worn her bra for a couple of days and she'd had the foresight to hang her white shirt over the back of a chair when she got in last night, so it wasn't too creased. Then through a process of untangling and sniffing, she selected a pair of tights from the pile on the floor before shimmying her way into a very tight, very stretchy, very short black skirt.

Jennifer was just easing herself into her motorcycle boots, a process which involved putting a carrier bag in them first to smooth her way, then pulling out the carrier bag, like a magician producing a rabbit from a hat, when she heard the phone ring.

She didn't want to answer it as it was sure to be either Dominic, her boyfriend or Mina, her academic supervisor. Jennifer was relieved that when she did pick up the receiver with a tremulous 'Hello?' it turned out to be Mina. Mina was currently the lesser of the two evils.

'Sorry I had to cancel our meeting last week. I've just been *so* busy,' Jennifer tried to sound like a very busy person might. 'And I'm almost out of the door. I have to be at work in forty-three minutes exactly.'

'I won't keep you long,' Mina insisted cheerily, which wasn't true. Mina really liked to talk. 'I just wondered if you'd had any more thoughts about transitioning your MA to a PhD.'

'Not really,' Jennifer said, phone clasped between ear and shoulder, as she tried to tug on her other boot. It was a lie. It was all that Jennifer thought about. It was the thing that kept her awake at night when she wasn't passed out in an alcoholic stupor. 'I don't know why I decided to write my dissertation on *Middlemarch* and reclaiming the Victorian novel as feminist text. So do I really want to spend another God knows how many years reading more Victorian novels and commentary about Victorian novels, which really aren't feminist texts at all . . . ?'

'We could discuss that,' Mina was now saying. 'Tweak things slightly . . .'

'It's not just that,' Jennifer insisted, eyeing the clock on the kitchen wall. 'Look, I really can't be late for work.'

'If it's money, then I'm sure there's a couple of grants you could apply for.' Mina's cultured tones were almost wheedling. Usually there was a lightness to her voice so even on the phone you could hear her smiling but now she sounded a little desperate. 'And if you're a PhD student, then you'll be able to pick up some undergraduate teaching.'

Jennifer made a silent, gagging face at the thought of having to teach any undergraduates. 'That's very kind of you, Mina. I really do have to go now.'

'Come and see me tomorrow. I'll be in my office from four.'

Jennifer said that she would, even though she was down for an evening shift tomorrow and would need to be at work by five, then hung up the phone. She grabbed her bag and denim jacket and headed for the door.

She raced down the rickety stairs, unlocked the street door, though one good kick would bust it open, and shrugged into her jacket as she ran towards the tube. It was a drizzly, grey February day. The kind of day where it felt like nothing nice was ever going to happen again. Christmas was long gone. Spring felt like it would never arrive, though as Jennifer raced past the dodgy kebab place that was never open because allegedly it was a front for money laundering, there wasn't much nature on display. No cheery daffodils or friendly crocuses poking through the cracks in the pavement.

Even so, Mile End wasn't quite the inner-city urban wasteland that Stan thought it was. 'They'd stab you soon as look at you,' he was fond of saying, and even though Jennifer would counter that by rhapsodising about the Regent's Canal and the sprawling verdant spaces of Mile End Park, she might just as well howl at the moon.

There was a train pulling into the platform just as Jennifer arrived, like it was her own personal transport. She loved it when that happened. At just gone eleven (and she really was going to have to get a wiggle on when she got out at Bond Street), there were plenty of seats free. Jennifer flopped down at the end of a row, put her bag on the empty seat next to her so that no one could sit there and allowed herself one minute to gather her thoughts before she pulled out her make-up bag.

It was the mark of a true Londoner to be able to put your face on while on a moving tube train. It was easier for Jennifer than most because, despite showering, she still wore the remnants of yesterday's make up and could use that as her base. Jackie always told her off for sleeping in her make-up and said that she'd get spots. She also said that about drinking too much and never eating any vegetables, but Jennifer still drank like a demon and never knowingly ate a vegetable and yet her skin was peachy soft.

Now, she slapped on some foundation, not even bothering to look in the grimy mirror of her powder compact to see if it was blended, then it was time to pile on the translucent powder. She didn't bother with the green corrector stick anymore – God, she hadn't had a clue when she was a teenager – and now relied on foundation and powder to tone down the red in her complexion.

Then she ran a pencil very lightly over her eyebrows, which were plucked almost to the point of extinction, and only paused as the train had pulled into Liverpool Street and someone was getting on and brushing past Jennifer to sit down opposite her. The doors closed, the train started to move and Jennifer fished out her liquid eyeliner. Never mind that she'd got a first in English Literature or that she'd been awarded a full bursary from the British Academy to fund her MA, Jennifer always thought her greatest accomplishment was being able to apply liquid eyeliner while a train jerked its way between stations.

She unscrewed the top, wiped the excess gloop off the tiny brush and with a rock-steady hand applied a sweeping line to the base of her upper eyelid, expertly flicking it up at the end for the desired cat-eye effect. The right eye was always easy. Being right-handed, it was the left eye that was a tricky bugger, but Jennifer repeated the same confident motion then lowered her lids to check that both eyes matched. They did. God, she was *good*.

Next, came mascara. She extracted the brush from the very gunky tube and held it up to her right eye when there was a sudden light touch on her knee, which could have been fatal. If the brush had been two millimetres nearer to her eye then . . .

'You could have blinded me!' She whipped away the mirror and then wished she hadn't and that it was still obscuring her view because sitting opposite her was someone she'd never expected to see again.

Those had been her explicit instructions the last time she'd clapped eyes on him.

Nick was leaning forward, his expression doubtful. 'Jen? I wasn't sure if it was you.'

For a second, Jennifer wasn't sure if it was her either.

Nobody called her Jen. When she'd started at Westfield College four years ago, it had been a new start. She was a new person. Jennifer. Jennifers were bookish. Got straight As. Didn't suffer fools.

She'd made a great Jennifer for approximately three days, until she'd met Kirsty and then she and Kirsty had met the two-for £1 jelly shots at a Fresher's event at ULU, the University of London's Student Union in Malet Street.

But Jennifer had still stuck, and she could brazen it out, deny all knowledge of ever having been Jen, but his hand was light on her knee again.

'I've thought about you a lot. Always imagined that I'd bump into you again.' He smiled ruefully, but there was something insincere about it like he'd practised that smile, the faint air of regret, over and over again. 'Can't believe it's taken, what? Four years?'

'About that, yeah,' she agreed and then to show that she was fine, just fine, Jennifer moved her leg so Nick had to move his hand and she returned, once more, to applying her mascara though her hand wasn't quite as rock steady as it had been before.

He was still staring at her. 'I hardly recognised you,' he remarked and Jennifer thought that his tone was appreciative, maybe even flirtatious, but was she just projecting what her sixteen-year-old self, even her eighteen-year-old self, had wanted to hear?

Jennifer was different now. And she looked different too. She was thinner, much thinner, because these days she preferred to drink her calories then sweat them out on the dancefloor. She'd dyed her hair jet black at the same time that Kirsty had dyed her hair white blond and they'd both cut in really short fringes. But it wasn't just the outside stuff. She was different on the inside too.

Different enough, that she could smile coolly and ask, 'So, how's life on the local paper?'

Another rueful smile (yup, he'd definitely worked on that in front of a mirror). 'That didn't work out in the end. I've got you to thank for that, actually.'

She was intrigued. She didn't want to be, but she was. Also, she had a few moves of her own that she'd practised, like the way she now arched one pencilled-in eyebrow. 'Oh?'

The train pulled into St Paul's station. The doors opened, but no one got off, and no one got on. It was just the two of them. Like old times. But Jennifer was different. She kept repeating it in her head as Nick shifted in his seat, crossed his long legs.

'I took your advice. Wrote some gig reviews, sent them off to the *NME*. Never heard back from them so then I sent them to *Melody Maker* and started freelancing for them,' he said, as Jennifer outlined her lips in red pencil then coloured them in. Her mirror was held in front of her but she could still see him, see how much he'd changed.

Gone were the indecently tight black jeans, the pointy-toed boots, the skinny T-shirt, the leather jacket that he'd worn come rain, come shine, come snow like Jennifer had worn her dad's old Crombie overcoat.

Nick was wearing jeans, desert boots, a plaid shirt with a T-shirt underneath and a fawn-coloured suede jacket. He no longer had that ridiculously unruly fringe to sweep back impatiently, though his dark hair was still long enough at the front to flop in his eyes as he explained how he'd progressed from tiny, inconsequential down page gig reviews to larger reviews, then being sent off to interview morose indie bands that Jennifer had never heard of. He'd jacked in the course at Harlow halfway through 'because having to sit in a Crown court all day taking down shorthand just wasn't my thing and then I was offered a staff writer position.' Now he was Features Editor on a new music magazine. 'It has the irreverent humour of *Smash Hits* but with the musical nous of *NME,* kind of like *The Face* but not so up itself. You didn't ever see my byline in *Melody Maker* then?' he added almost peevishly.

Jennifer shook her head as she pulled out her tube of red lipstick from her make-up bag. 'I hardly thought about you at all,' she said, which was such a gargantuan lie she was surprised that she wasn't struck down by a celestial thunderbolt. 'And I haven't read the music press in years. It's all a bit too teenage really.'

'You're still mad at me after all this time, Jen?' His smile now was much more familiar and wiped out four years just like that. Gone! He was still that beautiful boy. Maybe not quite so much of the boy now. As Jennifer tried to take up less space in the world, Nick had filled out just a little. He still had cheekbones that she wanted to cut her fingers on. Still had eyes as dark as oceans. Still had lips that she used to dream of kissing, even as they smirked at her in that annoying way that always used to make her roll her eyes and punch him on the arm. But then she thought of that revolting, slobbery kiss he'd stuck on her the last time she'd seen him; all teeth and tongue and it was enough to kill the rosy glow of nostalgia.

'It's ancient history,' she was proud to be able to say, because it was. But that didn't mean that there hadn't been nights, months of nights, when she'd replayed his smiles, his expressions, the sweetest things he'd ever said to her, because she had them all catalogued and saved up for best. Those minutes in the photo booth at Mill Hill East could have kept her going for years, in a way that a starving man could survive on crumbs if he had to. She still had that strip of photos in her purse, though Jennifer could hardly ever bring herself to look at them because all of those memories were ruined. What

Jennifer kept coming back to was sprawling on a dirty floor in a toilet in a Camden pub as she listened to Lucy and Linzi lay bare her soul; then that shameful, soul-scouring confrontation at Camden Town station and Nick admitting that she was pretty then shoving his tongue down her throat. Neither of those things that she'd wanted so badly had felt like a victory. More like the last prize in a raffle, like a stale box of chocolates, long past its best before date.

'I handled the whole situation badly,' Nick said, even though it *was* ancient history. Or rather, Jennifer had tormented herself for months and then pushed the whole heart-destroying, character-defining incident right to the back of her mind, where it could do the least harm. 'Between you and Lucy, there was never any real contest.'

'I knew that, so I don't know why I made such a fuss.' Jennifer pressed her lips together and then set about one final dusting of translucent powder. She felt much more in control now she had her face on. 'Of course, you would have chosen Lucy.'

'There's no "of course" about it. I'd have chosen you,' Nick said a little throatily and he hadn't lost the knack of staring deeply and soulfully at Jennifer so she felt like she was the most important person in Nick's world. But it wasn't true now and it certainly hadn't been true then.

'Oh, come on, we both know that's bullshit,' she said sweetly and closed her powder compact with a decisive click.

Nick shrugged as if to say that it had been worth a try. 'George said that you were still mad about it,' he muttered. 'I saw him when I went down to Brighton last month to interview a band – you wouldn't have heard of them – and we ended up talking about you. Not in a bad way. Remembering all the good times we'd had.'

'Glad to hear it,' Jennifer said, surprised that he'd kept in touch with George. Not that she had. She'd wanted to cast aside all her memories of college, leave everything and everyone behind, including George.

But last year, they'd celebrated Kirsty's twenty-first birthday with a weekend in Brighton. There'd been a whole gang of them and Jennifer had bumped into George as they'd been queuing to get into what looked like quite a tacky nightclub on the seafront.

George wasn't having that. He'd dragged them, six over-educated young women, all of them wearing stompy boots and red lipstick, to a gay all-nighter, Trade, at the Zap Club. Going to university in Brighton had been the making of George. Now he was out and proud and had been a dreadful influence on Jennifer that Saturday night. He'd plied her with drugs and made her dance on podiums. Actually, he hadn't made Jennifer do anything. She'd been a very willing partici-pant in both the drug-taking and the podium dancing. It had been one of the best nights of her life.

But it was interesting that George had never mentioned this ecstasy-fuelled encounter to Nick. Maybe George hadn't remembered it. He'd been absolutely off his tits.

They'd just left Holborn. Jennifer was getting off at Bond Street. Now that she'd finished putting her make-up on, she had nothing left to do with her hands but clasp them together and nothing to do with her eyes but try not to stare at Nick.

'What about you then?' He nodded his head once, giving Jennifer permission to drag out her own highlight reel of the last four years. 'I take it you didn't jack in your degree halfway through?'

'No, I got a first,' she said though Nick just nodded again. He was a features editor at a music magazine that wasn't up itself so he wasn't visibly impressed that she was one of only two people on her course to get a first. 'I'm living in Mile End and . . .'

'What's a nice girl like you doing in Mile End?'

'Mile End is actually a very nice place to live, there's the Regent's Canal . . . ugh!' She was going into the self-defensive spiel she went into every time Stan started on his own spiel about dragging himself out of the East End by his bootstraps. 'A year after I started at Westfield College just off the Finchley Road, still living at home, 113 bus from Apex Corner, all that jazz, it merged with Queen Mary's in Bow and . . . well . . .'

'No more 113 bus from Apex Corner?' Nick asked with a grin.

It was impossible not to grin back. 'Mum put up a spirited defence for still living at home even though she was already sick of me getting in at all hours, but I headed east. Apparently I've been written out of the will but I'm still hopeful that I might inherit her collection of Capodimonte figurines.'

'Yeah, you wouldn't want them going to one of your brothers. How are Martin and Tim?' he asked casually.

'I can't believe you even remember their names.'

Nick shrugged. 'Why wouldn't I? They tormented me often enough. Those kissy noises every time I came round.'

'They're a lot more evolved now. Well, Tim is. He's doing A levels, wants to go to university to study biomechanics, which apparently, according to Stan, is a much more useful degree than reading a load of novels.'

'What even are biomechanics?'

'I have no idea.' They grinned at each other again, as the train pulled into Oxford Circus. It had filled up as they'd reminisced and now more people pushed their way in, so Nick was suddenly obscured from view and Jennifer wondered if she'd just imagined it. Him.

'What about Martin then?'

Not a dream. He was leaning left, to peer around the middle-aged, suited man who'd suddenly come between them.

Jennifer leaned right. 'He's turned out to be the black sheep. Decided he'd much rather hang out in the Apex Corner subways, drinking and smoking, than studying for his GCSEs. He's at Barnet College, doing his retakes and an NVQ in something or other.'

She should ask after his older siblings. The twins. Francesca with her masses of pre-Raphaelite curls and a way of looking right through Jennifer, and Nick's brother with the Roman nose and who was as imperious as a Roman emperor on the rare occasions when Jennifer had encountered him. But she couldn't remember the brother's name and anyway . . .

'I'm getting off here.' She tried to stand up but middle-aged guy was so desperate for her seat that he wouldn't budge an inch. Jennifer had to make do with a half-crouch and the delight of treading on his foot as she elbowed her way past him.

She wasn't sure how to say goodbye to Nick. It hadn't been lovely to see him; it was actually deeply unsettling, but it didn't matter because he was right behind her.

'Going to pop into EMI to listen to an album,' he said a little too loudly, like Jennifer should be impressed about that.

She wasn't. 'Can't they just pop a tape in the post?'

Apparently they couldn't, because it was the new album from a very famous band and Nick would be frisked for any recording devices and then listen to the album and make his notes under the watchful eye of a publicist.

She glanced at her watch as they travelled up the escalator. 'Well, I'll say goodbye now then. I'm going in the opposite direction.'

'Trying to get rid of me?' Nick asked, still dogging Jennifer's heels as she inserted her card into the ticket barrier. 'Four years is a long time to hold a grudge, Jen.'

'There's no grudge-holding,' she insisted, though she hadn't even realised that she was still nursing a grievance until ten minutes ago. 'But you're going to take that exit for Manchester Square, it's at the back of John Lewis, right? I'm taking this exit because I'm going to Mayfair. And I'm late.'

Nick took hold of her elbow because they were being those two annoying people blocking the way for everyone trying to get through the barriers.

'It's been weird to see you again, but weird good,' Nick decided. He didn't smell like he used to. Of leather and Elnett. It made Jennifer feel sad. She could still conjure up that smell at will, would sometimes stand behind someone at a gig, someone who was wearing a leather jacket and huffing away on a Marlboro and she'd take great illicit whiffs of them. 'What are you doing in Mayfair? Something fancy? Have you gone up in the world?'

'Not really.' Jennifer made a sound that was half scoff, half world-weary chuckle. 'Waiting hand and foot on the bourgeoisie and the nouveau riche. And lunch service starts in ten minutes.'

'Oh, I won't keep you long,' said Nick with the absolute lack of urgency of someone who'd never been paid by the hour. 'Let's swap numbers.'

What's the point? Jennifer wanted to ask because she had enough problems in her life at this moment without Nick becoming another one of them. The whole time that they'd been talking, ever since he'd touched her on the knee, something had felt off. Wrong. Like she wasn't right in her own skin.

And now she realised, or remembered, that this was the way she always used to feel around him. As if she wasn't enough. Would never be enough. Would always be in love with someone who had no use for her love.

It was bad enough throwing her lot in with Dominic who'd

made her cry the last time she'd seen him; the last thing she wanted was to have Nick back in her life. She'd just have to tell him that. Straight. To his face.

'I can't phone you. Our phone ... it only accepts incoming numbers,' she explained. 'It's a whole thing with the landlord.'

'Bit like when Alan and Jackie wouldn't let you make calls before the six o'clock cheap rate,' Nick said with a grin.

'Don't exaggerate. I was allowed to make calls after one o'clock if it was an absolute emergency,' Jennifer reminded him and they both laughed and then she gave him her number. Of course, she did, because he was the first boy she'd really loved and the echo of those feelings still lingered as she watched him write the digits down in a proper reporter's notebook with his left-handed, curled scrawl that she knew so well from all the track listings on all those mix tapes that he'd made her.

'We should properly catch up,' he said as the world hurried past their little huddle for two by the ticket barriers. 'Wow. Jen Richards.'

'I'm Jennifer now.'

Nick shook his head. 'I don't know who this Jennifer is. You're Jen.'

'What I am is late,' Jennifer said, and she still didn't know how to say goodbye so she settled for gently punching him on his arm, then walking away without looking back.

And that was that. They were both living in London. Their paths had to have crossed at least once and now they had. It was simply a coincidence of their schedules, not to be repeated for at least another four years when their paths might cross on the Jubilee Line or in a queue for the ticket machines at some random tube station. Or maybe, just maybe, Jennifer would never see Nick again.

8

Friday, March 7th, 1992
Goodge Street Station

Two more weeks limped by with absolutely nothing to recommend them. Their landlord, Mr Chalmers, was on the warpath, because Jennifer and Kirsty had the temerity to complain that their ancient oven had finally died of old age.

The other man in Jennifer's life, Dominic, was still cold-shouldering her because she still hadn't committed to doing a PhD.

'You'll do some undergraduate teaching – it's not hard, they have very pedestrian minds – and get some funding so you can give up washing pots in that restaurant. Then you'll have more time to focus on academic pursuits,' had been his latest motivational speech.

'Oh, really? You didn't say anything about my pedestrian mind when I was an undergraduate and you were trying to get into my knickers,' Jennifer had countered. 'And I don't wash pots, as you know very well. Besides, I pretty much live off what I make in tips on a busy weekend.'

They'd been in their local, The Palm Tree, which Jennifer liked because they had lock-ins and Dominic liked because it was 'a perfect example of functional yet decorative 1930s design.' When Jennifer had brought up the fact that she couldn't realistically spend another three or four years of her life living in shitty rented accommodation and without a full-time wage, Dominic's perfect, patrician face became pinched and pursed in a way that Jennifer knew all too well. Then he'd shifted around on the banquette in the saloon bar so his back was to her and started talking to his friend Jason about how Liverpool was going to absolutely decimate Southampton in a first division match that weekend. That had been a week ago and Dominic hadn't said a word to her since.

It wasn't the first time that Dominic had stopped speaking to Jennifer. As usual, the first heady Dominic-free days were glorious. Jennifer was free to do what she wanted without having to justify herself to Dominic, who had an opinion on everything Jennifer did. From what books she read (and not just her set texts) to what she wore to what she had for dinner. At the beginning of their relationship – though he'd said that there was no need to put a name on it and let's just keep things casual – it had been lovely to have someone, a man, so involved in her life.

Dominic represented a marked improvement on Jennifer's two previous boyfriends. There'd been Bob, a maths student with white boy dreadlocks and a preference for his own natural odour over the synthetic, chemical-laden scent of mass-produced deodorants, who'd taken Jennifer's virginity and stuck around for a couple of months after that. Then in her second year there'd been Adrian, a ruddy-faced member of the Revolutionary Communist Party, who fucked in exactly the same way that he lectured Jennifer about the evils of capitalism: with great vigour but without any nuance or interest in what Jennifer might be thinking about either capitalism or the fucking.

Compared to them, Dominic was quite the catch and to start with, he'd acted as if she was truly fascinating, as if he'd never met anyone like her before. With hindsight, Jennifer suspected that it had been less fascination and more incredulity that she'd managed to live her life for twenty-one, nearly twenty-two, years without Dominic's expert guidance.

So, it was a relief to have some time off from Dominic's constant need to improve her. But as the days passed by and still no word, not even when Jennifer succumbed and wrote a genuflecting, apologetic note and stuck it in his cubbyhole in the faculty lounge, she grew uneasy. As if something unpleasant, like an invasive medical procedure or an exam, was looming.

'The unpleasant event is the telling off that you're going to get from Demonic, like he's some stern *paterfamilias*, before he makes you apologise,' Kirsty pointed out. 'No wonder he loves those dreary Victorian novels so much.'

But after the inevitable telling off, Dominic would behave himself for a while. He could really be quite sweet sometimes and if she were going to give in to pressure and do the PhD, then she really would need his guidance. So Jennifer just said wearily, 'I've told you not to call him Demonic a thousand times. One of these days, you're going to say it to his face by accident.'

'Oh no, it won't be by accident,' Kirsty had assured her with a sickly sweet smile and so when the phone finally rang at gone ten o'clock in the evening on the fifteenth day of Dominic's estrangement, Jennifer rushed to answer it.

'Hi!' she said a little breathlessly, stomach dive-bombing in anticipation of the lecture Dominic would have ready about how difficult and obstreperous she was being when he only ever wanted the best for her.

'Hi. Jen? It's Nick.'

Now, her stomach was hurtling towards the floor for an entirely different reason.

'Hi,' Jennifer said again slowly, even as her mind was racing. Why was he calling her? He wasn't meant to call her. He'd only taken her number to be polite. She'd put the whole awkward reunion out of her mind, easy enough to do when she had so many other unpleasant things to focus on and she was something of an expert at pushing away thoughts of Nick.

'Hi,' he repeated with a chuckle that sounded a little nervous, but that was just Jennifer projecting because Nick had never been the nervous type. Not then and not now that he was features editor of some music magazine that wasn't up itself. Although she hadn't been thinking about Nick, not at all, she had gone into the newsagent's across the road and pored over the music magazines until she'd found his name on a masthead, his byline on an interview with Mudhoney and had read half of the piece before the woman behind the till had shouted, 'This isn't a library. You read it! You buy it!'

'How are you?' Nick asked, breaking the chain of hi's. 'Such a trip to see you the other week.'

'Yeah, it was a blast from the past,' Jennifer agreed. The phone was in the kitchen and she sat down at the little table and crossed her legs, rotated an ankle so she could see the chipped red polish on her toenails. 'I didn't expect you to call.'

Even back then, even when she'd thought she was madly and secretly in love with Nick, she'd been able to be honest with him in a way that she couldn't be with Dominic. If she'd told Dominic that she hadn't expected him to call, there'd be sulks and recriminations, not another raspy little chuckle from Nick.

'Been working up the courage. Also, I was in the States for work. Went to Austin for SXSW,' he added, in case Jennifer really did believe that he was too scared to call her.

Jennifer didn't know where Austin was or what SXSW was, so she just made a noncommittal noise and ignored her stomach, which was still fluttering like a trapped bird. It wasn't nerves, she told herself. It was because she'd had nothing to eat since she'd wolfed down a bowl of soup ten minutes before she'd waitressed the lunchtime shift.

'Yeah, the actual bands weren't that great. Willie Nelson was the big draw but there were some good speakers, some good parties . . .'

'Right,' Jennifer muttered and she really didn't know why Nick had called, unless she was meant to be impressed that he was now the kind of person who got flown halfway across the world to cover what sounded like some quite dull music festival. 'So, was there a reason why—'

'You're probably wondering why I called you—'

'Sorry—'

'No, sorry, I interrupted,' Nick insisted. 'What were you about to say?'

Jennifer pulled a face at the dishes stacked in the drying rack on the draining board. 'Why are you calling? So we can catch up?'

'Well, yeah, of course I want to catch up,' Nick said, as if it should be obvious, as if they'd parted on the best of terms all those years ago. 'Over drinks, maybe? I always have a plus one so we could go and see a band then, you know . . .'

'No, I don't really know,' Jennifer said, marvelling at how she could be this upfront, this chippy with Nick when she couldn't voice even the mildest dissent with the man she was sleeping with. 'Don't you think some things are best left in the past?'

There was a moment's sticky silence. Jennifer began to sort through a pile of junk mail that had come through the door: flyers for Indian takeaways, pizza parlours, local cab companies, painting and decorating services, a small card advertising a local spiritualist healer promising 'good fortune and positive, healing lifeforce to all customers' until Nick let out a sigh, like he'd been holding his breath.

'The thing is, Jen, four years ago I was nineteen and I was an arsehole. And I'm probably still an arsehole now in completely new and different ways but I always regretted what happened between us . . .'

'There wasn't an us. Not really,' Jennifer said dully even as the pain she'd willed away sharpened.

'I just told Lucy what I thought she wanted to hear.' Nick wasn't listening to her and the last thing Jennifer wanted was to relive ten of the most humiliating minutes of her life. 'You were my friend, Jen, my best friend.'

'It's ancient history,' Jennifer said firmly. 'You're forgiven, absolved.'

'Then come and have a drink with me, for old times' sake,' Nick said in that cajoling, husky tone that Jennifer hadn't forgotten. It was the voice, which had fuelled a thousand teen fantasies. She was impervious to *that* voice now, surely?

'Well, OK, let's meet up but I'm bringing my friend,' Jennifer said, cross with herself because what she'd seen of this current incarnation of Nick, she didn't like very much, but God help her, the sixteen-year-old that she used to be was thrilled that she'd got Nick Levene to beg to spend time with her.

'Yeah, bring your friend.' He paused. 'What's she like?'

Jennifer was tempted to say, 'She's a he and he's built like a brick shithouse,' but she went for the more truthful, 'Kirsty's from Sheffield. She's very beautiful and doesn't tolerate racists, sexists or dickheads.'

'Just as well that I'm none of those things,' Nick said, which was absolute bullshit and he knew it because he laughed and it was odd that you could miss someone, look forward to seeing them, even while you still hated them a little bit.

★

Kirsty was more than up for going to see a band in the company of Nick, the breaker of teenage hearts.

'Meet the boy who did your tender, eighteen-year-old self wrong? Of course I want to meet him,' Kirsty had said with some relish. 'I'll make him rue the day and all that.'

'You don't have to . . .'

'But I know you'd do exactly the same for me if you ever met Ian Wallis who tried to snog me at a Wedding Present gig then told everyone that I kissed like a washing machine and I stuffed my bra.'

'It would be so much easier if we were lesbians,' Jennifer lamented, not for the first time. They'd even had an experimental kissing session, after a jelly shot promotion at one of the local bars, which had lasted for three excruciating minutes before Kirsty had called a halt and Jennifer had gratefully removed her tongue from Kirsty's mouth and her hand from Kirsty's breast.

'We both like dick too much,' Kirsty had said sadly, and Jennifer had agreed. Objectively she liked the idea of dick, but so far her subjective experiences with dick had been very disappointing.

That had been over three years ago and now they were doing what they did best: getting ready to go out and get into trouble. It was Friday night and they had both their stereos going full blast as they flitted between each other's rooms and wardrobes and the kitchen to get another refill of cheap supermarket-brand vodka and cheap supermarket-brand Diet Cola.

They were almost ready to go, Jennifer having tried on and discarded several garish crimplene dresses purchased from the charity shops of East London and still being taken up by Dorothy, but much shorter than when Jennifer had been doing A levels. 'Short enough that anyone can see what you had for breakfast,' her gran always said sorrowfully but she could never say no to anyone, let alone her eldest grandchild and besides, Jennifer was never seen in public without a pair of thick black tights on.

She'd decided on a dress whose black background was the perfect canvas for its squiggly graphic pattern in stinging shades of pink, green, orange, blue and yellow, like a test card on LSD. Then the ubiquitous black tights and motorcycle boots, her hair backcombed and teased into a messy bun, fringe trimmed over the bathroom sink and her eyeliner and red lipstick thicker than usual. Because it wasn't make-up; it was war paint and Jennifer was all ready for battle when she heard the doorbell ring.

Or rather someone was leaning on the doorbell to make themselves heard over the stereophonic cacophony of *Screamedelica* and *Nevermind*.

'Who is that?' Jennifer asked, as she sat cross-legged in front of the full-length mirror that was stuck onto her wardrobe door with Blu Tack and gaffa tape, applying yet more mascara and making no move to get up and answer the summons.

Kirsty, who was leaning over her, so they could both share the mirror, shrugged. 'Maybe it's baby-faced Andrews, the bastard butcher of Bow.'

'Well, he can bugger off,' Jennifer decided, but whoever it was wasn't buggering off and when she finally managed to wrestle the window open, she saw Dominic standing there, a pained expression on his face.

'I've been ringing for ages,' he complained. 'Come downstairs and let me in.'

'We're going out,' Jennifer shouted, buoyed up by cheap vodka and the anticipation of a proper night out. 'It will have to be some other time.'

The pained expression upgraded to a scowl. 'You were the one so desperate to get hold of me.'

'And you were pretty desperate not to be got hold of,' Jennifer pointed out at some volume, though she could already feel the first pinprick deflating her good cheer.

Luckily Kirsty was there to roughly shove her out of the way. 'She phoned you countless times. She even put a note in your faculty mailbox a week ago. All of which you ignored, so don't come round here and expect Jennifer to drop everything.'

'Note? I never got a note,' Dominic insisted.

'I watched her put it in. I suppose you never got the phone messages that she left either,' Kirsty said scathingly because she was so much better at hauling Dominic over the coals, and Jennifer was happy to, literally, hide behind her best friend rather than confront her own boyfriend. Which wouldn't do at all. She was a feminist. She had her own voice. Which could be very strident if she was dealing with anyone else.

Enough of this!

It was Jennifer's turn to elbow Kirsty aside so she had room to gaze down on Dominic. 'I'm so fed up with these games, Dom . . .'

'I've been very busy . . .'

'I doubt that there was a sudden Victorian literature emergency that needed all of your attention,' she snapped as Kirsty snorted with approval. 'I'm going to ULU to drink heavily subsidised alcohol and if you are over all this nonsense of freezing me out then we can meet on Sunday. You owe me cake.'

'Saturday's better,' Dominic said immediately even though he knew full well that . . .

'I'm working tomorrow. Sunday, three o'clock. If you come round with cake I'll let you in.' Jennifer didn't have a snappy closing line and it looked like Dominic was going to argue the point so she quickly withdrew to wrestle the window closed.

When they came clattering down the stairs five minutes later, Jennifer back in the party spirit due to an eye-watering, throat-catching shot of vodka, Dominic was nowhere to be seen. 'And I'll worry about him on Sunday,' Jennifer decided as she and Kirsty staggered to Mile End tube, passing a big plastic bottle of vodka and Diet Cola back and forth.

Jennifer felt quite giddy, as half an hour later, they staggered out of the lift at Goodge Street station, the vodka all gone but the buzz remained.

'So, this Nick . . . how do you feel about him? Friend or foe?' Kirsty asked.

'Not sure. Maybe a bit of both,' Jennifer said as they stepped out onto Tottenham Court Road. Even though they were five minutes late, Nick wasn't there and it instantly felt as if someone had played a practical joke on her. Maybe she'd imagined the encounter on the tube, the phone call.

Though back in the day, unless she was going to his house to run the gauntlet of Susan, he was always late. One Sunday, she'd waited half an hour outside Dingwalls in Camden for him and he'd just laughed when she'd raged at him. Told her not to be such a princess, as if she had nothing better to do with her time than wait for him. 'This is starting to feel like a bad idea.'

As soon as she'd said it, Nick appeared like the shopkeeper in *Mr Ben*. Materialising out of nowhere, or rather stepping out of a shadowed doorway, his hand raised in greeting.

'There you are,' he said easily, as if he and Jennifer hadn't spent the last few years apart.

His eyes glanced over Kirsty, who was worth a second glance. And a third or a fourth. She was wearing her going-out uniform of black bodysuit and red velvet hotpants over thick black tights and a pair of monkey boots because stilettos were a symbol of patriarchy designed so that women could hardly walk unaided. Also, Kirsty had weak ankles. A silver lurex scarf was flung casually around her neck, which matched her silver eyeshadow, her eyes huge in her pretty face. She was Twiggy by way of Sheffield; her tiny, bird-like figure at odds with her combative nature and her broad Yorkshire accent.

'Take a picture, pet, it lasts longer,' she told Nick. He blinked then smiled that lazy smile which had always made Jennifer yearn that little bit harder. Kirsty was made from much stronger stuff. 'So, you're Nick.'

'And you're Kirsty. Great to meet you,' Nick said, and he hadn't even looked in Jennifer's direction, so now she felt silly in her stupid day-glo clown dress, but then he gifted her a smile too. 'I've got you both on the guest list. No need to thank me.'

Kirsty rolled her eyes. 'God, what is he like?'

Now Jennifer was worried about the potential for awkwardness between her best friend and her ex-best friend who just happened to be a boy as the evening unfolded. Why couldn't she leave the past alone?

Nick held out his arm to her so she could tuck her arm through his and she really was pathetic. Clinging to those paper-thin adolescent dreams, but it was nice to huddle into him as they crossed over Tottenham Court Road, a bitter wind knifing through them and creating havoc with Jennifer's hair. She didn't even mind too much that Kirsty had taken Nick's other arm and was telling him that she only listened to music by female artistes. 'Though the music industry is inherently a misogynistic system,' she was shouting over the whistling of the wind. 'We're all just pawns of the patriarchy.'

'Yeah, good point, though I guess I do quite well out of the patriarchy,' Nick added cheerfully. 'Maybe I can subvert from the inside.'

'We all know you never will,' Jennifer sniffed but maybe the evening might turn out to be less excruciating than she thought.

For starters, being on the guest list was thrilling and they saved themselves the honour of having to pay five quid to see a bunch of whiny mope-rockers. 'We just need to stay for three songs while in the eyeline of the publicist,' Nick explained, having bought them both a vodka and Diet Coke and once they'd done their contractually obligated three songs, they sat in the bar and instead of talking about himself for several hours straight, Nick asked the questions.

'So, how did you two meet?' he wanted to know. Jen had been expecting another rehashing of the past or wanting to know what her future plans were. Topics that she wanted to avoid, but this one was easy to answer and made her grin.

'Freshers' Week,' she said. 'I'd already been annexed by this girl called Pru who'd decided we were going to be buddies, just because we'd sat next to each other in the orientation lecture.'

'But then I saw Jennifer across a crowded Freshers' Fair and she was wearing a Patti Smith T-shirt and glaring at the absolute rotters manning the Young Conservatives Society and I felt my heart skip a beat,' Kirsty chimed in as she put her hand on the very heart in question.

'So I'm standing there while Pru is telling me that she thinks we should join the Wiccan Society when suddenly this girl grabs my arm and says, "I really hoped that I'd finally find my people when I got to University . . ."'

'"And I have. You're my people," I said to Jennifer and instead of taking out a restraining order, she asked me if I wanted to get a coffee and we've been inseparable ever since.' Kirsty smiled at Jennifer with the affection that came from finding your people and knowing that no matter how annoying or wrong you could be at any one time, you had someone who was always on your side.

It had taken Jennifer eighteen years to realise that friendship could be so simple and unconditional. Such a difference from the friendship she'd had with Nick who was frowning as he looked at their clasped hands.

'And Pru?' he asked.

Jennifer shrugged. 'She did join the Wiccan Society and now she's living in a commune near Glastonbury on account of all the leylines.'

'So, what do you do now that you're not students?'

The two women shared a look. 'Do you want to tell him or shall I?'

'I'll break it to him,' Jennifer said with a sigh.

'Break what to me? What are you involved in?' Nick leaned forward, eyes gleaming. 'Is it something dodgy? Are you running drugs? Are you on the game? Jen! What would Stan say?'

'I think Stan would prefer that I was on the game, rather than *still* being a student. He says that I don't know the meaning of hard work, though he should try waiting tables in a Mayfair restaurant on the Friday lunchtime shift. Brutal.'

'We're just finishing up our MAs,' Kirsty explained. 'I'm doing mine on shopping lists.'

'Because she's a social historian,' Jennifer said a little defensively when Nick half laughed/half coughed. 'And I'm doing my MA on *Middlemarch* because I'm an idiot.'

'That doesn't sound like something an idiot would do,' Nick said but Jennifer could tell that this conversation, she and Kirsty, weren't the amusing diversion they had originally been. She was sitting with her back to the room and Nick's eyes were fixed beyond her as if he was waiting for someone or something far more entertaining. Then his eyes widened, even as Jennifer felt a displacement of the air as someone approached, and a heavy hand landed on her shoulder.

'I decided to join you,' said a familiar voice. *Dominic.*

Next to her, Kirsty huffed so hard that even the damp gig flyers on their table fluttered in the downwind. 'I thought you weren't invited.' Unlike Jennifer she had no problem with creating clear-cut boundaries and enforcing them to within an inch of their life.

'Didn't we agree Sunday?' Even to Jennifer's own ears, her voice sounded weak. She wasn't even the good drunk anymore, where she was loud and obnoxious and took no prisoners. Her teeth were numb, she felt vaguely nauseous in a way that would become more pronounced as time went on and her vision was blurry enough to add to the sensation that she was trapped on a boat in choppy waters.

But her vision wasn't blurry enough that she could mistake Dominic for anyone else as he stared down at her with the disapproving expression that she'd grown so familiar with. 'I wanted to see you now,' he said. In the early days of their courtship – Jennifer the still impressionable second year English Literature student, Dominic the dashing postgraduate and undisputed heartthrob of the English department – she'd been thrilled by such bold statements of intent, but now?

Now, it was just the five hundred and forty-seventh time Dominic wasn't listening to what Jennifer said because it didn't fit in with his immediate plans.

'What are you drinking or have you had enough?' he asked, because he couldn't even buy her a drink without point scoring.

It was on the tip of her furred tongue to tell him where to shove his drink but Kirsty never turned down free alcohol. 'Two vodka and Diet Cokes and what are you having, Nick? Another Stella?'

Nick nodded and Dominic nodded back. He probably thought that Nick was there for Kirsty – she had quite a high turnover of boyfriends – so not somebody that he needed to concern himself with.

The feeling wasn't mutual. As soon as Dominic was at the bar, Nick rubbed his hands together with what looked like glee. 'Is that your boyfriend, Jen?' Though Dominic had his back to them, Nick gave him an appraising look and Jennifer wilted because Dominic liked to dress as if it were 1935 and he was the young curate of a small parish church. He was wearing a tweed jacket, old fashioned trousers with turn-ups and was the only person Jennifer knew who sported the official Queen Mary's navy and yellow striped scarf. Even from behind, his short back and sides haircut was clearly evident and when he turned round with a tray of drinks, he had the air of a man who was always on the verge of asking that eternal question, '*Oh! Yet stands the Church clock at ten to three? And is there honey still for tea?*'

'Just a Diet Coke for you, Jennifer. You've had enough to drink,' Dominic announced censoriously as he placed the tray on the table. Kirsty kicked her but now wasn't the time to have it out with Dominic. Despite what he might think, Jennifer really hadn't had enough to drink to launch into an impassioned diatribe about the way Dominic was crushing her soul.

It was left to Nick to make the introductions. 'Thanks for the drink,' he said politely, holding out his hand. 'I'm Nick. I'm sure Jen has told you all about me.'

Dominic took the proffered hand like Nick had smeared it in dogshit first. 'I can't say that *Jennifer* has.'

It was Dominic's turn to give Nick a swift and assessing glance: the Chelsea boots, the tight jeans, the blue plaid shirt unbuttoned to reveal a tight black T-shirt underneath, the thick sweep of fringe that Nick brushed back with fingers adorned with silver rings. All capped off with that careless grin, always half a centimetre away from a smirk.

The effect on Dominic was instant and inevitable. Jennifer inwardly sighed as Dominic's shoulders lost their rigid set and he quickly tugged off his scarf. 'Anyway, mate, I'm made up to meet you,' he said in a voice, which was now much more Birkenhead than Brideshead.

Kirsty kicked her again and muttered 'Unbelievable,' under her breath but it was only too believable. When he wasn't being unbearably superior, Dominic loved to think that he was a man of the people.

When he'd first taken her out for a drink, after a two-hour private tutorial where his incisive commentary, half complimentary, half eviscerating, on her essay about *Mary Barton* had left Jennifer quite breathless – also, to be honest, quite turned on – his accent had got thicker and more pronounced until she'd said, 'Oh, I didn't realise you were from Liverpool.'

There was no reason that she should have because usually Dominic sounded like the poster boy for RP. 'I'm a bit of a paradox, me,' he'd confessed, ducking his head as if he were embarrassed. 'The scouser scholar.'

Oh yes, in the early days, Dominic had implied all sorts of things. That even though he was studying for a PhD on John Ruskin, he was still a scally deep down and was running some kind of typically scally scam to do with credits for the photocopiers in the library and something even more nefarious that explained the lovely flat overlooking the park. He'd also intimated *quite strongly* that his family were dockers and that Jennifer, being a poncy Southerner, was practically descended from royalty when compared to Dominic's own humble roots.

It was all utter rubbish. There was no scam. Dominic was entitled to free photocopies for his undergraduate seminar work. Everything else had become apparent late one Sunday morning as Jennifer was entwined in Dominic's arms in his big comfy double bed (no lumpy pillows and wafer-thin duvet from BHS for Dom) and resisting his efforts to push her head down because he wanted a blowjob. Suddenly they'd heard a key turn, then the front door open.

Was it the rightful owners of the flat? Maybe some Liverpudlian crime lord who'd been sent down for a ten stretch but had got out early for good behaviour?

Liverpudlian crime lords didn't call out, 'Dommy, darling? Surprise! It's Mummy and Daddy come to take you out for lunch.'

It quickly became apparent that Dominic's dad wasn't a docker, he was a High Court judge, just like his father before him. 'Though there's definitely some shipbuilding on Mummy's side of the family,' he'd hissed as Jennifer sat across from Mummy at the family's favourite table at Simpson's in the Strand. Which made it sound like a great-great-grandfather had spent long, arduous days banging nails into mainstays or whatever it was that shipbuilders did, rather than owning an actual shipyard, as his mother explained five minutes later.

'He's not even from Liverpool,' she'd told Kirsty, who had been weeping with laughter at the tale of how Dominic had been undone. 'He's from the Wirral. To think he accused me of dripping with privilege even though I was on a full maintenance grant and the first person in my family to do A levels.'

But by then, Jennifer was in too deep. Hurtling towards a first class honours degree. Being wooed by Dominic's supervisor, Mina, to sign up to the MA programme then a PhD after that. 'You and Dominic are such a great team,' she'd said, over tea and cake in the faculty lounge. 'I realise it can be a bit daunting, when there's no academic tradition in your family so you're very lucky that Dominic has taken you under his wing.'

Lately Jennifer felt increasingly unlucky that Dominic was so enmeshed in her life, especially as she listened to him talk to Nick about football because that's what real men did; Dominic's accent becoming even more guttural and phlegmy.

Nick was playing along, although in the two years that she'd known him, he'd never expressed any kind of interest in football. He was staring at Dominic, head tilted, amused and, oh God, it was so obvious!

This wasn't the first time she'd fallen under the sway of a charismatic, good-looking boy who wanted her in a supporting role while he took main stage. This thing with Dominic, which brought her zero joy, was just a tinny echo of all those complicated feelings that she'd had for Nick. Now Jennifer came to the sobering conclusion that, once again, she was very much the junior partner with nothing to offer. That she was expected to be pleased, even *grateful*, for the attention.

'Are you all right, Jennifer?' Kirsty asked urgently, peering at her friend's face. 'You look weird. Are you going to be sick?'

She was sick all right. 'I'm not doing a PhD,' Jennifer blurted out and saying the words was such a sweet, blessed relief even though Dominic broke off from the football chat to give her a stern look. 'I don't want to do a PhD. I want to work in publishing. That's what I've always wanted to do and, quite frankly . . .'

'Not this again.' Dominic had the audacity to smile in a long-suffering way at Nick as if to say, *You see what I have to put up with?* 'How selfish to squander all my time and energy then decide that actually you'd like to work in some dreary office stapling press releases about the latest romance novel.'

'Is that all that you think I'm capable of? Make your mind up, Dom. I'm clever enough to do a PhD but not clever enough to be able to do anything other than the most menial clerical duties. I guess I'm a *paradox*,' she added making the most bitter of air quotations with her fingers.

'Jennifer, we both know that you're not a very practical sort of person. You wouldn't survive ten minutes in the real world. At least in academia, you'd be cushioned from that.'

'Like I'm cushioned when I'm waiting tables on a double shift and reciting the specials while some creep puts his hand up my skirt.' Jennifer pointed at Dominic with a rigid, stabby finger.

'You were still reading Jilly Cooper novels when we first met,' he recalled with a little chuckle that was like ice cubes tumbling down her back.

Jennifer sucked in one furious breath. 'There is absolutely *nothing* wrong with reading Jilly Cooper novels.'

'Also, that's not very feminist of you, Dom,' Kirsty piped up at last. Jennifer was amazed that she'd managed to rein in her usually snarky asides for this long. 'You really are just a tool of the patriarchy, aren't you?'

Dominic chose to ignore the comments from the cheap seats. 'I don't know what's got into you . . .'

'Let's not do this here,' Jennifer said, aware of Kirsty keen to get off the ropes and take another swing. Even worse, Nick was leaning forward, not bothering to hide his amusement. It was all so humiliating.

'You're being very immature, Jennifer—'

'I just said, not here. Why do you never listen to—'

'Jennifer! Will you let me finish?' Dominic demanded, his right hand raised again like he was leading a seminar group. 'You're being ridiculous and not only are you embarrassing yourself, you're embarrassing me.'

'Oh my God, you're right, I am embarrassed. Embarrassed that I've let you snuff out every spark in me with your pompousness and your dull, *dull* Victorian novels where everyone dies.'

'Thank you for that, Jennifer,' Dominic said heavily. 'And I'll thank you tomorrow when you apologise for your appalling behaviour because you've had too much to drink and you're showing off in front of an old boyfriend.'

'Not an old boyfriend,' Nick said. Curiously he didn't have the look of a man who was mortified to watch two people who'd both read too many books really go at each other. On the contrary, he looked like he was having the greatest night of his life. 'We used to be best friends.'

Those days at college when Nick had been the centre of her world seemed like a lifetime ago. Jennifer wasn't sixteen, seventeen or even eighteen anymore. She was twenty-one, almost twenty-two. She'd left home. She had a demanding job as well as working towards her second academic qualification. She knew the difference between first and second wave feminism and she was glad that she was a third wave feminist because that meant she could wear fishnet tights and red lipstick.

She'd read *A Vindication of the Rights of Woman* by Mary Wollstonecraft and Luce Irigaray's *Speculum of the Other Woman*. She'd marched to take back the night and now it was time to take back the two years of her life she'd wasted on Dominic.

'I don't need to apologise for anything I've said,' Jennifer decided slowly. 'But I need to break up with you because I am never going to be the person that I want to be if we stay together.'

'Honestly, Jennifer, you make it sound like I'm some kind of domestic despot.' All traces of the Liverpudlian accent were gone now, every one of Dominic's syllables etched from glass. 'I've hardly oppressed you. Quite the contrary, I'd say that I've lifted you up.'

'Wow! That's kind of patronising,' Nick said, with that lazy smile that used to be Jen's undoing and certainly seeing it again, had precipitated the extrication of herself from this horrible relationship and consequently from the prospect of spending the next three or four years toiling away on a PhD dissertation. Still, she could manage perfectly fine by herself. And she could also find a way to tell Dominic that they were over, which might actually penetrate his thick skull.

'Oh just fuck off, Dom,' Jennifer said slowly, separating out the words with relish. 'Fuck all the way off and once you're there, fuck off some more.'

Dom stood up, all the better to look down at Jen with a bitterly disappointed expression like she'd muddled up her footnotes. He opened his mouth to say something, something boring and wordy, but Jennifer slumped back in her seat with an exaggerated groan and rolled her eyes dramatically.

'Why are you still here?' she asked and finally Dominic gathered up his scarf to his chest like it was a motherless child and left, weaving his way through the tables and chairs slowly enough that he must have heard Kirsty call after him, 'Bye bye, Demonic and not a minute too soon!'

Then she turned to Jennifer who was now slack-limbed in shock at what she'd just done.

'No, Jennifer. No regrets,' Kirsty said proudly. 'You were *majestic.*'

'Do you think I went too far?' Jennifer asked Kirsty but she was looking at Nick because he was looking at her in a way that he never used to. Not indulgent. Not amused. Not even exasperated. But with respect, as if she was his equal, but also not someone to be messed with.

Maybe that was why he now raised his almost empty bottle of lager in salute. 'I don't remember you ever being quite so mean, Jen.' He smiled. 'I like it.'

PART FOUR

1994

9

November 3rd, 1994
Hammersmith Station

The days were long at the Phillip Gill literary agency. It seemed to Jennifer as she climbed up the stairs to the office above a dry cleaners in Shepherd's Bush at 9.30 every morning, time began to slow down.

After a morning of photocopying, typing up Phillip Gill's long, ponderous, often incomprehensible notes to his authors and sending back unsolicited manuscripts with a terse form letter designed solely to crush the recipients' hopes and dreams, one o'clock had never been so welcome.

Jennifer got half an hour for lunch. She'd take her packed lunch to Shepherd's Bush Green and hope for an empty bench and some fresh air as lorries and buses and cars thundered past her on three sides.

On a cold November Thursday, when the sky was grey and there was a dampness in the air, even the petrol fumes were a welcome relief from the stuffiness of the little two room agency. Jennifer ate her cheese sandwich made from cheap white bread that wasn't designed to hold a filling, then pulled out her notepad to scribble a few lines on a letter to Kirsty.

Writing an MA dissertation on shopping lists had really worked out for Kirsty; she'd wangled her way onto a cushy research project on consumer habits at the University of Stockholm. 'Please send me some more of those Swedish fish sweets considering that you're literally being paid to go shopping. And no! Of course I'm not jealous, as I toil away at the coalface of literature in a draughty office while fighting off the advances of Phil Gill.'

Phil Gill, as Jennifer never called him to his face having been instructed to only ever address him as 'Mr Gill' or 'Sir' was the worst part of this job. Although, considering his agency was a one-man operation, it meant that all the job sucked.

Not that it really was a job, Jennifer reminded herself once she was back at her desk in the outer office that led through to Phil's inner sanctum. For it to be a proper job, surely she'd get paid. Instead, it was what the publishing industry called 'an internship' and what Jennifer called slave labour. She only got travel expenses though it was an ordeal to coax the money from the petty cash tin via Phil's fat fingers.

It had been quite the rude awakening to realise that the capital's publishers weren't rushing to employ Jennifer even though she had a first class honours degree in English Literature and an MA on the relationship between sex and death in *Middlemarch*.

Every Monday, Jennifer would comb through the *Guardian*'s media section. To start off with she'd been quite discerning; applying for editorial assistant and junior editor jobs. But as the weeks went by with barely even a rejection letter, just a deafening wall of silence, she became less picky. Sure, she could work in marketing or publicity or foreign rights then quickly make a sideways shift to editorial where they'd be wowed by her prowess 'as a self-sufficient self-starter who also works well as part of a team.'

All she'd managed to achieve were a few fortnight-long 'work experience' shifts, where she stuffed envelopes, did a lot of photocopying and suffered the pain of a thousand paper cuts with a sunny, ingratiating smile. She planned to make herself so indispensable that she'd be guaranteed the next junior position that became vacant. They might even create a job just for Jennifer. Jennifer, and all the other young women doing work experience who had names like Arabella and Araminta, had all gone to Oxford or Cambridge and didn't seem unduly concerned that they weren't bringing in a wage. Maybe it was that lack of concern, the blithe self-assurance that seemed to come as standard when you went to boarding school, along with the ability to play lacrosse and remember to say napkin instead of serviette, but it was the Arabellas and the Aramintas who got the jobs. Time and time again, Jennifer was told that she didn't have enough experience but then she couldn't get the experience without a job.

Hence, a six-month internship at the Phillip Gill literary agency, although Jennifer had been very firm with Phil; she could only work until six every evening and she couldn't work Fridays at all.

'You seem to think working is some kind of holiday,' he'd blethered in his blustery, blowhard way. 'You should be paying me for training you up, my girl.'

But there wasn't exactly a line out of the door waiting for a chance to slave over Phil's slushpile and do his filing. He even made her cut the Post-it notepads in half to save money. During her first week there, Jennifer had found a cut-up Post-it note in a drawer with 'God, I'm about to die from boredom!' scrawled on it; a message from beyond the grave or from her predecessor who was known darkly as 'that girl' by Phillip.

So Jennifer was resigned to spending the best, ripest days of her life imprisoned between the agency's nicotine yellow walls. Surrounded on all sides by filing cabinets and shelves of books, which initially had been quite thrilling until closer investigation revealed that the books were mostly about military history. Brick-like biographies of brigadiers, vast volumes on obscure military campaigns and a worrying amount of books about the Nazis.

The men who wrote these books (it was always men) were very terse when they rang to speak to Phil, who insisted that Jennifer take a message and more often than not he decided not to return their calls, so they'd ring again, even more terse. One day, not long after she'd started, the author of *The Other Battle of Britain: A Wing Commander's Memoirs*, called her a 'useless little scrubber', and she'd had to go to the poky, piss-scented toilet they shared with the debt-collection agency on the second floor and have a little cry.

Jennifer felt like having a cry now as she heard the slow, heavy tread of Phillip lumbering up the stairs. It was just gone four. He'd disappeared just before twelve to have lunch with an editor in Soho. A four hour lunch was pretty standard for Phillip. Jennifer could smell the alcohol fumes before he even shouldered open the door, his fleshy face and bulbous nose even more red than usual.

He snapped his podgy fingers at her. 'Coffee. Who's called?'

Jennifer picked up a small pile of cut up Post-it notes so he could snatch them from her. 'Selwyn, your accountant. He said it was very urgent.'

'Urgent.' Phillip made an actual harrumphing sound. He was the only person Jennifer had ever met, outside of books, who harrumphed. 'I dictated some letters in the taxi on the way back. They must go in the final post. They're very important letters.'

Jennifer doubted that very much. She took the Dictaphone from Phillip. It was hot and moist from where it had been clutched in his hand. She tried not to grimace.

'Well, I'll just be getting on with that,' she said, ignoring the way his eyes lingered on her breasts, because she was almost immune to it by now.

He stood there, swaying slightly for a few seconds, then righted himself, shook his head and blinked. 'Right. Yes. Selwyn. Also, I must have Henry Cormack's contract to peruse.'

Another snap of his fingers to indicate that Henry Cormack's contract took precedence over the letters then he lumbered into his office and left the door open. This would mean that Jennifer had to transcribe his precious letters while Phillip barked, spluttered and wheezed his way through his phone calls. Worse than that, he was already clipping the thick, fat cigar that he'd work on for the rest of the day, clamping it between his thick, fleshy lips and sending out a foul-scented fug that permeated everything, but especially Jennifer's hair, her clothes, even the contents of her handbag.

'I'll just shut the door, shall I?' she asked hopefully.

Phillip sucked wetly on the cigar for a second then removed it from his gaping maw. 'Leave the damn thing open, so I can keep a beady eye on you, girl.'

Nobody would ever believe exactly how odious (even odorous), Phil really was. Jennifer didn't have any friends in publishing who'd encountered Phil at some swanky literary lunch and could empathise. She didn't have any friends in publishing, full stop. All her other friends just thought she was exaggerating to get laughs.

Still, there was something satisfying, even soothing, about the clunky sound of the ancient electronic typewriter (no swanky computers or even a word processor had made it over the threshold of the Phillip Gill agency) as Jennifer got into her rhythm. She'd taught herself to type one summer with an ancient Pitmans book and her mother's old typewriter and it had proved to be a far more profitable skill than anything she'd learned at university.

Her fingers thundered over the keys like the Gadarene swine, until Phillip appeared in his office doorway, bushy brows beetled, and shut the door. Jennifer stuck her tongue out at the frosted glass panel, at the lumbering shape hurrying back to his desk.

By quarter to six everything that needed to be typed was typed. With a deep and unhappy anticipatory sigh, Jennifer knocked on Phillip's door, didn't wait for his grunted assent, which rarely came, but opened the door herself and advanced forward under the weight of Phillip's scowl.

He took the phone away from his ear and held a meaty paw over the receiver. 'What now?'

'You need to sign these letters so they can go in the last post,' Jennifer told him, proffering the letters and a pen because it would take ages to find a working ballpoint in the debris on Phillip's desk.

There could well be all sorts of glaring errors in the letters but time was on Jennifer's side. Phillip signed with his slashing signature, grumbling all the while and Jennifer was almost free and clear when he coughed as she was about to close his office door.

'And I'll see you first thing tomorrow.' It was an order not a question and they played this game at five minutes to six every Thursday evening.

'You know I don't work Fridays,' Jennifer said without flinching, though her first couple of weeks at the agency, she'd cringed where she stood. 'Have a good evening,' she added brightly and she fled, picking up her coat and bag on the way and stuffing the letters into their respective envelopes as she ran down the stairs.

Her multitasking skills were second to none. Jennifer could see the post office van pulling up at the postbox, which glowed dull red under the streetlights, and picked up her pace.

'Could set my watch by you,' said the friendly driver, opening his sack so Jennifer could drop her letters in.

She was still in forward motion, running through the rush hour crowds to get to the tube station. It was only two stops and it would have been cheaper to take the bus but Jennifer didn't have time to crawl through the clogged streets. She'd rather strap-hang, hot and flustered as a colony of butterflies had taken control of her stomach at the thought of what the evening had in store for her.

Jennifer reached Hammersmith far too soon. Then it was a short walk from the tube past handsome Victorian houses until she came to a building that had once been a school but was now an adult education centre.

She shouldered her way through the door, wincing at the old school smell of disinfectant and savoury mince. Jennifer climbed the stairs up to the second floor and made her way down a corridor, classrooms on either side, until she came to the last one. Although she was early, there were already a handful of people setting up their workstations.

It's really not so bad once you get into the spirit, Jennifer told herself although the spirit was elusive as she entered the room, a tense smile already on her face. Not that anyone paid her any attention as she scurried through, head down, until she reached a door at the back of the room. She supposed that once it must have been a stationery cupboard because she was sure that the lingering scent of chalk dust was catching at the back of her throat as she shut the door behind her and dumped her bag on a tiny chair more suited to a small child than an adult woman.

Five minutes later, she was still skulking in the cupboard. Through the door Jennifer could hear the hum of conversation so the classroom must have filled up. Skulking wasn't going to get the job done. She pulled off the rest of her clothes, her lovely warm clothes, folding her jumper neatly and placing it on the chair followed by tights, bra and knickers. Then she grabbed the voluminous and fluffy robe that she'd had stuffed in her bag all day.

It was her favourite item of clothing because since she'd left home she'd never once managed to live anywhere with central heating. Right now, it was covering everything that Jennifer wanted to keep covered as she scooped up her hair with one hand and secured it into a ponytail with the other. She'd grown out the short fringe and the black hair dye and it was back to being sort of red and sort of brown and sort of wavy. She'd also stopped wearing make-up for the day-job, all part of trying to present the world with the perfect candidate for a job in publishing. Now she looked in the small speckled mirror that someone had sellotaped to the wall and scrutinised her bare face.

Considering that she ate all the wrong things and didn't sleep for long enough, her skin was still in pretty good shape apart from the shadows under her eyes and a tightening of her lips that Jennifer worried might be permanent. Not that anyone here was expecting great beauty from her. She was just a face, a body, a collection of curves and straight lines. And when she thought about it like that, it was easier to open the door and come out from her cubbyhole.

'How do you want me?' she asked Russell as she climbed up onto the small dais, where the teacher's desk must have originally been because there was still a blackboard fixed to the wall. Now it was home to a stool. Not a very comfortable stool either.

Russell was a tall, white-haired man with a stoop, a kindly face and a penchant for double corduroy. Tonight he was wearing maroon jumbo cords and a fawn corduroy jacket over a thick pullover.

'Some quick standing poses, I think. The caretaker's trying to dig out a heater so we can have you seated for a long pose after the break,' he said, rubbing his hands together. Not in anticipation, he wasn't that type, but because it was perishing cold in the repurposed classroom. 'So, um, if you wouldn't mind taking off the robe . . .'

It was like plunging into a swimming pool or taking off a plaster. Best to get it out of the way. Jennifer unbelted the thick plush towelling dressing gown and then shut her eyes and inhaled as she slipped it from her shoulders and handed it to Russell. Instantly, her poor nipples exposed to the chill atmosphere shrivelled into hard painful buds and it was impossible to see where her skin ended and the goosebumps began.

'He really has promised to find a heater,' Russell said apologetically as Jennifer tensed her muscles and tried not to shiver.

'You said quick poses,' she reminded him and he nodded and turned to the dozen or so people half obscured by their easels. Thank God.

'People! Let's get started,' he called out. 'Some lightning quick sketches so poor Jennifer doesn't freeze to death where she stands.'

Russell guided her through a repertoire of quick poses. Hands behind her head. Hands on her hips. All her weight on one leg, hip cocked. Back arched, one hand behind her head. And so on. Halfway through there was a knock on the door. It was the caretaker with not one but two heaters, though he refused to come in the room 'on account of the naked young lady, guv.'

Jennifer was so cold that she was surprised there wasn't tiny droplets of ice clinging to her pubic hair and she wouldn't have cared if a coachload of caretakers had suddenly descended. Also, she'd been doing this – standing naked in a room full of strangers – for eight weeks now, and although she'd be the first to rail against the objectification of women, Jennifer had quickly realised that she didn't mind this kind of objectification.

Her body, in all its glory and with all its many flaws, was scrutinised, studied and then sketched. If anyone was concerned about the slight dimpling of cellulite on the back of her thighs or the fact that her left breast was larger than the right (half a cup size the lady in John Lewis had said the last time Jennifer had been properly fitted) or that she had the faint silvering of stretch-marks over her hips, it was only how best to render these personal defects with charcoal onto paper.

Which was preferable to the man who'd casually stuck his hand up her skirt and rested it proprietarily around her upper thigh when he'd ordered his dinner last Saturday night. Or the other man who'd cornered her outside the gentleman's loos and said, 'The contrast between your white apron and the shortness of your skirt when you turn around is unbearably erotic. I'd like to fuck you. I'll make it worth your while.' Or even the men, it was always the men, but especially Phillip Gill, who addressed all their remarks to Jennifer's breasts. Compared to all that, this was as innocent as a vicarage tea party. Not that Jennifer had ever been to a vicarage tea party.

The heaters were ceremoniously brought in and despite some argy bargy when Fiona, a middle-aged woman who clearly prided herself on being artistic, judging by the sheer amount of Indian scarves, bangles and tie-dye she was draped in, tried to claim one of them, soon Jennifer was both freezing and in danger of third degree burns on the bits of her body directly in line with the heaters.

She was relieved when it was time to take a break and she could bundle herself back in her robe and let Russell get her a chalky hot chocolate from the vending machine.

'If you wouldn't mind revisiting the pose you did last week so people can continue with the paintings they've already started,' he said when he returned.

Clutching her hot chocolate, she wandered around the room to get her circulation going and to look at the sketches. A lot of them hadn't even bothered drawing her face, not that Jennifer minded, and it was fascinating to see her body through their eyes. But then she got to Fiona and it was horrifying rather than fascinating to see the painting begun the week before clipped to her easel.

'What do you think, then?' she asked Jennifer in a challenging tone. As well as fancying herself as artistic, Fiona was one of those people who considered herself honest to a fault ('I speak as I find,' she was fond of saying, one of the reasons why Jennifer half-heartedly hated her). She was pretty sure that Fiona had been behind the campaign to get her to stop shaving under the arms. Poor Russell had delivered the request with some explanation about texture but Jennifer had been quite firm in her refusal and Russell had flapped his hands and backed off.

Now she stared at the painting, where Fiona, like a TV camera, had added ten pounds to Jennifer's frame. At least. Jennifer was sitting on the stool, hunched over so that the students could capture the line of her spine (they were really into sketching vertebrae) and Fiona had made her breasts dangle like five-pound bags of potatoes. Her face looked like she had a bad case of mumps and also, 'Um, I'm very *green*,' Jennifer ventured because Fiona had painted her skin a fetching shade of chartreuse, which reminded Jennifer of the green concealer stick of her youth.

'You don't like it.' Fiona sounded almost triumphant. 'That's because I paint the true essence of people, which can be very confronting if you've never done much work on yourself.'

'Right. Interesting . . .' Jennifer longed to tell Fiona that if anyone needed to do some work on themselves it was her, but Russell paid an unbelievable fifty pounds a session for his life models. Most classes paid a maximum of ten an hour and fifty quid a week put a major dent in Jennifer's rent, so she turned away with what she hoped was a contained smile.

The other paintings were much nicer – even the efforts of a middle-aged man who could never look Jennifer in the eye but was obviously going through a Cubist phase and had given her buttocks right angles. In the furthest corner of the room was the easel belonging to a young man who Russell had said was a Fine Art graduate from the Slade or Chelsea School of Art, Jennifer couldn't remember which. He always gave off a vibe that wasn't unfriendly but wasn't encouraging either. He'd taken advantage of the break to hurry out for a cigarette (Jennifer was *gasping* for a cigarette but she wasn't also *gasping* for hypothermia) five minutes ago and she couldn't resist taking a look.

It was definitely her. But a version of Jennifer who had all the grace and litheness of a Manet nude; her features exquisite and heartbreaking.

'What do you think?' asked someone from behind her in a lilting Welsh accent. Jennifer looked around. It was the former Fine Art student, a tall man not much older than she was, biracial, with close cropped hair, strong, uncompromising features and a soft, gentle voice.

'Is it yours?' she asked though she already knew that it was.

He nodded. His gaze fixed not on his painting but on Jennifer with her hair scraped back and her cheeks red from the heater, as if she were utterly fascinating. That was the thing with artists, she supposed. Everyone must be fascinating to them.

'I don't look like that,' she said ruefully, with a smile so he wouldn't think she was offended. 'You've made me look far too beautiful.'

'Ah, but like Fiona, I paint the true essence of people, which can be very confronting if you've never really worked on yourself,' he said, as solemn as an Easter Island figure so Jennifer couldn't tell if he was joking or was serious or was absolutely coming on to her.

She didn't have a chance to find out because the last stragglers trooped through the door bringing with them the glorious smell of freshly smoked cigarettes and the moment was lost.

★

His name was Gethin. With a th-sound, not an f. He was from Barry in the Vale of Glamorgan and said that the way Londoners pronounced his name as Geffin made him want to cry. But he didn't say all this until the next week when he didn't go out for a smoke but stayed behind, patiently waiting for Jennifer to reach his little corner of the room as she made a show of intently studying the art on display.

At the end of the class, when Jennifer was stiff and sore, she came out of her little cubbyhole back in her clothes to find Gethin still in the classroom. Russell was also there waiting to pay Jennifer. 'I'm really sorry about this but I've had another request about the underarm area,' he said, flustered and flapping again.

'Russell, please. My body, my choice.' It was the most effective thing to say to a dyed-in-the-wool Leftie, because Russell reared back so the fluorescent strip lights glinted off the CND and Stop Pershing badges on his lapel.

'Yes! Of course, yes. You're absolutely right. I won't ask again,' he said and all the while Gethin was in the back of the room very slowly packing his paints and pens and brushes into his bag so that just as Jennifer was leaving, he was right behind her.

'That last pose looked uncomfortable,' he said a little too loudly as if he'd been working the words over in his head again and again.

'That stool is my arch nemesis.'

'I thought Fiona was your arch nemesis.' Again, he was absolutely straight-faced.

'I have many arch nemeses,' Jennifer said, as they went down the stairs, Gethin slightly ahead of her.

'Can you have more than one?'

'Oh, I do,' Jennifer assured him. 'I update my list of nemeses regularly. Weekly. Sometimes daily.'

He held the street door open for her, the frigid night rushing to greet them. Already there was the glint of frost on parked cars and privet hedges.

'I don't think I'd like to be on your list,' Gethin decided and certainly, he hadn't done anything to deserve a place among the ignoble, the impossible and the just plain bloody rude.

They'd come to a halt outside the school, their breath ghosting in the air. Jennifer thought of her little bedsit in Shepherd's Bush without much affection. It was almost as freezing inside as it was outside.

'So, I'll see you next week then?' she suggested because it was too cold to simply stand there, jiggling from foot to foot. 'Where do you live? Are you getting the tube?'

'Um, Brixton,' Gethin said as if he'd only just remembered where he lived. 'By tube. And you . . .'

The bus stopped practically outside her building as opposed to a long, cold walk from the station. Jennifer had planned to pop into the chippy opposite the bus stop, just before it closed, for a battered sausage and chips. It would be too late if she got the tube, but the hopeful look in Gethin's dark eyes was so inviting.

'I'm getting the tube too. Shall we walk together?'

Gethin didn't say much, which was a pity because Jennifer could listen to him sounding out words in that melodic Welsh accent all night. Once, in a long ago English A level class, Nick next to her sighing like it was too boring for words, Mary had played a recording of Dylan Thomas reading *Under Milk Wood* and Jennifer had been rapt, transported.

They stood shivering at the entrance to the tube station before they went in different directions. Jennifer would catch the pink Hammersmith and City line, while Gethin had to walk across Hammersmith Broadway to another part of the station where he'd be able to catch the District line then change at Victoria.

'I could wait with you until your train comes,' Gethin suggested, which was a nice thing to do. Far too nice. In Jennifer's experience, men were never that selfless, which instantly made her suspicious. Did he think that she'd invite him back to her place? Did Gethin make a habit of coming on to impressionable life models? If he did, then he was going to be sorely disappointed.

'You don't need to do that,' Jennifer said quite firmly, even though a tiny little bit of her was a tiny little bit tempted. 'I'll see you next week.'

Gethin made no move to leave but shoved his hands into the pockets of the old RAF flying jacket he was wearing, the sheepskin lining disintegrating at the collar, the leather cracked at the cuffs and elbows.

'So, um, do you want to go out tomorrow night? Go for dinner or something?'

'What?' Jennifer grunted ungraciously because she hadn't expected him to ask her out. On a date. She'd imagined that all he was after was a quick bunk up with a girl who got paid to take her clothes off in front of strangers every Thursday evening. But apparently, his intentions were honourable, which made a change. Then she remembered an important fact about tomorrow night. 'I can't. I'm working.'

'Saturday night?' he asked again, his voice hesitant.

'Sorry, working Saturday night too,' Jennifer said with a sigh.

She saw him swallow as if were trying to get past a lump in his throat. 'You have a boyfriend, don't you? I should have known you wouldn't be single.'

He sounded dismayed, crestfallen. It was a balm to her soul. 'No! No boyfriend. I really do have to work.' She hadn't told him that she worked unpaid during the week. But then she hadn't told anyone. Not family or friends, because it was too shameful to admit that after eighteen months of job hunting, she *still* hadn't found a full-time job in publishing. Better to have to work evenings than listen to everyone say, *I told you so.* 'That literary agency I mentioned. I mean, it doesn't pay very well.'

'Right.' Now he sounded sceptical. However, it was such a novelty to be asked out – for dinner – and there was something about the way Gethin looked, and the way that he looked at her, that made Jennifer really want to go on a date with him. 'OK.'

'I'm free Sunday,' she said quickly. 'Even God took Sunday off, right? Unless, you're religious.'

She didn't know much about Wales but didn't it have a lot of chapels and male voice choirs singing hymns?

'Don't tell my mam, but sometimes I question the existence of God,' Gethin said, smiling now that he was on safer ground. 'Sunday lunch, then?'

'Sunday lunch sounds great,' Jennifer agreed enthusiastically.

'We could go to Chinatown for dim sum?'

'Perfect.' Jennifer was still waiting for her more sophisticated palate to emerge with age. She didn't like Chinese food – all those indeterminate vegetables floating about in gloopy spicy sauces – but she loved egg fried rice and she couldn't keep turning him down. 'Shall we meet at Leicester Square tube station, the entrance next to the Hippodrome?'

'Sounds great. One o'clock?'

One o'clock on a Sunday was like 8 a.m. on a weekday but she nodded eagerly. 'It's a date.'

'It really is,' Gethin said with a slow, sweet smile that she wanted to eat off his face. 'Until Sunday then.'

10

November 5th, 1994
Oxford Circus Station

Before Sunday, there was a double shift at the restaurant on Friday, then another double shift on Saturday. Friday lunchtime was a bloodbath of businessmen taking long, boozy lunches with absolutely no intentions of going back to their offices. But they tipped well, and so they should because they never, ever kept their hands to themselves. Friday lunchtime tended to bleed into the dinner service, punctuated by the staff meal at 4.30, when Jennifer ate better than she had all week. Loading up on pasta drizzled with truffle oil, she shared war stories with her colleagues, before slipping her biker boots back on, tying a fresh snowy white apron round her waist and heading back into the restaurant to do it all over again, from six until at least midnight.

Then Saturday was Groundhog Day but without the handsy businessmen at lunchtime.

Jennifer had been working at Ciccone's for four years. Four years! It was the longest she'd stuck at anything.

She'd started her waitressing journey at a small family-run trattoria in the nicest bit of Mile End when she'd moved out of the parental home and realised that the precious maintenance grant really couldn't maintain her. After a couple of months at Il Positano, it was clear that £5 an hour, plus tips from the good folk of Mile End wasn't going to keep her in a style to which she'd like to be accustomed. But if Jennifer swapped Mile End for Mayfair and its coked-up advertising execs and media whizzkids with large expense accounts, on a good weekend, she could take home a hundred quid in tips.

By now, Ciccone's felt like family. The staff were young. They worked hard then partied hard and Jennifer was no exception. Except lately, she was starting to feel like a veteran, one of the old guard. There was a fast turnover. Potboys saving up enough to go travelling. Sous chefs going on to be commis chefs somewhere else. Her fellow waiters getting their degrees and finding well-paid jobs that meant that they didn't end Friday night soaking their feet in a washing-up bowl of hot water and Epsom salts.

Four years felt like Jennifer had outstayed her welcome and was going to end up like Luis, the head waiter, who'd worked at Ciccone's for twenty years and had once sucked off a really famous 80s' popstar in the wine cellar after Saturday lunchtime plating. He was still dining out, quite literally, on that story twelve years later. And though Jennifer had never sucked off any of the customers, always politely declining, she didn't like the thought that if she stayed at Ciccone's much longer, she too would become a salutary tale for any wide-eyed students who thought that a little part-time wait-ressing would supplement their student loans until they got proper jobs.

During her eighteen months in the job-hunting wilderness, Gaston, the general manager, had even offered to train her up so she could step into his shoes one day. Jennifer had politely declined that too.

But in the gap between Saturday lunch and the Saturday evening service, she didn't decline the line of speed that Darren, one of the commis chefs, offered her. In fact, she'd been counting on it because she was fading fast and all she wanted to do was find a quiet corner of the storeroom and take a nap, using one of the sacks of semolina flour as a pillow. It took the edge off Jennifer's exhaustion nicely so that come eight o'clock, she was on her A game.

Ciccone's was tricked out like it was still the roaring twenties and flappers in silk dresses were going to perform a quick Charleston on the black and white chequerboard tiles. There were six sections, each consisting of eight tables with chic aquamarine velvet club chairs fanning out from the huge, ornate bar in the centre of the main dining room. Plus the coveted booths lining the far wall.

After four years, Jennifer had earned waitressing rights to the second-best section, consisting of a mixture of tables and booths, which were tucked away from the entrance, not too near the kitchens or the bathrooms. They were reserved for prized customers, who were usually big tippers and she earned every single one of those tips with a cheery smile, remembering names, birthdays and dietary preferences. Flattering the women, gently flirting with the men. All the while carrying plates up her arm with the skill of a virtuoso.

It was midnight before the last bloody diners had stopped lingering over coffee and cigarettes and were shown the door, handing Jennifer a couple of twenty-pound notes, which she dutifully decanted into the tip jar, an old cigar box behind the bar, which was ceremonially removed to Gaston's office as things were packed away, tables and floors wiped down.

Then while those who were hurrying home hurried, everyone else had a quick drink in the staffroom to get themselves lubricated for the night ahead. Jennifer disappeared into the staff loo to tear off her skirt and blouse, spritz under her arms and then wriggle into a shell-pink nylon slip edged with synthetic lace that she'd picked up in a charity shop. She loved the easy, transformative power of a chuck-it-on dress, although she had to put up with a lot of comments about going out 'in her nightie' from people who didn't know Courtney Love from a bag of spuds.

Then she backcombed her hair, spritzed that too (if anyone came too close with a naked flame, what with the Elnett and the nylon, Jennifer would go up like a roman candle) and threw make-up at her face. The liquid eyeliner that she could expertly apply even in a blackout, mascara, more mascara, and just when she decided that that was quite enough mascara, she added some more. Powder to tone down the hectic flush on her cheeks, even though the night was about to get a lot more hectic and her cheeks would bear the brunt of it. Lastly, the red lipstick that had become her thing: Clinique 100% Red, a bluey sort of red that made her teeth look really white and her mouth like she'd been attacked by a swarm of bees.

Jennifer peered at herself in the mirror and decided that objectively she looked good. As waifish and sexy and as mysterious as she'd always wanted to look when she was peering at herself in mirrors as a teenager, ineptly applying make-up and hoping that it would change her into the person that she always wanted to be.

Although Jennifer didn't really know who this person was anymore. Two or three years ago, going-out Jennifer with big hair, racoon-like eyes and fuck-me lips used to be her truest self, but now it felt as much like fancy dress as the sober skirt and blouse and shoes that she wore to the literary agency every day. Probably the truth, the real Jennifer, was somewhere in between but Jennifer wasn't going to search for her now. She had much better things to be doing.

'Come on! Come on! Time's a wasting! Let's go!' she squealed as she burst into the staffroom a minute later, her ratty leopard-print faux fur coat over one arm, her overnight bag slung across the opposite shoulder. 'Get your arses into gear!'

It was the usual motley Saturday night crowd careering through the back streets of Mayfair, passing round a bottle of vodka they'd nicked from work, an IOU note left in its place. They arrived at their destination: a nondescript alley halfway down Regent Street and a nondescript building that looked like it housed some deathly dull offices. Jennifer led the way through the door and down the steps to a subterranean pleasure dome, a nightclub that in its heyday had entertained the likes of Judy Garland and Errol Flynn. Now, in the brash 1990s, after a refit which included a light-up dancefloor ('Yes! Just like the one in the "Billie Jean" video!'), it was frequented by skinny boys in bands, the skinny girls who idolised them and a supporting cast of characters who were all glitter, feather boas and polyester clothes from charity shops. Going-out Jennifer fitted in here perfectly. Hand-stamped by the door whore, she said a vague goodbye to her erstwhile colleagues then fought her way through the crowd to her usual table, her usual people.

'There she is!' Nick was sitting between two girls: tiny blonde things, because he still had a type, but he held out his hand to Jennifer so the one on the right had to scooch over, with a very put-upon air, to make room for her. 'Took your time.'

'But I'm always worth waiting for.' Jennifer sat down and let Nick put an arm around her and pull her in for a messy kiss on the cheek. 'You're in a good mood.'

'Chemically induced,' Nick said, lifting up his dark glasses to reveal eyes that were all pupil. He was suited and booted in silvery grey '60s Italian menswear and a white Fred Perry shirt, his hair ruthlessly short back and sided but still he clung on to that floppy fringe so that when he swept it back from his face, the tiny blonde thing on his other side sighed a little.

Jennifer could still remember what it was like to sigh rapturously every time Nick had brushed his hair back with those long fingers, to get a contact high just from being so close to Nick, tiny little brushfires igniting from his thigh touching hers.

But Nick was annoyingly still . . . Nick. As pretentious and as infuriating as he had been when he was seventeen. Even worse now, because he was an editor, an actual fucking editor, of a music magazine at the tender age of twenty-five, and success and being sucked up to by bands and managers and publicists had gone straight to his head. If only Nick wasn't so pretty, it would make Jennifer's life much easier. And if only he hadn't decided two years ago, that they were going to pick up the reins of their friendship again and really run with them.

Jennifer had been conflicted. She would never forget the night of her eighteenth birthday and Nick's role in her down-fall, but she'd decided that, on balance, she'd rather have Nick in her life than banished to just a bad memory. Also, lessons had been learned by both of them. She wasn't just his adoring lapdog anymore; she'd earned some respect. If any of the little blonde things got the wrong idea and tried to push Jennifer to the sidelines, Nick got shot of them pretty quick.

There'd been one last year, Nancy, who'd come up to this very table and threw a drink at Nick and Jennifer, though it had mostly hit the new little blonde thing on Nick's other side and spat, 'You are a pair of fucking dark wrong 'uns. Why don't you just do everybody a favour and fuck each other? It's obvious you want to.'

It wasn't obvious at all. There were no secret yearning looks this time because there was no secret yearning. Jennifer would like to state for the record that she wasn't in love with Nick anymore. She could appreciate him on an aesthetic level, and he could make her laugh so hard that she snorted vodka and

Diet Coke out of her nostrils, but the older he got and the more successful he got, the more arrogant he became and the arrogance wasn't at all attractive. Jennifer knew for a fact that in ten, fifteen years from now, Nick would transform into the sort of man who tried it on with her at Ciccone's every Friday and Saturday evening when his wife had slipped to the powder room.

But arrogant arsehole that he was, she liked Nick. She liked hanging out with Nick. She liked being friends with him.

And as for Nick? It was clear that Jennifer absolutely wasn't his type, being neither little nor blonde, and also because she could crush him and his ego with one pithy sentence if she wanted to.

Neither of the current little blonde things looked like they'd have the stones to throw a drink anywhere near either of them, Jennifer decided as she rummaged in her bag for cigarettes and lighter.

'So, how was the evening shift?' Nick asked, though he couldn't really be very interested.

'A drunk, crying woman in the bog tipped me twenty quid when I gave her a tampon,' Jennifer said because the drudge-y reality of waiting tables wasn't ripe with funny anecdotes. 'And a man pinched my arse so I made sure that his dinner plate was piping hot and placed it right at the edge of the table so he got burnt when he leaned forward.'

'Scratch Jen Richards and you draw your own blood.'

'As it's written on my personal crest,' Jennifer said. 'Anyway, now we must wait for my second wind.'

'Oh, I can help with that.' Nick rummaged in the inside breast pocket of his suit, though it wasn't as if Jennifer had been dropping hints. He turned away from her slightly for a second then turned back, sliding his hand up her back to cup her neck and bring her face closer to his. 'Open wide,' he whispered and then he snaked his tongue into her mouth, transferring the small bitter pill onto Jennifer's tongue then retreating. She dry-swallowed the tablet.

'You could just have put it in my hand,' she said mildly, though the way her nerve endings had sung as his tongue slid against hers had been far from mild. But old habits die hard.

He shrugged. 'Where's the fun in that?'

One of the foundations stones of their friendship was a flirty banter that confused everyone except George who suddenly launched himself at Jennifer.

'Babes!' he cried joyfully. 'Babes, I'd just about given up on you.'

If Nick was in a chemically enabled good mood, then George must have swallowed the contents of several chemistry labs. He lay across the table, drinks that hadn't been drunk now flung to the four corners, dressed in silver PVC trousers and a brocade jacket with nothing on underneath, his bleached blond hair teased into a little Tintin quiff. He was wearing almost as much eye make-up as Jennifer.

The chubby little indie kid she'd known at college had gained several inches and shed several stone. Now that he was back in London, George worked in an advertising agency by day and by night, did a metric fuckton of drugs and had the same predilection for little blond things as Nick did. Though George's little blond things came with a penis as standard.

'Get off the table, darling,' Jennifer said, patting him on the head. 'You're getting beer on your Jean Paul Gaultier jacket.'

'Not the jacket,' George cried in genuine alarm as he levered himself up off the table. 'Where's your second wind, Jen?'

'She's working on it,' Nick said and Jennifer held up her hands because second winds couldn't be rushed and if she started to panic that she wouldn't come up, then inevitably she wouldn't come up.

'Suck that cigarette down like it's a juicy cock, that helps,' George said. 'I'll get you a drink and then I'll throw you about the dancefloor. If you haven't come up by then there's no hope for you.'

Two more cigarettes, a double vodka and Diet Coke and being lifted up under her armpits by George and spun round in a circle while 'Babies' by Pulp played, gave Jennifer her second and her third, maybe even a fourth wind.

She stayed on the light-up dancefloor, lost in the music, hands in the air, hips swaying, feet skipping until the music stopped and the lights came on.

Oh, the humanity!

It always made her feel sad, that everyone looked so beautiful, so luminous, and then the harsh fluorescents came on and all she could see were pale, grubby faces, jaws clenched, eyes slightly dead.

It was time to call it a night.

11

Sunday, November 6th, 1994
Mornington Crescent Station

And that was the last thing she remembered until she was pulled out of sleep a scant six hours later by something or someone nudging against her hip, hot breath blasting the back of her neck, a hand trying to find purchase on her breast, which was shrouded in slippery, flammable nylon.

Nick.

Jennifer was in bed with Nick. So, he obviously hadn't pulled one of the little blonde things last night.

'Stop feeling me up.' He just pulled her in tighter so she could feel him snuffling her neck now like a pig rooting for truffles. 'You're asleep and you won't even remember this when you wake up,' she added a little sadly.

She got a grunt in response and with a sigh and a sharp elbow in Nick's rib, she rolled over so she was facing him and he was no longer nudging her with his hard-on or treating her left breast like it was an executive stress toy.

It was an arrangement set in stone: on Saturday nights, after clubbing it, pilling it, having it, rather than make the journey back to Shepherd's Bush on unreliable nightbuses or in an unlicensed minicab, Jennifer made the short journey back to Nick and George's flat in Camden, but the nice bit of Camden; a long curved terrace of Georgian houses between the High Street and Regent's Park. She slept in the same bed as whichever one of them hadn't pulled and if both of them had got lucky, she slept on their sofa, which was still a hundred times more comfortable than her own narrow bed, which she was sure her landlord had bought as part of a job lot from her near neighbours at Wormwood Scrubs prison. Of course, sometimes she pulled but only sometimes because Nick had an annoying habit of cock-blocking her. 'No, Jen,' he'd say firmly, when she was dead set on going home with some random guy she'd been snogging on the dancefloor. He'd take hold of her hand just as firmly. 'We both know that I'm saving you from a Sunday full of regret and an STD.'

More often than not, Nick preferred to leave the club without a little blonde thing in tow, so Jennifer usually ended up in his bed. And she'd also usually end up little spoon to Nick's big spoon, their legs entwined, his arm tight round her waist, sometimes his cock nudging insistently against her arse but they were a boy and a girl sharing a bed so sometimes stuff like that happened. It didn't mean anything. It was just biology. It was the price that Jennifer paid for getting to spend one night a week in what amounted to luxury.

Murky daylight leaked in from the gaps in curtains that hadn't been properly closed so that Jennifer was free to gaze at Nick's face as he slept on. It felt like a violation to see him like this; unguarded, vulnerable. His features were relaxed and he looked younger than she'd ever seen him. She knew his face even better than she knew her own, had catalogued every smile, every one of his enviably long eyelashes, every mark, every blemish, that tiny beauty spot that still persisted just above his top lip on the right.

Things that you did in that half-life between Saturday night and Sunday morning, sleep and awake, didn't count. Jennifer pressed the tip of her index finger to that freckle with ideas above its station and didn't take it away, not even when Nick's eyes opened and he stared back at her, steady and alert, so she wondered if he'd just pretended to be asleep.

'Hi,' he whispered.

'Hi,' Jennifer whispered back.

Then, just like the night before when he'd cupped the back of her head to bring her closer so he could pass her the pill, his fingers were tangling in her hair even as their legs tangled together and his tongue was in her mouth again.

Jennifer closed whatever distance she'd put between herself and Nick, so they were cleaved together as they kissed. It was sticky and sweaty but she didn't care and when Nick's thigh pressed between hers, she was glad because it gave her something to grind against.

Jennifer could feel her insides melting. She needed the hand that was skimming her hip to move a crucial few inches and to press and rub and make all her nerve endings come alive. Nick's hard dick nosed eagerly against her belly and actually she wanted that even more than she wanted his fingers on her, in her.

'Hang on,' she breathed against his mouth, and she reached down to hook one finger into the waistband of her knickers, to tug them off . . .

'No, wait . . .' Nick mumbled.

'No waiting, that's the point!' Jen reached for Nick's lips again but he turned his head and she realised, with a sickening sort of dread, that the hand he had on her hip was pushing her away so there was suddenly an ocean of bed between them.

'This is not a good idea,' he said softly but with more resolve than Jennifer had ever heard from him before.

She was eighteen again. The sting of rejection smarted and burned all over again. 'You don't want me,' she said flatly, because it was a fact, not a question.

'It's not about that.' Nick's voice was muffled because he was practically face down in his pillow, so desperate was he

159

not to look at Jennifer. 'Neither of us needs this kind of complication.'

'Yeah, fine, ok.' Jennifer was just saying words to fill up the silence. 'I'm probably still drunk or whatever.'

'Right.'

'Right.'

'There you go then.'

It wasn't right. It was all wrong. She lay back down, a metre separating them, and now it seemed like a fever dream, the kiss, the hands, the *grinding*.

Oh God . . .

She risked a glance at Nick but he gave every appearance of having fallen back to sleep because what had happened was no big deal unless Jennifer chose to make it one. Then what? They wouldn't speak or see each other for years again, until she'd got over the pain, the humiliation. What a fucking idiot she was when . . .

BRRRRRIIIIINNNNNNNGGGGGGGG!
BRRRRRIIIIINNNNNNNGGGGGGGG!
BRRRRRIIIIINNNNNNNGGGGGGGG!

The shock of the insistent and penetrating ring of the old-fashioned alarm clock on the other side of the room was enough to make Jennifer flail her limbs.

'Make it stop,' she moaned, trying to sit up and failing.

'You make it stop,' muttered Nick, touching her once again but only to prod her shoulder this time. 'Seriously, make it fucking stop. You were the one who made me set it and put it over there so you'd have to get out of bed to turn it off.' He paused to groan dramatically. 'So why aren't you getting out of bed to turn it off?'

On the third attempt Jennifer managed to sit up and wished she hadn't as the room ricocheted around her. She peeled back the duvet and on unsteady legs staggered across the room to where his old-fashioned alarm clock was still shrieking. It was a wonder that George, a notoriously light sleeper, hadn't burst in and screamed at them.

Usually, she cherished their Sundays. She'd have a long, hot shower, which was the only time of the week when she felt properly clean. Then once whomever they'd pulled had been sent packing, the three of them would go to the big Sainsbury's to stock up on food without any discernible nutritional value and fizzy pop, maybe some booze depending on how big they'd had it the night before. Then to Blockbusters to stand around arguing for up to an hour about what videos they were going to rent. Nick always wanted to get something foreign and subtitled, George always wanted to rent either *Breakfast at Tiffany's* or *My Beautiful Launderette* and Jennifer wanted something simple and uncomplicated with pretty people in it and a happy ending.

They'd spend the rest of the day slumped under blankets on the huge sofa in the huge living room, eating crap. Sometimes if she'd organised her overnight bag properly, Jennifer would stay a second night but, more often than not, she'd crowbar herself off the sofa at around eight to go back to her cold, inhospitable little bedsit.

But not today. Today, she fumbled with the alarm clock until it stopped shrieking. For a moment, Jennifer was tempted to crawl back under the covers, despite what had happened a few moments ago, but it was already past eleven.

'Oh, shit!'

Lunch with Gethin. That was why she'd forced Nick to set his alarm. So she could pretend that she liked dim sum and awkward conversation and there was absolutely no way that she wanted to go on a date with him anymore. Not now. Not after this.

Jennifer debated phoning Gethin and pleading a sudden

illness but they hadn't swapped numbers. She could stand him up but then come Thursday night, she'd be naked in front of him and already she didn't like the vibe that she was getting just thinking about how that would feel. Vulnerable, exposed, kind of icky.

She already felt kind of icky; the way she always did coming down after Saturday night. Like there was grime and disco dirt in every crevice; even her soul felt grubby. Jennifer had slept in her charity shop slip last night and it smelt ripe. *She* smelt ripe. No wonder Nick was repulsed by her.

'I need a shower,' she said but Nick just grunted in reply and pulled the covers over his head.

Physically, at least, Jennifer felt much better after a shower, the water staying hot and not running cold like Jennifer was used to. Even when she had to wash her hair twice to get rid of the smell of stale cigarettes. Back at her bedsit, she had to run a bath in the shared bathroom by boiling up endless kettles of water, which really ate into the leccy. One day she too would live somewhere with a power shower and electricity that just was and didn't need a charge key topped up at some out of the way newsagent's.

Jennifer didn't like to think about how much Nick and George must be earning that they could afford a lovely flat where nothing was broken. No cracked windows, no sagging drawers, no door handles that got stuck. Also, Nick and George had an actual shower instead of a shower over the bath and a cleaner who came twice a week.

Freshly scrubbed, she now pondered her outfit options. Jennifer of the day before had had the foresight to pack clean underwear and tights, but not anything that constituted date wear. Gethin had seen her naked and then in her buttoned-down work clothes. He wasn't ready for stinky second-hand synthetic slips and besides, Jennifer couldn't bear to put it on again. The blouse she'd worn in the restaurant had red wine splatters from a punter gesticulating wildly and sending their glass of Merlot all over her.

In bra and a black bandage skirt, she wandered back into Nick's room. 'Can I borrow a T-shirt?'

There was no reply, he was probably pretending to be asleep to avoid her, but technically she had asked his permission first so she knelt down in front of his chest of drawers to see what he had to offer.

T-shirts were in the bottom drawer. Neat, serried ranks, no doubt ironed and folded by the cleaner. The oldest, most faded ones, once black, now a smudgy grey, gave Jennifer a Proustian rush. The Smiths. Pixies. Jesus and Mary Chain. She'd been there when he'd bought some of them, packaged like albums in HMV and Virgin Megastore. So much had happened to them while Nick had worn these T-shirts. The gigs they'd been to, the long afternoons in English lessons, or bunking off to chain-smoke cigarettes in the college canteen or on the grass in the park, taking an earbud each to listen to *Substance* or *Surfer Rosa*. Those evenings in the little back-rooms of Camden pubs, half a mile and a lifetime away. Nodding their heads in time to the music, sharing a smile because both of them got it. Then rushing to catch the last tube back to Edgware and even Nick's dad, Jeff, being terse to the point of rudeness as he gave her a lift home, couldn't break the spell. They had so much history between them that maybe Nick hadn't meant to be cruel, but to be kind, when he'd called a halt to what would probably have been an unsatisfactory, hungover shag that they could never come back from. It still hurt though.

Jennifer carefully rifled through the folded cotton until she came to a white T-shirt bearing the logo of *The New York Herald Tribune*, just like Jean Seberg wore in *Breathless*. He *really* was pretentious. It was too big on her, but she could gather it up and knot it, and though a white T-shirt was quite unforgiving when she felt so rough, it was better . . .

'What are you doing? Take it off!'

Nick was sitting up in bed, hair going in fifty different directions as he scowled at Jennifer.

'I asked first,' she said, twisting to see how she looked in his big mirror. She looked all right. She'd look better when she had some make-up on.

'Doesn't count if I'm asleep. Seriously, Jen, your tits will stretch it out.' He was such a grouch in the morning, verging on afternoon. Also, it seemed that the way he was going to deal with their almost shag was to pretend that it had never happened.

'Go back to sleep,' she snapped.

'I'm awake now, aren't I?' Nick sounded close to tears. 'What are you doing up so early anyway? Why did you make me set the alarm?'

She knelt down to retrieve her make-up pouch from her bag. 'Didn't I tell you last night? I'm sure I did.'

'Sure you didn't.' Nick folded his arms. He was bare chested, but Jennifer already knew that. Objectively, he was quite weedy really. He looked better in clothes. 'We always spend Sunday together. It's our thing.'

'Not every Sunday,' Jennifer said, smearing globs of foundation onto her face. It wasn't that having a date was a big secret, but it would lead to all the other secrets that she'd kept from Nick and George, from everyone really. Even Kirsty in Stockholm and there had been a time when Jennifer had told Kirsty everything. And how could she tell Nick that she was going on a date when not even an hour before, she'd been trying to take her knickers off so he could put his dick inside her? She couldn't. 'Sometimes we both go back to our Mill Hill residences for Sunday lunch.'

'We haven't been home in *ages*,' Nick noted and Jennifer even thought about saying that that was where she was headed now, but then he might decide to come with her. He was quixotic and annoying enough to do that. 'So, where *are* you off to?'

'Meeting someone for lunch,' Jennifer said, as she put concealer, a lot of concealer, under her eyes. 'No one you know.'

'I know everyone you know,' Nick said arrogantly but also truthfully because he'd met her university friends and the crew from Ciccone's and there were no new people in Jennifer's life. Or there hadn't been up until a couple of days ago.

'Someone I met through work.' Jennifer rummaged for her eyebrow pencil.

'It's not that awful bloke in charge? What's his name? Is he your sugar daddy? Or is it an up-and-coming writer of military memoir? Is he going to bang on about Churchill in the hope that you'll bang him?' Nick was sounding much more alert. Their eyes caught in the mirror. (Jennifer didn't want to know why the big mirror faced Nick's bed.) He was wearing his most infuriating, shit-eating grin. Why was it always like this between them? One moment she wanted him, the next, she wanted to punch him in the face.

'Yes, Nick. I get really hot for paunchy middle-aged men in tweed who love nothing more than regaling me with tales of Monty's Desert Rat campaign,' Jennifer said in a deadpan voice and rolled her eyes for good measure, which was a tricky manoeuvre when she was also applying mascara. 'Who says it's even a he?'

'But it is a he?' Sometimes, Jennifer wondered what exactly it was that Nick did for a living, to achieve such wealth and status because he never kept proper office hours. But when he was like this, persistent and relentless, she had to concede that he was probably very good at getting celebrities to spill their guts.

She hoped she was made of sterner stuff. Because she didn't want to tell Nick that she'd met Gethin in an art class, that she'd stood naked in a former primary school classroom while he drew her.

Why on earth are you getting starkers for cash, Jen?

Because you're short of money?

But what about that job in the literary agency?

The one that took you eighteen months to find?

Oh, so you don't actually get paid? Right. OK. That's a bit shit, isn't it? I thought you said that you were still working at Ciccone's because you liked the buzz. Didn't know that it was paying the rent.

Kind of a waste of all those fancy letters after your name.

No, she really didn't want to have that conversation. But Nick had lost interest now. He was getting out of bed. Scratching his chest. Any second now he'd put his hand down his shorts and scratch his balls, the kind of thing you did in front of one of your best mates, even if she was a woman.

'Where are you meeting this mysterious, maybe-a-he lunch date?' he asked as he reached past her to grab a T-shirt and boxers from his drawers. He smelt as ripe as she'd done pre-shower.

'Leicester Square tube at one.' There was no harm in telling Nick that. And it was good to say something that wasn't a lie or a prevarication.

By the time she'd finished putting on her make-up, it was only noon. She'd have to walk to Camden Town and it would be busy. They'd shut Mornington Crescent to do repairs but that had been two years ago and it still hadn't reopened. It always creeped Jennifer out the way the trains slowed down as they went through the empty station. She always expected to see a ghostly apparition on the platform trying to flag down the train. But even given the Camden Market crowds and closed tube stations, it would still only take her half an hour to get to Leicester Square and she was nervous now. Her stomach fluttering though that might have been because it was a long time since that bowl of pasta between the lunch and evening service.

If only they weren't having dim sum. She couldn't really remember what Gethin looked like now. Or half of what they'd talked about. Or why she'd even fancied him.

But hanging out with Nick, their usual Sunday routine, cosy and comforting even though they'd spend most of the day gently bickering, wasn't an option today. Give it a week and, like Nick, Jennifer would be able to pretend that nothing was wrong, but today she couldn't bear the white hot heat of embarrassment when she remembered the grinding. God, she really needed to stop thinking about the grinding.

She'd stay for one bowl of egg fried rice and that was it. Jennifer's mind was made up by the time Nick sauntered back into the room in jeans and an old Creation Records T-shirt. Jennifer was still kneeling in front of the mirror to fiddle with her hair and he bopped her on the head with a rolled up copy of *Time Out*, which made her hiss and narrow her eyes.

'I'd completely forgot that George pulled while we were waiting for a cab,' he announced.

'News to me,' Jennifer murmured, but not surprising news because they always got a cab from Old Compton Street and it was always packed with nubile young men spilling out of the bars and clubs and George was very pretty, especially in his silver PVC trousers. The only surprising thing was that it had still seemed like a good idea to sleep in Nick's bed once they got home. 'Sorry that we're both abandoning you.'

Nick sat down on the edge of his bed. 'Unlike you, I like dim sum. I could gate-crash your lunch date,' he said casually. Far too casually, like he'd been working on his lines while he showered.

'Absolutely not,' Jennifer said in what she hoped was a tone of voice that brooked no argument. Not even trace amounts of argument.

'I knew you'd say that.' Nick sniffed, like Jennifer's predictability was beyond contempt. 'OK, I'll come with you as far as Leicester Square station.' He held up *Time Out* even as Jennifer raced through all the reasons why Nick couldn't journey into town with her and tried to find one that might stick. 'There's a French film on at Metro that I wanted to see anyway.'

12

Sunday, November 6th, 1994
Leicester Square Station

Over an hour later – she was fifteen minutes late and count-
ing – Jennifer climbed the first set of stairs to exit Leicester
Square station with Nick pretty much glued to her hip.
They turned the corner to the second set of stairs and
Jennifer caught sight of Gethin peering anxiously down the
street.

She'd forgotten how tall he was, how broad he was – he
looked over her shoulder, a smile lighting up his face as he saw
Jennifer – how very pleasing to look at he was and her stomach was fluttering again, but not the good kind of flutters
because Nick was still next to her.

'Are you meeting the old dear in the orange cagoule? Or is
it that gaggle of Japanese tourists?'

'Jennifer!' Gethin exclaimed as she reached the top of the
stairs, slightly breathless with nerves, her cheeks pink.

'Hi! Hey! Yes, hello. Sorry we're . . . sorry I'm late.' She
smiled, a manic stretch of her lips. 'So sorry.'

'You only need to say sorry once, Jen.'

Anyone but Nick would have discreetly disappeared off
into the depths of Soho to see his critically acclaimed French
film. But Nick just stood his ground, giving Gethin an assessing look, a smirk on his face.

Gethin was busy assessing too. Looking from Nick to
Jennifer and then back again, with a slight frown.

'We're in everyone's way,' Jennifer said, grabbing hold of Nick's arm and shoving him none too gently away from the exit, so the three of them were huddled at the mouth of the alley that ran behind Leicester Square.

Then there was silence and Nick and Gethin still eyeing each other up with very little enthusiasm.

'Sorry to be late,' Jennifer said again, everything inside of her cringing. She tried again. 'Gethin, this is Nick, an old friend, we did our A levels together, and he's just about to head off to the cinema.' That sounded innocuous, innocent, and wasn't an inaccurate way to describe how Nick was enmeshed in her life. 'And Nick, this is Gethin, a new friend who's a wonderful artist.'

They shook hands without any discernible displays of macho strength or trying to crush each other's fingers. Jennifer let herself have one sigh of relief, because she knew that Nick could be a tricksy bastard and all that she really knew about Gethin was that he was an unknown quantity.

'You're going for dim sum, right?' Nick queried and Gethin nodded.

'Yeah, there's a little place on Leicester Street. Lots to choose from,' Gethin said and how could Jennifer have forgotten the way he talked. How he rolled the words in his mouth like they tasted amazing. In other circumstances by now Jennifer would be experiencing the good kind of fluttering, but she still managed to smile up at Gethin who smiled back so it was as if it really was just the two of them.

'Bad idea, mate. This one hates Chinese food,' Nick said crushingly. He put his arm around Jennifer, who stood rigid-backed and furious. 'She has the blandest palate of anyone you've ever met. Won't eat fish that's too fishy, or cheese that's too cheesy, anything spicy and she acts like her mouth is on fire. Complete nightmare.'

'I don't hate *all* Chinese food,' Jennifer insisted. She wriggled her shoulders to be free of Nick and then turned her back on him so she could give all her attention to Gethin who now wasn't looking quite so delighted to see her. 'Anyway, shall we go?'

'We don't have to have dim sum,' Gethin said.

'No, really dim sum is fine. Dim sum is great!'

'Well, I'll leave you two kids to it,' Nick said and at last he was sauntering away, with a careless hand raised in salute. Jennifer couldn't remember the last time she'd been this angry with him. Or was it easier to be angry with Nick than to be angry with herself?

'He really is a gigantic dick,' she said venomously.

Gethin was frowning again. 'You said on Thursday night that dim sum was a good idea. You should have said that you didn't like it,' he said, his tone gently reproving. Jennifer had thought him reserved, even shy, but he wasn't having any trouble in holding her to account.

'It was just that I'd already been picky about dates and I didn't want you to think that I wasn't interested ...' She stopped. She didn't even know if this was a date date. They hadn't kissed. God, he hadn't even tried to feel her up. She was a monster because not so long ago, she'd been with Nick, but now the thought of Gethin feeling her up brought on that liquid sensation inside of her, like she might just melt into the pavement. She really would too if he kept smiling at her like he was smiling at her now: sweetly but with a gleam in his eyes.

'So you are interested, then?' he asked. 'I wasn't absolutely sure.'

Jennifer nodded. 'Very interested.' She blinked slowly once. Then twice. Christ, she was actually batting her eyelashes at him.

'We don't have to have dim sum,' Gethin assured her and that was fine by Jennifer. Maybe they could just skip straight to the bit where she was naked again but this time, he'd have his hands on her. She couldn't remember where she was in her cycle, maybe that was why she was so desperate for a shag. She could just blame *everything* on her hormones. 'We could go to the Stockpot.'

The Stockpot, just around the corner on Old Compton Street where Jennifer had loitered only a few hours before, was a low budget London institution, serving huge plates of cheap stodge and the kind of wine that stripped the surface off your tongue. Many was the time that Jennifer had been almost incapacitated by a vast, glutinous serving of spaghetti Bolognese. Even her fussy palate could find no fault with The Stockpot though it wasn't very sexy. Not like feeding each other morsels of exotic food with chopsticks – though Jennifer didn't have the required hand to eye coordination to have mastered the art of feeding herself with chopsticks, let alone anyone else.

'The Stockpot sounds great,' she said, which was another prevarication because what she really wanted to say was, 'I'm going to die pretty soon if you don't put your hands on me.'

She had to settle for Gethin taking her by the elbow to guide her to The Stockpot, protecting her from the jostling throng of tourists, filmgoers and Christmas shoppers who weren't deterred from their plans by a chilly November afternoon. He even walked on the road side of the pavement to protect Jennifer from any swerving traffic, which none of her other dates had ever done.

The Stockpot was heaving so they didn't get to sit in the faded, tacky main restaurant with its faint echoes of a Soho now almost gone, but downstairs where they were hemmed in like battery hens. Gethin's legs wouldn't even fit under the table so he had to sit side saddle and apologise every time someone tripped over his feet.

But apart from that, it was actually, surprisingly, perfect. Gethin had penne carbonara and a glass of red wine, which made him wince every time he took a sip while Jennifer had a grilled chicken breast with bacon and chips and a Diet Coke on the side. It was ages since she'd been on a first date, maybe not since the days of Dominic, and back then she'd have been far too nervous to horse down a big plate of food. But she was still coming down from the night before and Gethin had a way of looking at her, like she wasn't quite flesh and blood, but something more otherworldly and divine, so she even ordered pudding. 'Just apple crumble, with ice cream, not custard, please. Can you write it down? No custard.'

'You don't like custard?' Gethin shook his head but he was laughing with her, not at her, when Jennifer pulled a face as she tried to articulate her feelings about custard.

'Too gloopy. Too wet.'

'But isn't the ice cream wet?'

'It's a completely different kind of wet.'

While they waited for their puddings, Jennifer gently interrogated him.

She already knew he was from Barry, a small Welsh seaside town. 'Barrybados, we call it,' he said with a smile. His father, Henry, was from Nigeria and had worked on the Barry Docks, and his mother, Primrose, was a midwife and neither of them knew why Gethin was so artistic. 'Like it's a bad flaw I inherited from one side of the family.'

Gethin had come to London to study Fine Art at the Slade at the same time as Jennifer had hopped on a 113 bus to start her English Degree at Westfield College, but they'd never bumped into each other at ULU. 'Because I'd have definitely remembered you,' Gethin said, but he'd have remembered a

Jennifer with different coloured hair and different clothes and whenever she'd gone to ULU, she'd usually ended up falling down drunk so she decided not to pursue the point.

He'd graduated with a first and a well-received final show and then . . . 'Tumbleweeds. I don't feel right if I'm not painting every day but then you start to realise that there's not that many people who are going to pay you to paint every day.'

Now Gethin worked in a big art supplies shop in Covent Garden four days a week and painted the rest of the time.

'And that's me,' he concluded, dipping his head as if he was embarrassed and maybe he was because Jennifer couldn't stop staring at him. There was something about him, the beautiful way his face was arranged, his steady gaze and quiet stillness, which drew the eye. And his voice! She could happily listen to him recite shopping lists as if they were sonnets for hours.

Afterwards, they sat in a secluded little booth in the Coach & Horses, and though Gethin still hadn't even kissed her, Jennifer found herself telling him everything. Once she started, she couldn't stop.

That all she'd ever wanted was to work in publishing, to be the conduit through which writers would find their readers, but she couldn't remember the last time she'd even read a book. About how the job at the literary agency wasn't even a proper job despite all the months she'd spent searching for it. Which was why she stripped for strangers on a Thursday evening and got through double shifts on Friday and Saturday at Ciccone's by doing bumps of speed.

How she'd go out with Nick and George on Saturday night and do more drugs and though they were her friends, she could see how the three of them were becoming hard, brittle people and she didn't want to become that kind of person but she didn't know how to stop it.

The one thing she didn't tell him was that no matter how

much she denied it to other people, to *herself*, she was still in love with the boy who was her friend, but not a boyfriend, who'd broken her tender heart when she was eighteen. That if Nick hadn't rejected her that morning she'd never have turned up to meet Gethin for lunch.

And because she didn't confess that awful truth to Gethin, he continued to look at her like she was someone worthy of his time, the weight of his gaze, his tender expression.

'I had all these big dreams of what my life would be like and they've all slipped away and I'm stuck in this place with no idea how to get out,' she said finally, her tongue loose from the vodka and Diet Coke she was drinking and the last vestiges of the MDMA (and whatever it had been cut with) still slowly trickling through her veins. 'Not even stuck. I'm lost. So lost.'

Then, finally, she was silent and she couldn't even bear to look at Gethin, because she'd completely fucked *this* up. She shouldn't have gone out last night. Shouldn't have taken anything. Shouldn't have slept in Nick's bed. Shouldn't have placed the tip of one finger on that tiny little mole that she adored. Shouldn't have kissed Nick. Shouldn't have rocked up to meet Gethin with Nick. Shouldn't have spilled her guts.

Her whole life was paved with fucking shouldn'ts.

Gethin didn't say anything. Instead, he took Jennifer's hand which was resting limply on the tabletop and threaded his long fingers through hers and squeezed gently as if he were trying to gift her some of his steadiness, his quiet.

'Sorry,' Jennifer muttered. 'I'm sorry.'

'You don't have to be sorry about anything,' he said softly. 'And you don't have to be lost either. How can you be lost when I've just found you?'

PART FIVE

July 1995

13

Saturday, July 22nd, 1995
Paddington Station

On Saturdays, Jenny was meant to finish work at six thirty. But at six, she rang Gethin to say that she was going to stay behind for an hour or so. 'Let's say eight. Meet me at eight.'

Gethin sighed a little because he was used to Jenny calling him just as he was about to leave his big dusty house share in Brixton to delay him.

That done, Jenny went back to the little pile of books she'd assembled and ran her fingers along the spines. She'd been asked to put together a starter library as a sixteenth birthday present for the goddaughter of one of their customers. Said customer thought nothing of buying twenty copies of a newly published book so there'd be one in every guest bedroom of her big house on the Gloucester/ Somerset border and in the London house on Cheyne Walk too.

But Jenny wasn't going above and beyond just because The Honourable Lydia Featherstonehaugh (pronounced Fanshawe – posh names were rarely pronounced as they were spelt, solely to trip up the lower orders) spent as much in a year at Cavanagh Morton as Jenny earned in a year at Cavanagh Morton.

She was going above and beyond because this was a dream assignment. Jenny would have loved a fifty-volume starter library when she was sixteen.

'I wouldn't be cross if you wanted to leave that until Monday morning. Haven't you got somewhere more fun to be?' Hetty asked, as she came out of the back office.

Hetty was Henrietta Cavanagh, daughter of Henry Cavanagh (another thing about posh folk was that they liked to name their children after themselves) who had founded the Mayfair bookshop in 1929 with his partner and fellow Old Etonian, Percy Morton. 'Two days before the Wall Street Crash, Daddy never did have good timing,' Hetty had said at Jenny's interview.

'This doesn't even feel like work,' Jenny said, which was how she often thought about bookselling. Though not when she was hefting boxes of new releases up the narrow winding stairs from the cellar storeroom. And not when they got a large collection of unsorted books from an estate sale and she had to weed out the mildewed ones while cross-referencing non-mildewed ones in the shop copy of *A Buyer's Guide to Rare and Collectable Books*. 'And I am going out tonight. Geth and I are going to a party on the Circle Line.'

Hetty clasped her hands together and looked thrilled in the way that she always did whenever Jenny revealed some small detail of her life outside the bookshop. 'The Circle Line? Is that a new nightclub?'

Jenny caught the eye of St John (pronounced Singeon) who was closest to her in age though he'd circulated Save the Date cards from Asprey's for his fortieth birthday at the beginning of the week. St John smiled sympathetically as Jenny shook her head.

'No, Hetty. It's a party on the actual Circle Line.' They'd had a similar exchange at Jenny's job interview when Nancy, daughter of Percy Morton, asked her which three books, published that year, she'd recommend to the president of Iceland.

Jenny had been caught off-guard. 'What? Iceland, the frozen food chain?'

Nancy had looked appalled. 'No! Iceland as in the country.'

Maybe it was the nerves, the desperation to get a job, a paid job that was something to do with books. These two frightfully posh, elderly but sprightly women, so different to Jenny's own grandmother Dorothy, trying to make sense of her grubby, lower middle class reference points.

Jenny had started to giggle. Tried to hide it with a cough but the more Jenny tried to rein them in, the more they burst forth, until she was sitting there, tears streaming down her cheeks, her ribs actually hurting from laughing so hard.

It had taken her a little while to realise that Hetty and Nancy were laughing too. 'Well, you might not be our usual type, but you do have an encyclopaedic knowledge of books about military history.'

Somehow, probably by osmosis, a lot of Jenny's neuron space was imprinted with an extensive bibliography of boring books about war. This came in very handy at Cavanagh Morton. There was a certain type of upper-class gentleman who was absolutely obsessed with reading any book about Winston Churchill that he could get his hands on.

So, though she wasn't their usual type, and they certainly weren't hers, Jenny had begun to blossom after she started work at the legendary London bookshop. It had been seven months now and she still felt as if she hadn't quite reached full bloom.

'How wonderful!' Hetty exclaimed. 'I do like it when you young people have adventures.'

The adventures would have to wait another couple of hours. While St John and Hetty dealt with the last customers of the day, stragglers who were inclined to linger without buying anything, Jenny went back to her starter library.

I Capture the Castle. Bonjour Tristesse, not in the original French because Jenny was sure that The Hon Lydia Featherstonehaugh's goddaughter couldn't be such a try-hard as Jenny had been at that age. *Emma,* because *Pride and Prejudice* was too predictable. *The Dud Avocado. Harriet,* because there had to be a Jilly Cooper in the mix. *The Pursuit of Love.* Then of course, the two books that had shaped Jenny's own adolescence, *The Bell Jar* and *The Catcher in the Rye,* and no library for any discerning young woman could be complete without a copy of *The Collected Dorothy Parker.*

Jenny was just checking the shelves to see if they had a nice edition of Louis MacNeice's *Autumn Journal* when Nancy came up the stairs from the basement storeroom and kitchen with two bottles of champagne, Patrick who guarded the antiquarian rooms like they were his first born, bringing up the rear with a tray of champagne coupes. One of the many important life lessons that Jenny had learned since she started at Cavanagh Morton, as well as the correct way to address a marchioness, was that champagne shouldn't be served in fluted glasses but in coupes. 'Apparently their shape was modelled on the left breast of Marie Antoinette, but I remain sceptical,' Hetty had said when she first instructed Jenny on the subject of suitable receptacles for the serving of champagne.

There was the triumphant pop of a champagne cork as Nancy expertly and smoothly opened the first bottle.

'What are we celebrating this week?' Patrick asked because there was always a good, if sometimes spurious, reason for their Saturday champagne. A birthday, an anniversary, a very profitable week, it was fifty years since VE Day. Any excuse.

This week, Hetty gestured for Jenny to come forward to take the first glass. 'We're celebrating darling Jenny's maiden voyage as a published writer,' she said, as Nancy held out a glass of the bubbling pale gold liquid that to Jenny smelt and tasted like cat's piss. Not that she'd share that with the group. And right now she was blushing with pleasure and ducking her head.

'It was only a three-hundred-word piece because something had dropped out,' she insisted but she still couldn't think about seeing her name in print, above the three hundred words that she'd agonised over, and not feel thoroughly delighted.

'Well, let it be the first of many,' Nancy said, her usually quite austere features suffused with softness as she smiled at Jenny. 'We had a young man working here. Sometime in the mid-Sixties. Had one of those Beatles haircuts and always used to come back from lunch positively reeking of marijuana . . .'

'His father was an archbishop, so one supposes he was rebelling against the establishment,' Hetty mused. 'Anyway, he went on to become editor of the *Times Literary Supplement*. So, from such tiny three-hundred-word acorns, mighty literary oaks are born, Jenny, just ponder that.'

Jenny's career path was already far from the straight line to literary glory that she'd imagined. She still wanted to work for a publisher, to become a publisher one day, but working at Cavanagh Morton had reignited her love of books.

Despite its grand clientele who had libraries rather than bookcases, both Hetty and Nancy insisted that a love of books was something that brought everyone together. To that end, they had several shelves of second-hand Penguin Classics at the entrance to the shop, all priced at 50p, which were treated with the same care and reverence at the till as if the customer was buying a signed first edition.

Now, Jenny got first pick of those Penguin Classics that she'd collected as a teenager; the sight of a tattered orange spine in a charity shop always giving her a little frisson of anticipatory delight. Lately, thanks to the shop's impressive collection of Penguin Classics, she'd discovered Angela Thirkell, Monica Dickens, Dorothy L. Sayers and many more, which had led to an enthusiastic conversation in the shop with an editor from the *London Review of Books* about how much they both loved Dorothy L. Sayers' titled sleuth, Lord Peter Wimsey.

When the editor had got back to the *LRB* offices, she'd rung up the shop and asked Jenny if she could 'knock out three hundred words on why Lord Peter is the perfect metro-sexual. It's just something else has fallen through and we go to press tomorrow morning. I can bung you fifty quid for it.'

And that was how Jenny had become an actual published writer. Maybe she'd end her career several decades from now as a venerated lady of letters, she thought as she took a sip of champagne and tried not to pull a face at the sour taste.

By the time Gethin tapped on the door, only Nancy, Jenny and a dribble in the second bottle of champagne were left. Jenny was pleased to see him as he came into the shop and was also pleased that he was holding a thin striped carrier bag, which clinked slightly as he held it behind him, although what-ever he'd got from the offy on the way here was going to be several rungs below the vintage champagne. He kissed Jenny on the cheek. 'Do you want to pop home first or are you good to go?'

Jenny said she was living in Kilburn because Kilburn Park station was the nearest tube. Her grandmother, Dorothy, now also her landlady/septuagenarian flatmate, insisted it was Maida Vale because Maida Vale ran parallel to their road for about five seconds before it became Kilburn High Road. Jackie said it was Paddington because Paddington Recreation Ground was just round the corner and Gethin insisted it was St John's Wood because Abbey Road Studios where The

Beatles had recorded, um, *Abbey Road* was less than a mile away.

Either way, Jenny had been delighted to swap the very limited charms of her Shepherd's Bush bedsitter, especially when her landlord started to refer to it as a studio flat and wanted to put the rent up. Dot's duplex council flat in a sprawling low-rise, had central heating, plentiful hot water and a balcony, so on balmy summer days Jenny could have her morning coffee al fresco while gazing out at the little garden square (actually more of a rectangle) opposite.

From the loud hum of the ancient Kelvinator fridge, which was older than Jenny, to the bright red floral carpet in the large lounge/diner, which clashed with the brown and orange Dralon three-piece suite, it was familiar in a way that Jenny hadn't even realised she wanted or needed.

The Kilburn flat had been a second home when she was growing up. It was where she'd sat at the dining room table for three long hours when Stan wouldn't let her get down until she'd eaten everything on her plate. On her plate were kippers, horrible hairy kippers, so she'd sat it out until her parents came back from a Saturday afternoon Up West and had been furious. With Stan, not with her. As Jenny remembered it, she was compensated with a KitKat.

It was also where she and Martin and Tim had spent afternoons at the playground on the roof of the block. It seemed unbelievable now that everyone was obsessed with Health and Safety, that it had ever been okay to let small children play unsupervised on the deathtraps that were rickety swings and a rusting roundabout when they could also plunge to their deaths from a great height. But the only time Jenny had injured herself was when she'd been left to happily swing on the bars at the entrance to Sainsbury's on Kilburn High Road and had fallen off and cracked her head open.

'There was blood everywhere,' she recalled with some relish as she and Gethin cut through Hyde Park on their walk to Paddington station. It would take them half an hour but it was a sultry, high summer Saturday evening. Even though the Oxford Street traffic was only five minutes away, they could no longer hear the rumble of engines and the impatient toot of car horns. They were no exhaust fumes to catch at the back of their throats. All was a glorious, redolent green, broken up by groups of picnickers. 'See that little dent just by my temple.'

'I've already catalogued that little dent,' Gethin said, pressing the tip of his finger to it. 'It's one of my favourites of all your scars.'

They'd been together ten months now. Gethin had had some weird notion that he was going to woo her, though Jenny really hadn't needed to be wooed. Either way, they hadn't had sex for the first three torturous months. Some rubbish about respecting her too much.

Gethin had still been quite happy to sketch her naked in his big, dusty room in a big, dusty shared house on Brixton Hill. Jenny had wondered if that was his kink. A look but don't touch kind of deal. But after thirteen weeks and four days, she couldn't bear it any longer and had got up off his bed where she was laying on his crumpled sheets, approached the stool where he was sitting and had straddled him, rubbing herself up and down like a cat in heat. She could probably have got herself off just like that, but it turned out that Gethin wasn't made of alabaster, like the cliffs of Penarth near Barry that he'd pointed out when he'd taken her home to meet his parents a couple of months ago.

No, Gethin was made of flesh and blood like everyone else and he'd managed to last two minutes of rubbing before he'd given in and finally put his hands on her.

That first time, he'd used those talented fingers and his even more talented mouth to reduce Jenny to nothing but white heat and sensation. It was the foreplay she'd heard so much about but had never experienced in the flesh.

Several hours later, he'd put Jenny in the bath and washed the charcoal smudges off her because there wasn't even a millimetre patch of skin that had escaped his attention.

Jenny still got misty-eyed at the memories. Just thinking about it, as she once again breathed in the fumes of the Saturday night traffic clogging Praed Street as they crossed over the road, was enough for her to get that feeling between her legs that was both languid and urgent at the same time.

She loved living with her grandma, but it did mean that during the week, she hardly saw Gethin at all. Certainly, he wouldn't stay the night and she couldn't stay the night at his. Dot had never spent a night on her own in her life and she was too old to start now.

Fortunately, on Friday evenings, Dot went to stay with Jackie and Alan for the weekend, otherwise Jenny and Gethin would never be able to have sex. Just thinking about what lay in store for the rest of the evening made her take Gethin's hand and squeeze it tightly.

'I reckon we'll do one circuit. How long will that take?' she asked.

He considered the question for a moment. 'About an hour? It can't take more than an hour.' He looked at her hopefully. 'We could always jump out at Victoria, then it's only a couple of stops to Brixton.'

Jenny frowned as the great lumbering beast that was Paddington station came into view. 'But it depends which direction we're heading.' She stopped to gesture with her hands. 'If we're going left, then Victoria isn't that far from

Paddington, but if we're going right, then that would be the long way round and it would probably be OK if we ducked out early.'

'But there isn't a left or right on the Circle Line; it's east or west. Which one's which?'

'I have no idea.' She pressed the button at the crossing and waited for the green man to appear. 'George is going to have to know these things. They go by east and west in New York, don't they? Like, you have the Upper West Side and the Lower West Side. So confusing.'

The green man appeared and they were soundtracked across the road by a short series of beeps.

'At least, New York is built on a grid system, not like London which is built on, I don't know, a spaghetti system. Very confusing to a young lad from the valleys, his first time in the Big Smoke,' Gethin said, slowing his words down and thickening his accent, then grinning when Jenny gave a little huff of annoyance.

'I don't think London's that confusing,' she said with all the self-assuredness of a born and bred Londoner who had no trouble navigating through the city's spiderweb of streets and roads and alleys and yards and cul-de-sacs and dead ends. Stan had been a cabbie though, so maybe The Knowledge was hardwired into her DNA.

Paddington wasn't the hurrying, scurrying place that it was during the week but the concourse was still quite crowded as they entered the station only long enough to head in the direction of the tube. Turning their backs on the platforms that carried people westwards to Somerset and Gloucester and beyond that, Devon and Cornwall.

As Gethin queued for the ticket machines, Jenny pulled out the flyer that George had faxed to the bookshop.

There was a large London Underground roundel with the

words 'Rave On The Circle Line' where the name of the station should be.

Start spreading the news. I'm leaving today.

Yes, it's true! I'm leaving for New York in a week to bring a touch of London street cred to Madison Avenue so let's have one last almighty blow-out before I go. We are going to party on the Circle Line, like it's 1999.

When: 9.30 p.m., Saturday, July 22nd.

Where: Paddington Station, Eastbound Circle Line platform (heading towards Baker Street).

Dress code: Fucking fabulous, darlings – something you can dance in and then run away in if we get caught by the fuzz.

The Plan: Bring booze, bring pills and powders, bring your best moves and let's see if we can do a whole circuit of the Circle Line before we take this party overground.

Be there or, literally, be square.

Love, George.

Jenny folded up the fax and stuffed it back in the front pocket of her bag. She wasn't even sure how George had known where she worked in order to send a fax.

Things had become quite strained between them. No, that wasn't right. Things had become distant. Very distant. Jenny regretted that distance, especially as George had become completely absent from her life and was now heading to New York to wow the Gothamites with his fabulousness, and this fax was the first she'd heard of it. Although this time last year, Jenny would have said that George was one of her best friends.

One of her other best friends had been Nick and they'd similarly drifted apart. There was so much going on in Jenny's life; every aspect of it had changed and she'd changed too. She was a different person now. A much happier person.

Then the fax had arrived and so had the churning in her stomach when Jenny thought about seeing Nick again. Not the good, anticipatory flutter of butterflies but something a bit more nauseous.

'You all right?' Gethin was back with his ticket and the air of a man about to walk to the electric chair.

He hadn't wanted to come. He wasn't really a party person. He didn't dance. Certainly didn't do powders and pills, which Jenny was glad about because she didn't do them anymore either.

'We really don't have to do a full circuit,' Jenny told Gethin, though it felt more like she was reassuring herself. 'If it's awful or there's a very real chance of being arrested, we can jump out at any time.'

'We could jump out now,' Gethin said hopefully. Jenny was tempted. But just because you weren't looking forward to something was no reason to bail. 'I do want to see George before he goes. I mean, he might not come back. I might never see him again!'

Gethin sighed in capitulation and guided Jenny forwards to the ticket barriers. 'You could go to New York, you know.'

'Unlikely.'

They'd gone to Paris for Easter, not realising that everything in Paris shut for Easter. Gethin, though he'd grown up in a small Welsh town, had been abroad many times. Package holidays to Spain. Interrailing the summer after he'd done his Art Foundation. He'd even gone to Prague just for a weekend, just for the hell of it.

He couldn't believe that Paris was the first time Jenny had gone abroad. She had to get an emergency one-year passport because it had never occurred to her that she might need a passport. As a kid, there hadn't been enough money for foreign holidays, not even package ones. Instead, Alan would load up the car and Jackie would pack a coolbox and they'd go and stay in Alan's parents' chalet in a holiday park in Cromer.

So, the prospect of five days in Paris had blown her mind. They'd got on the Eurostar at Waterloo and within two hours, about the same amount of time that it took to get to Manchester, they'd arrived in Paris. France. Full of people talking French. The lovely blue street signs edged in green, the Art Nouveau font of the metro stations. Tartine for breakfast every morning. A place that was very clearly not England.

And now Gethin was talking about New York. Jenny shook her head as they descended the escalator.

'Maybe if I get a Christmas bonus, we could go to New York,' she dared to say, fingers crossed behind her back because it felt a lot like tempting fate that by the end of the year she'd still have a job she loved, somewhere to live that she loved and a man that she loved.

OK, neither of them had declared their love but they didn't really have to. That was another thing that people only really did in books. Love was Gethin never minding that she worked late, or that she'd passed up living with him in favour of living with her grandmother.

Love was the slow, steady beat of Gethin's heart when he slept with Jenny in his arms. The sweet smile that not many people got to see but Jenny saw it all the time. Then there was the wicked glint he got in his eyes – Jenny hoped she was the only person who ever saw that.

Love was the comforting weight of his hand at the small of her back as they got off the escalator. Not to guide her but just to say, 'here I am' as they followed the signs to the eastbound Circle Line platform.

Things were much livelier underground. It was Saturday night; people were travelling home to the furthest ends of the tube after dinner or a film. Then there were the other people, in their weekend finery, spilling out of trains, hurrying up escalators so as not to waste a minute of their precious Saturday nights.

Even before they'd reached the bottom of the stairs, Jenny could hear the shrieking and the sound of thumping Handbag House. When they finally reached the platform it was easy to spot the glitteriest, giddiest collection of party people that London had to offer: girls in feather boas and sparkles, the boys primped and peacocked.

'Jesus wept,' Gethin said faintly.

Jenny and Gethin were not sparkling or primped. She'd been working all day and although there wasn't a dress code, Nancy and Hetty expected a certain standard of sartorial decorum from their staff. Gone were the unflattering blouses and skirts of her Phil Gill days, and the nothing-to-the-imagination tiny skirts of her waitressing days too. More recently, Jenny had taken inspiration from that other bookshop girl, Audrey Hepburn in *Funny Face*, and wore skinny-fit black trousers with Dunlop Green Flash trainers, jumpers in winter, and in summer a collection of vintage tops. Today she was wearing a sleeveless, silky sixties shell top with a scalloped print in different shades of green, which had a bit of a shimmer to it. As they crept closer to the party people and Jenny caught sight of one woman in a lurex romper suit, she came to the unhappy realisation that tennis shoes and a sedate second-hand top would not do. They would not do at all.

Gethin had been working all day too, in the art supplies shop. He was wearing jeans and had swapped the red branded T-shirt he was expected to wear for a navy blue T-shirt. Gethin didn't do fancy. He expected his clothes to be functional and eventually end up with paint on them.

Still, they were here now and Jenny could see George in the midst of the throng, wearing an actual ringmaster's red tailcoat with a top hat perched on his head.

'We're getting on the next train,' he yelled and Jenny raised her hand to get his attention but he'd already turned away to hug two boys in matching skinny suits who looked like they might be in a Britpop band.

There was a displacement of air, a ripple, and when Jenny tilted her head and stared into the darkness of the tunnel beyond, she could see the faint glimmer, which became two beams of light. The ripple became a gust of wind as the train hurtled into the station. It usually gave Jenny a tiny thrill no matter how many times she'd experienced it, but not this evening.

'Maybe we will get off at Victoria,' she said to Gethin as they didn't so much climb on board as get swept up in the party's forward motion, Jenny almost knocked in the face by a ghetto blaster carried aloft on someone's shoulder, which was now blasting Barbara Tucker's 'Beautiful People'.

'Watch it!' Gethin snapped, but the ghetto blaster and whoever was holding it was already halfway down the carriage to the bemusement of the people already in situ.

Jenny wasn't quite sure how a party on the Circle Line was going to work. If there'd be an easing in period; standing around holding their drinks, making polite conversation, that sort of thing. But as soon as the train doors slid shut, the other invitees were instantly raving and raving hard. Dancing like everyone was watching, hands in the air, hips gyrating, someone was blowing a whistle, someone else shouting out 'Woo woo!' in time to the music.

There wasn't a single person that she recognised, apart from George. As if he'd shrugged off all his old Saturday night friends. Maybe he'd shrugged Nick off too. And just like that, just thinking his name, had Jenny up on tiptoes, craning her neck, peering down the carriage and tensing for the moment that she saw his face. She couldn't see Nick so she let Gethin guide her to two seats which had been vacated by an appalled-looking middle-aged couple, who were clutching carrier bags from the National Portrait Gallery gift shop and theatre programmes from *Elvis: The Musical.* They'd clearly had their nice day out in London ruined.

'Let's have a drink,' Jenny decided.

'Or we could get off at the next stop.'

'I haven't even spoken to George yet. I need a drink before I do that,' Jenny said firmly as Gethin pulled out a familiar slim copper bottle and handed it to her.

'Hold that, I'll open it in a minute,' he said, taking out a can of Stella for himself.

Not long after they'd started dating, Gethin had sat Jenny down for a serious talk. He'd explained, gently, that as she was an adult, she really couldn't keep drinking vodka with fizzy pop to hide the taste of the alcohol. Even worse, she'd recently switched her allegiance to peach schnapps and lemonade, a drink so teeth-rottingly sweet, there was every chance she'd be toothless before thirty. It had taken a lot of research, many anguished cries of 'are you actually trying to poison me?' even some retching, but eventually Jenny had found her drink: a ready mixed Moscow Mule, a combination of vodka, ginger beer and lime, which only faintly tasted like cough medicine and came in a lovely copper-coloured bottle. Also, it didn't make Gethin wince as he retrieved his key ring and opened the bottle for Jenny with the implement he always had on hand for her. He was so thoughtful like that.

The train pulled into the next station, Bayswater. Everyone froze like they were playing Statues, though the Handbag

House was still going strong. Most of the non-partying travellers including the appalled-looking middle-aged couple got off and apart from one tired-looking man in a hi-vis jacket who realised his mistake only as the doors were closing, no one dared enter the carriage.

'We'll definitely get off at Victoria,' Jenny said again as the dancing and the shrieking started again.

'Definitely,' Gethin echoed. 'Maybe you should have that word with your friend sooner rather than later.'

'I suppose,' Jenny agreed without much enthusiasm as she heaved herself out of her seat to approach the middle of the carriage where George was twirling around with his arms outstretched. Absolutely off his nut as usual, Jenny thought, as she tugged at his tailcoat.

'George! Hey! Hi,' she said her voice loud so it could be heard over the music. 'How are you?'

George stopped twirling, stopped everything; the beatific expression on his face gone so abruptly it was as if someone had taken an eraser to it.

'Oh, it's you,' he said thinly, looking at Jenny like she was a final demand that had arrived unexpectedly in the post. 'Hi.'

'I can't believe you're going to New York,' Jenny persisted, despite her rising irritation. 'It's amazing. Congratulations! How long are you planning to stay there?'

'You'd know all about my plans if you'd actually been around.' Jenny's hand was still on his arm and he twitched in annoyance so he'd be free of her touch. 'We never thought you'd be one of those sad girls who dumped all her friends the minute they got a boyfriend,' George sneered, so Jenny couldn't even see the echo of the plump, sweet, *shy* boy she'd first met, God, could it really be nearly ten years ago? Also, that was such an unfair accusation.

'Excuse me for wanting to spend a little time with Gethin . . .'

'Oh, whatever!' George turned his back on Jenny. She felt as if her insides were plummeting to the grimy floor of the carriage.

'So, this is it? You're not even going to say goodbye and have a nice life?' she demanded, catching hold of his arm again. 'George!'

He tugged himself free. 'Jesus, Jen, you're completely bringing me down.'

The train was slowing as it approached Notting Hill Gate station and jerking slightly, so Jenny had to make a panicked swipe at the yellow grab rail above her head. 'Why did you even invite me?'

'He didn't invite you, I did,' said a voice from behind her. Even over the sound of Blackbox's 'Ride On Time' and the grinding of the train gears as it slowed even further, that voice made Jenny tense and her hands clutch tighter to the handrail and the clammy bottle of Moscow Mule.

She had a notion that if she turned around, she'd be transformed to stone.

Still, Jenny turned around to look into Nick's pale, sweaty face.

14

Saturday, July 22nd, 1995
Victoria Station

'Against my better judgement,' George snapped in the background but Jenny had already decided that he was a lost cause.

'Nick,' she said, her voice deadpan because she didn't know if Nick was going to be inexplicably cross with her too. She hoped not because what she had with Nick, their friendship, it was deeper, always more complicated. 'You look . . . well.'

He didn't look well. He looked as if Jarvis Cocker was about to send him a cease and desist letter for stealing his look. He was wearing a brown suit with wide lapels, which looked second-hand, and that had nothing on the wide lapels of his orange paisley shirt. Then there was the new shaggy haircut and the sideburns and the blue tinted sunglasses even though it was nearly ten on a Saturday night and they were in an underground train carriage.

Even after all this time, if forced under pain of death, Jenny would have to admit that the still glorious jut of his cheekbones would always make her feel a little lightheaded and swoony. Overall though, he looked like a total idiot, she decided a little smugly, a little sadly, until she realised that Nick was giving her a swift but thorough once-over too. But because he was wearing those stupid glasses it was hard to know what he thought of the changes in her appearance since she'd last seen him, which had been over six months ago, at a Christmas party at the club on Regent Street.

She'd still been waitressing and Ciccone's had been ferociously busy in the run-up to Christmas and Gethin had been working all day too. They'd stayed just long enough to show their faces, have a couple of drinks then make their excuses and leave. Nick had cold-shouldered Jenny that night, barely spoken to her, and when she and Gethin had left, she saw him and a little blonde thing practically having sex against the cigarette machine. He'd caught her eye and Jenny had looked away and was glad that she was done with that scene. Done with him.

Now she no longer had to hide the ravages of too much work and partying and not enough sleep. Her hair was caught up in a simple ponytail and, inspired by Audrey Hepburn again, she'd cut her fringe back in. She wasn't getting through a tube of foundation and one of mascara every three weeks and though she'd give up on liquid eyeliner and red lipstick only when some cruel person prised them out of her cold, dead hands, her lighter look was much less time consuming and, Jenny thought, much more flattering.

'You look . . . different,' Nick said, like he didn't think it was flattering at all.

'Well so do you,' she countered and when the train doors closed, Nick gestured to the empty row of seats at the other end of the carriage.

'Shall we?'

For one moment, Jenny wondered if there was even any point and a glance behind her took in Gethin sitting slumped, as he took a pensive sip of his lager. But she'd known Nick for nine years, with gaps, so for old times' sake and all that.

'All right then.'

They sat. Jenny tried to assemble her thoughts, to think of something to say, but a good opening line eluded her.

'See that girl over there?'

Jenny followed Nick's pointed finger to where a group of four girls were taking turns to gyrate against the pole in the centre of the carriage.

'Which one in particular?'

'The really pretty one in the denim hotpants . . .'

The 'really pretty one' had accessorised her tiny denim hotpants with a silver and gold-striped lurex tank top with nothing else on underneath and, even though she wasn't *that* much younger than Jenny, knee-length socks and pigtails. Jenny didn't like to pass judgement on another woman's appearance but it took every ounce of strength she had not to purse her lips in disapproval. She was also tiny and blonde so it really shouldn't have been a surprise when he said, 'She's my girlfriend. Clara.'

'OK . . .'

'She's in a band. They're all right, I suppose, if you like that whole bubblegum pop kid thing,' he conceded, so clearly love may be blind but it wasn't deaf too. 'They supported Echobelly on a couple of dates. *NME* rates them, anyway.'

'Well, if the *NME* rates them.' That came out much tarter than Jenny intended and she couldn't blame Nick for flaring his nostrils. 'So, how are you? How's work?'

Nick shrugged. 'I'm feeling like the whole music magazine thing is played out. There's only so many ways you can describe the sound of a guitar, and being an editor isn't that much fun. Too many boring meetings about budgets,' he said casually, as if being an editor of a magazine, a mass market magazine sold in every newsagent's and supermarket in the country, was beneath him. 'I'm going to make the move to a style mag. It's not official yet, but I interviewed for deputy editor on *Cravat* and I just got the nod that the position is mine.' Another shrug. 'I mean, it's kind of a sideways move. Maybe even a backwards move, going from editor to deputy editor but . . .'

'No, it's a brilliant move,' Jenny insisted. She was relieved that she could feel pleased for him. Before, there had always been a tiny but powerful throb of resentment at each new announcement from Nick whether it was a week's trip to the States to hang out with a band or an exclusive interview with someone mega famous that ended up being syndicated. Even though Jenny had no interest in doing what Nick did, his triumphs were always a reminder that she had no triumphs, just a hard slog, day in and day out, and still she was getting nowhere fast. But that had all changed now. 'Congratulations. You're going to be amazing.'

There was silence. Nick dipped his head in acknowledgement of how amazing he was going to be. The train was approaching High Street Kensington, only five more stops to Victoria, and then Jenny could go. He was so self-involved. Always had been. He couldn't even be bothered to ask her how she was, how her job . . .

'So, how is life in *retail*?' When he said it like that, like retail was a nasty, grubby word for a dubious profession, Jenny wished that he'd shown no interest at all.

'It's fine, thank you. Better than fine actually bec—'

'I can't believe you've settled for so little,' Nick continued. He leaned forward and Jenny followed his gaze to where Gethin sat, still slumped, still looking as if he wished he were anywhere but here. Nick didn't mention Gethin by name but then he didn't have to. The implication was as loud as if he'd shouted it.

'I haven't settled at all,' Jenny bit out. 'I *love* my job . . .'

'You said that you wanted to work in publishing. Instead you're working in a bookshop . . .'

'There's nothing wrong with working in a bookshop!' Jenny finished her drink with three long pulls. 'Cavanagh Morton is a London institution. Virginia Woolf had an account there.

Cyril Connolly once passed out drunk in the window! I put together book collections for people and organise author signings . . .'

'You're a shop assistant paid by the hour. What is the point of that fancy MA now?' Nick asked and he wasn't even getting heated in the face of Jenny's rising anger and increased volume, which was even more infuriating.

'Fuck you!' she snapped. 'Fuck you for being so bloody superior when you have no idea what it's like to struggle.'

'You don't have the monopoly on working hard, Jen,' Nick said, his voice tightening a little. 'I work hard.'

'Staying up until six in the morning writing up an interview that you were flown to LA to do isn't working hard. Try working six months for no pay for a lecherous literary agent and having to pull double shifts at a restaurant to pay the rent where even more lecherous men would shove their hands up my skirt and say vile things to me . . .'

Nick shifted in his seat and wriggled his shoulders as if he didn't like where this conversation had gone. 'You never said that you were working for free,' he pointed out.

'Because you weren't really that interested and I was ashamed that my glittering career, the career I wanted so badly, hadn't panned out. So, yeah, I'm working in a book-shop but I'm getting paid and I'm happy so you can take your superior attitude and shove it!'

Jenny struggled to her feet as the train pulled into Gloucester Road. The party was *still* raging, everyone looking as if they were having the best of times and Jenny was bitterly disappointed that the London Transport Police weren't waiting on the platform to storm the carriage and pull the plug. She waved manically at Gethin to indicate that they should get off the train *this instant*, but he was now talking to an elderly man in an anorak and not looking at her.

'Jen! Jen, sit down,' Nick said urgently, tugging on her wrist. She pulled away.

'Don't touch me!' she hissed.

'I'm sorry. I was being a dick,' he muttered so she thought she'd misheard him because Nick didn't ever apologise. That would make him accountable. 'I'm sorry, OK?'

He really had apologised. Twice! This must be the day that Satan went to work on ice skates.

She sat back down with a huff. 'It's not OK.'

More silence. Nine years ago, Nick had known her better than anyone. There'd never been silence. But that had been a lie too. Had they ever really been friends in a good, pure way? Jen didn't think so and it was ridiculous to keep chasing an ideal that had never been real.

'So . . . you still living in Shepherd's Bush, then?' Nick interrupted Jenny's unhappy train of thought.

'What? No.'

'You moved in with lover boy?'

'His name's Gethin as you know very well and no, I haven't moved in with him.'

Nick tipped his head back and exhaled. 'God, give me something to work with, Jen! I'm trying here.'

Neither of them should have to try to maintain a civil conversation, an interest in each other's lives. Or sneer at the other one's life choices.

'Maida Vale. Or Kilburn, really. I'm living with my nan.' Jenny tilted her chin in a challenge. 'I'm sure you've got something to say about that.'

'You're living with Dot and Stan?' Nick asked incredulously and Jen was incredulous too that he could still remember her grandparents' names.

'Just Dot.' She sighed. 'Stan died five months ago.'

'I'm sorry . . .'

'Don't be. He had a massive heart attack in the bookies when his seven-way accumulator bet paid out.' She smiled ruefully in a way that had become a part of how she told this story. 'Died with a grin on his face, apparently.'

'He was . . . I know it's a cliché but they really don't make them like your granddad anymore.' Nick nudged her arm gently. 'Do you remember when I met him that time and he asked me if I was an Arthur or a Martha and it wasn't even like my hair was that long or I was, you know, wearing a dress?'

Jen shook her head and this time her smile was more genuine, less a part of the act. 'Yeah, I remember.'

'And when we went upstairs, we heard him say, "So, he's queer then, is he?"' It was Nick's turn to look down the carriage to where Gethin was still talking with his new best friend. 'What did he think of lo . . . Gethin?'

'You mean because he's Black?' Jenny queried a little defensively, because she'd walked in Gethin's shoes now, or rather she'd walked down the street with him numerous times and heard people say disgusting things to him and about him daring to hold hands with a white woman. Jenny really had thought that she lived in a tolerant, liberal society, but then Stan had hardly been tolerant or liberal . . . except. 'Actually, he loved Geth. Took him a while to get his head round the fact that someone could be Welsh and Black. But when he found out that Gethin could draw, he was utterly besotted.'

They'd been out to celebrate the twins' twenty-first birthday. It was only the second time that Gethin had met the family en masse and the first time, Stan had hardly been welcoming. It was painfully and unbelievably awkward and Jenny was steeling herself to have words with her grandfather when she could get him on her own, but before that she gave Martin his birthday card. The birthday card that Jenny had designed and Gethin had drawn, which featured the words

'Happy Birthday! (Subject to contract)' and a cartoon of Martin leaning against his pride and joy, the Mini Cooper that was emblazoned with the logo of the estate agent where he'd worked since leaving college at seventeen. He was carrying a mobile phone the size of a cereal box and punching the air as he liked to do when he'd successfully sold a house.

'It looks just like him!' Stan had marvelled with child-like wonder. 'It's better than that Rolf Harris.'

For the rest of the lunch, he'd pestered Gethin to draw various family members and Gethin had obliged and ever since that, Stan had been like a teenage girl with a crush on a popstar.

'He's a good lad,' he'd say whenever Gethin came up in conversation. 'She could do a lot worse. He'll never be short of money with a talent like that.'

Stan had gone to his grave harbouring the delusion that people with a knack for figurative drawing could pull in the big bucks. Gethin had recently increased his hours at the art supplies store but he was still focussed on his art. 'Actually Gethin's doing really well. He's having an exhibition in November,' Jenny told Nick, who nodded but didn't comment, though Jenny was meant to have been impressed that he was seeing some girl with a Lolita complex who was in a minor indie band. OK, the exhibition wasn't in some slick Mayfair art gallery but a café in Camberwell, but still it counted for something.

'Do you miss him then, Stan?' Nick asked though Jenny didn't know why he was persisting in talking about her dead grandfather while a party raged around them.

But it was a question that no one else had asked her. 'Considering how much we fought, especially in the last few years, I do miss him. He was such a huge part of my life,' Jenny said, thinking that even now when she walked through the front door of her grandparents' flat, *her* flat now, she still expected Stan to be sitting in his armchair, with his fags, *Racing Post* and a cuppa on the go on the little side table next to him.

'Look what the cat's dragged in,' had been his usual cheery greeting, followed by a brutal critique of her outfit ('that skirt's so short, I can see your kidneys') and her life choices ('so how much money are you earning thanks to those two fancy degrees of yours? Waste of bloody time.')

There'd been no rapprochement. No softening of Stan's opinion of her. No whispered, 'I'm proud of you,' whenever Jen had brushed her lips against his cheek as she said goodbye.

So, she didn't know why she missed him so much and why it felt like there was a gaping hole in the middle of her world.

'Nan hardly misses him at all,' she told Nick. 'At first she did because she didn't know how to do anything. She'd never written a cheque or paid a gas bill. Hadn't even spent one night on her own in her life so me moving in was a bit of a lifesaver. Not that I'm complaining.'

'Cheap rent, then? Full bed and board?' Nick nudged her again. 'Bet she does your laundry too, doesn't she?'

Jenny nodded. 'Even irons my pants. Says that she's happiest looking after someone else and I don't moan as much as Stan or use foul language when Arsenal loses. And with what was left of his winnings, she went and bought a freezer because he'd always said that they didn't need one and she filled it with ice cream.'

'Ice cream?'

'She loves ice cream and she has trouble sleeping so in the middle of the night, if I hear a noise and I get up, it's just Nan helping herself to a bowl of rum and raisin.'

Nick pulled a face 'Not even nice ice cream, then?'

'It's the worst flavour, isn't it?'

They grinned at each other and Jenny rested her hand on top of Nick's, where he gripped the armrest because even when things were scratchy and they had nothing left in common, they still had that connection. Probably always would.

'So, you've had a lot of life stuff going on, then? You didn't just dump your mates, me, because you got a boyfriend?' Nick sounded chippy again.

'The world doesn't revolve around you, Nick,' Jenny told him drily. 'It's only July and so far this year, I've got a new job, lost my grandfather, moved in with Dot, who's needed a lot of TLC, and yes, I do occasionally want to spend time with my boyfriend. I'm sorry about that.'

Jenny's footing on the moral high ground wasn't quite as secure as she made out. Yes, she hardly partied at all now or hung out with her old crowd. But Gethin preferred it when it was just the two of them. When they were an us. It wasn't a crime to love being one half of an us when Jenny had been on her own for so long.

Also, she couldn't have carried on the way she'd been going. Partying so hard then feeling so wrecked afterwards. All the pills and drink hadn't filled the aching chasm inside her. Neither had hanging out with George and Nick. Especially Nick, because for all the bravado and the brave face she put on it, when she'd hung out with Nick she'd still felt sixteen, clumsy and shy. Had still been his sidekick, his plus-one, his support act, rather than her own person.

'I have to tell you something,' Nick said now, his voice uncharacteristically hesitant.

Jenny raised her eyebrows. Neither encouraging or discouraging, not even that curious because it would just be another boast about his brilliant career or the girlfriend that dressed like some charity shop Baby Doll. 'Go on then,' she said gesturing with a hand like she was back at Ciccone's and ushering someone to their table.

'I am . . . I was . . . when we were hanging out before him,' he jerked his head in the direction of where Gethin was still having a very animated conversation with the old man.

'You were what?' Jenny asked even as she inwardly cringed because she knew, she just *knew*, that whatever Nick's revelation was, she wasn't going to like it. He'd probably shagged one of her friends.

'I wanted you so badly,' he said, which wasn't at all what she'd expected him to say.

Her mouth fell open and she turned to stare at him in disbelief. 'You what? No, you didn't!'

'I did,' Nick insisted and he tried to take her hand but Jenny stopped him by the simple act of folding her arms and fixing him with a hard but hurt look. 'There were all those nights when we slept in the same bed, except I couldn't sleep because all I wanted to do was fuck you.'

'You have never wanted to fuck me,' Jenny said a little bitterly, because even before *him*, before Gethin, she'd tried so hard to tamp down any feelings she might have had for Nick. Had accepted that they were friends, only friends. 'You never said or did anything to indicate that you were gagging for me.'

'Oh, I think I did,' Nick snapped. 'I barely looked at another girl that whole time.'

Jenny made a scoffing noise like a motorbike that was having trouble starting. 'Not true. There were countless little blonde things. Every week there was a new one.'

'But I hardly shagged any of them and I could have,' Nick pointed out and if that was proof of his devotion to Jenny then he really was going to have to do much better than that. 'And I stopped you from shagging at least half a dozen guys because

I knew they were bad news and I couldn't bear the thought of you with someone else. Someone who wasn't me.'

There was a catch in his voice that Jenny had never heard before and when she risked a glance sideways, he'd taken off the stupid glasses and was staring at her with what looked like sincerity.

'Well, why didn't you say something then?' she implored him, though she didn't know what she'd have done if he had.

Nick shrugged, not in a standoffish way but as if he'd asked himself the same question over and over and had never managed to come up with an adequate answer. 'I don't know, I was waiting for a sign that you felt the same way,' he admitted. 'It was easier when you used to blush every time I looked at you. Now you're quite a hard person to read.'

'I really am not,' Jenny said in surprise. Though she still longed to be mysterious and enigmatic, she was mostly realistic these days. 'I'm an open book. Not even a very long book either.'

'And maybe because I knew you were in a bad place,' he said softly. 'I didn't know that you were working for free or anything like that, but you seemed kind of brittle and I didn't want to be the one to break you.'

He was so different from Gethin who'd seen exactly the same quality in Jenny but had wanted to be the one who put her back together, though Jenny liked to think that she'd saved herself. She was the one who'd got the job at Cavanagh Morton. Also, moving in with Dot and getting the security and stability and home cooked meals that she'd secretly been craving had been a huge step towards getting happy. But before that there'd been Gethin looking at Jenny like she was someone who deserved to be happy and he was going to do everything in his power to make that happen.

'See, the old Jen would have sneered "Ha! Like you could break me. Don't flatter yourself",' Nick pointed out a little sadly.

'I'm not the old Jen anymore. Actually, everyone calls me Jenny, even Kirsty,' Jenny said and though she'd railed against being Jenny in the past, now she didn't mind the perkier, jauntier version of the Jennifer that was on her birth certificate.

'To me you'll always be Jen. You were Jen when I first knew you.' Nick put his hand on her elbow, though her arms were still folded tightly. 'I shouldn't have said anything. I wish I hadn't now.'

'I didn't know . . . I'd never have guessed.' Jenny should have felt pleased, shouldn't she? Vindicated. Validated. But mostly, she tried to ignore the pulse of lust that had quickened within her, when Nick had said that he'd wanted to fuck her. Not make love. Not even have sex. But to fuck her. It was a crude thing to say but it had lit a fire in her belly that she now desperately wanted to stamp out. But still, there were some things she needed to know before they never, ever talked about this again. 'Is that why . . . that morning when we . . . You pushed me away and I thought . . .' She couldn't seem to form sentences but she could still remember the scorch of embarassment because she was feeling it now, all over again. 'I thought you didn't want to.'

'Of course I did,' Nick said, his cheeks suddenly stained with red too as if this conversation was as mortifying for him as it was for Jenny. 'I wanted it more than anything. But I didn't want to take advantage of you, not just because we were still pilled up but because you just . . . you were so fragile, Jen, and I knew it would be a mistake, that you'd end up hating me.' He shrugged again. 'But you ended up hating me anyway.'

'I don't hate you,' Jenny said, exasperation replacing embarassment. 'It works both ways, being friends with someone. It's not like you've made an effort to stay in touch with me.'

'You haven't called me once, Jen, since you paired up. Not once. And forgive me for being pissed off with you that you went straight from my bed to *his* . . .'

Jenny rolled her eyes. 'It wasn't like that!' Except now that Nick was pointing it out to her, it had been exactly like that. Though it hadn't seemed like that at the time. She was back to feeling mortified again. 'You know, you really should have told me how you felt instead of letting me think we were just mates.'

'If I had, would you still have got with him?'

Jenny shook her head. 'God, don't ask me that . . .'

She couldn't begin to know the answer and when she looked up for divine guidance . . . Gethin was standing there.

'Victoria,' he said, his face and voice utterly expressionless and Jenny realised that they'd been through several stations and the next destination was where she said goodbye.

'Right.' She got to her feet. 'I guess this is goodbye then.'

'You're not staying?' Nick crossed his legs and put his shades back on so it was impossible to see the truth in his bloodshot eyes any longer.

'I don't think so.' Gethin had already moved to the doors. 'Really only came to see George off and he's furious with me so . . .'

'He's off his nuts right now. I'll talk to him tomorrow,' Nick offered as the train began to slow down. 'Though I'm planning on getting off my nuts quite soon so I might not remember.'

'If you could.'

They were coming into the station now and there was nothing left to be said.

'It was good seeing you, Jen,' Nick said. 'We shouldn't leave it so long.'

'Absolutely,' she agreed. 'You still in Camden?'

'I'm moving out when George goes but you can get me at the office . . .'

'I'll do that,' Jenny said quickly. The doors had opened and with the most perfunctory of smiles and a little wave, she hurried to jump off the train and catch up with Gethin who was already halfway down the platform. 'Geth! Hold on!'

He came to a halt, his face still impassive, which usually meant that he was quietly seething about something and it would take ages for him to reveal what was bothering him. Not that Jenny needed any clues this time.

'It's done,' she said and she brushed her hands together like she was wiping away chalk dust. 'And I won't be doing that again.'

'Doing what?' Gethin asked, as she tucked her arm in his and they walked down the platform.

'Seeing those people. Nick,' she added, just in case Gethin was in any doubt. She'd chosen him over Nick that Sunday at Leicester Square tube station and had never once regretted it. What she had with Nick had always been something insubstantial, with built-in obsolescence. Like a washing machine or a vacuum cleaner. He might want to *fuck* her, but what she had with Gethin was so much more than that. 'There's no point. Just because we were friends when we were teenagers doesn't mean that we have anything in common, except memories, and a lot of them aren't good memories.'

'If you wanted to still see them, him, then I wouldn't mind . . .'

He absolutely would but it was a measure of his sweetness that Gethin insisted otherwise. 'I don't want to,' Jenny said. 'I mean, there's work time, there's Nan time and God help me if I'm not home by ten o'clock on a school night . . .'

They were approaching the Victoria line platforms now and, miracle of miracles, Gethin was smiling. 'She worries about you . . .'

'I want the rest of my time to be Gethin time, so you don't have to worry about anyone else making demands on me.' Jenny caught his hand and threaded her fingers through his so she could bring it to her mouth and kiss it. 'OK?'

Gethin nodded. 'OK.'

'Because I do love you,' Jenny said and she wished she wasn't saying it for the first time as they squeezed through people coming off the Brixton train that they wanted to catch.

'We're going to miss the train.' It was a rush and a push to jump on before the doors closed. 'So, I didn't tell you, I was talking to this old guy . . .'

'Yeah, I saw you . . .'

'He was at the Royal College of Art with Eric Ravilious and Eric Bawden.' Gethin let out a low whistle. 'Studied under Paul Nash. Incredible, isn't it?'

Jenny agreed that it was though she didn't know who any of those people were but that was OK, because Gethin proceeded to tell her. As he talked, she couldn't help feeling despondency, a gloom, settling over her at the thought of that rushed, guilt-ridden, final unsatisfying goodbye then saying 'I love you' to someone who hadn't even attempted to say it back to her.

PART SIX

1996 – 1997

15

Friday, October 18th, 1996
Heathrow Terminals 1,2,3 Station

'So, is that what all the best editors are wearing this year?' Kirsty asked as Jenny hefted one of her friend's suitcases onto the escalator. 'I thought you'd look more, well, bookish.'

Once Jenny had made sure that the suitcase was secure on its stair, she gave a little shimmy. 'This is the unofficial office uniform.'

This was a strappy black vest, a fine-knit pale blue cardigan, grey hipster trousers and Jenny's trusty Dunlop Green Flash trainers.

'Of course, when I'm not helping my friend cart half her worldly goods across London, I dress a bit smarter. If I'm having lunch with a writer or agent, something like that.'

Kirsty dared to take a hand off the suitcase that she had propped on the step behind her so she could pat Jenny's shoulder. 'Get you! Doing lunch with fancy writing folk. Do you have a company credit card?'

'Yes! I can hardly believe they've trusted me with one.' Jenny couldn't pretend to be blasé about it. Besides, she was reunited with Kirsty who wouldn't expect her to be. 'Even better than that, I have my own business cards. I'll give you one once we're on the tube.'

'I'm so proud of you. Jennifer Richards, editor. Such a nice ring to it.'

'Editor, I still can't believe it,' Jenny said, because she'd started at Lyttons in January as an Assistant Editor but through a combination of being over-qualified for the job, a couple of editors leaving and the sheer luck, for once, of being in the right place at exactly the right time, she'd been promoted to Editor by Easter.

She was still very much learning the ropes but the three writers she'd inherited and the one writer she'd acquired hadn't yet turned round and said, 'Excuse me, but we'd like a proper editor and not this ... this imposter!'

But today was all about Kirsty. Which was why Jenny had booked the afternoon off to meet her best friend and her best friend's two suitcases and assortment of big blue IKEA bags. Kirsty was back in town. For good this time. Her strapping boyfriend, Erik the Viking (actually he was a leading expert in Urban Studies), whom she'd acquired while she was in Stockholm, was following at a later date. 'Never mind my company credit card, I have a best friend who's the new curator at a top London museum.'

'Assistant curator at a museum in the back of beyond that no one's ever heard of,' Kirsty insisted, but she took her hand off her suitcase again to prod Jenny in the back. 'We're not doing too bad, are we?'

'We are not,' Jenny confirmed and she was just about to list the itinerary she had planned for Kirsty's first weekend back in London: back to Jenny's flat in Notting Hill to dump Kirsty's stuff, dinner at The Seashell in Lisson Grove, the best fish and chip shop in London. Tomorrow they'd explore Portobello Road market, then head over to Covent Garden to meet Gethin from work and back to Brixton where some friends of his were having a party ... when she glanced over at the down escalators and the words caught in her throat.

He had his head turned so she wasn't sure if it was him. A tall, lean dark-haired man talking to two people he appeared to be with: a short middle-aged woman wearing linen in various shades of taupe who was gesticulating so wildly it was a wonder she didn't plunge to her death, and a man dressed all in black carrying a camera bag and tripod. Even the faintest suggestion that it was him was enough to make her heart thump so loudly that Jenny was sure it could be heard over the trundle of the escalators, which echoed in the cavernous hall.

Then he turned slightly, adjusted the big holdall on his shoulder, and it was definitely him. Nick. His hair was a lot like it had been when she'd first known him; a long fringe, which he pushed back impatiently. He was wearing jeans, though Jenny hadn't seen him wear anything as ordinary as a pair of jeans, a T-shirt, a leather jacket, for ages.

But a lot could happen in a year. A year was long enough for Jenny to leave one job, start another and already have a promotion under her belt. To still work some Saturdays at Cavanagh Morton while Gethin worked Saturdays at the art supplies shop but also because she missed bookselling; putting books into the hands of people and knowing that in some small way each book would change their lives. To write ten more pieces for the *London Review of Books*, three articles for the *Times Literary Supplement* and a double-page spread on her beloved Jilly Cooper for the *Guardian*'s book section.

A year was long enough move in with Gethin to the big, dusty house in Brixton then move out a month later because of the dust, the mice, the silverfish, the housemates who were too pretentious and too obsessed with their art to ever run a vacuum over the place.

A year was long enough to get over the hurt that Gethin really didn't seem that bothered when she'd moved out to share a flat with her work friends Charlotte D and Charlotte W in Notting Hill (which was across London from him but much nearer to her offices in Kensington.)

A year was long enough to have invested in proper plump pillows, two sets of bed linen and The Duvet. The Duvet wasn't even from Marks & Spencer, the pinnacle of consumer achievement as far as her mother and grandmother were concerned. The Duvet was from John Lewis (despite the fact that the Richards women only ever went to the more upmarket John Lewis to get fitted for a bra) and it wasn't even a duvet but TWO duvets. 'A thin one for summer and a medium one for mid-season then you clip them together to make a heavy duvet for winter,' Jenny had explained as the three of them had stood in the soft furnishings department of John Lewis in Oxford Street.

'Who would even think such a thing was possible?' Dot had wondered aloud because she was still firmly wedded to a top sheet, blankets and a candlewick bedspread.

'It's so practical and not much more expensive than a regular duvet,' Jackie had said, looking at her daughter with what Jenny liked to think was new respect. 'Do you get a lot of things from John Lewis, then?'

Jenny had shrugged. 'Well, they are never knowingly undersold.'

So, a year was also long enough for her parents and grandmother to finally treat her like a proper adult.

A year was long enough to finish growing out her fringe, then cut it back in again. And break the two littlest fingers on her left hand after slamming a minicab door shut on them. Slightly related, during this year, she'd found a new socially acceptable alcoholic drink: vodka and cranberry, 'the red drink' as it was known to her friends. 'Practically a health drink,' Jenny would tell people because she'd only had one bout of cystitis since she'd adopted it.

A year was long enough to go back to Paris with Gethin to try and rekindle what they'd had but nothing could compare to the thrill of the first time. There'd been three long weekends in Stockholm to visit Kirsty. A booze cruise with her brothers to load up on cheap alcohol for the secret 30th wedding anniversary party they'd thrown for Jackie and Alan. A week in Ibiza with Kirsty though they'd quickly realised that they weren't cut out for a week in Ibiza.

A year was long enough for a couple of pregnancy scares. One that she told Gethin about and wished she hadn't because her period arrived a couple of days after that but his quiet, brooding fury lasted for weeks. And one that Jenny didn't tell him about, not even when a pregnancy test confirmed her worst suspicions and she booked two days off work and went to the doctor for a prescription for Mifepristone.

A year was long enough to realise that she was no longer stuck. Not only had she found herself but she was becoming the person she always wanted to be.

A year was long enough for Gethin to become lost but the difference was that he didn't want to be found. He didn't paint or draw or smudge charcoal on paper anymore. Didn't smudge charcoal on Jenny either. He just worked five days a week, sometimes six, as assistant manager at the art supplies shop. He worried about inventory and staff productivity and every single person that came in to buy paper, paint or some other medium by which to make art with was a bitter reminder of the person that he used to be.

A year was long enough for Gethin's disappointments to coalesce into resentment.

A year was long enough to see the light slowly dim from Gethin's eyes when he looked at her.

A year was long enough that Gethin should have said he loved her at least once. Even if he didn't mean it.

A year could be such a long time. Long enough for Jenny's life to change beyond all measure. For it to be a different life to the one that it had been the last time she'd seen Nick. But despite all this change and growth and far too many red drinks, there hadn't been a single day during that year that she hadn't thought about Nick at least once. About what they'd had. What they hadn't had. What might have happened if things had been different.

Now, he was going down while Jenny was going up. She momentarily thought about calling his name but he was too far away. Going in completely the opposite direction. Nick didn't notice her though Jenny turned her head as far as she could without losing control of her suitcase until he disappeared from view and she was back in reality, in the present, in the here. The moment was hers and hers alone.

'Are you all right?' Kirsty was asking. 'You haven't been listening to a single word I've said. They were good words!'

'Sorry, I'm fine, just ... I thought I saw someone I knew.' They'd reached the top and had to haul their heavy load off the escalator. By the time they were sitting in a stationary Piccadilly Line tube train waiting for it to depart, Jenny had found some calm and a smile that was decent enough to fool Kirsty.

'So, these good words, what were they?' she asked.

'I was just wondering how things were with you and Geth?' Kirsty asked delicately. 'You said last time we spoke that things were a bit dicey.'

They were more than a bit dicey. But neither of them wanted to be the one to admit that after two years they'd grown apart rather than grown together. She'd say it soon, Jenny decided. If not next week, then the week after. But Kirsty had just moved her entire life across half a continent and it was her first weekend back in London, plus she'd already said that she had the beginnings of a hunger headache.

So Jenny pulled out another half decent smile. 'Nothing that you need to worry your pretty little head about. Now, how do you fancy me treating you to the best fish and chips of your life?'

'Poncy London fish and chips, where the fish isn't fried in beer batter, the mushy peas are substandard and you have no change left out of a tenner?' Kirsty sniffed though she'd been living in Sweden for God knows how long and had regularly eaten moose so she couldn't really play the hardy Northerner anymore.

'One and the same.'

'Sounds like heaven,' Kirsty said rapturously. 'Do you know that in Sweden they serve boiled potatoes with practically every meal? Even breakfast?'

'Yeah, you might have mentioned it once or twice,' Jenny said as the doors closed and the train began to speed them back into town, to a tumultuous two weeks that would break Jenny's heart but continue to shape her into the person she wanted to be.

16

Friday, September 5th, 1997
High Street Kensington Station

It had been a really trying morning.

An edit back from a newbie author who'd disagreed with every single one of Jenny's suggestions and didn't seem to realise that it was in Jenny's best interests to make their book as good as it could be. Not to 'stifle and strangle my creativity'.

There'd also been final offers on a book that Jenny was desperate to acquire but Valerie, her boss, wouldn't let her go above a certain figure, so she'd lost to her opposite number at Penguin. How she hated her opposite number at Penguin!

Then there'd been a very long interdepartmental meeting about the email system that was finally going to be installed on the new iMacs they were getting. They had to draft up a company internet policy because Sinclair, the MD, was terrified that no one would ever do any work ever again because they'd be too busy 'doing the internet'.

Jenny actually had the internet on her home computer but didn't have the heart or the courage (he was famously short-tempered) to tell Sinclair that you could do the whole of the internet in an hour.

Of course the meeting had overrun and now she was running late, fighting her way through the lunch-time crowds. Kensington Arcade had never been so busy. But it had been like that all week. People surging through the ticket barriers in their hundreds with grim, set faces and clutching huge bunches of flowers.

Much like Jackie and Dot, waiting for Jenny by the entrance to Boots, and despite the bright, late summer weather were both dressed in muted colours. Dot always had her hair set on a Friday morning and her white curls were as rigid as her lips. She was wearing the navy crimplene dress that she'd had for as long as Jenny could remember and which did for funerals, important meetings and hospital appointments. Dot had worn the dress a lot in the weeks after Stan had died, accessorising it, like today, with her best big black handbag.

Jackie was slightly less formal but was wearing her good black 'dress slacks' and a pristine white blouse with a grey check blazer and court shoes. It was a look she'd suggested Jenny might adopt to get ahead at work, which was probably why she was frowning as Jenny approached in her trusty vintage blue and white polka dot dress and ubiquitous tennis shoes.

'Oh, Jenny, you might have made more of an effort,' she said as Jenny kissed Dot on the cheek. 'We're meant to be paying our respects and you look . . . You look very cheerful.'

'I told you that I'm out tonight,' Jenny explained. 'And I am sombre on the inside, believe me.'

She'd been sombre ever since last Sunday morning. She'd been having her usual indulgent, lazy Sunday morning lie-in, cocooned in good quality bedding and vowing to get up in another ten minutes, when Jackie had rung. Charlotte D was at her boyfriend's, Charlotte W had gone to her parents for the weekend, so the phone had rung and rung until the answerphone had picked it up.

Jenny was already getting out of bed, because the phone's rings had pierced her sleepy haze and she realised that she needed a wee so when she opened her bedroom door, it was in time to hear Jackie's frantic message echoing down the hall.

'Jenny? I can't believe you're still in bed! Call me back immediately!'

Jenny didn't call her back immediately. She had a wee. Brushed her teeth. Made a cup of coffee and had a couple of puffs of her first cigarette of the day before she rang Jackie, who didn't even bother with a hello and how are you. 'I can't believe the news,' her mother said in a croaky voice. 'It's so shocking. I keep thinking it's a dream and I'll wake up. That poor woman. Those poor boys.'

'What woman? What boys?' Jenny had asked, imagining it was one of Jackie's friends or a neighbour.

'Diana!'

'We don't know any Dianas.'

'Princess Di! She was in a car crash in Paris with that Dodi Fayed. He's dead too.'

It was as if the whole world had tipped off its axis though Jenny would have sworn, had sworn, to her friends that she was an ardent Republican and that the Royal Family were parasites and anyway 'people shouldn't be born into great privilege; they should fucking work for it.' But last Sunday morning, a chill had immediately enveloped her and she'd almost dropped the phone. She was so shocked that all she could say was, 'I can't talk right now,' and hung up. Then she'd burst into tears.

Diana's death had cast a pall over the week, had pierced the national psyche. It was why Kensington was so busy, with people coming to pay their respects and lay down flowers at the gates of Kensington Palace, where Diana's body (Jenny could barely comprehend that Diana was just a body now, rather than a glowing, golden girl who had been omnipresent in Jenny's life ever since she and Charles had first got engaged), currently lying in state at St James's Palace, would return that night ahead of tomorrow's funeral.

Jenny always came out of the tube and turned left along Kensington High Street to get to work but now, flanked by Jackie and Dot, she turned right in the direction of Kensington Palace and its gardens.

She wasn't prepared for the scent of the flowers that hung in the air as soon as they crossed over Kensington Church Street. The fragrance grew stronger and stronger as they joined the end of a long, meandering queue of people, most of them holding bouquets, cuddly toys, large envelopes.

Jenny had seen the scenes on the news but nothing could prepare her for the sight of the thousands and thousands of flowers and tributes, stretching from the gates of the Palace and all along the Broadwalk.

Both Jackie and Dot were uncharacteristically quiet as they lay down their white carnations and chrysanthemums. They weren't ones to cry, not in public, unlike a lot of other people, not just women but men too, who were sobbing quietly. One woman decked out in black with a full lace mantilla was howling and Dot gave her a flinty-eyed look. 'Some people just go to pieces in a crisis,' she murmured and hoisted her big black handbag further up her shoulder.

Afterwards, even though the three of them were still subdued, they retraced their steps to the High Street. 'We'll go to Barkers for tea and cake,' Jenny said. 'My treat.' She would never get bored of having enough disposable income that she could treat her parents or her grandmother. Also, there were few things Dot loved more than afternoon tea in a department store.

Since Stan had died, Jackie and Dot had become even closer. 'She's my best friend,' Jackie often said, then would give Jenny a slightly pointed look. 'That's how it should be. You should be best friends with your mum.'

If Jackie knew how many times Jenny and Kirsty had got rid of each other's one night stands that had outstayed their welcome or held each other's hair back while they'd thrown up, she wouldn't be so keen to have a best friend instead of a daughter who only told her things on a need to know basis.

But when Jenny did make a threesome with Jackie and Dot, it wasn't like a friendship threesome where someone was always the spare. It was different with the people you shared DNA with. Jenny was always welcomed with open arms and great delight. Now that she was a proper grown-up with a duvet for all seasons, Jackie and Dot were always seeking out her opinion and were wide-eyed with wonder at all the new things Jenny had introduced them to.

There'd even been a very jolly weekend to Brighton just after Jenny had broken up with Gethin. Instead of staying in the cheapest B & B they could possibly find, Jenny had wangled them a suite with sea views at The Grand from a deal she'd found on a new website that specialised in last-minute hotel deals. The nascent respect they had for Jenny had tripled, at the very least, when they'd arrived at their suite to find a complimentary bottle of champagne and a plate of chocolate-dipped strawberries.

Now, they both enjoyed the illicit thrill of afternoon tea on a Friday afternoon. 'Even though it isn't even anyone's birthday,' Dot marvelled. 'I still can't believe you get every Friday afternoon off, Jenny.'

'Every other Friday afternoon,' Jenny explained for the umpteenth time.

It was both a perk and a quirk of working at Lyttons. While not one of the Big Five publishers, they were a thriving independent company that prided itself on catering for a more literary reader – no glitzy bonkbusters or lurid crime novels for them. Lyttons was still a family run company and, like the Lyttons who sat on the board, believed that most of their staff must have houses in the country they were keen to return to for the weekend. Or, at the very least, liked to spend the weekend with friends who had houses in the country. Hence, the Lyttons staff got every other Friday afternoon off.

Jenny had only ever spent one weekend in the country and that was at the invitation of Sinclair Lytton himself, MD, and great-grandson of the original founder. Last March when she'd just had her second promotion to Commissioning Editor, she was invited down to the family seat, a huge honey-coloured house just outside Chipping Norton and was very glad she'd spent her youth reading Jilly Cooper novels so she had half an idea of what to expect. She'd much rather be eating scones with clotted cream and jam with Dot and Jackie than having to worry about the social minefield of whether the jam or the cream went on first. (Though anyone who put jam on first was obviously a monster.)

Once the three of them were seated, they talked about what they usually talked about and though the repetition, the careful assembly of family myth-building ('And who would have thought that Martin would have come good in the end. When I think of the sleepless nights he gave us') should have been frustrating, Jenny found it comforting in its familiarity. Her life moved so fast, making up for all that time she'd squandered after she finished her MA, and she was always so focussed on smashing her adult milestones, that listening to Dot recount, yet again, the tale of how she'd been in the crowd at Buckingham Palace on VE day, was kind of relaxing.

All too soon it was time to go their separate ways. They came out of Barkers by a side door as they debated the best way for Dot and Jackie to go back to Kilburn where Alan would pick them up later.

'Get the bus,' Jenny said firmly. 'Jump on the 328 and it will take you practically door to door.'

'But the traffic's so busy and I'm not sure my bladder will hold out,' Dot said.

'You've just been to the Ladies, Nan!'

Jackie shook her head. 'I told you not to order that second pot of tea.'

This well-worn back and forth was definitely more frustrating than familiar.

'If you get the tube, you'll have to change at Paddington. It's gone four now, Paddington will be carnage,' Jenny announced and it had been *hours* and she couldn't hold out for a cigarette any longer, even though she'd told Jackie and Dot that she'd practically given up. For good this time.

But she really needed a nicotine hit because she was going to have to squeeze on a rush hour Circle Line train to Embankment, then change to the Bakerloo or Northern Line just to go one more stop to Charing Cross. Next, Jenny would have to fight her way through the commuter hordes to get to the concourse of Charing Cross mainline station so she could catch a train to New Cross. Not even a tube train but an actual proper train because the little East London line, which used to serve New Cross, had been closed for the last two years.

Jenny pulled a face at the very thought of New Cross – she loved Kirsty but she'd been tempted to dump her rather than have to make the arduous journey across London every time Kirsty insisted that they meet at hers. To add insult to injury, Kirsty lived a good fifteen minute walk from the station.

As Jackie and Dot argued the merits of bus over tube, Jenny gratefully relinquished the albatross around her neck or rather the heavy, shoulder-denting canvas tote bag full of manuscripts, proofs and books that was her constant companion.

She rummaged in her handbag for her cigarettes but before her hand had even closed around the packet of Consulate (she was back to smoking the menthol cigarettes of her adolescence in the vain hope that they were healthier than normal cigarettes) and the clunky silver Zippo that she'd got for her eighteenth birthday, she heard someone haltingly call her name.

Or rather they called out a version of her name that no one used. 'Jennifer Richards?' A smartly dressed woman, the older side of middle-aged, was waving at them from further down the street.

Jackie glanced over her shoulder. 'Who's that?'

Jenny shrugged. 'Search me.'

'Jennifer!' the woman called out again. The woman crossed the road and came closer, a lilac and blue floral dress billowing in the breeze, her dark, greying pre-Raphaelite curls secured in a bun, a slightly querulous look on her face. She did seem familiar.

Jenny raised her hand in greeting and wondered if that would be enough but no, the woman was almost upon her and holding out her arms like she expected a hug. Like they were two people who knew each other well enough to hug.

'Jennifer Richards,' the woman said again. 'You haven't changed a bit!'

Jenny let herself be gathered in a quick, stilted embrace and, oh, she was expected to brush the other woman's cheek with her own as they air kissed.

'Hello,' she said, wondering whether to bluff this one out or simply admit that she didn't have a clue who this woman was, when the woman gave her a swift once over in a way that made Jenny feel like she was seventeen again and standing on the doorstep of a big Arts & Crafts house in Mill Hill, not entirely sure that she was going to be granted admittance.

'Susan. Mrs Levene,' she said and Jenny was no longer a teenager, she was a grown-up who really needed a cigarette, now more than ever, and there was absolutely no reason why she couldn't just light up. It wasn't as if Susan was going to bust out a can of air freshener, like she'd used to when she'd suddenly wrench open the door of Nick's room and exclaim, 'I knew you two were smoking in here! How many times do I have to tell you that I can smell it all over the house?' But somehow, Jenny wasn't getting out the Consulate but smiling thinly at Nick's mother. 'It's been, what, ten years since I last saw you?'

'Susie. I always said that you should call me Susie,' Nick's mum said, because she'd always been Nick's mum to Jenny, not a person in her own right but a disapproving presence. It was quite hard to reconcile her with this woman who was smiling and generally acting as if she was pleased to see Jenny. 'I can't get over it. You really haven't changed. In fact, I even recognise that dress.'

Jenny looked down at her blue and white polka dot dress as if she couldn't remember what she'd put on that morning. It was part of the stash of five-pound vintage dresses that she'd bought as a teenager, which had languished in her parents' loft as she lived in a succession of rented rooms in shared houses. When she moved into the shared Notting Hill flat the year before with big fitted wardrobes and no damp or mould, Jackie and Alan had insisted that she finally clear out her stuff and she'd been reunited with all of her favourite frocks, which still, miraculously, fitted. Even though she never bicycled anywhere anymore and she drank far too much wine, which led to eating far too many crisps, once Jenny's puppy fat had gone, it had stayed gone.

'You look the same too,' Jenny said, which wasn't really true. Susan – she would never be Susie – was greyer, rounder and also seemed a lot happier. 'Still living in Mill Hill?'

'Oh yes. You and Nick don't keep in touch?' Susan raised her eyebrows in surprise. 'Though I suppose if you did, you'd have more interesting things to talk about than your parents. It was ever thus, right?'

Jenny nodded, though to be fair back in the day, they had talked a lot about their parents. Or rather complained about their parents' fascistic, small-minded and totally unfair domestic policies. Before swiftly moving on to complain about what a raw deal they both had in possessing twin siblings who always got all the attention simply because there were two of them.

The tidal wave of memories threatened to knock Jenny off her feet or maybe it was the very unsubtle prod of Jackie's hand at the small of her back. Jenny dutifully made the introductions.

'. . . this is Susan . . . Susie, Nick's mother. Nick, who I was friends with at college,' Jenny prompted when both Dot and Jackie looked blank at the mention of Nick's name. Jenny hadn't been very good at keeping them updated on her life, career and friendship group during her lost years so they didn't know that Nick had been close friends with Jenny for a long period after her MA. But now Jackie was nodding in recognition.

'Oh, Nick, yes! The pair of you used to be inseparable,' Jackie said, which was a slight exaggeration. 'Such a pity that you lost touch with each other.'

'He still keeps tabs on you. Said you were working as an editor now and writing for the *Guardian*. Which publisher are you with?' Susan asked, without any of the edge, any of the barely veiled disdain that she used to have, either because Jenny had proved her wrong or because Jenny had been projecting her own adolescent insecurities, distrust of authority and complicated feelings about Nick onto his mother. Something to ponder at a later date. For now, Jenny gestured at the bulging tote bag at her feet.

'Lyttons.' She couldn't ever answer that question without feeling a sense of gratitude that she'd made it to the other side of the curtain. Even though she didn't have the right accent or an Oxbridge degree, she was working for one of the oldest, most highly regarded, publishers in the country. And she *almost* felt as if she belonged there.

'Jackie, you must be so proud,' Susan said warmly and Jackie agreed, just as warmly, that she was. She'd long got over her confusion and anger about Jenny having two degrees but squandering her education by mostly waitressing.

Jenny gave her mother a copy of every book that she'd worked on. Not that Jackie read them all, but she'd turn to the acknowledgements page to see what the author had said about her daughter – it was usually very complimentary – smile approvingly and then put the book on a shelf that had been ordained for that very purpose. 'Jenny's books,' Jackie always said as if Jenny hadn't just edited and commissioned them but written them, typeset them and even printed them.

'You must be proud of Nick too,' Jenny said because it was easier than admitting that she'd deliberately ejected him from her life. Though, to be fair, however much he might have kept 'tabs' on her, he hadn't made any effort to keep in contact either.

'Well, he's an editor of a bestselling men's magazine,' Susan agreed grudgingly, her lips curling over the words. 'But why there has to be a half-naked woman on the front cover of every issue is something that he can't adequately explain.'

He was obviously an editor of one of the lads' mags, which always had a woman on the cover wearing a tiny pair of pants and cupping her breasts like her hands had been repurposed as a bra. 'I guess sex sells,' Jenny said, shrugging but then she felt guilty because it sounded like Nick had only said nice things about her. 'But still, he's done so well and he's not even thirty yet. Talk about a glittering career.'

Susan nodded and Jackie and Dot were shuffling impatiently and Jenny's allotted smoking time was now long over. If she continued to dawdle, she'd get to Kirsty's much later than planned, but Susan was rifling through her bag with one hand, her other hand held in front of her in an unmistakable command that Jenny was to stay put.

'Talking of proud . . . I'm now a grandmother three times!' she exclaimed joyfully and another five minutes was spent showing them pictures of these three grandchildren. The eldest, who belonged to Nick's brother, Daniel ('he's just got silk') and his wife ('an absolutely lovely girl, she's a barrister too') was a chubby little toddler with a mop of dark curls and dimples that you could stick your fingers in. The other two ('because, as we all know, twins run on Jeff's side of the family') were six-month old girls who looked like little old drunken men. Nick's sister had birthed them in a break from her job as a very successful ear, nose and throat consultant because 'we always wanted one of them to go into the family business.'

'Nick's a long way off from adding to the grandchildren?' Jenny asked casually, but her stomach lurched in anticipation of the answer. Tucked into her own purse was that strip of photo booth pictures they'd taken at Mill Hill East station on her eighteenth birthday. Every time she changed over purses, Jenny wondered why she still kept them but never wanted to examine the answer too closely.

'To have children, he'd have to find a woman who was willing to put up with him,' Susan said crushingly.

Jenny smiled weakly, though on the inside she was cringing. 'He's only twenty-eight. That isn't old. Still plenty of time.'

'Are you seeing someone?' Susan asked, carefully putting

the pictures back in their protective wallet. 'A pretty girl like you must have been snapped up by now.'

'I'm just dating. Casual dating,' Jenny said, because since she'd broken up with Gethin, it was very hard to find the impetus to want to be in another relationship. She hadn't just broken his heart, according to his pretentious friends in the big dusty Brixton house, but made him leave London and return to Barry where he was doing his PGCE so he could qualify as an art teacher. It was a much better use of his skills than selling art supplies but Jenny still felt guilty. A guilt that had lingered throughout the several dates she'd been on with men who weren't as much fun as a night in with a good book.

'Our Jenny's a real career girl,' Dot piped up, sensitive to any criticism of her granddaughter, who was living a life she could never quite fathom. By the time Dot was twenty-seven, Jenny's age, she'd been married seven years, had two kids – both born during rationing – and when Stan had died, it turned out that she didn't even have her own bank account. 'She's about to buy a flat.'

'In Kentish Town,' Jackie added.

'Lovely,' Susan said in a neutral voice then she brightened. 'Daniel and his wife, have I mentioned that they're both barristers, bought a beautiful place in Finchley, by the golf course, and Francesca and Seth, they're living just round the corner from us in Edgware.'

Jenny could see from the way that Jackie's jaw was working furiously that her mother was trying to think of some maternal boast about her own children, but there was no point. None of the achievements of the Richards' kids could compare to barristers, homes next to the golf course in Finchley or cherubic grandchildren.

'Well, Martin, our youngest . . .' Jackie said but Jenny

actually stepped in front of her mother, so she could say quickly, 'That all sounds lovely, Susan. You must be so proud. Anyway, we won't keep you and we don't want to get caught up in the rush hour crowds.'

There was another prod in the back from Jackie, which Jenny ignored as Susan was nodding in agreement. 'It's a pity you're not Jewish, I know some lovely boys I could set you up with,' she said. 'Doctors! Who ever heard of a poor doctor?'

Back in the day in his bedroom, Nick would do a savage impersonation of Susan as she queried his ambition to be a writer. 'Be a dentist,' he'd exclaim, his voice going full Yente, the matchmaker in *Fiddler on the Roof*. 'Whoever heard of a poor dentist? People will always need things doing to their teeth. You'll want for nothing!'

Jenny had to thin her lips to stop herself from smiling at the memory. Also, the very thought of herself ending up with a doctor. How boring. How staid, though Dot murmured, 'Well, we wouldn't mind if you wanted to convert.'

Talking of Jenny's long-term romantic plans, Jenny's requested presence at Kirsty's dinner party was largely so that her friend could throw some guy called Michael into Jenny's path. Michael, apparently, was 'sort of Erik's boss but not, they have a very non-linear hierarchical staff structure at Goldsmiths, and he's really fit in a handsome older man kind of way.' Kirsty was firm in her belief that Jenny should just be over Gethin by now and going out with someone more befitting of her intellect and her pay grade.

'I really have to love you and leave you, ladies, I'm due in New Cross in an hour.' Jenny brandished her Marks & Spencer's carrier bag containing wine and chocolates – you couldn't buy a bunch of flowers in Kensington for love or money. 'Dinner party.'

'Who would live in New Cross? It's miles from civilisation,'

Susan said in scandalised tones. This was something that all the women could agree on.

'We were just saying to Jenny that she'd better make sure that she leaves early enough that she'll be able to get home on public transport,' Jackie recalled.

'We said, you'll never get a black cab south of the river that time of night,' Dot chimed in.

Jenny shrugged. 'My friend, her boyfriend teaches at Goldsmiths . . .'

Susan shook her head. 'I won't keep you then.' She held up a bunch of lilies. 'Jeff and I are going to a concert at the Albert Hall but I wanted to pay my respects first. That poor woman . . .'

'Those poor boys,' Jackie added.

Jenny heaved her tote bag aloft once more but Susan stilled her with a gentle hand on her heaving arm. 'Have you got a business card? I could pass on your details to Nick. It would be lovely for you two to catch up.'

It wouldn't be lovely. They'd grown apart like ice floes and their shared history was full of conflict and complications. Jennifer couldn't really explain that to Susan, or to Jackie and Dot, so she just retrieved one of her business cards from her purse and handed it to Susan with a weak smile. 'I'd like that,' she said with enough sincerity that Susan beamed and insisted that they have another hug before they parted ways, Susan to join the mourners at the gates of Kensington Palace, Jackie and Dot to nip back into Barkers because Dot really needed to visit the Ladies again, and for Jenny to arrive at Kirsty's later than she planned but still in enough time to avert disaster.

17

Friday, September 5th, 1997
Charing Cross Station

Erik let her into their tiny but charming Victorian terraced house miles from New Cross station (and civilisation) with a smile and hug. He was a strapping six foot five inches, so Jenny had to stand on tiptoe and peer over his shoulder to confirm her suspicions. Yes. Jenny now had a clear line of sight to the kitchen where Kirsty was standing over an uncooked chicken, an open jar in her hand.

'I brought wine and chocolate,' Jenny called out to soften the blow of what she had to say next. 'What is in that jar? Are you putting it on the chicken? Why would you do that?'

'It's harissa paste. It's a cornerstone of North African and Persian cuisine,' Kirsty explained through what sounded like gritted teeth. 'It has a very gentle heat. You'll hardly notice it.'

'It will burn my mouth,' Jenny all but wailed as she rushed into the little kitchen, which really was only big enough for two people. 'I've come *all* the way to New Cross, you're not even on the tube, Kirsty, and you're going to hurt me with your spicy paste.'

'Which is why we got you a separate piece of chicken that we're going to roast without any harissa on it,' Erik said calmly from the kitchen doorway. He was the calmest, most unflappable person Jenny had ever met, unless you were playing Monopoly or doing a pub quiz with him and then he turned into a monster. 'Have you added any more vegetables to your repertoire since we last saw you?'

Jenny shook her head. 'Nope. Just cucumber and tomato as always, but not sundried tomatoes, and green beans but only if I have a forkful of meat to eat with them.'

'How you don't have a serious vitamin deficiency, I'll never know.' Kirsty picked up a palette knife and began to slather the poor chicken in the paste. 'So, we're also having orzo.'

'What's orzo?' Jenny narrowed her eyes even as she wished that her palate had got a little more sophisticated with age. Training herself to like white wine had taken a good two years. Though like was maybe too strong a word. Tolerate would be more accurate and she still couldn't go near red wine without very bad things happening.

'It's tiny rice-like pasta,' Erik said from the doorway of the sunny yellow kitchen, where every available surface, both horizontal and vertical was covered in cooking equipment. From jars and bottles of fancy and exotic ingredients (that Jenny was having nothing to do with) to copper-bottomed pans of all shapes and sizes and cooking utensils, the majority of which looked like torture devices. Erik and Kirsty fancied themselves as foodies and Jenny knew that she was cramping their style, but she just couldn't help herself.

'Well, I like rice and I like pasta but I'm not sure I'd like a hybrid of the two,' she said in what she hoped was a suitably apologetic manner.

'It IS pasta!' Kirsty snapped. 'Pasta the size and shape of rice, for fuck's sake!'

*

'And I said, "It's just as well that I'm such charming company",' Jenny explained to the assembled guests a couple of hours later when a Sociology lecturer called Mansoor wanted to know why Jenny was eating a 'really Spartan version of what we're eating?' and Kirsty had launched into a largely good-humoured rant about how Jenny was the 'pickiest, fussiest person I've ever met and her palate would be a lot more sophisticated if she'd actually *try* new things.'

But now everyone laughed, then Erik offered up an anecdote of eating some chocolate-covered ants as part of a research project into alternative, sustainable sources of protein.

It was a lively group of mostly young academics. The conversation had veered from the death of Princess Diana and Erik's new mobile phone, which had a colour screen, to the latest Oasis album and their expectations of the Labour government now they'd been in power for a few months.

Jenny joined in or rather she smiled and nodded a lot, but mostly she thought about Nick. These days she'd hardly allowed herself to think about Nick at all but now she revelled in the luxury of trying to get into his head in a way that she hadn't since she was a teenager and desperately wanted him to see her. Really see her.

Had he thought about Jenny ever since their last goodbye on that Circle Line train? He must have done if he could give his mother a vague account of her career trajectory. Would Susan go back to him, full of praise about how well Jenny was doing? Would she mention that Jenny was single? Was Nick single?

So many questions and when Nick was handed her business card maybe he'd call her and give her some answers. Or maybe he wouldn't and the past was best left behind her.

'. . . not a South Londoner either?'

Someone was talking to her from across the table. Michael, Erik's sort-of boss.

Jenny smiled. 'I'm sorry. I didn't catch that.'

Michael smiled too. He was about ten years older than Jenny and everything Kirsty had said he was: funny, charming, handsome. He had exquisite bone structure, patrician, as one of Jenny's authors might describe him. Dark hair swept back from a broad forehead, strong brows, piercing blue eyes, an aquiline nose and thin but beautifully shaped lips. He could have looked quite stern but the piercing blue eyes had a mischievous gleam to them and his lips always seemed to be either smiling or on the verge of smiling. He reminded Jenny of Christopher Plummer in *The Sound of Music*. Captain Von Trapp had been one of her first and formative crushes. Christ, that explained a hell of a lot.

'I was asking if you lived in South London,' Michael said and Jenny pulled an appalled face much as she had when she'd been handed a bowl of salad coated liberally in some spicy dressing studded with peppercorns.

'God, no!' she said, without thinking how tactless that might sound because she *had* managed to acquire a tolerance for white wine and was already on her third glass. 'I mean, I'm sure it's nice . . .'

'It really is,' Kirsty piped up.

'And some of my favourite people live here,' Jenny frantically tried to backtrack, 'But I was born and brought up in North London. If I moved South, I'd be excommunicated from my family. Do you live locally?'

'God, no!' Michael echoed with another one of those wicked smiles. 'Civilisation ends just beyond Pimlico. If you fancy some company on the journey home . . . unless you're getting a cab?'

'A cab from New Cross to Notting Hill would bankrupt me,' Jenny admitted, her mother's words ringing in her ears. 'Besides, you'll never get a black cab south of the river . . .'

'. . . at this time of night,' Michael finished for her and they both grinned.

'That is so blatantly not true,' Kirsty said but she had a glint in her eyes as she looked first at Jenny then at Michael. The glint was still there as she waved them off at a very respectable ten o'clock because 'it would actually be easier and probably take less time to get to Edinburgh than to the other side of London,' Jenny said. She was glad of Michael's company as they walked along narrow streets of narrow Victorian houses to get to the station. It was late and the streets weren't that well lit, but it meant that they could pass the joint back and forth that Erik had given them as a going-home present as the South London contingent of guests were staying behind to drink coffee and skin up.

'How long have you lived in Notting Hill?' Michael asked as the station came into view.

'Just over a year, but I'm buying a flat in Kentish Town.' Even saying the words out loud still didn't make the concept of Jenny buying a flat any more real. She wasn't earning a fortune. £25,000 pounds wasn't a fortune, but it was enough to get a mortgage on a £68,000 two-bedroom basement flat. She'd saved up all the money she'd made from her little bits of journalism for the deposit. Jenny was very proud of that. She worked with people who seemed to have been handed their own London flats in posh postal districts as a matter of course after graduating, but Jenny hadn't taken a penny from Jackie or Alan. 'One of my younger brothers is an estate agent and he heard about this flat, it's a repossession, and it wasn't properly listed so I was able to swoop in. I did feel a bit guilty about taking advantage of someone else's misfortune until I saw the flat and realised that they'd taken everything that wasn't nailed down.'

Michael quirked an eyebrow at her, as they walked down the steps that led to the platform. 'That bad?'

'Worse actually, because they took everything that *was* nailed down too. They even removed the skirting boards.'

They talked house renovations as they waited twenty minutes for a train to take them back into town.

It would be an easy journey for Michael once the train arrived. One stop to London Bridge, then he could switch from mainline rail to the tube and it was only a few stops to Angel on the Northern Line. Whereas Jenny needed to head back to Charing Cross, then take the Bakerloo Line to Oxford Street so she could change onto the Central Line and it was still four of five stops until she'd reach Notting Hill and finally be able to collapse on her sofa.

She was a little sad that she'd only spend another ten minutes or so with Michael. He was both easy and fascinating to talk to; an architectural historian who'd travelled and worked in places as far-flung and exotic as Buenos Aires and Kyoto, but he wore his knowledge lightly and didn't keep 'well, actually'-ing Jenny every time she spoke.

She liked the twinkle in his eyes, that ready smile, and she wouldn't mind if Kirsty invited them both to some other function. Though hopefully not another dinner party in the bowels of South London. By that time she might have pushed Nick back to the furthest, dustiest recesses of her head but tonight he was very much at the forefront of her mind and even circling around her heart again.

'You know, Islington and Kentish Town aren't that far apart,' Michael said once they were on the train. Although her feet were killing her, even in her trainers, Michael was only going one stop so it seemed a bit rude to sit down.

'Not as far as the crow and the Northern Line flies,' Jenny agreed, looking up at Michael, because he was really tall. Maybe he'd make good on his vague assurance that he could give her some advice on reinstating the period details that had been ripped out by the previous tenants of the flat.

'We're almost at London Bridge, lucky you.'

'I thought I'd stay on to Charing Cross,' Michael said casually. 'I can get the Northern Line just as easily from there.'

It wasn't just as easy. He'd have to go all the way to Euston to change to the Bank branch.

But when Jenny pointed that out, he just shrugged. 'I really don't mind.'

Michael talked about books the rest of the way to Charing Cross. Or rather he asked Jenny about her job, about her authors, and really listened to her replies. The stations, the dark night outside the train windows, just whizzed by and soon they were at Charing Cross.

As they walked across the concourse, Michael took Jenny's elbow and shielded her from a lurching, loud pack of drunk men and she was grateful that he'd changed his travel plans. Now that she thought about it, he'd probably lengthened his journey time just so that he could do this changeover with her. It was very considerate of him.

'Thank you for coming with me to Charing Cross,' she said once they'd made it to the tube station in one piece and were travelling down the escalator, which led to the platforms. 'I didn't realise just how many pissed up people there'd be waiting for trains. It's very kind of you.'

Michael shrugged again. 'It's nothing. Though, I confess, I did have an ulterior motive.'

He was standing behind her and Jenny couldn't keep craning her neck to turn and look at him, so she waited until they were off the escalator before she arched an eyebrow. 'Ulterior motive?' She hoped he wasn't touting for work because she really couldn't afford an architect.

'Yes, I'd really like to see you again,' he said smoothly. No muss, no fuss, no prevaricating, which was . . . refreshing.

'Oh . . .' Jenny came to a halt.

'I've been thinking about kissing you all evening,' Michael

continued, his cut glass vowels a little huskier than before, though that might have been the after-effects of the joint. 'Would you like me to kiss you?'

Jenny considered the question. It had been nearly a year since she broke up with Gethin; a respectable amount of time had passed. It was two years since she'd last seen Nick and her life was better, happier, calmer, without him in it. Her head would be happier and calmer without him in it too, so this was just the distraction she needed. Besides, Michael was really handsome in a wickedly sardonic way that made her think of all those Byronic heroes in the racier Victorian novels she'd read for her MA.

Jenny put down the laden tote bag that she'd been carting around for most of the day. Then she pursed her lips and tucked her hair back behind her ears. 'Yeah. I think I would like you to kiss me. I think I'd like that quite a lot.'

PART SEVEN

1999–2000

18

Wednesday, March 17th, 1999
Old Street Station

There were over two hundred and fifty stations that made up the London tube network and Old Street was Jenny's least favourite.

Unfortunately, it was the nearest tube station to Hoxton, and Hoxton was the current centre of the universe. Its old factories and warehouses had been converted, seemingly overnight, into industrial live/work spaces; all huge windows, steel beams and wooden floors, where hip photographers and graphic artists worked and lived and skinny young people with statement glasses, statement haircuts and vintage Japanese Levi's all did something in New Media start-ups. New Media. New Meedja. That was what the internet was called now.

Even the publishing industry, which didn't like to stray too far away from Soho and Bloomsbury, had been tempted east for book launches in what used to be electricity showrooms. Or meetings in pie and mash shops with these New Meedja people who were keen to tell them that the novel was dead and they should diversify and synergise and harness the power of information architecture.

'They've been saying that the novel is dead since the days of Sophocles and yet, somehow, the novel has managed to survive,' Jenny had said at the last of those meetings that she'd attended.

If it weren't for the people who were turning it into a hipster's playground, Jenny would have quite liked Hoxton and Shoreditch and its surrounding areas. Her roots were East End after all. Though her father, who'd literally been born within the sound of Bow Bells, wasn't having any of it.

'You go to Hoxton after dark and you'll end up with your money gone and your throat slit,' was his pithy summing up. 'You want to be careful, Jenny. I'm going to get you the rape alarm I saw in the latest *Innovations* catalogue.'

Jenny had her own reasons for wanting to steer clear of the area. And not just because of the time she'd witnessed a drive-by shooting when she'd been having a drink with an author in The Bricklayer's Arms. No, it was because Old Street station had eight exits and she could never work out which one she needed.

Now, on a wet Wednesday lunchtime in March, she trudged up the steps to street level to discover she was on the wrong side of the massive roundabout above the station. She trudged back down the steps, a tattered A to Z clutched in her hand, and tried again. Maybe exit eight instead of exit three? The fairly useless sign said that exit eight was the exit for Moorfields Eye Hospital.

Was Moorfields Eye Hospital near the address on the call sheet her assistant had printed out? Jenny peered at the correct page in her A to Z, which showed tiny street after tiny street. Then she retraced her steps to the map of the local area in the ticket hall, which was already being colonised by a man and woman, both of them annoyingly tall and blocking Jenny's view.

'I swear to God, every time I come to this station the exits have all swapped places,' the woman was saying in the home counties drawl that Jenny had never managed to acquire.

'I'm pretty sure they multiply too,' the man said and he had that drawl too, though he hadn't grown up in the home counties. He'd grown up in NW7, just like Jenny.

She was already backing away but it was too late. The woman had half-turned. 'Sorry. Are we in your way?'

Jenny's flight instinct made her back up a couple more steps until she managed to get it under control. Adrenalin was still coursing through her as she forced a smile. 'It's OK. I can wait.'

'Jen? Wow!'

She wasn't sure that her look of surprise was that convincing. 'Nick! God, what a blast from the past.'

'Yeah, it's been donkey's years. How are you?' Nick asked and apart from that first initial glance when Jenny had made sure to open her eyes really wide in feigned shock, now she couldn't bring herself to look at him. She stared down at his shell-toe Adidas trainers instead.

'Great. Good. Lost though.' She could only manage monosyllables.

'Us too,' said the woman. 'What is it with this tube station?'

'Honey, this is Jen. One of my oldest friends though we kind of drifted apart. What was that about?'

Jen shrugged while still staring down at the ground. She forced herself to look up, her gaze getting as far as Nick's chest. He'd broadened out. 'I don't know. Life?'

'And Jen, this is Honey, who's, well, what are we exactly, Hon?'

'We? I'm an entirely autonomous being last time I checked,' Honey said, with a defiant tilt to her chin. She was beautiful. She could have been named for her hair, which was a honey-ish, tawny-ish blonde, mostly obscured by a black baker's boy cap, which hadn't diminished her thick, blunt cut fringe in the slightest, though Jenny knew that her own fringe was inevitably curling at the edges. She had perfect features too: wide-spaced, cornflower blue eyes, an imperiously retroussé nose and full, pouty lips.

The whole effect was effortlessly chic. Undeniably cool. Like Marianne Faithful in *Girl on a Motorbike* but the motorbike had been substituted for a monthly travelcard. Or Françoise Hardy if Françoise Hardy had swapped Paris for Dalston. Though neither Marianne Faithfull or Françoise Hardy had the same careless, heavy-lidded arrogance to their beauty as Honey.

Nick might have progressed from little blonde things to this stunning giantess of a blonde thing (Honey had to be nearly six foot and she wasn't even wearing heels), but he'd always shied away from the difficult girls and yes, Jen, would have put herself in that category. Now, however, he smiled, indulgently, tenderly.

'As well as being an entirely autonomous being, Honey used to be the sex and relationships columnist on the magazine, until she deserted us for the *Observer.*'

'Because they pay me an annual salary, none of this wordage rubbish, and the byline pic isn't me in my underwear,' Honey explained, which had to be for Jenny's benefit because she was sure that Honey and Nick must have already discussed this in great detail.

Jenny hated it when couples used random, helpless passers-by as props for their own dramas. Gethin's housemate Paloma had loved having loud noisy fights with her boyfriend, Danus in the communal areas of the Brixton house solely so they could have loud, noisy make-up sex in their own room. So Jenny was going to nip this in the bud and then be on her way.

'I'm a big fan of your *Observer* column,' she said, which was true and now that Jenny had got over her shock, she'd have recognised Honey without Nick even introducing her. 'I loved the one you wrote about why women with daddy issues shouldn't date men with mummy issues.'

Even the most insolent-looking beauties stopped looking quite so insolent when you praised them for something other than their beauty. Honey beamed. 'Thank you. Though my actual mummy and daddy hated that column.'

'Probably an occupational hazard when you write about sex a lot,' Jenny ventured, and Honey smiled again.

'It is. I'm always desperate for material especially as Nick has forbidden me to write about our sex life,' Honey revealed, clearing up any lingering doubt that she and Nick were just ex-colleagues. 'Even my friends won't dish the dirt without issuing a disclaimer that they don't want to see their sordid secrets in the *Observer*.' She pouted a little. 'I don't suppose you have any sordid secrets.'

'Christ, Hon . . .' Nick said. He'd been silent all this time; Jenny had been painfully aware of his gaze, though she still steadfastly refused to look him in the eye. She was also painfully aware of how she must look in comparison to Honey's insouciant chic.

She was flushed and flustered at the prospect of being late. She was growing out her fringe again. And she was wearing a red wool princess coat, black tights and black lace-up brogues. Like some kind of frumpy spinster of the parish, who volunteered with the mobile library service and cared a little too much about whose turn it was to do the church flowers.

Then Jenny remembered that she wasn't a spinster of the parish. She too was an autonomous being whose daily life didn't revolve around what Nick Levene thought about her or her lifestyle and sartorial choices. Also, not a spinster and Michael liked the way she dressed. 'Ah, it's Jane from Occupied Europe,' he'd say when Jenny stumbled downstairs each morning, more usually wearing a vintage dress, cardigan and clompy shoes. 'What's on the agenda for this morning? Are you going to meet some SOE agents who were parachuted in last night?'

'I don't know what you mean,' Jenny would say. 'I'm just a simple French country girl.'

It was one of her favourite ways to begin the day. It was how she'd started this very day. Though Jane from Occupied Europe was hopefully more adept at map-reading. Once again, Jenny brandished her A to Z and the crumpled call sheet.

'Let's not talk about my sex life,' she said crisply. 'Though if you have any suggestions on which exit I need for . . .' She peered at the paper. 'Juniper Street?'

'We're going to Juniper Street too,' Honey exclaimed. She struck a pose, all her weight on one foot, hip sticking out, finger on chin. 'Are you one of the *Evening Standard*'s Thirty Most Creative Londoners?' She pointed at herself. 'I'm The Columnist. Nick here is The Editor and you are?'

Jenny shrugged. 'The Publisher, apparently. Though technically I'm an Editorial Director.' It had been quite the meteoric rise, considering the last time she'd seen Nick, properly seen him, she'd been working in the bookshop. (Where she still clocked in on occasional Saturdays because how could you know what books people wanted to read unless you actually asked them?) But in the interim, she'd worked bloody hard, had a couple of lucky breaks and published seven *Sunday Times* bestsellers.

'Jen published Aaron's novel,' Nick said. 'For her sins.'

'You must be a very patient person.' Honey looked to the heavens. 'After five minutes of Aaron, I want to punch him in the throat.'

So did Jenny, but she just made weird scoffing sounds like Aaron wasn't difficult at all and had never once phoned her at three in the morning threatening to set fire to himself and his manuscript.

'Aaron never mentioned that he knew you,' was what she did say, risking a quick look at Nick's face. He was still studying her intently but he raised his eyebrows like he and Aaron had better things to do than discuss Jenny but they must have discussed her at least once or how else would Nick know that she was his friend's editor? And if she was going to overanalyse what Nick had or hadn't done in their years apart, he must have discussed her with his mother. At the very least, Susan would have said that she'd bumped into Jenny and given Nick her business card and Nick had chosen to do . . . *nothing.* 'Which is weird because he mentions a lot of things that I really wish he wouldn't.'

'Who can even know the inner workings of Aaron's mind?' Nick asked and Honey shuddered.

'I certainly wouldn't want to.' Jenny turned back to the map. 'Come on, we're three reasonably intelligent people, we should be able to find the right exit for Juniper Street.'

It took one more false turn before they managed to exit the station and find themselves on the correct side of the roundabout. Then they couldn't very well go their separate ways, not when they were heading for the same destination. But thankfully, Honey didn't seem to do awkward. She was bright and amusing and said audacious things ('So, you two have never fucked? Just so I know, because there was a very embarrassing incident with a cocktail waitress once . . .') for the sheer pleasure of saying audacious things. There didn't seem to be any malice or intent behind words. More that she liked to think that she was an *enfant terrible*, an *agent provocateur* or some other French phrase, which would sum Honey up as a woman who liked pushing boundaries.

Next to Honey, who walked into the photographic studio like she was walking onto a yacht, Nick seemed subdued, a little less than he used to be. He even looked different. He'd filled out a little, lost that elfin, feline quality to his face, his movements. His hair, fashioned into a regulation Hoxton fin, was shorter than Jenny had ever seen it. He was wearing a skinny-fit black wool suit, which couldn't disguise its designer credentials even though he'd paired it with a T-shirt advertising some obscure Northern Soul record label and the Adidas trainers. He was a man. An adult. An actual adult.

Though to the outside world, Jenny supposed she was an actual adult too. She was a Serious Book Publishing Person who knew her own mind and wasn't afraid to speak it. Which was why the fashion stylist, despite the very thorough pre-shoot briefing they'd had, was instantly contrite when Jenny told her very politely but very firmly that she was absolutely not going to be wearing any of the tight, Azzedine Alaïa dresses hanging on a rail in the dressing room. As was the picture director, the art editor and the features writer who were all despatched to see if Jenny had changed her mind and wanted to be shoehorned into a dress designed to be worn by a woman at least two stone lighter and six inches taller than her. Someone a bit like Honey, who was also having no truck with the bandage dresses either and had changed into a very sexy version of Nick's suit, the jacket unbuttoned to reveal the sides of her very perky breasts.

Jenny, however, was not going to be revealing any part of her moderately perky breasts. Eventually they compromised on a dress very similar to the vintage dress Jenny was already wearing: high necked, long sleeved, with a huge flounce to the hem, but this Miu Miu frock was in a camouflage print, which apparently was very 'on trend', whatever that meant.

She'd imagined that having her photo artfully shot wouldn't take more than a couple of hours, but she'd been wrong. The photo studio, on the top floor of what had once been a shoe factory, was a cavernous, industrial space, with a vaulted ceiling to showcase the original metal beams and huge windows letting in as much overcast daylight as possible.

At one end the photographer and his very large entourage of assistants fiddled with lights and the colourama and at the other end was a kitchen alcove and a table laden with salads, quiches, artisanal bread with lots of seeds clinging to it and finally progressing to brownies, lemon drizzle slices and a huge bowl of Wotsits. There were four squashy leather sofas arranged in a square where a couple more of The Thirty Most Creative People in London (The Milliner and The Florist) had apparently been waiting all morning for their photo to be taken.

Through a small archway was a dressing room with clothing rails and several make-up stations. This was where Jenny quickly found herself, sitting next to Honey, and having industrial amounts of foundation applied to her face by a young woman whose clear-faced beauty didn't need industrial amounts of foundation. Meanwhile a man with a hairdryer and several hairbrushes in an over the shoulder holster picked up a strand of Jenny's hair and pulled a face.

'So, the fringe.' He made a twirling movement with his index finger. 'What's going on there?'

'I'm growing it out,' Jenny said, because when was she not? Except those brief moments when she didn't have a fringe, forgot all the pain and upkeep that a fringe took when your hair wasn't thick and straight like Honey's, then eventually caved and cut one in again.

'You can grow it out after you've had your pictures taken because there's nothing here I can work with unless I trim your regrowth,' she was told.

Honey gave her a sympathetic look in the mirrors. They were authentic and very unforgiving dressing room mirrors with lightbulbs around the frame. 'I swear, having a fringe is harder work than having a baby.'

Obviously it wasn't but it had to run a close second. They sat in silence for a couple of minutes until Jenny decided that it was silly to put it off any longer. She made sure to catch Honey's eye in the mirror. 'So, have you thought about writing books? Maybe a collection of your columns to start with, then perhaps a novel?'

Honey fluttered her now sooty lashes. 'A novel? Like a proper writer?'

'You're already a proper writer,' Jenny said because she knew Honey could turn a phrase but more importantly, she was the whole package. Pretty, connected, gave a good quote. If she wrote a novel about sex and relationships, probably a very thinly veiled piece of auto-fiction, it would guarantee lots of press and lots of sales. It might even turn out to be a very good novel from a very good writer. But Jenny was realistic, if not resigned. Not every book could be a beautifully crafted piece of prose that encompassed deep truths about life and the universe. Besides, that wasn't the kind of book she was interested in publishing or reading. There was a reason why she still preferred Jilly Cooper to Iris Murdoch.

'If you're interested,' Honey fashioned her hands into little paws and panted so Jenny guessed that she was interested, 'send me a two-page outline for a novel that you'd like to write; if you wanted to have a crack at a couple of chapters, even better. You'll need an agent . . .'

'Oh, I have agents contacting me all the time,' Honey said blithely, not realising that there were hundreds, if not thousands, of writers toiling away in garrets and basements dreaming of the time that they might get something back from an agent that wasn't a standard rejection slip and their manuscript returned in the stamped, addressed envelope that they'd had to provide. 'Do I really need one?'

'You absolutely do,' Jenny said unequivocally. She leaned forward to retrieve her handbag, grimacing an apology as the woman doing her make-up who'd been blending in several different shades of brown eye shadow had to pause. She retrieved one of her business cards from an inner pocket. 'Send me an email with the names of the agents who've contacted you and I'll tell you who the best three are. Not all agents are created equal.'

'That's really kind of you.' Honey tucked the card away and they lapsed into another brief silence until Honey decided to move to the next item on the agenda. 'So, you and Nick?'

It was hard to feel a chill of foreboding when a man was aggressively blow-drying your hair straight. 'Me and Nick?'

'We've only just met, so I don't know you very well, but I know Nick very well and it seems like there's unfinished business between you two.' This was very rash of Honey considering she was talking to a woman who'd just mooted the idea of a book deal to her.

'Not unfinished business,' Jenny said a little tightly. 'We used to be friends but life happens fast and sometimes things, and people, get lost in the slipstream.'

'Right, right.' Honey nodded vigorously much to the annoyance of the woman who was doing *her* make-up, though it really was a case of gilding the lily with a very light hand. 'But even so, you must know Nick very well too.'

'I haven't seen him in *years* . . .'

'I'm dying to know what he was like as a teenager. Was he very spotty and did he find it impossible to talk to girls?'

'Yes, Jen, what was I like as a teenager?' asked Nick who was leaning against the archway, who knew for how long?

And where to even start with that one?

Funny haha.

Funny peculiar.

Beautiful.

Heart-breaking.

Cruel.

'Pretentious,' Jen decided with a grin. 'Oh my God, you were *so* pretentious.'

'Ha!' Honey clapped her hands in delight. 'Still is.'

Nick shrugged, a hint of a smile tugging at his lips. 'You say pretentious, I say discerning.'

'Which is exactly what a very pretentious person would say,' Jen pointed out as Nick put up his hands to ward off the double-pronged attack.

'I don't know what you mean,' he insisted, folding his arms. Then he jerked his head back. 'Hon, they're waiting for you on set.'

There was a final flurry of activity from the woman doing Honey's hair and one last slick of barely-there lipstick then Honey disappeared through the arch with a careless, 'Be good. We don't want to have to separate you two.'

It had taken no time at all to transform Honey into a tousled sex-kitten, but Jenny's metamorphosis from a frazzled twenty-eight-year-old woman to someone fit to have their picture taken was clearly going to take much longer. Her face had been smeared with so much product for the last half hour that she currently looked like a blank version of herself, albeit one with a very even skin tone. Now the make-up artist was wielding blusher and a big brush.

'Please make me look like I have cheekbones,' Jenny murmured as Nick unpeeled himself from the archway and came to sit on the stool that Honey had vacated.

She was in no position to talk to him, as first her cheekbones were revealed then she found herself in a tussle with the make-up artist who seemed to think that Jenny might want some barely-there lipstick too.

'Red lips,' Jenny insisted. The lips in question were stretched tight in an awkward smile because there'd been the dress and now this and they probably all thought that she was a bitch. 'I understand that models wear what they're told but I'm not a model. I'm an ordinary woman who always wears bright red lipstick. It's my thing.'

'It is,' Nick confirmed, though Jenny didn't need him, or anyone else, to fight her battles. 'She's known throughout London for her red lipstick.'

Jenny gave him a warning look in the mirror from under lashes stiff with several coats of mascara.

'Well, you can take it up with the art director if he doesn't like it.'

'I will,' Jenny assured her, reaching forward once again for her handbag so she could pull out her trusty Clinique 100% Red lipstick.

Then she had to hold her mouth very still, lips parted, as lip pencil then lipstick was applied and all the while, Nick made no attempt to disguise the fact that he was staring at Jenny again as if someone would be asking him questions later on her appearance.

'Right, I'm done,' the make-up artist announced like there really was nothing more she could do under the circumstances. 'I'm going to have a cigarette.'

Jenny could have murdered a cigarette. But she was four weeks and three days into her latest attempt to stop smoking. Besides, as soon as the woman left the little dressing room she was free to get off the stool so she could lean right into the mirror and assess the damage that had been done.

'Christ, she's blended out half my lips,' she grumbled, because her mouth now looked very small and very pouty.

'Keep an eye out for me,' she added as she took out her own make-up bag.

'This takes me back to the time that you'd make me stand watch while you shoplifted nail polishes from Boots,' Nick remarked as he adjusted the stool so he was turned towards Jenny rather than her reflection.

'That must have been some other girl. I've never shoplifted in my life,' Jenny said, as she drew the corners of her lips back in with red pencil.

'Every time we went into a Woolworths, you grabbed a handful of pick 'n' mix. Said that was why you only wore dresses with pockets.'

'Stealing pick 'n' mix doesn't count. They take into account that people help themselves when they decide the price. Besides, who doesn't take a handful of pick 'n' mix when they're in Woolies?'

'I never have.'

It was true. Nick never had. Less to do with the principle and more that he was terrified of being caught. Back then, it was one of the few things Jenny had over him.

'But I always gave you some of mine,' Jenny recalled, as she reapplied her lipstick. 'God, she hasn't even flicked out the end of my eyeliner.'

Jenny tutted to herself as she rooted in her make-up bag; she had a look that had been working for her for a good ten years. If she was going to have to have her picture taken to appear in a newspaper then it was going to be looking like her best self and not some unrecognisable, on trend version of herself.

Lately, Jenny felt that she'd settled into her face. That all the component parts that she used to obsess over – that her nose was too large, her eyes were too small, her eyebrows were never going to grow back after plucking them to oblivion in the early part of the decade – were suddenly in proportion. (Though her eyebrows were never going to be bountiful.)

She no longer thought of herself as hideous. In fact, objectively, she thought of herself as pretty. Especially when she was wearing make-up because she knew how to make the best of her features now rather than using cosmetics to paint a completely different face on. She even liked how she looked first thing in the morning, all sleepy and smudgy.

But today? Today, not so much.

'So, Jen, how have you been?' Nick asked, when her make-up bag was put away, her hands were still and she was no longer muttering under her breath.

'You mean you don't already know?' She raised her newly tweezed and shaped eyebrows. 'I bumped into Susan a couple of years ago and she was all up to speed on my move from bookselling to book publishing. Said you'd been keeping tabs on me.'

'It's not unusual to want to keep track of old friends,' Nick said. Now that she was seeing him up close, she was noticing the shadowed look in his eyes, echoed in the shadows under his eyes. The dimples at the side of his mouth were grooves now. There was a suggestion, faint but present, of what he would look like ten years from now, twenty, even thirty. 'I'm always seeing your byline in the *Guardian* arts section. And well, there's Aaron. Our mutual acquaintance. Your name came up a couple of times.'

Jenny subsided a little at that. 'OK. Though I don't really think that you are friends with someone if you never see them or talk to them anymore.'

As ever, it seemed to Jenny that what they meant to say to each other was hidden beneath and between the words that were actually coming out of their mouths.

'I'm talking to you now, aren't I? Wanting to know how life is treating you – or am I not allowed do that anymore?' There was an edge to his voice, which made Jenny subside a little more.

'Of course you are,' she said softly. 'And life is . . . good. Yeah, it's good.'

It was. Career was on track, finally. She was getting paid to do something that she loved.

Home. She actually owned a home. Had fixed up that two-bedroom basement flat in Kentish Town. Nick didn't need to know that though she'd been involved in eight-way, six-figure book auctions, she'd had an absolute meltdown in the mortgage broker's office, which culminated in her snotty nosed and sobbing, 'But what if my salary goes down?'

She didn't actually live in the flat that she was so proud of buying because she'd moved in with Michael while the builders were in. Against Jenny's better judgement, because they'd only been seeing each other for a couple of months, but Jenny quickly realised that living with Michael was easy, in the same way that being with Michael was easy. Once the builders had left, she rented the flat out and continued living with Michael in his industrial loft, once the top floor of a grain workhouse, which overlooked the Regent's Canal.

Which meant that her love life was on track too.

But Jenny didn't want to give Nick specific details though she wasn't sure why. Maybe she didn't want Nick to pick over the bones of her life at some later date, cast judgement on her decisions, find fault with her achievements. But that wasn't fair. If anyone had the right be on the defensive, it was Nick.

'I'm glad,' he was saying but Jenny put a hand on his arm, fingers resting on the fine wool and able to feel the tension in his bones, to quiet him.

'Those last months that we were in contact, I'm ashamed of my behaviour,' she said without preamble because she'd often thought about what she might say to Nick if their paths crossed again and she'd realised that it would be more of an apology than anything else.

'You don't need to be,' he said immediately, untruthfully but the wary look in his eyes said otherwise.

'I do. I was that horrible cliché of the girl who gets a boyfriend and immediately dumps everyone else in her life, but it was more like I was trying to dump the person who I used to be.' Jenny sighed. 'I didn't like that person very much.'

'That person was great, I had some good times with that person,' Nick said softly. 'Though, yeah, I guess a lot of those good times were chemically enabled.'

'You said I was broken but now when I look back, I think we were all a bit broken, weren't we?' Jenny asked because the Nick sitting down next to her today might be older, might look more tired, but he also seemed whole, in full working order.

'I said a lot of things the last time I saw you too, Jen.' He was looking her straight in the eyes, which was brave of him because Jenny really wanted to look anywhere but at Nick's face, his expression open, his gaze warm as he reminded her, without saying the actual words, that he'd wanted to fuck her. Even the memory of it made her feel hot and heavy though she'd never aspired to be the kind of woman that men, that Nick, just wanted to fuck. What she had with Michael, even what she'd had with Gethin, was so much more than just sex. 'But it's been four years. A lot happens in four years, right?'

Jenny nodded slowly. 'I just wanted you to know that I was sorry. I hope you've forgiven me.'

'Absolutely nothing to forgive. Both of us were dickheads back then and I was a much bigger dickhead than you were,' he said with a grin, like he was steering them to less choppy waters. 'And don't try to claim that you were a bigger dickhead than I was because we both know that's not true.'

'I wasn't going to,' Jen protested with a matching grin. 'It's true. You *were* a much bigger dickhead than me. Anyway, I just wanted you to know that I was sorry.' And then because she couldn't bear to talk about the past any longer: 'Honey's lovely.'

'But I'm punching above my weight?'

'I never said that!'

Nick's smile was as wry and wicked as ever. 'You were thinking it though. But yeah, she's lovely. Doesn't put up with any of my nonsense.'

'I'm glad to hear it,' Jenny said, as Nick pulled a packet of Gauloises from the inner pocket of his jacket. God, she really could *murder* a cigarette and God, he really was still pretentious after all these years. Which was kind of comforting. 'Where are you living? Are you still in Camden?'

There was a pause while Nick lit up, took a long drag on his cigarette and when he spoke, it was on the exhale so Jenny could get a sizeable hit from passive smoking. 'Moved to Stoke Newington a couple of years ago.'

Jenny wasn't sure that she'd heard him correctly. 'Stoke Newington?'

'Come on, Jen, you've lived in London all your life. You know where Stoke Newington is.'

'I know where it is but I can't believe that you moved somewhere without a tube station. Your eighteen-year-old self is appalled.' Jenny put her hand over her heart. 'I'm appalled.'

'I can afford taxis now,' Nick grumbled, a scowl clouding his features as if he was genuinely offended. 'I suppose you live *next door* to a tube station.'

The Kentish Town flat was 0.2 miles from Kentish Town station according to the estate agent particulars and Michael's lovely light loft overlooking the canal was a five-minute walk to Angel.

'Not next door but pretty damn close,' Jenny said, still not that keen to get into specifics. 'Never again will I miss the encore at a gig because I live miles away from the tube.'

'OK, OK, no need to rub it in.' Nick gestured with the hand holding his cigarette and Jenny's nostrils twitched like she was one of the Bisto Kids. 'When was the last time you even went to a gig?'

'I don't go to gigs in Camden backrooms anymore. I don't want anyone spilling beer over me,' Jenny admitted. 'Also, I like to be able to sit down.'

Nick shook his head sadly; that teasing light back in his eyes. 'You've changed.'

'I have and I haven't even told you about my cheese epiphany,' Jenny said, shifting on her stool so she could still get a contact high from his Gauloise.

'Before you do, would you like a cigarette? Because you're looking a lot like a Victorian street urchin with their face pressed up against a sweet shop window.' Nick's cigarettes were sitting on the counter and now he pushed them towards Jenny.

With a sigh, she pushed them back. 'I really am trying to give up.'

Nick pushed them towards her again. 'Are you sure?'

Jenny pushed them away. 'Quite sure, Nic O Teen, now do you want to hear about my cheese epiphany or don't you?'

'Go on then.' He tucked the cigarettes away, out of sight, and even moved the Coke can he was using as an ashtray so it was sitting on his other side. 'Do you like cheese that actually tastes of cheese now?'

'I absolutely do! No one is more surprised than me,' Jenny added, when Nick pretended to choke. 'Went to Paris and had dinner with friends who'd already had quite enough of my bland palate by the time the cheese plate arrived.'

'So, you succumbed to peer pressure . . .'

'I was *forced* to try a sliver of Comté on a cracker and it was actually all right,' Jenny said in a low, urgent voice. 'Then I was *browbeaten* into trying a morsel of Brie with a scraping of apricot compote, and I quite liked that, and I realised that maybe I didn't mind cheese that tasted like cheese anymore. Then when we got back to London, I experimented with cooked cheese . . .'

'Which you always said was an invention of the devil . . .'

'Well, I was young and foolish then. But now I'm older and wiser and I bravely tried some lasagne and I liked it. Actually, I loved it and then I wondered whether I should try something else, which featured cooked cheese just to see if it was a fluke or not and it turns out that I love pizza,' she finished proudly. 'Only your basic Margherita though.'

'Well done, you.' Nick clapped his hands mockingly. 'So now you're horsing down Stilton and Époisses?'

Jenny pulled a face. She could have sworn she felt her make-up cracking. 'No blue cheese, no oozy cheese, no cheese with ash on it.'

'And what are your feelings about fishy fish?' Nick asked, the shadows gone from his face, his dark eyes gleaming. 'Do you eat spicy food now? If you tell me that you're now a curry aficionado, my entire belief system will be destroyed.'

Jenny paused to tease the moment out. 'Are you kidding me?' She relented at last. 'I might like a strong cheddar but I'm still very anti-fishy fish. The thought of sushi makes me want to cry. Still can't do anything spicy. Even some strong salt and vinegar crisps are enough to take the roof off my mouth.'

'I can sleep easier tonight,' Nick said, and Jenny didn't mind the way he looked at her now. Or maybe she'd got used to the way his eyes never seemed to leave her.

It wasn't just Nick either. Every time she glanced over at him, she was assessing the changes, both big and infinitesimal. From the hair and the way that he had broadened out, seemed to take up more space in the world, to the faintest concertina of lines at the corner of his eyes when he smiled, and a caginess to him that he'd never had before. As if he was less confident about his place in the world, even though he had all the outward trappings of success.

'Are you happy, Nick?' Jenny found herself asking, her stomach swooping down to the floor in expectation of his reply. 'You're still an editor, right?'

'Yup, editor,' he confirmed, as if the title, the status, didn't give him much pleasure. 'Britain's best-selling men's magazine. I'm everything that's wrong with modern civilisation according to your mates at the *Guardian*.' He took one last extravagant drag on his cigarette, before stubbing it out with great precision on the Coke can. 'Am I happy? Maybe. Yeah. Why not? I'm happy.'

'I'm glad.' It was the truest thing she'd said ever since their paths had collided at Old Street station a few hours ago.

'And what about you, Jen? When you were in Paris, sampling the delights of the cheese plate, were you with someone?' he asked.

Jenny nodded but she'd already decided she wouldn't be drawn in. The problems she'd had with Gethin, their disconnect, had been entirely of their own making, but right from the start, from that meeting at Leicester Square, Nick had cast a long shadow over their relationship.

'Is he kind? Does he make you happy?' His voice was low, his gaze intent.

'Yes and yes, but my happiness isn't just defined by who I'm seeing. I can be, *I am* happy in my own right.'

'Good,' Nick said. 'Good. Then I don't need to worry about you.'

The connection between them, like a static charge, seemed to vibrate. Jenny was happy and Michael was a huge part of that happiness and she needed to stop *this* right away.

'You never needed to worry about me,' she said with all the assuredness of someone who was going to leave her turbulent twenties behind in eighteen months and she couldn't wait. 'I'm fine. You're fine. Everything worked out.'

And after today, she'd walk out of Nick's life with a much lighter heart and conscience. And who knew when they might bump into each other again? It could be years, even decades from now.

19

December 31st, 1999
Angel Station

'I thought it was a good idea an hour ago, but now I'm not so sure,' Jenny confessed, as they clattered down the escalator at Angel station. It was the longest escalator in the underground network. Sixty-one metres. Sixty-one bloody metres. Two hundred feet if, like Michael, you still remembered imperial measurements. Michael and Erik had decided that they were going to walk down, so the others had to walk down too. Jenny had been happy to stay standing on the right until Kirsty told her off for dawdling.

It was left to Honey to accompany Jenny, one hand on her elbow, as if she was steering a very elderly, very infirm relative.

'It's still the best idea ever,' Honey said. 'Maybe if you let me take the bottle, you could use that hand to, you know, grab hold of the rail.'

'You'll drink it all, I know you!' Jenny kept a tight hold on the neck of her bottle of Waitrose champagne and continued her perilous climb down the escalators in the silver T-bar Mary Janes with a three-inch heel, which were only ever meant to be worn around the house. Or, if she really had to, from car to bar, then she'd spend the entire evening shifting her weight from one foot to the other because the balls of her feet were on fire.

'Your problem is that you missed your heel window,'

Honey had said to her during one of those painful evenings (dinner and drinks at Soho House to celebrate Honey's 'significant' two-book deal). 'While the rest of us were spending our adolescence learning to walk in high heels, you were stomping about in clompy boots and looking down on us. Nick has shown me the pictures. Who's laughing now?'

'I'm not laughing right now because I'm in a thousand agonies but I will allow myself a little chuckle in the distant future when the bunions and the plantar fasciitis and the nerve damage have kicked in,' Jenny had said, which was no way to talk to her star signing. In a strange turn of events, which she didn't entirely understand and had originated from a mammoth bar crawl in Hoxton after their photo shoot, she'd rekindled her friendship with Nick, which meant a new friend in Honey. Which in turn led to both Nick and Honey falling madly in love with Michael: his cool, calm demeanour was in such contrast to the frantic, frenetic way they both lived. Then Kirsty and Erik had naturally been added to the mix and the six of them had become a tight little group. So tight that it was only natural that they'd spend the New Year together. Not just any New Year but the New Year to end all New Years.

Michael had said that the likelihood of the Y2K bug actually happening and all their appliances blowing up and planes falling from the sky was highly unlikely. 'Highly unlikely isn't definitely,' Jenny countered, which was why they now possessed enough bottled water and IKEA tea lights to see them well into the millennium after this one.

But the bottled water and the tea lights (plus the AA batteries and quite a lot of tinned tomato soup) were back at their flat. While Jenny and her guests were on a hare-brained, champagne-addled scheme to get to Primrose Hill before midnight so they'd have a front row view of the fireworks that would illuminate the darkened skies of the city.

'Get a wiggle on, ladies!' Kirsty shouted from the bottom of the escalator. 'We've got half an hour!'

'You just have to rise above the pain,' Honey hissed, hooking her arm into Jenny's so she could haul her down the last stretch of escalator. 'It's all part of being a woman.'

Each step was murder on her poor squashed, chafed toes. Jenny's champagne buzz had buzzed off and her smile had become a grimace a hundred metres ago. By the time she got to the bottom of the escalator where four of her dearest friends and her life partner were impatiently assembled, she was pretty sure that she was doing a good impersonation of Edvard Munch's *The Scream*.

'I forgot you were wearing your indoor shoes,' Michael said, his face concerned but his tone of voice positively jaunty because much as Jenny valued his empathy and compassion, he was a man and he had no idea, no fucking idea, how much she was currently suffering. 'Once we get to Chalk Farm, it's not *that* far to walk.'

'Yes, by my reckoning, we have twenty minutes to get to Chalk Farm, then another ten minutes to reach the summit of Primrose Hill by midnight,' Erik said, glancing at his watch for the umpteenth time.

'Darling, it's not a mountain. Just a gentle slope,' Kirsty said, taking Jenny's other arm, so she was bookended and they could frogmarch her to the northbound platform. 'We can always give this one a queen's chair.'

Nick had been the only one to protest the Primrose Hill expedition on account of it being cold 'and hate to break it to you, but we are never ever going to find a cab free.' Getting a cab had been the original plan, but half an hour shivering on Upper Street had put paid to that. Now he sighed and gave

Jenny a more sympathetic look than anyone else had mustered. 'Or we can grab an arm and leg each and carry you up that way.'

'Due to the extenuating circumstances, I would absolutely let you do that,' Jenny agreed as they wound their way around a sizeable number of revellers rushing to be somewhere more exciting come this auspicious midnight.

As they reached the platform, a train mockingly sped past them. There was more bad news when they looked at the indicator boards. All trains were going via High Barnet and they really needed a train going via Edgware in 'the next two minutes', according to Erik, who had a determined glint in his eyes like he was about to make them coordinate watches and go on an enforced *run* through North London.

Jenny collapsed onto the nearest row of seats. 'This is all giving me a hideous sense of déjà vu. All those nights when we really needed an Edgware train, remember?'

Nick nodded. 'Our youth in a nutshell. So, shall we get on the next train and change at Camden?'

'Or we could go back to ours?' Jenny suggested but it was hope over expectation as the others hadn't lost their champagne buzz due to their footwear and seemed quite undaunted at the prospect of changing at Camden.

There was a train due in one minute. Jenny reached down to unbuckle her shoe, maybe ease one foot out for a couple of blissful seconds . . .

'Don't you dare!' Honey growled. 'You'll never get them back on.'

Michael sat down next to her so he could take one of Jenny's hands and give it a gentle squeeze. 'Do you really want to go home?' he asked softly, and she knew that if she really wanted to, he'd come home with her, even though he seemed very invested in this increasingly ill-fated excursion to Primrose Hill.

'I do really want to,' she whispered for his ears only. 'But I'm going to put a brave face on it and pretend that nothing would give me greater pleasure than breaking the land-speed record to see in the New Year on the frozen wastelands of Primrose Hill.'

'That's my girl,' Michael said, leaning forward to kiss her forehead. 'We can huddle together for warmth.'

He stood up and held out a hand as a High Barnet train came shrieking onto the platform. Jenny tried not to wince as her feet took her weight. She liked to think that she had a poker face, especially in fraught meetings with the finance director or difficult author/agent lunches, but now she wasn't so sure.

She limped onto the train, which wasn't as busy as it would normally be this close to midnight on a Friday. Kirsty came and sat down next to Jenny and patted her arm, as Nick and Honey dropped into the seats opposite and Erik looked at his watch again. 'I should have made you board the last carriage so we could change over at Camden via the back way,' he fretted. 'Now we'll have to go through the busiest part of the station so it's imperative that we stick together and nobody gets left behind.'

'I've never wanted him more,' Kirsty drawled. Usually, Erik was laid-back and affable but tonight he was working every single one of Jenny's last nerves and Kirsty's too from the sound of it.

They had three stations to go until Camden and the stretch between King's Cross and Euston station was a long one so Jenny was going to make the most of every precious moment. 'Let's open one of the bottles of champagne now! Keep the party spirit going.'

'Oh, yes, let's!' Honey agreed. She'd been leaning into Nick, the way she always did, which reminded Jenny of Bob Dylan and Suze Rotolo on the cover of *The Freewheelin' Bob Dylan*, but now she launched forward eagerly. 'Shall we open ours too?'

They'd left the flat with three bottles of champagne between them and disposable cups so they could toast appropriately at the midnight hour. But breaking into one bottle couldn't hurt.

'I don't want you all drinking champagne and falling behind on the changeover,' Erik fussed, but Jenny had already ripped off the foil on her bottle and was unwinding the delicate wire so she could prise off the cage. 'Jenny, I said no!'

Jenny ignored him and with her thumb eased the cork out of the tilted bottle with a jubilant pop and no spray. She held the bottle to her mouth, tried not to sneeze as the bubbles tickled her nose and took several long gulps.

Then she held the bottle out. 'Honey?'

Honey took the bottle as Jenny held a hand to her mouth and burped distinctly but she hoped, delicately. Not delicately enough because Nick smiled and shook his head. 'Can't take you anywhere.'

The bottle was ceremonially passed to Kirsty, who made a great show of wiping the neck with the sleeve of her coat. 'I can't trust that neither of you have backwashed. You're sloppy drunks.'

'I'm never sloppy,' Honey said grandly brushing her fringe out of her eyes.

'Anyway, the alcohol sterilises the germs,' Jenny added as the bottle was passed back to her and she waved it at Michael who was standing by the doors.

'Oh go on, then,' he said though Jenny knew that it was more to make her happy than because he really wanted a drink.

Then the bottle was back in her custody and they were pulling into Euston, the platform almost deserted. As soon as the doors closed, Erik checked his watch again. 'We can do this, people, but we only have a minute to complete the change-over.'

'But you don't know if there will be an Edgware train,' Nick pointed out, the lone voice of dissent, though on the inside, Jenny was also dissenting.

'They're meant to be running every two minutes, according to the *Evening Standard*,' Michael said.

'A London Transport minute is a unit of time quite differ-ent to an ordinary minute,' Nick argued.

Jenny had been very conscientious about her hostess duties: making three dishes from Nigella Lawson's *How to Eat*, sending Michael out at eight that morning to forage for fresh raspberries for the Bakewell tart and a bottle of Noilly Prat for the spaghetti carbonara, and fussing that everyone had enough to eat and no one got stuck with the wobbly one out of Michael's Eames chairs, which he'd been meaning to get fixed for ages. Then there had been the preoccupation with her footwear and it was only now that she realised Nick's mood was slightly off.

Not off enough that anyone else had noticed, apart from maybe Honey. But if Honey had noticed then she was doing a very good job of pretending not to as she stood up at Erik's command, clicked her heels together and saluted.

Jenny had noticed because there would always be a small corner of her heart reserved only for Nick. She loved Michael without question. He was kind and funny, talked to her about books and films and art but never patronised her; he had a particular way of smiling at her that always made her come undone; he made love to her without ever making her feel compromised or exploited, and he could plumb in a washing machine. If a more perfect man existed, then Jenny hadn't met him.

Nick was far from perfect, but he was the man she'd loved first and the echo of that love lingered on, so she was aware of how taciturn he'd been for most of the evening. And when Honey had been leaning into him, he hadn't leaned into her but had sat tightly tucked in, arms folded, mouth a straight tight line.

'OK, people, positions please!' Erik's announcement broke through Jenny's reverie. The train was almost imperceptibly slowing down as it did when it approached a station, and any Londoner, either homegrown or transplanted, could sense this change.

With an unhappy sigh of anticipation Jenny rose to her feet along with Kirsty, Honey and Nick to join Erik and Michael who were already at the double doors.

They came into Camden Town station, which by its usual Friday night standards was deserted. Erik puffed out his chest. 'Less people to get in our way,' he said, his hand on the door like he was going to force it open while the train was still moving.

The train came to a halt, the doors opened and Erik took off like he was attempting a four minute mile. 'Let's go!' he called over his shoulder. 'Pick up the pace!'

The others leapt from the train as if they were greyhounds chasing the rabbit at Walthamstow Dogs. Hampered by heels, handbag and open bottle of champagne, Jenny descended with more care and a lot less grace.

'Come on, Jenny!'

To show willing, Jenny broke into a gentle jog – this was all unpleasantly reminiscent of the dreaded cross country run at school – trying to sidestep past a man intent on catching the tube that she'd just vacated. For several agonising seconds they were caught in a ducking, dodging dance, until the man shouldered her out of the way with a furious, 'Stupid bitch!'

Jenny was knocked into the wall, ricocheted off another desperate reveller and managed to stagger another couple of steps before she found herself pitching forward, her foot and her shoe, the buckle already half undone, parting ways. She managed to right herself and, more importantly, the bottle of champagne . . .

She looked up to see how far ahead the others were. They'd disappeared from view so they must have raced up the two short flights of stairs that led to the patch of no man's land at the bottom of the escalators and were probably fast approaching the Edgware-bound platform. Jenny hobbled over to her shoe and swayed on one foot as she tried to put it back on but she was still holding the champagne bottle and her fingers seemed to have been replaced with sausages and there was no time . . .

'Jen! Just take off the other shoe!' She looked up to see Nick's head, then his shoulders, and then the rest of him as he climbed back up the stairs and hurried towards her. 'Quick, there's an Edgware train coming!'

'Fuck my shoes and the horse they rode in on,' Jenny muttered under her breath as she all but wrenched off her other shoe. Nick took the bottle of champagne from her, tutting impatiently as she picked up her shoes, then grabbed her other hand.

'You're going to have to run like you've never run before,' he advised.

Jenny had time for one heartfelt 'Ugh!' and then she was half running/half being pulled along by Nick. Not so much dodging past the couple of stray souls in their direct path, but aiming right for them so they scattered.

As they entered the passageway that led to the Edgware platform, the train arrived. Jenny tried to pick up the pace but they were suddenly surrounded by a surge of people streaming off the train, hellbent on reaching street level and their destinations before midnight.

Over the sound of people chattering and a gang of girls harmonising a version of Shania Twain's 'That Don't Impress Me Much', Jenny could hear Erik bellowing, 'Faster! Faster!'

'Fuck, fuck, fuck, fuck, fuck,' Nick gritted between his teeth, as they weaved through the crowd and yes! The train was still there, their friends crowded at the open doors.

Kirsty made frantic beckoning gestures. 'They're about to close!'

'Come on, guys! You can do it!' Honey squealed. 'Come o—'

The doors shut just as they reached the platform and all Jenny could do was stare at the four shocked faces looking back at her for one, two, three seconds before the train pulled away.

Then she wrenched her hand free of Nick's and doubled over, panting. Even though she'd successfully given up smoking for over a year now, she'd had three 'social' cigarettes on their balcony over the course of the evening and now she was suffering for every low-tar drag that she'd taken.

'Next train isn't for another seven minutes,' Nick informed her.

'So much for them being every couple of minutes!'

Once Jenny felt a little less like she was about to throw up her Nigella Carbonara, she sat down on the nearest bench. The platform was now empty.

'What's the time?' she asked Nick, who was pacing. 'Come and sit down. Reserve your energy for our mad dash once we get to Chalk Farm.'

'It's already gone ten to twelve. We're not going to make it.' He sat down next to Jenny and handed her the champagne bottle.

'They still might.' Jenny frowned. 'If they make it to the top of Primrose Hill before it's midnight, then I won't be too mad that they didn't wait for us.'

Nick shook his head. 'They're *never* going to make it. It was a shit idea from start to finish.'

Jenny took a ruminative gulp of champagne, which was none the worse for being jiggled about during their platform-to-platform dash. 'They might though.'

'They won't,' Nick said finally. Crushingly.

'So, what shall we do? Go to Chalk Farm and phone them from there?'

Nick shrugged. 'I haven't got any better ideas. But good luck getting your phone to work when everyone else in the country is phoning people to wish them a happy New Year's Eve.'

His bad mood was contagious, or maybe it was the dawning realisation that they wouldn't be seeing in the new year in style. It wasn't just the new year. It was the next bloody millennium, a defining moment, like remembering what you were doing when you heard about Princess Diana's car crash or, more relevant in their case, when The Smiths had split up.

'So, Jenny,' someone might say twenty years from now. 'What were you doing at the dawn of the new millennium?'

'Well, I was in the bowels of Chalk Farm station, separated from both my life partner and my friends,' she'd have to reply. Still, there were some silver linings. Her parents, Martin and his fiancée, Bethany, were currently at the Millennium Dome, waving Union Jacks about and doing whatever people were doing at the Millennium Dome for New Year's Eve. No one really seemed sure. Still . . .

'This is not how I planned to spend this most momentous of moments,' she mused and decided that another swig of champagne was called for.

'Technically, it's not actually the new millennium until two thousand and one,' Nick said in his most sneery voice, the one that she hadn't *actually* heard for years. Not since they were teenagers.

Once again, she was knocked sideways by a sense of déjà vu. This scenario: a station platform late at night, the two of them sitting side by side, fretting about the time and waiting for the next train, Nick being an absolute, sneery-voiced pretentious bastard. It was so painfully, and yet lovingly, familiar.

Jenny did what she would have done when she was seventeen and gave Nick such a hard shove that he almost slid off the bench.

'Fuck off,' he snapped.

'You fuck off with your "uhhhh, it's not *actually* the new millennium for another year" bollocks,' Jenny sing-songed. She thrust the bottle at him. 'Have a drink. Have several drinks. Stop being so annoying.'

If she were a good friend, she'd ask him what the matter was but she wasn't sure that she wanted to know the answer.

They sat there in a spiky silence, passing the bottle back and forth, until finally the departure board indicated that the Edgware train was imminent. 'At last!' Jenny nudged Nick gently. 'What's the time now?'

'Time you got a watch.' Nick pulled back the sleeve of his jacket with a beleaguered air. 'After five to twelve. Maybe three minutes to twelve?'

'This is the best new year ever!' Jenny clasped her hands together in mock delight then got to her feet as she saw the dim ghostly glow in the depths of the tunnel.

'I don't know. Kind of fitting that you and I would be on an Edgware-bound train come midnight,' Nick said, with the first genuine smile that he'd managed to crack for hours. 'Old times' sake and all that.'

'Such unparalleled glamour.' Jenny decided that she needed to let it go. Nick had been right. At least she was warm and dry and didn't have her painful shoes on, as opposed to being cold and legging it through Primrose Hill on a fool's mission.

The almost empty train pulled into the almost empty station and as soon as the doors opened, Nick ushered her on board, with great ceremony. 'After you, madam.'

There was no point sitting down so Jenny leaned against the central pole and, once the doors had closed, stared at her warped reflection in the glass. She looked wan, her face pale against the red of her lips and the sparkly black material of her dress. Nick came to stand behind her and he too stared at the Jenny and Nick in the glass, like they were two entirely separate entities from the corporeal Jenny and Nick.

20

January 1st, 2000
Chalk Farm Station

In no time at all, they reached Chalk Farm, the only people to
get off the train. Jenny was about to ask what the time was but
Nick was already looking at his watch. He held up his hand.
'Five seconds to midnight.'

There was nowhere else to go.

'Four . . . three . . . two . . . one . . .'

'Happy New Year!' Jenny said with more enthusiasm than
she actually felt. 'Best one yet, right?'

'If you say so,' Nick said but he was grinning and when he
held out his arms, Jenny stepped up close so she could hug
him, stand on tiptoe and kiss his cheek. He turned his head so
she ended up brushing the corner of his mouth with her lips
and bumping noses.

Jenny laughed. 'Awkward!' but when she tried to pull free
she couldn't because his hands were on her arms, holding her
gently but tightly.

'We should rewind,' Nick said. 'It's bad luck to screw up a
New Year's kiss.'

'I'm sure it's not,' Jenny said, and she had other things to
say, but Nick bent his head and kissed the words right out of
her mouth. Her mouth. Not her cheek.

It was a soft but insistent kiss, sure but exploratory, as if
Nick was testing his boundaries as well as the topography of
her lips.

And Jenny? She kissed him back because this was a moment out of time. One year rolling into the next. One century becoming another. The boy she'd known almost half her life, whom she'd loved, then hated. Now her feelings for him existed in some shadowy in-between space, like this kiss.

One kiss, one kiss to wipe away the bitter memories of their first kiss and their second kiss. Third time was the charm. One kiss, a last kiss, couldn't hurt.

She tilted her head back, let Nick deepen the kiss, but when his hands slid from her arms to her hips and his tongue slid into her mouth, she pulled free.

'Happy New Year,' Jenny said again and already she was regretting what had just happened. She couldn't look at Nick so she simply followed the 'Way Out' sign.

Nick caught up with her at the lifts, a hand on Jenny's shoulder to stop her, pull her back and pin her against the wall. The shoes she was holding hit the floor because there was nothing soft or exploratory about it this time. It was a hard, demanding kiss, his tongue fucking into her mouth, his hands in her hair, cupping the back of her head, holding her captive while his body pressed against hers.

Her first instinct, and every instinct after that, was to melt into him. To throw her arms around Nick, to give in, to arch against him, to encourage him with throaty little moans. Because, God help her, she loved every filthy thing his mouth and hands were doing.

But Jenny forced herself to stay still, to tense all her muscles, until Nick finally took the hint and stopped kissing her. He didn't let her go, his eyes boring into hers, as he panted slightly.

'No,' Jenny said, and she shook her head.

'But I love you. I still love you. I've always loved you. And you've always loved me.'

'No, you don't. I don't.' She went to gesture at the bottle of champagne, but they'd left that behind at Camden Town along with their rational selves. 'You're drunk.'

'I am *not* drunk.'

'You're drunk,' Jenny repeated again, a little desperately this time.

Nick reached for her again but this time she did flinch away. The moment had passed. Grim reality and the consequences it always brought had set in. 'I've never been more sober. I love you, Jen.'

It was everything that she'd ever wanted him to say on all those nights in all those other train stations. But not here. Not now. 'I love Michael,' Jenny insisted. 'And you love Honey and if you don't, then this is a shitty way to try and extricate yourself.'

She felt a momentary pang of sympathy for Honey but Honey was a smart woman. She'd figure it out.

Nick was still crowding her, still looking Jenny right in the eye while she wished that she could look at anything besides him. 'You don't love him.' His voice was urgent and low.

'I do love him,' she insisted, because it was the truth, though even talking about Michael after kissing Nick felt like a betrayal. Another betrayal.

'He's not your forever.'

This was more than she could bear. Jenny thumped Nick on the shoulder and he finally stepped back, gave her room to think, to breathe again.

She ducked away from him and dived for the open lift, hit the button to close the doors but before they could, Nick was in the lift with her.

'Jen . . .'

'No!' she snapped. 'I've given you a get-out clause, take it. You're drunk. Tomorrow when you've sobered up, you can send me a text to say you're sorry and then we're never going to talk about this again.'

'Or else, when you stop lying to yourself, you can send me a text to say that you love me too and I'll drop everything, drop her . . .' His voice was low, urgent. 'I'll come and get you . . .'

Jenny shook her head to deny his words, the picture in her head of Nick ringing her doorbell while she stood waiting for him, bags packed. 'No! Stop! Please, Nick, will you just stop? I'm not going to do that. I don't know why you're being like this.'

'You know why.' His eyes burning into her.

Jenny turned her back on him and he sighed as the pips signalled the doors closing then the lift began its juddery ascent to street level.

God, it seemed to take forever and like Lot's wife, Jenny couldn't look around, was half terrified, half longing to feel his hand on her shoulder again.

The lift doors opened and Jenny stumbled out through the open barriers of the ticket machines and there huddled at the entrance were Erik, Kirsty, Honey but she only had eyes for Michael, who looked relieved to see her for, his eyes lighting up, a smile on his face. Then he frowned.

'I'm so sorry,' she said to him. 'I've ruined everything.'

'Where did you get to?' he asked, rather than being quick to dismiss the idea that Jenny had ruined everything.

'Well, we missed the tube,' she reminded him. 'You were there to see the doors closing in my face.'

'The next tube was due seven minutes after that, but we've waited for you for fifteen minutes,' Erik, ever the reliable time-keeper, reported.

'We thought that, at least, we could see in the New Year together even if it was outside Chalk Farm station,' Honey said, her frown a perfect match for Michael's. 'But you never showed up. Not for another eight minutes.'

Were they really kissing for eight minutes? That was ... excessive. Also, wrong. A world of wrong.

'Well ... We already discussed, didn't we, that a London Underground minute is completely different to a normal minute.'

The kiss, the kisses, hadn't even been Jenny's idea, yet now she was being forced to lie to cover up the fact that they'd happened.

'And where are your shoes?' Kirsty asked.

'I've got them,' said Nick from behind her. 'It's why we're late. Left them at Camden. Had to go back for them.'

Michael's frown deepened. 'Why didn't you say that?'

Jenny flapped her hand. 'You didn't give me a chance.'

This was awful. It wasn't how she wanted the year to begin or the night to end. Because it had ended now. Everyone flat and disappointed, despite the pop and crackle of fireworks dancing across the night sky.

Kissing the wrong man at midnight. Then having to lie about it.

'Look, I'm sorry,' she said again, and it should have been the easiest thing to fold herself into Michael, tuck her arm in his, and give him a belated New Year's kiss, much like Nick was doing with Honey even though Honey stage whispered, 'I'm really pissed off with you,' before she proffered her cheek.

But how could Jenny snuggle up to Michael and kiss him when she could still feel the phantom touch of Nick's hands on her, her lips still tingling and kiss-sore. Christ! She hadn't even checked to see if her lipstick had withstood the onslaught, but a quick glance at Nick who was whispering in Honey's ear while she giggled and swatted him away like a fly, showed that he didn't seem to have a suspiciously Clinique 100% Red mouth.

'I want to go home,' Jenny said and she knew that she was behaving like a brat, like the worst seventeen-year-old incarnation of herself, but she couldn't help it. She turned and headed back into the station, without even waiting to see if there was a general consensus.

★

Jenny still felt scratchy and out of sorts, hours later. It was three the next afternoon. Michael was grouchy. He wasn't one to shout and bang his fist when he was annoyed but today his silence was like a weapon. Or maybe it just cut like a blade because she was feeling so guilty.

Still, a shrug had been the only response to Jenny's determinedly cheerful enquiry about what Michael wanted to do about lunch and so now she'd taken herself back to bed with a generous slice of leftover Bakewell tart, two paracetamol and a can of full fat Coke to puncture her hangover. She never used to get hangovers, but now she did and they were bloody awful.

Not as bloody awful as Nick had been last night. As Jenny snuggled down in her nest of pillows, duvet and cashmere blanket, she was indignant all over again. He'd been rude and dismissive all night. Emotionally he'd regressed back to the sarky, snarky Nick of their college days.

And he'd kissed her. It had been entirely his idea. His fault.

Except, she'd kissed him back because she'd spent the half of her life that she'd known Nick, even when she was loved up with someone else, imagining what it would be like to kiss him again. It hadn't been a constant thought, but it had been there; a little daydream that she'd come back to occasionally. Now Jenny knew that she'd play last night's first kiss, then, especially, that second demanding, dominating kiss, on a loop until the tape wore thin.

Also, he'd said that he loved her. That he'd always loved her and she couldn't even begin to process that information, because she'd always loved him. It was an uncomfortable truth that she could only admit to herself on a day when she was already feeling vulnerable and laid bare.

She loved Nick. Not in the way she loved Michael and she did love Michael. Michael was her lodestar. Her better half in so many ways. He made Jenny feel protected, cherished and adored and Nick didn't make her feel like that at all.

But those kisses and Nick's desperate 'I love you. I've always loved you,' was making Jenny contemplate the unthinkable. What would happen if she did text Nick to tell him that she loved him? She'd be throwing a hand grenade into the happy, safe life that she'd built and destroying it for what? What was Nick offering her in return?

A teenage fantasy finally fulfilled. Exciting, dangerous kisses that made her forget who she was. The look in Nick's eyes that promised Jenny everything. But they were all ephemeral things. They couldn't compare to the very real, very tangible, very safe life she had with Michael. Besides Jenny had known Nick for long enough that she knew full well that even though his eyes might promise her everything, odds were that she'd actually end up with a fat load of nothing, except more heartache.

Jenny burrowed deeper into the duvet as that one stubborn thought kept going round and round in her head like a hamster on a wheel.

But *what if?*

But what if I told him that I loved him?

But what if he came to get me and take me away?

Then, somewhere deep in the folds of the duvet, came the imperious two-note tone of her Nokia alerting Jenny to a text message. Probably Kirsty asking if she was ready for a debrief on last night, though she couldn't ever tell even Kirsty what had really happened.

Jenny groped for her phone and when she saw she had a text from Nick, it was like a sense memory of his lips pressed against hers, his tongue dipping in her mouth, his hands hard on her hips and she could feel her face heat up, her stomach dip deliciously.

And then . . .

Sorry about last night. I was really drunk. N

PART EIGHT

2001

21

Sunday, September 9th, 2001
Howard Beach Station, NYC

Jenny had been in New York for over two months and it was like everything she'd imagined. It was also like nothing she'd ever imagined.

When she'd arrived late on a Friday afternoon in late June and staggered out of JFK airport, she'd been knocked sideways by the filthy, filmy humidity of the New York summer. It was like walking into a wet, hot fog, as brutal as the noise and the frenzy of the city itself.

The cab ride through Queens, then Brooklyn had been bewildering, disorientating. The low flat houses, the high rises, the strip malls, even the other cars and trucks sharing the road were unfamiliar. Then they'd crossed the Brooklyn Bridge into Manhattan itself and all of a sudden, New York was as familiar to Jenny as Mill Hill Broadway.

The wide streets that stretched further than the eye could see. The steam rising from the manhole covers. The yellow taxi cabs. The pretzel stands on street corners. The bustling crosswalks.

It was *Breakfast at Tiffany's*. It was *When Harry Met Sally*. It was *Annie Hall*. It was even *Friends*. It was every movie and TV show set in New York that Jenny had ever seen and that car ride, eyes unblinking so she didn't miss a thing, mouth hanging open in awed stupefaction, was when Jenny had fallen in love with New York.

She was there on a three-month job swap with her opposite number, Heather, at a venerable US publisher that, like Lyttons, prided itself on its independent status and the big list of award-winning authors it published. Jenny and Heather had acquired so many of each other's books that in the end, Jenny had proposed that they enter into a reciprocal 'first look' arrangement. That had been a couple of years ago and had proved so successful – a 'special relationship' as *The Bookseller* called it – that the two publishing houses had now entered into a more formal agreement, which had resulted in Jenny and Heather swapping jobs for three months.

Even though Jenny loved her job, she didn't live for work, she worked to live. And she was currently working and living in New York where there were drinks to be had in chichi hotel bars on the Upper West Side and little dives in Greenwich Village. There were bookshops to explore and rails of vintage dresses to rifle through. For the July 4th weekend, she was even invited to the Hamptons by the company MD so Jenny could talk books with his wife (a former Rhodes scholar now interior designer) and attend a cookout on the beach to watch the fireworks where she was introduced to a Kennedy and a man who said he was the inspiration behind Carly Simon's 'You're So Vain' but he didn't want to talk about it.

On the rare occasions when she was left to her own devices on the weekend, when there were no visits from friends or family over from London to take advantage of a free sofa bed and a strong pound, Jenny would ride the F train all the way from West 4th and Washington Square to Coney Island at the end of the line so she could paddle in the Atlantic Ocean, or stroll along the Boardwalk listening to Lou Reed on her antiquated Walkman.

She'd buy doughnuts, maybe go to the Circus Sideshow then have another paddle in the ocean before getting the subway back to the West Village, along with the real New Yorkers. Families with sticky, sunburnt kids, lunches packed in Duane Reade bags, the kind of people who didn't go to their summer houses at the Hamptons or the Berkshires on the weekends, but on Sunday afternoons when they didn't have to work, they could afford a $1.50 subway ride to the beach.

But on this Sunday afternoon, though Jenny was getting the train from the end of the line back into Manhattan, she hadn't been slowly strolling along the Coney Island boardwalk, but had been at the airport to see Michael off.

It had been a . . . different kind of weekend. It was his third trip to see her. On the two previous occasions, even though Michael had been to New York many times before, they'd done all the tourist things. The Circle Line tour. The Met. The Whitney. The Guggenheim and, of course, MOMA. They'd had brunch at Sarabeth, dinner at the Rainbow Room and drinks at the 21 Club.

But this time when Michael arrived at Jenny's West Village apartment on Friday evening just five minutes after Jenny had got back from the office, he'd cut her off mid-sentence as she was explaining that someone in the office knew someone who knew someone who might be able to get them stalls seats for a new production of *42nd Street*.

'Can we not?' he'd asked in a weary voice. 'I've come to see you not the sights. Also, you know I hate musicals. Let's just be flaneurs.'

So they'd spent the entire weekend simply pottering around the West Village.

Michael was thrilled to just stroll along the banks of the Hudson, hand in hand. To have a long, lazy Sunday morning in bed without ever making it to brunch and so it was a mad rush to get him packed and on his way to the airport to catch the redeye back to London.

'I feel like I've got my Jenny back,' he said, as they sat next to each other on the subway, holding hands. Michael would never get a cab because the traffic was too unpredictable and it was much easier to get the train. Some seed of superstition meant that Jenny would always come and see him off. She couldn't let Michael get on a plane, fly however many miles in a tin can with wings, without a hug and a kiss and an 'I love you,' at the gate. Or maybe she'd just watched too many movies.

'I've been here all the time,' Jenny said. 'Yes, there's been the whole of the Atlantic Ocean between us but emotionally, I haven't gone anywhere.'

'That's good to know,' Michael said, and he lifted her hand to his mouth so he could dust her knuckles with a kiss.

Which was lovely, so romantic, but it made what Jenny had to say even more difficult.

'But whatever's on your mind, I wish you'd just come out and tell me,' he continued and once, just once, it would be great for Michael not to be all knowing and perceptive. 'You can tell me anything. You haven't fallen in love with a Wall Street banker called Trip, have you?'

'I've been trying to think of a gentle way to drop that bombshell on you,' Jenny said, leaning into Michael so hard, that it was more of a nudge. 'But seriously, there was something I wanted to talk to you about.'

Michael glanced at her briefly but warily. 'That sounds a little ominous.'

That depended on your politics. 'So, I've been offered a job. Here. In New York.'

'OK,' Michael said in a voice that was so neutral it was beige. Then he didn't say anything for a little while because he wasn't one for making rash statements until he had all the facts to hand.

She waited for what seemed like hours but could only have been a couple of minutes before Michael had processed. 'I thought this was just a three-month job swap.'

'It is. It was, but someone's leaving and they've asked if I'm interested in stepping into their role. It would be a big promotion,' Jenny tried to keep the passion, the eagerness out of her voice. 'But it wouldn't be forever, I wouldn't want to move to New York permanently. Mum would have a fit and Gran's getting on, but I was thinking, three years would be a fair crack of the whip. So, that was what I wanted to tell you.'

'Tell me. Not ask me,' Michael said in that same flat voice and sometimes Jenny wished that he'd get angry. Proper fucking furious. Not this flat, toneless automaton routine, which always left Jenny floundering and instantly on the defensive.

'I'm talking to you about it, aren't I? I want to know how you feel about this . . . development. I'm not going to make any decisions until *we've* explored all the options.' Jenny forced herself to push down her anger and yes, also her guilt and to be as calm and as rational as Michael was or was pretending to be. 'I mean, we could do the long distance thing. But I was thinking, hoping, that maybe you could move over here.'

'Really?' Michael said, with the merest millimetre elevation of his eyebrows. 'That's what you were thinking? Goodness.'

'I don't even know if I'm going to take the job.' Jenny could feel herself slowly deflating so she was sure that she was now a little sack of bones and internal organs in a nice summer frock. The job offer had been validating, exciting, and yes, there were a lot of factors to consider, but now it seemed daunting. Maybe they'd only offered her the position to be kind . . .

'Three months on a job swap in a rent-free West Village apartment is very different to the realities of working here permanently,' Michael explained patiently, even though Jenny did know that. 'Most of your salary will probably go on rent and you'll need to find out what the tax implications are. No NHS either, if you get run over or your appendix suddenly ruptures . . .'

'Wow,' Jenny mouthed, because Michael had just made being offered a job, a promotion, with a renowned New York publishing house, like the worst thing in the world. 'Oh, what's that noise?' She held a hand to her ear, though all she could really hear was the rumble of the train over the tracks. 'That's the sound of you crushing my dreams under your feet.'

'There's no need to exaggerate, Jenny,' he said and then he didn't say anything and neither did Jenny. They simply sat there, next to each other, silent.

They were just transferring to the shuttle bus at Howard Beach station after sitting in that fulminating silence for a good twenty minutes, when Michael spoke. 'The thing is . . . where do you see yourself in five years' time?'

'I want to be a Publisher. Or Publishing Director, even better,' Jenny said immediately because that was the easy part. It was the other areas of her life that were unsure. Even Michael, these past three months, always so sure and so steady had become something of an unknown quantity. 'I think I'd be in London. Hopefully with you. In a house. A proper house with period details. Practically next door to a tube station.' She smiled hesitantly, but Michael didn't smile back.

'You did say when we first met that you didn't want children,' he reminded Jenny, hoisting his black leather weekend holdall over his shoulder, when they got off the bus at the airport. 'But you were twenty-seven then and that was four years ago.

I was wondering if that was still the case now that you're in your thirties.'

'I've only *just* turned thirty-one.' Jenny realised that wasn't the point. 'I still don't want children. Not now. I'd want to have my career in really good shape before I took time off to have a child. Or children.' It would probably be children. So that would be six months or, more likely, a whole year off and no sooner were you back to hitting your stride at work again, then you'd be disappearing off to push another human being out of your vagina. Things were meant to have improved for women in the workplace but tell that to Sinclair Lytton, who'd been heard to say when one of the publicity team left to have her third child, 'Christ, hasn't she learned how to cross her legs yet?'

It was the twenty-first century and there had been men on the moon, always men, and measles and polio and other diseases had been almost eradicated. The world had changed so much and yet if you were a woman, you still had to choose between a really glittering, fulfilling career or being a present and devoted mother. It was such a fucking con.

'So, you would want children in five years or so?' Michael persisted and Jenny had thought about taking his arm as they walked into the airport but now decided against it.

It wasn't yes. But unlike when they'd talked around the subject when they first got together, it wasn't an emphatic no either. 'Children might be a possibility, a lot can change in five years,' Jenny said, and she thought, hoped, they were done with this because it was making her antsy and uncomfortable.

'I'm forty-one,' Michael said calmly, because he really did have nerves of steel. 'In five years' time, I'll be forty-six. That means that this first hypothetical child would turn eighteen and I'd be sixty-four, sixty-five. Ready for retirement.'

'Don't say that,' Jenny begged. 'Look at the Rolling Stones, they're still getting women pregnant and they pretty much are *at* retirement age.'

'Please don't compare me to Mick Jagger ever again,' Michael said and there was the faintest glimmer of a smile playing on his lips now. But then it disappeared. 'While we're putting our cards on the table . . .'

'Oh God, what fresh hell?'

Michael shifted his bag onto his other shoulder. 'Well, in five years' time, I'll definitely be looking to move out of London.'

Jenny couldn't hide her surprise or her horror. She screwed up her mouth like she had a bad taste. 'Why? Why would you do that?'

'Because I've done twenty years in London and it's not somewhere I want to live when I'm old and it's certainly not somewhere that I'd want to bring up children. Wouldn't you like to live somewhere with a pastoral view or fresh sea air?'

'Quite frankly, I'd rather die,' Jenny said, because the country was boring and the sea was bracing and neither of them could compare to "the swing, tramp and trudge; in the bellow and the uproar; the carriages, motorcars, omnibuses, vans, sandwich men shuffling and swinging; brass bands; barrel organs; in the triumph and the jingle and the strange high singing of some aeroplane overhead was what she loved; life; London".

'Are you quoting Virginia Woolf at me to try and win this argument?' Michael was smiling properly now as they joined the end of a long queue at check-in. He even leant down to press a kiss to Jenny's sweaty forehead.

'Not an argument. A discussion,' Jenny said firmly. 'Which is ongoing.'

'Well, if it's a discussion then we can discuss it when . . . I was going to say when you get back from New York, which was meant to be the end of this month, but that's debatable now, is it?'

'I haven't decided for definite if I'm going to take the job . . .'

'If you wanted to, I wouldn't stand in your way. I'm sure we could find a way to make it work,' Michael said, pulling Jenny in for a hug. 'Just as long as it's not forever.'

But what if it was forever? What if she loved the job and working in New York even with its astronomical rents and lack of socialised healthcare? What if, after two years, she was offered an even better job? Would she have to choose between her career and Michael, whom she regarded as her forever? What would forever look like if it weren't with Michael?

These big, life-altering questions spun round and round in Jenny's head all the way back into New York.

22

Sunday, September 9th, 2001
Delancey Street Station

Jenny was meant to be going out to dinner, which was now the last thing she felt like doing. Though actually when Jenny thought about it, the very last thing she felt like doing was going back to her borrowed apartment, which had currently lost all its charm, and carrying on with her existential crisis.

There wasn't time to freshen up and change so she repaired her make-up on the train. That was a constant in her life that she never wanted to change: Jenny travelling underground while applying liquid eyeliner on a moving train.

She painted on her best face and dragged on a smile as she pushed open the door of Katz's Delicatessen on East Houston Street. As soon as she stepped inside the diner, her smile became wider and brighter.

It had everything to do with the brightly lit space: the basic Formica tables and booth seats, the old-fashioned counter and the backlit menu above it. The Pepsi signs and the wall of photos featuring the great and good who had eaten there. It was busy and bright and bustling and there was the tempting aroma of fried food, which was a reminder that Jenny hadn't eaten all day.

But best of all was the man waving at her from a table tucked into a corner. Jenny waved back, her smile no longer something that she'd put on even though it didn't really fit.

She already had her first line cued up as she slid into the booth opposite him. 'I'll have what she's having!'

'Bloody tourist!' George said, reaching across the table to squeeze Jenny's hand. 'I'd figured that you might not have crossed this off your list of New York landmarks that you *had* to visit.'

'I'm thoroughly ashamed to admit that I hadn't even put it on the list.' Jenny gazed around the restaurant, which had been immortalised in *When Harry Met Sally*, one of her favourite films. 'God, I'm starving.'

'We're waiting for a couple of people: Nick, and a surprise guest.' George smiled faintly. 'If Nick bothers to turn up what with him jetting over for Fashion Week so he can interview lots of famous people.'

'It will be a miracle if he deigns to mingle with us common folk.'

Though Jenny couldn't be too down on Nick because he'd reunited her with George. George had rung her on her first day in the New York office and insisted that they meet for drinks at the Algonquin Hotel. 'So you can live out all those Dorothy Parker fantasies that you used to have.'

Jenny had been touched that George could even remember the nonsense that she'd spouted as a teenager and agreed to meet him the following night.

George wasn't the eager to please boy that she'd first known and he wasn't the acid queen of their early twenties, but some delicious combination of both. He was also a practised New Yorker now with a fancy corner office in an advertising agency in SoHo and a loft apartment on Bleecker Street, which he shared with his boyfriend, Luca, who worked in merchandising at Condé Nast. He was there for practical help like how to open a bank account, get a mobile ('except they call them cellphones, God knows why') and also for moments when she felt unbearably homesick. Despite the fact that it had been so acrimonious the last time they'd seen each other in London, in New York George and Jenny had slipped into an immediate, comfortable familiarity.

Now they shared an eye roll at the thought of Nick at his most obnoxious if he decided they were worthy of his company. Nick was unbearable when he was in work mode, dropping names like they were old receipts and cutting people off mid-sentence to take a phone call.

'Fashion Week? How could we even begin to compare to the charms of some teenage Eastern European model?' Jenny asked.

'We won't,' George said, handing her a menu. 'I sat here so we can have waiter service. Otherwise, there's this whole thing with ordering from different counters that I still haven't been able to figure out. Are you drinking?'

'I am very much drinking,' Jenny muttered darkly.

'Not a successful weekend with your beloved?' George had met Michael a couple of times, which wasn't enough to really gain a deep impression. Though they had reconnected and were fast friends, they hadn't reconnected enough or were fast enough that Jenny was going to unburden about the current state of her relationship. 'They don't serve wine. It's beer or hard soda.'

'I'll have a hard lemonade then. You said special guest. Is Luca joining us?'

George shook his head. 'It's a surprise,' he said with a smile, running a hand through his perfectly on point hair: short back and sides and expensively streaked on top.

George had also introduced Jenny to a level of grooming that she hadn't ever experienced before. She'd declined an appointment with the aesthetician who gave George a little bit of Botox every six months of so, but she did have and now actively enjoyed a mani/pedi every two weeks. She'd even got waxed in anticipation of Michael's visit though he'd raised his eyebrows in some consternation when he'd seen that she was now depilated of 90 per cent of her body hair. And on the days when Jenny had a really important meeting or a lunch, she got up early so she could go to the hair salon opposite the offices and have a big, bouncy blow out – thank God her fringe was currently grown out.

'The higher the hair, the closer to God,' as her assistant, Cindy from Dripping Springs, Texas was fond of saying.

'I'm not sure I like surprises,' Jenny said.

George shrugged. 'Too late,' he said, his eyes sliding past Jenny who had her back to the door. She swivelled round to see a tall, pretty woman in a crisp white summer dress walking towards them, her hand raised in greeting and her glossy dark hair bouncing like Jenny's never did, not even on the days when she had a blowout.

'Is that . . . ? It can't be.' She turned back to George. 'Not cool.'

'It *is* cool. We're all cool now,' he assured her, as the woman reached their table, her megawatt smile dimming a little as she met Jenny's eye. 'Hi babes! You remember Jen.'

'Of course I do.' Priya licked her lips nervously, though Jenny couldn't think what she had to be nervous about. Back in the day, she'd had absolutely no shame. 'Hi Jen, how are you?'

'I'm good,' Jenny said slowly. 'And how are you?'

'Feeling like I should let you give me a slap so we'll be even or something,' she said with a tremulous smile. Then she put her shoulders back. 'Though in my defence, I was seventeen; I wouldn't let myself eat more than five hundred calories a day, but I was still sure that I looked like an absolute moose and my only validation came from having boys fancy me!'

'You didn't look like a moose. You were the most beautiful person I'd ever seen in real life. And you know what? We were teenagers, we were all unhappy and we took it out on each other,' Jen decided in that moment that she was going to let it go. Yes, there had been a time when she'd spent many long hours seething about how Priya had done her wrong. But that was literally half a lifetime ago and she'd barely given Priya a thought for at least a decade, until here she was standing in front of Jenny. 'I think we should hug.'

It had already been established that Priya was still beautiful but she was even more beautiful when she no longer looked like she was expecting Jenny's right fist in her face.

It was a surprisingly sincere hug though Priya still felt fragile and insubstantial, like she might blow away on a stiff breeze or be crushed to death by Jenny's entirely substantial arms. Then Priya sat down next to George, who was looking unbearably smug about the success of his surprise guest, so she could take Jenny's hands in hers.

'God, Jen, you got really, really pretty,' Priya said, gazing at Jenny as if Jenny's face was giving her immense viewing pleasure.

'Oh, stop it!' Jenny waved the words away but secretly she was pleased that Priya had noticed that she was no longer covered in spots, trowelled in foundation, which still didn't cover the green tinge from her complexion corrector stick, and amorphously blob-like. 'And you haven't changed at all! Have you got a portrait stashed away in your attic like Dorian Gray?'

It was true. Like George, Priya had the polish and gloss that came with age, sophistication, a good salary and some of New York's finest aestheticians on speed dial. But she still had the same delicate features and huge doe-like eyes, which looked even more luminous than they had done in the college canteen all those years ago.

'The price of New York real estate means that no one has an attic unless they work for Goldman Sachs,' Priya said.

'So, where do you work?' Jenny asked. 'What are the odds that both you and George ended up in New York?'

They had to apologise to their waiter three times for not being ready to order as Priya caught Jenny up with the last thirteen years of her life.

Post-college, she'd gone to drama school and had even managed to get an agent and a three-episode role in *The Bill* afterwards. Mostly she'd temped and attended auditions up against girls who were prettier than her, or more experienced than her, 'or, let's be honest, less Indian. So, I decided that if I was going to be a temp then I might as well be a temp somewhere exciting and I have an aunt who married a guy who works at one of the big investment banks who sorted me out a visa.'

Now Priya had given up any thought of being an actress and was making six figures as Vice President of Client Relations for a financial services agency. When she wasn't toiling away in the South Tower of the World Trade Center, she was living in recently married bliss on the Upper East Side with Sanjay, a software developer, the nephew of her mother's best friend, who'd been trying to set them up for years.

'All those years of blind dates and answering ads in *Time Out*! I should have given in much earlier and got my mum on the case,' said Priya, as Jenny handed back the photo Priya had pulled out of her Gucci purse of the very handsome Sanjay sunning himself on their Bahamian honeymoon. 'Honestly, Jen, if you ever find yourself single, your parents will be much more useful than the lonely hearts column.'

'Not single,' Jen said, though after this weekend, she no longer felt as if she and Michael were as rock steady as she'd imagined. She started rummaging in her vintage, pink leather purse for the picture of Michael at Kirsty and Erik's wedding earlier in the year. He looked particularly handsome and Captain Von Trappish with a Swedish lake in the background. 'If Jackie and Alan were in charge of my love life, well, it doesn't bear thinking about.'

'They'd definitely pick someone very boring for you,' a voice behind her agreed. Then Nick slid into the booth next to her, so Jenny had to scoot closer to the wall, but even so his thigh brushed against hers. She promptly tucked her purse away because although she was having trouble finding the picture of Michael that she knew was in there somewhere, she knew exactly where the strip of four pictures taken in a photo booth at Mill Hill East station thirteen years ago were. Lurking in the same compartment as her foreign paper money, nestled against francs and guilders and deutschmark notes, though Michael said she should get them all changed before the euro came in. 'Just so you know, I could have been hanging out with models and film stars but I decided to have dinner with you losers instead. Hi, Pri, still gorgeous as ever.'

'Nick, still pretentious as ever,' Priya sniped back, but she was grinning and it set the tone for the rest of the evening.

Nick ordered huge amounts of 'the food of my people', even though George didn't eat carbs anymore and Jenny suspected that Priya still subsisted on not much more than five hundred calories a day as she only picked at the tossed salad that was about the only green thing on the table.

There were two rounds of pastrami on rye and corned beef on rye though it was nothing like the depressing chopped meat in cans that Jenny had always refused to eat when Jackie was making sandwiches to take with them to Southend for a sand-logged picnic. Nick, who'd suddenly become very Jewish and even exclaimed, 'Oy vey!' when Jenny reminded him that she didn't like pickles or mustard or condiments of any description, said that in the UK, his 'fellow Heebs' called it salt beef. Either way, it tasted delicious. So did the potato latkes, even though Jenny would have sworn that she knew every delicious thing you could do with a potato. But she'd never thought of grating one, mixing it up with a little onion and deep-frying it.

It was quite hard to concentrate on eating when the four of them were reminiscing about their glory days. Of those endless free periods doing the rounds of the charity shops and checking out the 60p singles box in Harum Records. And the people they'd known. Jenny snorted hard lemonade out of her nose when Priya did a wicked impersonation of Miguel, who Jenny had sat next to in English, doing one of his patented toneless, emotionless readings from *The Taming of The Shrew*. 'Tranio, I burn, I pine, I perish,' she intoned like she was reading a shopping list.

'Do you remember Linzi and Lucy?' George asked, though it wasn't likely that Jenny would ever forget them.

'I wonder whatever happened to them,' she murmured and George, who was delicately picking his way through a bowl of split pea soup, shot Nick a knowing look.

'I wonder if Lucy ever found out that you shagged Linzi at that birthday party in Hadley Wood?' he mused.

'You shagged Linzi?' Jenny couldn't keep the hurt out of her voice. Her throat throbbed with it.

'Yeah, I know. A bit too close to home,' Nick murmured, making no effort to deny it. And why should he? It had happened thirteen years ago. When she'd secretly loved him with a fervour unlike anything she'd known since.

If Nick had been shagging people he shouldn't, then

would it have killed him to make all of Jenny's teenage dreams come true? Then she thought about the wet-mouthed reality of that first kiss he'd landed on her at Camden Town station and the painful reality of losing her virginity a couple of years later with Bob, the deodorant-eschewing maths student. If that had happened with Nick, then it would have been even more humiliating. Besides, she'd have been relegated to the long list of girls that he'd shagged and they probably wouldn't have been friends then or friends now.

Still, she couldn't help but give him a look. A narrowing of her eyes and a pursing of her lips that let him know that yes, she was angry with him but mostly, she was disappointed.

'You dirty little slut,' she said, which made George clap his hands in glee and Priya clutch the table because she was laughing so hard.

And that was that. Nick ordered dessert, even though George and Priya weren't going to be gobbling down slices of New York cheesecake or babka and Jenny was sure that the seams of her Sixties black and white check cotton shift dress were about to burst.

'So, Jen, how long have you got left in New York?' Priya asked because, after the whole shagging Linzi reveal, it was time to put the conversation on a more neutral footing.

'Another two weeks,' Jenny said though she couldn't imagine being back in London in time for the slide into autumn, leaves crunching under her feet, trying not to put the central heating on until the clocks went back, but always giving in by the end of September. 'Although . . .'

'You got the New York bug.' George nodded his head. 'You either love it or loathe it.'

'I was going to give New York a year and that was five years ago,' Priya added.

'I have been offered a permanent job. Not permanent. I'd only want to stay two, maybe three years,' Jenny said, but it still didn't seem real. Not just because Michael was far from onboard with the idea, but also because she often still felt like the awkward teenager that the three people sitting with her remembered so well.

There were times when her career, her list of authors, her achievements, her sales figures, all seemed like a trick that she'd got away with. Surely, there couldn't be any other editorial directors who had to run cold water over their wrists before important meetings in an effort to calm down and be able to talk without squeaking? Or who felt physically sick when they got involved in a bidding war for a book?

Jenny would not be surprised, in fact she was expecting it, if one day she arrived at work and one of the security guards (not even someone in management) tapped her on the shoulder and said, 'You know you're not meant to be here. Clear out your desk so I can escort you from the building.'

But now there was no tap on her shoulder, just Nick throwing her his own version of the little bit angry but mostly disappointed look. 'Congratulations,' he said flatly. Then he sighed. 'How am I meant to manage without you?'

'You'd manage perfectly fine,' Jenny said, because it wasn't like Nick depended on her for anything. Honey was his significant other, so significant that they were buying a home together. Not even a flat, but a house with lots of bedrooms to put lots of babies in.

At one time, Jenny had suspected that Nick and Honey might be on the outs. Around the time of the New Year's Eve kiss. Not that they ever talked about the kiss. Sometimes, Jenny even wondered if it had really happened or if it was just something she imagined, especially when Michael wasn't around and she was bringing herself off on the memory of Nick pressing her against the hard, unyielding tiled wall of Chalk Farm station, his body just as hard and unyielding as it seemed to touch every inch of her. That delicious combination of guilt and wrong would make her come every time.

'Maybe I should get a job in New York too,' Nick pondered later when they were standing outside the diner and getting ready to say their goodbyes. 'I could, you know. We're launching a US edition of the magazine . . .'

'Then my plan to relocate to New York to get rid of you would all be for nothing,' Jenny said. She clonked him with her heavy bag of leftovers. 'Ruined!'

'So mean.' Nick pouted and put a finger to his face as if he were tracing the track of one lonely tear.

'I can never work out if you want to kill each other or secretly shag each other's brains out.' George tilted his head.

Jenny decided not to dignify that remark with a reply, though she could feel that flame in her belly ignite at the thought of Nick shagging her brains out. It was only because reuniting with old friends had made her remember what it used to be like when she'd first known him. When she'd been so in love with him that just the inconsequential brush of his hand when they walked side by side was enough to keep her going for weeks. It had nothing to do with the quite perfunctory sex she'd had with Michael the night before; more of a maintenance shag than the throes of passion.

Also, it might just be indigestion.

It was Nick's turn to tilt his head and consider Jenny as she stood in front of him. 'Probably a bit of both, wouldn't you say, Jen?'

'No, I wouldn't say.' She turned to hide the sudden blush.

'The trouble with you two is that you could never get your timing right,' George murmured, not in his usual teasing way but in a more serious tone. 'You can never manage to be in love with each other at the same time.'

'Not love. It was a teenage crush.' If she said it firmly enough, then it was true. She couldn't bring herself to look at Nick.

'And now we're in love with other people,' he said lightly, unable to look at her too. 'So that ship has long sailed, right, Jen?'

'It's sailed all around the world and has now been broken down for scrap.'

'So, you never even got off with each other when we were at college?' Priya wanted to know, because the pair of them were fucking relentless.

'Stop it!' Jenny said. 'The only man I wanted to get off with was Morrissey and Nick, by the sound of things, was too busy shagging most of the girls in North London *and* Hertfordshire.'

'No wonder you did so badly in your A levels, Nick.' Priya grinned as she rummaged in her purse and pulled out a business card, which she handed to Jen. 'If you are only here for another two weeks, I'd love to see you again.'

'I'd love that too,' Jenny said, and she really meant it.

'You should come and meet me from work so you can see the view from our offices. We're on the seventy-eighth floor.' Priya spread her hands wide. 'Then we can go to Century 21 across the street to look for half-price Marc Jacobs.'

'Talking of which, I'm off to the New York Fashion Week launch party,' Nick said, pulling out a crumpled white A5 card from the pocket of his jeans, which he was wearing with a Bettie Page T-shirt and dinner jacket. 'Anyone fancy it?'

'Not on a school night,' Jenny said, though she would never ever fancy going anywhere that was wall to wall models.

'Some of us have to be at our desk by eight,' George added.

'Seven-thirty,' Priya countered.

They said goodbye in a flurry of hugs and kisses. George and Priya leaving to catch the subway uptown, Jenny consulting her map to plan her walk back to the West Village.

'I'm only here for a couple of days,' Nick remarked casually when it was just the two of them. 'I'm staying at the Pantheon House.'

'Fancy.' The Pantheon House overlooking Central Park was proper old school New York elegance.

'I'm a very fancy boy.' Nick stepped closer to Jenny as she frowned down at her map then folded it up.

'Actually, what you are is a dick,' she said, because she was still reeling from the news that he'd shagged Linzi back in the day.

'I know I am,' Nick agreed, still not making any move to go on his merry way to mingle with models. 'Shall I walk with you for a bit? I need a cigarette. Oh my God, what is *that* and why isn't it in a museum?'

Jenny looked down at the object in her hand that had met with Nick's derision.

'It's my old Walkman,' she said, holding it out for Nick's closer inspection. It wasn't actually a Sony Walkman but a generic portable cassette player from Curry's, which she'd dug out before she'd come to New York. 'I didn't want to cart a whole load of CDs with me and actually, I've been listening to a lot of my old tapes. Remember this one?'

She opened the cassette player and gingerly prised out the tape so Nick could see that she still had the tape he'd made her years and years ago with Lou Reed's *Coney Island Baby* on one side and *Street Hassle* on the other.

'I haven't listened to either of them for years,' Nick said, falling into step with Jenny as they turned left onto East First Street.

'Lou Reed is my New York soundtrack. Well, him, Patti Smith and a bit of Stephen Sondheim.'

Nick nudged Jenny slyly with his elbow. 'You always did love a showtune.'

'That's between me and my God.' Nick had once heard her singing 'I Could Have Danced All Night' from *My Fair Lady* while she'd been having a shower at his old flat in Camden Town and had teased her about it for weeks.

'Your secret's safe with me.'

Nick was the keeper of so many of Jenny's secrets.

She glanced at him, his face in profile, skin garish from the reflected neon lights of a pharmacy they were passing, cheeks hollowed as he took a drag of his cigarette. 'Do you miss writing about music, Nick?'

It was his turn to glance at her with a smile tinged with regret. 'Every day. But all those music magazines have folded. All the ones I used to write for anyway. I'm like the Typhoid Mary of magazines.'

'Hardly. You're now the editor of a very well-respected, well-read Sunday supplement.' She wasn't one to massage Nick's ego; it was one of the healthiest things about him, but his swagger was temporarily absent and now that it was just the two of them and he didn't have to pretend anymore, he seemed dejected. 'Youngest editor in its history, apparently.'

'So they say.' Nick took Jenny's elbow as they crossed over a side street, his fingers cool on her bare skin. Then he let her go. 'I don't do any writing anymore, Jen. It's all putting out fires and budget meetings. I'm not even going to schmooze models at the Fashion Week launch party, I'm there to schmooze advertisers.'

He sounded so sorrowful that Jenny wanted to laugh, but instead she said something soothing, chimed in with her own bitter disappointment at how many finance meetings she had to attend, and by now they were at Hudson Street.

'You should get a cab from here,' Jenny said and Nick nodded and stuck out his hand.

It would have taken ages to find a black cab with its light on in old London town on a Sunday night but here it took less than a New York minute before a yellow cab was bearing down on them.

'I reckon you're allowed to schmooze at least one model,' Jenny said teasingly, but Nick didn't smile back.

'I miss us,' he said, stepping back onto the kerb so the cab could come to a halt alongside them. 'I miss being a teenager and how I got to spend hours hanging out with the person I liked the best. Hours, Jen, when we just listened to music and talked and talked.'

It was these words, these sweet words, which pierced Jenny's heart so something warm and comforting oozed into her bloodstream. All those precious hours when they'd bunked off afternoon classes and gone back to Nick's to listen to whatever album had come out that week; that was real. Not something that either of them could ever replicate with someone else, somewhere else. It had been them and then, but still she said, 'You get to spend hours hanging out with Honey.'

'It's not the same thing. There's a lot more chat about interest only mortgages and whose turn it is to take the bins out.'

Michael always took the bins out. It was one of the reasons why Jenny loved him. 'I'll see you when I get back to London,' Jenny said, because she didn't like where this conversation had ended up. Or maybe she liked it too much.

'*If* you get back.' Nick climbed into the back of the car. 'Don't stay away too long, Jen. I'd be fucking miserable without you.'

Then he slammed the door shut, the car easing into the traffic before Jen could muster a suitable reply.

23

Tuesday, September 11th
Cortland Street – World Trade Center Station

On the Monday night it had stormed and thundered like the city's heart was breaking. But on Tuesday morning when Jenny stepped out of her apartment building onto Horatio Street, the sky was impossibly blue and the sun was glinting off the Hudson River as she began the forty-five minute walk to her office on West Broadway.

If she could bear to get up half an hour earlier and slip on her trainers a la Melanie Griffiths in *Working Girl*, or rather her trusty Dunlop Green Flashes, she preferred to walk to work rather than cramming into a hot, crowded subway car, usually rammed up against someone's armpit, someone who eschewed the need for antiperspirant. Whether Jenny was in New York or London, *plus ça change, plus c'est la même chose*.

But she was very definitely in New York, carrying her blue take-out cup of coffee from the deli on her block, though she found it almost impossible to walk and drink at the same time. Jenny worked her way through Lower Manhattan, keeping the river in her sightline until it was time to turn into Chambers Street, then Broadway and her office, which was in a sixty-storey skyscraper a couple of blocks away from City Hall Park. Sixty storeys was nothing in New York, but Jenny still felt her stomach lurch as the elevator ascended with a whoosh. She stepped out onto the fifty-seventh floor where her colleagues were hunched like hamsters in their little cubicles.

People were just not meant to go about their business hundreds and hundreds of metres up in the sky, Jenny thought, not for the first time, as she made her way to her office. She didn't merit a window to the outside world but gazed out at more and more cubicles, more and more hamsters.

Jenny logged into her computer at exactly 8.30, and opened her email programme. She always started the day with a quick email to Jackie. They did try to speak on the phone once a week or so but only a minute would pass before Jackie would exclaim in horror, 'Christ, this must be costing a fortune. I'll let you go, Jenny. Love you!'

Now, Jenny filled her in on their favourite topic, the weather. 'It thundered so hard last night that at one stage I thought a bomb had gone off . . .'

As soon as she typed those words, there was a loud bang outside. It sounded like a sonic boom. Jenny could have sworn she felt the building shake, but this was New York. It was always something. She turned back to her screen, to memories of her near sleepless night.

'Thankfully, it's all clear today – a beautiful, sunny morning. I wish I didn't have a business lunch because I'd love to get a sandwich and sit in the park.

'Anyway, not much else to report but let's talk tomorrow? I'll call you around your lunchtime.

'Must go or I'll be late for the Monday morning mee—

'I'm coming, Cindy,' Jenny said to her assistant, without looking up from her computer. Cindy could always be relied upon to appear at Jenny's open door five minutes before any meeting that required Jenny's presence, wafting the scent of CK One and hairspray Jenny's way. 'Hang on! I still have my trainers on.'

That was Cindy's cue to say, 'You mean sneakers. You've gotta talk American,' in her slow soft, Texan drawl, but this morning she didn't. She coughed, spluttered really, and when Jenny looked up it was to see that the younger woman was crying hard enough that a sooty stream of tears cascaded down her face.

Jenny was on her feet in an instant. 'What's the matter? What's happened?'

Cindy shook her head, hands flapping in front of her face in an effort to stave off the tears. 'A plane,' she sobbed. 'A plane's flown into the World Trade Center.'

'What are you talking about?'

Cindy didn't answer but left Jenny's office, cannoning off the doorframe in the process. Jenny took off in pursuit, following Cindy to the boardroom where their meeting should have been about to start except it was full of people, eyes wide, hands to mouths, as they gazed at the TV screen, and beyond the TV screen to the skyline outside the huge floor-to-ceiling windows. The familiar sight of the Twin Towers, silhouetted against the beautiful blue sky, the sun reflected off the glass. But that was where normality ended because there was a huge hole in the side of one of the towers, smoke billowing from it to join the cumulus clouds of ash and debris, which wreathed the top of the building.

'It's eight fifty two a.m. and we have a report, so far unconfirmed, that a plane has hit the World Trade Center. There is limited information at this time.'

Everyone was talking. Exclamations and variations of 'Oh my God,' and 'I can't believe it!' When Jenny asked, 'Which tower is it? My friend works in the South Tower,' her voice seemed deafeningly loud, yet no one answered. Cindy was shaking with the force of her sobs; she wasn't the only one crying. The MD, Gerry, a man of few words, most of them caustic, was ashen, one hand clutching the edge of the table.

Jenny tried to remember what floor Priya said she worked on. How many floors were there? Too many. God, they were just standing here and watching as a few blocks away in that tower, people were trapped, injured, *dead*.

She turned away and in that moment there was an almighty BOOM! so loud, so hard, that the windows, the view, warped. The noise of that bang reverberated around the room, the floor shook under her feet and without even being aware of what she was doing, Jenny was suddenly on her knees under the table, hands over her head, but still able to hear the panicked voices coming from the television.

'Oh my God, another plane has just hit the other building! It flew right into the middle of it.'

'Oh my God!'

'Oh my God!'

'That's a second plane. It's just exploded.'

'Oh my goodness! Oh my goodness! There's another one!'

'This seems to be on purpose.'

'This has to be a terrorist act.'

Jenny curled herself into a little ball, braced for impact, braced for she didn't even know what until someone reached under the table and grabbed her arm.

It was Graham, one of the desk editors who sat outside her office. A man who wore shirt, tie and sleeveless pullovers even on the hottest days. He was wearing one now. 'We have to evacuate the building,' he said, pulling Jenny up when she crawled out from under the table.

'My bag, my stuff . . .'

'Out! Everybody out!' Marcus the facilities manager, never seen without a huge bunch of keys and a screwdriver, appeared in the doorway. 'Take the emergency stairs. You need to leave the building NOW, people.'

'But my bag . . .' Jenny realised that she didn't even care about her bag, about any of it, other than getting out of the building as fast as possible. Being on the ground, not with floors and floors of glass and steel in the way.

It was safer on the ground.

She let herself be herded through the fire door and into the stairwell where there was already a mass exodus from the upper floors hurrying down the concrete stairs.

'I'm so scared, Jennifer,' said Cindy, who was still hiccupping and crying, her pretty face a mess of tears and streaked make-up. Jenny had told her not to call her Jennifer a hundred times. 'What if a plane flies into us?'

'It's not going to happen,' Jenny said firmly, though she'd been thinking the exact same thing. She took Cindy's clammy hand in her own. 'We're going to walk down the stairs and soon we'll be outside. Everything is going to be fine.'

As they made their slow way down the stairs, resisting the urge to panic and run, Jenny could hear her own voice reassuring Cindy. 'Everything is fine. You're OK. We're going to be OK.'

By the fortieth floor, Jenny didn't think they'd ever reach street level.

The thirtieth floor, the back of her cotton dress was drenched in sweat, her fingers slipping against Cindy's.

The twentieth floor, she felt as if she couldn't take another step but the press of people behind her carried Jenny on.

Then the tenth floor, legs wanting to buckle, but, 'We're nearly there, Cindy. I said we'd be fine and we are.'

The fifth floor and Jenny imagined that she could already see daylight, smell that peculiar New York street smell: flat, sulphurous like rotten eggs, which always made her long for exhaust fumes and the iron scent of London.

Fourth floor.

Third floor.

Second floor. Jenny had forgotten that in this topsy-turvy world where planes flew into buildings the first floor was the ground floor.

'We've made it, Cindy,' Jenny said, and she dropped her assistant's hand so she could stumble down the last two flights of stairs and plunge into freedom, daylight, away from a building that could suddenly turn into a fireball, a coffin, when you least expected it.

The surge of people that followed her outside pushed Jenny across the street and she began to choke on the air, thick with smoke and ash. The noise was deafening: the shriek of emergency vehicles, sirens wailing, people crying. So many people, standing and staring and pointing.

Jenny couldn't look. Wouldn't look. But then, she turned and saw those terrible towers, much nearer than they'd seemed before. Their tips were almost shrouded in smoke and she could see . . . she couldn't quite believe what she was seeing.

There were people jumping from the upper storeys. They seemed to hover gently in the air, like swallows, before gathering speed to plummet down below.

Jenny didn't know how long she stood there, frozen in place, but the smoke intensified, until she couldn't see the people jumping anymore, everything was engulfed in the pillowy clouds of ash and soot and dust. All Jenny could do was stay rooted to the spot, a hand to her mouth, as she watched the building gracefully concertina and collapse in on itself, the smoke puffing out, coming closer . . .

'Holy shit! Run!'

Someone took her arm, pulled her along, and Jenny began to run, to outpace the dust cloud that was racing towards her like some kind of mythical monster; she could feel the heat and the force of it at her heels. She kept running, still being dragged along, as it rained down on her, choking her, coating the back of her throat, her teeth, her tongue. Ash and soot and God knows what else in her hair, sticking to her skin, under her nails so that Jenny knew that it was in her blood, that she'd never be free of it, and still she kept running.

Eventually, with her lungs about to burst because she couldn't force air into them, Jenny slowed down then stopped. The man who'd been pulling her along, he was a young kid really, couldn't have been more than eighteen, nineteen, though it was hard to tell when he too was covered in the same thick grey dust, also stopped.

Jenny looked behind her again. The long city streets stretching further than the eye could see had disappeared from view to be replaced by thick dust and fallen masonry, thousands upon thousands of pieces of paper floating in the air like confetti.

'You saved me,' she said, but could hardly get the words out of her mouth. 'Thank you. Thank you.'

'I can't believe this shit,' he said, shaking his head at the devastation they'd left in their wake. He was slight, not much taller than Jenny, but wiry, though his strength had felt superhuman when he'd been pulling her along block after block. 'Just can't believe it. Fuck!'

They both leaned against the nearest building, a bank, which was solid enough that it probably wouldn't fold in on itself. Jenny put her hands on her knees and tried to get her breath back. Her companion/saviour spat out a mouthful of black phlegm.

Then he straightened. 'I gotta go,' he said and was gone. Running in the opposite direction from where they'd come, a hand raised in salute.

Jenny stayed where she was for a couple more minutes. Her thoughts were choppy and uneven. She thought about Cindy. About her handbag which she'd left in her office. Whether their office building was still standing. Then she thought about Priya; beautiful, redeemed Priya with her handsome, loving husband and her high-paying corporate job, which meant that she had to be at her job on the 78th floor of the South Tower by 7.30 a.m. Maybe, maybe, maybe she'd made it out.

There was a rumble behind her; the dust was still too thick to see anything, but the ground beneath her feet began to tremble and Jenny began to run again as a mile away, the North Tower crashed to the ground.

24

Tuesday, September 11th, 2001
59th Street – Columbus Circle Station

Jenny couldn't tell how long she'd been running. Or when she'd stopped running and started walking, though she didn't have a clue where she was going. What she really wanted was to go home. Not to the little apartment on Horatio Street. Nor the converted warehouse overlooking Regent's Canal that she shared with Michael.

When she really thought about it, her mind focussed on one sharp point of clarity, home was the tiny little box bedroom in Mill Hill with the green and yellow floral-sprigged wallpaper and the narrow single bed, where she'd spent her formative years. She wished that she were there now, aged sixteen and listening to The Smiths and writing bad poetry. Nick lounging on the bed, while she perched on the end, her elbows resting on the windowsill, the door open and Jackie's tread on the stairs as she brought them up Ribena and biscuits, but really to check that there wasn't any funny business going on. Which there never ever had been. Not even once.

That was home; thousands of miles away and fifteen years in the past and no matter how much she wished for it, Jenny couldn't find her way back there. So, she kept on walking up Broadway, heading north. Passing cross street after cross street. Not aware of the people staring at her, asking if she were all right, not even the woman who tried to give her a bottle of water.

Jenny knew that if she carried on walking along Broadway then sooner or later she'd come to Central Park. Later rather than sooner, it turned out. She could see treetops in the distance and that brilliant blue sky; people were waiting in line to get lunch, sitting at tables arranged outside restaurants, like this was a normal day.

The trees got nearer and nearer until they were just across the street and Jenny thought that she might need to walk around the park, however long that might take her, but as she turned the first corner onto Central Park South, there it was.

Pantheon House.

A tall art deco building like a white wedding cake.

The closest thing there was to home.

Jenny sidestepped the uniformed doorman, who said something to her punctuated by a concerned 'Ma'am?' and pulled open the heavy glass door all by herself.

Her feet, which were hot and sore after fifty-seven flights of stairs and pounding sidewalks for over two hours, glided over a terrazzo marble floor towards a gleaming mahogany reception desk, manned by a man and a woman, both dressed in black, sleek-haired, their polished faces and practised smiles dropping as Jenny approached.

'Nick,' she said in a voice that wouldn't work properly. She could taste the dust, like she'd gone to sleep with her mouth open and not woken up for a hundred years. She couldn't even remember Nick's surname, though somehow she'd managed to walk halfway across Manhattan to his hotel. 'Nick from London.'

Then, because her legs were shaking so hard that she didn't think they'd hold her up for much longer, Jenny leaned her elbows on the desk and slumped forward to rest her head on her hands.

'Ma'am, are you all right?'

'I need Nick,' Jenny mumbled. 'Could you find him, please?'

She didn't know how long she stayed there using the reception desk as a pillow, but eventually, she heard a familiar voice.

'Jen, there you are! Jesus!' He sounded like he'd been looking for her everywhere and not the other way round. 'Oh, Jen . . .'

Then there was a hand on her shoulder, lifting her off the desk, turning her round so she could see Nick's familiar face, which was so crumpled and concerned that it hardly looked like him.

'Hold me,' Jenny said and then she didn't have to look at him anymore because she was in Nick's arms, her head tucked under his chin.

For the first time since Cindy had appeared in her office doorway there was no longer panic rising up in her like bile. Her mind, all the voices in her head, the thoughts each one worse than the last, quietened.

Nick swayed slightly, so he could rock her back and forth. 'You're all right now. I've got you,' he murmured along with other similar sentiments until, still with his arms around her, he stepped back a little.

'Are you hurt?' he asked.

'I don't think so.' Jenny frowned. Her feet, her legs were sore, chafed. Her shoulders and back ached. Her head was pounding. 'I mean, everything hurts.' But none of that was important. 'The whole building it . . . it disintegrated. It was there and then it wasn't. Then the other one came down. It just fell down. Buildings shouldn't just fall down.'

Her voice was so hoarse and scratchy that she could hardly understand her own words but Nick nodded, his eyes never leaving her face.

'But you're all right, that's the important thing,' he said, his arms tightening around her again. 'You're here. I'll take care of you.'

'I was meant to have a lunch today,' Jenny suddenly remembered. 'With a literary agent. I need to cancel but I don't have my diary. I don't have . . . My bag, it's in my office.'

'The lunch is cancelled,' Nick said firmly, steering her towards the lifts and their elegant, engraved gold doors. 'Everything's cancelled today.'

The lift doors opened as soon as Nick pressed the button and Jenny stepped into the elevator. She gasped as the doors shut and she could see herself reflected in the mirrored walls.

Every inch of her was covered in a thick layer of sludgy grey grime. Not dust, which would brush away with a flick of her hand, something dirtier and harder than dust. Her eyes and hair were wild – she didn't recognise herself in the person staring back at her.

'It will wash off,' Nick said and he was staring at her reflection too. His jeans and black T-shirt were filthy too from where she'd been pressed against him.

Jenny gazed down at the dress she'd put on that morning. It had once been white with green geometric shapes scattered over it. 'I don't think it will.'

'It will.' Nick repeated, put his hand on her waist, almost as if he knew that Jenny's legs wanted to give way. When the lift stopped at the fifteenth floor, he put his other hand on her arm and shuffled her out of the lift and down a panelled corridor of gleaming wood and plush carpet until they came to his room right at the end.

'Got a park view suite. I mean, that's when you know that you've truly made it.' Nick reached around her to slide his key card in the lock. He said it without any of his usual bravado but more as if he didn't know what to say and when they were in his park view suite, he stared helplessly at Jenny who stared just as helplessly back at him.

'What do you need?' he asked.

'I don't know.' She gestured at herself with the smallest of hand movements. 'I don't want to make a mess and ruin everything.'

Nick nodded. 'You should have a shower. Wash your hair. Bathroom is on the right and if you leave the door ajar . . . In case, you . . . I'm just out here, if you need me.'

The bathroom involved more mirrors. Too many mirrors. And a shower that might just as well have been the control desk at NASA with all its buttons and knobs.

'I can't do this,' Jenny called out, sitting down heavily on the edge of the tub, the hard rolltop rim digging into her thighs. 'Can you help me?'

Nick turned on the shower and then he knelt down and tugged off Jenny's trainers and socks because he was a brave man, who didn't even flinch when her feet were exposed. They were as red and raw as slabs of meat in a butcher's window.

Nick pulled Jenny up, turned her round and unzipped her dress and, with the most clinical yet expert of touches, unclipped her bra. Then he gently pushed her in the direction of the shower cubicle where the water was beating down like a tropical rainstorm.

'You can do the rest,' he said unsteadily, giving Jenny another little push. 'Shower gel and shampoo and whatnot are already in there.'

Jenny walked into the shower in her clothes and let the water beat down on her, eyes closed so she wouldn't have to see the water turn black before it circled the drain. When she finally peeled her eyes open, the water was running clear and she struggled out of her sodden dress and underwear, almost toppling over as she kicked them to the other side of the cubicle.

It took three separate applications of shampoo and a whole bottle of shower gel before Jenny felt clean. Then swathed in a fluffy hotel robe and with her hair wrapped up in a towel, she padded back into the room.

Nick was sitting on one of the three sofas in the room staring out at the park views from the double aspect windows. Jenny was glad that they were only fifteen floors up; it still felt too high.

'I'm not going back,' she said. Nick turned at the sound of her voice. 'Even if the office is still there, I can't be fifty-seven storeys above the ground. And what if it's not there? My bag. It's got my passport in it. My purse. It's why I walked. I've no money, but then I didn't even think to get the subway. Is the subway running? All I could do was keep walking. Also, very sorry about this, but I had to use your toothbrush. Do you think I'm in shock?'

Nick didn't even have to think about it. 'Yes. Come here. Come and sit down.' He patted the sofa and waited until Jenny collapsed on the seat next to him. He took her hand. 'You wouldn't have been able to get on the subway even if you had your purse. The entire network has shut down. My cellphone isn't working. Planes aren't flying.'

At the mention of the word 'plane' Jenny shuddered. 'I heard a bang when the first plane hit the tower but I didn't know what it was. I was writing an email, thinking about the Monday morning meeting. Then the second plane, we were in the boardroom by then, seeing it on the telly at the same time as we watched it happen outside the window . . .'

She talked hoarsely and without stopping because it suddenly seemed very important to document exactly what she'd experienced that day and by the time she got to the part when Nick had entered stage right, her voice was croaking and cracking.

'I'll get you some water.' Nick tried to prise Jenny's fingers from their vice-like grip on his hand. 'Though sweet tea is meant to be good for shock.'

'Just because I'm in shock doesn't mean that you can trick me into drinking tea,' Jenny said. That felt more like her. Nick grinned, which was more like him. 'Though I am freezing and look!'

She held up the hand that he was no longer holding so he could see it shaking. 'Brandy's good for shock?' he suggested.

'I don't like brandy either.'

'Brandy with full-fat Coke or hot, sugary tea, it's your choice.' Nick peered at a control panel on the wall by a desk, which was covered with stiff white envelopes. 'I have no idea how to turn down the air conditioning. I'll get you a blanket.'

He disappeared through a door into what had to be the bedroom because he reappeared with a waffle-knit blanket the colour of milky coffee, which he proceeded to tuck around Jenny, like she was his geriatric maiden aunt. She felt like she should protest, but it was easier to curl her legs up underneath her and burrow into the thick folds.

'Thank you. I'm sorry, Nick, for all this fuss . . .'

'Stop it!' He held his hand up. While she was in the shower, he'd changed into an old Pixies T-shirt that she hadn't seen in years. It was faded now but still like coming face to face with an old friend. 'I'm glad you're here. I was worried about you. I knew your office was close . . .'

'Priya.' Jenny said her name like a sigh.

Nick swallowed hard. 'I know.'

Thinking about Priya made Jenny want to cry but her eyes were dry and she couldn't force out even a single tear though she was sure that over the course of the morning (was it only one morning?) her heart had shattered several times and been hastily patched back together.

Nick opened the mini bar under the desk and pulled out a can of Coke and a miniature of brandy.

'In separate glasses, please,' Jenny said because she wasn't going to have her Coke ruined by the addition of brandy. He hissed in annoyance, which was familiar and comforting.

'You are *such* a princess.' He put down the brandy and the Coke then made a big deal of huffing and puffing as he fetched two glasses and placed them on the coffee table in front of her with exaggerated care. 'Now, are you going to eat something?'

Jenny shook her head. 'I couldn't.'

'Something plain?' Nick suggested, though he wasn't usually so indulgent of Jenny being 'a fucking fussy pain in the arse'. 'Some toast?'

The thought of food made Jenny's stomach roil and she burrowed deeper into her blanket den. 'No food. Not yet.' Another random thought popped into her head. 'All those leftovers from last night. Should I go back to my apartment?' She glanced over at the desk, which Nick was perched on as he sifted through a clutch of stiff white envelopes. 'Don't you have a fashion show to be at or a celebrity to interview? I'm taking up so much of your time. I'm sorry, but I didn't really know where else to go.'

'You already said that and I already said that you were right to come here,' he said. 'And the fashion shows are cancelled, the parties are cancelled, the schmoozing is cancelled. All the celebrities are staying in LA because there are no planes. It's a total shutdown.'

Jenny nodded. Then she stuck one cold hand out of the blanket to reach for the miniature of brandy but she was still shaking too much to be able to unscrew the top, let alone pour some in a glass.

'I'll do it.' He stood over her, poured the brandy into one of the glasses and paused. 'Do you want ice?'

Normally Jenny would have wanted ice but she was cold enough already. 'I'm good, thanks.' She tried to take the glass from him but he held on.

'You have to come out of your blanket fort so I can see the way you screw up your face when you take a sip of brandy,' he said. 'I really could do with something to make me smile.'

Jenny stuck her head out of the blanket but couldn't even summon up a glare. Not even a narrowing of her eyes. But when she did finally take a sip of brandy she couldn't hide her displeasure as the neat spirit made contact with her taste buds. It was harsh and astringent, no matter that people always said it was mellow, and it burned all the way down. As far as Jenny could tell it did absolutely nothing for her shock.

Nick sat at the other end of the sofa from her, his body turned towards her, his eyes on her face as she gulped down the Coke to get rid of the taste of the brandy. 'You know, George was nearer.'

Jenny hadn't even thought about George or that she'd have been within a couple of blocks of his office as she passed through SoHo. 'You were the closest thing to home,' she said, though usually she wouldn't have been so unguarded in front of him. Not since that New Year's Eve kiss. 'Home home. Mill Hill. My little bedroom.'

'Some of my happiest hours were spent in your little bedroom.' Nick leaned his head back and smiled. 'Jackie popping in every now and again to make sure I wasn't ravishing you.'

'Chance would be a fine thing,' Jenny said, which, again, was far, far too unguarded even for these extenuating, exceptional circumstances on this weird, horrible day. 'I could go home. Back to the West Village, I mean. Should be able to get a cab. If you lend me say thirty dollars, I'll pay you back.'

'Don't be a twat, Jen,' Nick said gently. 'Of course you're staying here. It works both ways. You're the closest thing to home that I have right now.'

It was then that she got it; the enormity of it. That Nick might not have been there, close enough to see the Towers unfold and crash down in front of his eyes, to coat him in its deadly dust but after today, everyone and everything was changed.

They were silent after that. Two people bound together by all the years they'd known each other, all the good and bad they'd put each other through, but also quite separate. Both lost in their own little worlds.

25

Tuesday, September 11th, 2001
59th Street – Columbus Circle Station

Jenny must have fallen asleep because she woke up to find the skies outside the windows were streaked pink. Nick had gone but left a note on the coffee table.

> *Popped out for a little while.*
> *You should call your Mum and Michael.*
> *Order anything you want from room service. N x*

She called Michael first. He answered the phone on the first ring and said her name like it was a prayer.

'Yes, it's me.'

'Well, thank God for that. Are you all right?'

'I'm fine.'

'That's what you always say even when you're not fine. Especially when you're not fine,' Michael pointed out, not that Jenny needed reminding of the many times she'd spat out, 'I'm *fine*,' when they'd just had words.

'Well, I'm alive and really happy about that.' Her voice broke. 'It was just . . . unreal but too real. It's hard to explain.'

There was no point in going into the horrific details over the phone and now that they'd established that she was alive, that she was fine, there didn't seem much else to say.

'So, I'll see you when you get back,' Michael said heavily

and Jenny was sure that she was being over-sensitive; she currently felt like a raw nerve, but it seemed to her ears as if Michael was treating her return as if it was something vaguely troublesome, like a dental appointment or a complicated form to fill in. 'You are coming back?'

'Yes, I'm absolutely coming back. I'm not taking that job.' Jenny didn't even have to think about it. The decision had been made for her the moment the first plane has flown into the first tower. 'If I could, I'd be on a plane tonight.'

'I wish you were.' Michael no longer sounded as if Jenny was an unpleasant task. 'I wish I was there to wrap my arms round you.'

'I wish that too,' Jenny said, because of course she did. She loved Michael. He was a source of immense comfort and joy even if they didn't know whether they wanted the same things anymore. 'But when I do come back, I'm not ready for kids or living in the countryside. I might never be ready for that.'

'Why are you talking about this now?' Jenny couldn't blame him for his incredulity. 'None of that is important right now. The important thing is that you're all right, though it sounds like you're in shock. Where are you anyway? At your apartment? Is it safe?'

Physically Jenny was in shock. Still freezing cold and the hand that was gripping the phone couldn't stop trembling but her mind felt as clear as glass, as she told Michael that she was staying with a friend because 'I really don't want to be alone.' Which was true. Not a word of it was a lie, but she knew there was no good reason not to mention that the friend was Nick. Knew it, but still didn't feel inclined to share that information with Michael.

She rang off with assurances that they'd talk tomorrow 'when you're feeling more like yourself'. Then, with squinched-up face, Jenny drained what was left of the brandy and called her mother.

The phone was snatched up halfway through its first ring and answered with a tearful, tremulous, 'Yes?'

She was still on the phone to Jackie half an hour later, Jackie still tearful, when Jenny heard the click of the keycard then Nick was there in the doorway. He didn't take a step forward until Jenny beckoned him in.

'Look, Mum, I'd better go . . .'

It was another five minutes before Jenny could put the phone down because every time she tried, Jackie would say, 'Yes, I won't keep you . . .' and then launch into another barrage of questions and declarations of maternal love.

Nick had gone into the bedroom to give her some privacy but he emerged once Jenny was finally off the phone. He was holding a large bag from Gap and a black zipped pouch, which he put down on the coffee table.

'From the hotel,' he said, sitting down next to her and stretching out his long legs. 'Toiletries and stuff. They have them for when people lose their luggage.'

'I hope there's a toothbrush in there because I owe you one,' Jenny said and even a gesture of goodwill from a major hotel chain made her eyes smart. She wondered what would be the small act of kindness that would finally break her today and make her cry.

'I got you some clothes,' he said uncertainly when usually Nick's certainty could always be relied upon. 'The dress you left in the bathroom; you can't wear that again, Jen. You wouldn't want to.'

It was true. No amount of scrubbing could get the stains out and there was a rip right across the bodice, though Jenny had no memory of how it had got torn.

'Thank you. I'll settle up with you when I can get . . .'

'Honestly, any more talk about owing me or paying me

back and I will smack you,' Nick said, tipping his head back so he could pinch his nose.

'I'd like to see you try,' Jenny muttered. She stood up on unsteady feet. The room swam about her. She blinked and everything came back into focus.

'Are you all right?' Nick checked himself. 'Of course, you're not all right but are you more all right than you were before?'

'I think so. But I really need another drink. A proper drink. With alcohol.' Jenny was all right, that had already been established, but she felt so spiky, so scratched, that she needed something to numb the pain a little.

'You're not having any more alcohol until you eat something . . . what the fuck are you doing?' Nick reared back in alarm as Jenny placed her hand on his forehead.

'I thought you must be ill. All this being sensible, it's completely out of character.' His forehead *was* hot to the touch, though not hot enough for him to be running a fever. Jenny stroked Nick's hair back from his face in a way that she would never have dared to do at any other time during their long history and Nick let her until his fingers looped around her wrist and pulled her hand away.

'I think one of us needs to be sensible,' he said, his eyes dark as they fixed on her. 'Now, what shall I order from room service?'

The thought of eating. Chewing. Swallowing. It was exhausting. 'All I really want is toast and butter,' Jenny said, which would surely be enough ballast if she wanted a proper drink. 'But I'm only going to eat something if *you* call *your* mum.'

Instantly Nick dropped his gaze. 'I don't think she'll even remember that I was meant to be in New York.'

'Yes, she will. Call her.' He was still holding her by the wrist, but Jenny tugged herself free so she could fold her arms and glare at him. This, Nick being an arse and Jenny having to call him on it, was also just like old times. 'I'm going to change while you call Susan. Then we'll order some toast and proper drinks. OK?'

Jenny went into the bathroom to give Nick some privacy and investigated the bag of clothes he'd bought. A couple of black T-shirts and leggings. A denim shirtdress. He'd also obviously checked the size of the ruined clothing that had now disappeared because he'd even got her a couple of black bras and a multipack of black knickers, a little skimpier than she'd normally wear. It was disturbing to think about Nick making his selections and thinking about what underwear she might like. What she'd look like wearing them.

Then Jenny was disturbed to realise that actually it wasn't *that* disturbing. Ever since that New Year's Eve, despite the not talking about it and the stalwart pretending it had never happened, there'd been something different between them. A simmering flirtation, which was better suited to their teen years rather than two people in their early thirties.

By the time Jenny emerged from the bathroom in black T-shirt and leggings, trailing the towelling robe because she was still cold, Nick was *still* on the phone to Susan.

'I have to go ...' he said, rolling his eyes at Jenny as it was clear that, much like her own mother, Susan was physically incapable of understanding and acting on the words. 'I have to go.'

Not wanting to intrude or seem like she was earwigging, Jenny sat down at the desk and leafed through the hotel information pack on 'things to do and see during your stay in the Big Apple' to a soundtrack of 'Yeah, but I really do have to go now, Mum ...'

She was wondering how much longer she'd have to stay in New York; if it would be possible to get a flight home before her final two weeks were up on the job swap and if, during that time, she'd want to spend hours 'exploring historic Harlem', when Nick hung up the phone with a beleaguered sigh.

'If I wasn't already emotionally drained then I am now,' he said stretching his arms above his head so he could knit his fingers together and groan.

'She must have been relieved to hear from you though.' Nick wouldn't concede that point but asked her to find the room service menu, which was buried under his fashion show invitations on the desk.

Nick was absolutely unyielding on the topic of dinner and how toast and butter 'was a side, maybe a starter at best. You have to eat something more substantial than that.'

Despite a lot of spirited backchat, he ordered a plethora of the plainest items on the menu for Jenny, a tomato and cheese pizza, chicken Milanese, a burger without any garnishes, trimmings or sauces and said he'd mop up whatever she didn't finish.

Jenny had one slice of pizza before declaring it too soggy then made a sandwich out of the toast and some fries, which she argued constituted a main meal. 'George would have a fit. I'm triple-carbing and if that doesn't line my stomach then nothing will.'

Nick had also ordered everything they'd need to make Moscow Mules including a prohibitively expensive bottle of Grey Goose vodka – his room service bill was going to be absolutely ruinous, but he didn't seem to care. All he seemed to care about was Jenny, that she'd eaten enough, that she wasn't drinking too much and when she flicked through the TV channels and couldn't find anything to watch that wasn't footage of the two towers collapsing, he calmly took the remote from her hands and quickly found a station that was showing reruns of *I Love Lucy*.

Three Moscow Mules and four episodes of *I Love Lucy* later and Jenny was feeling the good kind of buzz, but far from receding, the horrors of the day were still there, playing out in full technicolour and surround sound. It might have been the vodka, the shock, but Jenny was sure that there must be some way that she could press rewind on the whole day and find herself back in her bed on Horatio Street all ready for a do-over.

'Jen?' Nick put his hand on her arm, his touch setting off wave after wave of goosebumps, enough to make her shiver. 'You're cold. You must be tired. It's so late. Go to bed. I'll take the couch.'

Jen supposed it was late. The sky outside was jet black but she didn't want to go to bed to be alone with her thoughts without the distraction of Lucille Ball and cocktails.

Or maybe she just didn't want to be alone.

'Don't be silly,' she said in a voice that suddenly seemed as sultry as an August day in Savannah. 'We can share a bed. We've done it in the past.'

Nick sighed. This time when he touched her arm, it was slow and deliberate, and Jenny turned her head to see that the look he was giving her was slow and deliberate too.

'We both know that if we share a bed tonight neither of us is going to get much sleep,' he said, his voice deep enough that it made something low down in Jenny's belly stir.

She didn't drop her gaze. 'I don't have any problem with that,' Jenny said, getting up from the sofa, her leg brushing against his as she did so, and by the time she came out of the bathroom, she expected Nick to be waiting for her in the bedroom but he was still sitting on the sofa, leaning forward, his arms resting on his legs, his chin in his hands. He'd turned off the sidelight so it was impossible to see his face, to know what he was thinking. As Jenny hurried to the bedroom, she tried to convince herself that even the sting of rejection was better than feeling numb.

The bed was huge and on a dais so that it was like being on a stage set. Jenny didn't know how to close the curtains, didn't even have the energy to try, so she sat on the end of the bed staring out at the night. It never really got dark in New York; the buildings lit up, the rumble of traffic, people bustling, but tonight the city seemed as silent as the grave.

Then Nick was there in the doorway, still standing in shadow. 'I don't want to take advantage of you,' he said.

'But I want you to take advantage of me,' were the magic words to make Nick step into the room and walk, stalk, towards her. 'I want to feel something, anything, that isn't the way I feel right now. And let's not forget that you were the one who kissed me that New Year's Eve and you were the one who said that . . .'

Then thank God, Nick kissed the words right out of her mouth, chased them away with his tongue until all there was was him. Hard in all the right places and soft where the memory didn't hurt.

Jenny scrambled to her feet, to meet him more than half-way, rucking up his T-shirt so she could feel his skin, his body, warm under her fingers. She deserved this. She needed this. And so did he. Two lost souls finding themselves in a mess of tangled limbs on tangled sheets.

Jenny made an inarticulate noise and yanked at his shirt. 'Off. Take it off.' But when Nick tried to pull away to shrug off the offending garment, she pulled him close again.

Don't let me go.

Nick's mouth travelled down to her neck, she felt his tongue cool and wet in her ear and gave in to the damp tickle of it as one hard thigh worked its way between her legs. Even between two layers of cotton, she could feel herself getting swollen and soaked.

'If you only knew the things I've wanted to do to you,' he whispered in her ear. 'The things I've wanted you to do to me. I promise I'm going to make you feel something.'

Then he pulled his T-shirt over his head and the febrile glitter of his eyes burned brighter than the city lights outside the window. The sound of the buckle and then the faint hiss of his leather belt sliding through the loops of his jeans was deafening in the quiet of the room.

Another kiss, long and languorous, just enough wet heat to turn the passion up another notch, Jenny's hands wound in the sticky silk of his hair, her fingers full of promises and traces of hair gel.

'Let's see some flesh then, Jen,' he muttered against her mouth and without ceremony she tugged her own T-shirt over her head. Then she pushed down her leggings and her knickers without any grace, struggling to free herself from the restraining folds of black cotton as Nick dropped to his knees in front of her. His lips were frantic as he placed ravenous kisses across her skin, a long, low swipe of his tongue into her belly button that made her buck her hips.

The fifteen years they'd known each other all came down to this moment on a warm September night when sleep was impossible and grief was scratching at the door. For fifteen years Jenny had wondered what it would feel like to have Nick make love to her. But the reality of him pushing her down on the bed and parting her quivering thighs, then his hands touching her with such purpose there where she was wet and aching for him was something beyond even her most fevered dreams. She'd never imagined his mouth following the path of his fingers, his tongue determined to wring every last drop of pleasure out of her.

How long had she wanted this? Too long. Oh God, so long.

'Just let go,' Nick murmured against her flesh and Jenny could feel it coming; a tsunami that started in the pit of her belly and whooshed outwards, until she was mindlessly grinding into his face and clenching everything she could. She finally came undone when his fingers found the maddening, unbearable place inside her while the tip of his tongue rubbed against her clit.

All her insides turned to liquid and it was never going to stop. She'd die with Nick on his knees in front of her, her fingers weaving into his dark hair the last thing she'd see before her vision went blurry. Only the steady hold of his hands against her writhing flesh stopped her from toppling forwards as she continued to arch her hips against his beautiful, clever, wonderful mouth.

There was a ringing in her ears as she floated gently back to reason. His tongue gently lapped at her clit, savouring each one of the tiny ripples that he took as his due.

At last, Jenny managed to sit up. 'That was what I needed to feel,' she murmured, leaning down to place tiny kisses on whatever part of Nick's face she could reach.

'No, don't touch me . . .' Nike groaned but he hauled himself up onto the bed and didn't stop Jenny from running a hand down the contours of his chest, lingering only to press her fingertips against the hard points of his nipples before continuing the journey downwards so she could brush against the bulge in his jeans.

'All those things you thought about me doing, let's make them real,' Jenny whispered and licked his lips so she could taste herself.

She raised herself up on her knees so she could straddle him. 'It's all right. You don't have to,' he said in between more filthy wet kisses, which made that pulse between her legs thrum to life again.

'But I want to.' And before he could protest and state his preference, she tugged at his zipper and grasped his hard length in her hot hands. 'Now, what shall I do with this?'

'Nobody likes a tease,' Nick moaned and threw his neck back as Jenny ran a languid hand up his shaft and pressed her thumb against the head. She was about to take him in her mouth when Nick rolled her over and she felt the brush of his knuckles against her clit as he guided his cock into her.

He had to be the first man in the history of the human race to turn down a blow job. 'You don't want me to . . . ?'

He shook his head, eyes glittering as he stared down at her. 'I want this more.'

'I've wanted this for so long,' Jenny mumbled brokenly, as Nick pressed inside her by inestimable degrees, until he was fully sheathed and she squeezed him tight, her legs coming up to lock round his hips. 'Don't move for a second, OK? I just want to feel you inside me.'

Oh, never let me go.

She concentrated on the weight of him, how solid and safe he felt in her arms, the curve of his ear against her cheek as he licked along the damp sweat that dotted her collarbones. She felt truly alive for the first time that day.

'Jen . . .' he urged her. 'Let me . . . oh, you feel so good.'

He shifted restlessly and her muscles fluttered against him. 'Go on, then,' she said, locking eyes with him. 'Please.'

Nick thrust deep into her, pulling back until Jenny was scared that he was going to go and then plunging forward, grinding his pubic bone against her clit as he entered her making sure to rub against that little mound of nerves on the down-stroke.

'We should have done this years ago,' he told her, resting his forehead against her. 'All the time we wasted.'

'I don't want to waste time anymore,' she said, tilting her pelvis up to get even more of that delicious stimulation. 'I've dreamed of this ever since you kissed me that New Year's Eve.'

'I wanted to do more than just kiss you,' Nick said, and she couldn't quite believe that this was happening. It was all so shockingly new and yet familiar too, because this was Nick. He'd seen the best of her, the absolute worst of her. She'd loved him. She'd hated him and now as he reached between them so he could roughly stroke her clit, she didn't think she'd ever be able to live without him. 'God, you feel amazing.'

'I've never felt like this,' Jenny gasped, her hands clutching at Nick as she felt the hard, violent waves begin to consume her again. 'Not with anyone else.'

Nick didn't hold back, just drove into her hard. 'I've always loved you. I wish I didn't, but I do. I love you.'

She wanted to tell him not to say things like that but he was coming in violent bursts, arching deep into her even as Jenny tightened around him again. Nick collapsed on her, knocking all the breath from her. Her legs slid down, still splayed out and she brought one limp hand up to brush the damp curls from his forehead.

They lay there without moving until Nick pulled out of her, soothing Jenny's soft cry of protest with the brush of his finger against her mouth.

She'd never felt so content as she did at that moment.

26

West 4th Street – September 14th, 2001
Washington Square Station

They spent the next three days making love and sleeping. Though making love made it sound sweeter, more romantic than the way they'd come together so frantically, with such edge and desperation. At times when Nick was driving into her or she had him pinned to the bed, doing things with her hips that she hadn't even known her hips could do, it felt to Jenny more feral than anything else.

But all good things, even good things forged from something terrible, had to come to an end. And on the fourth day when Jenny woke up, kiss-bitten and sore, she knew that, like everyone else living in New York, she had to find some new semblance of normality.

'What's so good about normality?' Nick asked, pulling her towards him when she mooted the idea. 'Why can't we just stay here forever?'

'We'll get bedsores if we stay here forever,' Jenny pointed out, wriggling to get free. They really needed to get up, get out, let Housekeeping in. Jenny was sure that the ripe, pungent smell of sex permeated every single thread of bedding and they couldn't even crack open a window because most windows in this town didn't open.

Yet somehow those brave people, she thought of them as brave, had managed to open the windows of the World Trade Center and not wait for death, but left on their own

351

terms. That was what Jenny kept coming back to. The jumpers.

'Don't, Jen,' Nick advised, reaching for her again so he could press a sweet if unnecessary kiss to her shoulder. 'Stop thinking about it.'

'Hard not to.'

'That's another reason to just stay here,' Nick said, his hand sliding down her tender flesh, which had been so well primed for his touch that all her nerve endings began to sing.

It took a great effort but Jenny pushed him away. 'Enough. I need at least a twenty-four-hour recovery period.'

'I suppose. Not since I was fourteen and found an Electric Blue video under my brother's bed . . .'

'Please don't finish that sentence,' Jenny begged, clamping her hands over her ears.

Nick laughed all the way to the bathroom, leaving Jenny alone so, with a sense of impending doom, she could phone the office.

Her call was rerouted to the cellphone of Marcus, the facilities manager. Their building was still closed until the structure had been declared safe, but he'd been allowed in to collect people's belongings.

An hour later, Jenny's handbag was couriered to the hotel and an hour after that, freshly laundered and wearing clothes for the first time in days, she and Nick took the E train to the West Village, because the C train had been suspended since September 11th.

Much as she never wanted to set foot in another skyscraper, Jenny wasn't looking forward to travelling underground either. Not since she'd heard that the subway station under the World Trade Center had collapsed too. Nick had suggested that they get a cab, but though she could avoid skyscrapers when she was back in London, not ever going on the tube again was untenable.

'If you come with me, the first time, then it won't be so bad,' she said as they passed through the barriers at 7th Avenue station and walked to the platform. It felt normal. Using the subway was something she'd done practically every day while she was in New York, when she wasn't battling with her huge street map and trying to walk to places.

The subway was as quiet as Jenny had ever seen it. She and Nick sat side by side on hard, plastic seats, which made a girl nostalgic for the soft moquette-covered seats of a London tube train. He held her hand but neither of them spoke.

As the train took Jenny nearer and nearer to her destination, the world came rushing back at her, her head crowded with thoughts all bumping up against each other.

There were the leftovers in the fridge that needed to be chucked out. She'd meant to go and fetch her dry-cleaning after work on the Tuesday. The man who worked there was a grumpy old sod at the best of times. And she needed to call Jackie, she hadn't spoken to her since that Tuesday. Then Jenny needed to call Michael too.

Oh God, Michael.

Just saying his name in her head made Jenny grow immediately cold and clammy. Nick had his fingers threaded through hers, his thumb absent-mindedly brushing the back of her knuckles and he gave a start when Jenny pulled her hand free. Like he hadn't even realised that they'd done a terrible thing to the two people they loved.

'We've fucked it up, Nick. Absolutely fucked it,' Jenny muttered, which made Nick turn to look at her in surprise. 'All I wanted to do was to get back to London and now I'm dreading going to back to London.'

'I thought you'd been offered a job here,' Nick said.

'I had. I mean, I have but I'm not going to take it. Not now.' Jenny turned to look at Nick again, taking in his tense jawline, the way he swallowed convulsively. 'How could I stay here?'

'You never thought to mention it once during the last few days?' he asked softly.

They hadn't talked about anything important over the last three days and especially the last three nights. Nick had whispered absolutely filthy things into her skin and Jenny had risen to the challenge. They'd reminisced about the past. Made a decision to live in the here and now. And absolutely hadn't talked about the future.

'I'm mentioning it now.'

'I thought that we were both on the same page,' he muttered and then he wouldn't look at her.

'Oh, and what page would that be?' Jenny winced at the shrill edge to her voice.

'That you were moving to New York and that I . . . I already said that I could probably get a job here. We could leave all that difficult stuff behind us. Honey. Michael. They'd be in London. We'd be here.' He shifted on the seat so his knee bumped against her but when he tried to take Jenny's hand, she folded her arms across her chest. 'Why are you looking at me like that?'

'You know this can never be anything, don't you?' Jenny asked him.

'This?' Nick echoed. 'What do you mean exactly?'

Jenny pointed at herself and then at Nick, who looked at her finger like it was a poisoned dart. 'This. Us.' Her voice rising so that a woman in an MTA uniform opposite them slumped against the seat divider, half asleep, came to with a start. 'Christ, Nick, you and Honey are exchanging contracts on a house next week.'

'Wow! I hadn't realised that my real estate ambitions were so important to you. Obviously, Honey and I . . . the timing sucks and yeah, I suppose I love her, but not in the same way that I love you.' Nick lightly touched Jenny on the arm, and even that light touch made her want to clutch him and kiss him until she couldn't think straight. Which wouldn't help matters, it would just make everything even worse. 'I've been trying to do the whole relationship thing with her; taking out life insurance and paying fifty grand more to buy a house in the catchment area for the best local school. But that isn't me. I'm not built that way and neither are you. What we have is passionate, elemental. Like Scott and Zelda or Sid and Nancy.'

'What the fuck are you taking about? F. Scott Fitzgerald was an alcoholic, Zelda was clinically insane and Sid and Nancy were heroin addicts who died in a murder suicide pact. Great relationship models.'

'But I'm not talking about a relationship, about being tied down with endowment plans and a membership to *Which* so we can choose the most energy efficient washing machine. I don't want to live like that.' Nick fixed her with that unwavering stare that always made her skin prickle. 'You weren't worrying about Honey, or Michael for that matter, when you were begging me to fuck you.'

Jenny should be furious that he was offering her nothing more than a vision of the two of them together that bore no resemblance to any kind of reality. But the reminder of how she'd clung to him, how desperate she'd been to have him inside her again, made everything below her waist quiver in lustful anticipation again.

She tried to soften her features, which she felt sure had set into harsh lines. 'What we've just done, it's not real . . .'

'It felt pretty bloody real, Jen.'

'It was lovely but it was a moment out of time,' she tried to explain though she didn't have the right words to describe the past three days. Wasn't sure she ever would. 'A pause on our everyday lives.'

It was Nick's turn to fold his arms. 'Did you think this was a lost weekend? That it was just a pity fuck? That I felt sorry for you?'

Jenny flinched from the force of each question. 'It was an itch, fifteen years in the making, that we were both desperate to scratch.'

'OK, right, you were just putting me out of my misery,' Nick said tartly. His shoulders sunk. 'You won't even consider leaving him, leaving Michael?'

'I *love* Michael. But it's not even about that.' Jenny did love Michael. She really did. Though the thought of getting back to London, unlocking their front door and having to look him in the eyes and tell him . . . what? She shuddered. Only one thing was certain: she had to shut things down with Nick right now. To make him see sense. Otherwise, God knows what he might do . . .

'I'm just pointing out that we've both committed to other people,' Jenny said in a slightly more conciliatory tone. 'It's been an odd few days. Emotions were heightened, very heightened and . . .'

'So, now you're saying that I shouldn't have started this . . .'

'Don't be ridiculous! I'm not some impressionable teenage virgin . . .'

'But you have been in love with me since you were sixteen,' Nick pointed out like it was his trump card. The MTA lady was leaning forward now, not even bothering to hide the fact that she was listening and enjoying herself immensely. 'And in my own way, I was in love with you too then. I've never stopped loving you, Jen, and now . . . enough is enough. Let's just jump and not worry about where we're going to land.'

It was everything she'd ever wanted Nick to say. Yes, when she was sixteen and yes, even now when she was old enough to know better. But loving Nick Levene was about loving a memory, a dream, an idea, rather than the feckless, careless, irresponsible man himself. 'Your friendship is really import-ant to me,' Jenny said carefully.

'Are you saying that you don't love me?' Nick sounded as bitter as a bag full of lemon drops. 'Because, I'm sorry to keep bringing it up, but when we were living out every single one of your teenage fantasies, you said that you'd never felt like that before. That I was the best that . . .'

'Don't, Nick, just don't.' Jenny was desperate to stop him from saying something that they couldn't come back from. Though, maybe they couldn't come back from this. Shouldn't. Wouldn't. 'George nailed it the other night when he said that it was never going to be the right time for us. But we have such a great friendship and I don't want this to ruin it.'

They'd reached 34th Street and the MTA lady got up, shaking her head at Jenny and Nick, as she exited the car. Her place was taken by a young black guy, headphones firmly in place, eyes fixed on the floor, who had no interest in the row that was taking place. Because, yes, this had now officially become a row.

'You weren't loving me as a friend when you let me . . .'

'Enough!' Jenny snapped, her hand in front of his face, like she was directing traffic. 'Let me remind you about the last time you confessed your undying love for me. I was *this* close' – she snapped her fingers in an act of sheer aggression that made him blink – 'to throwing away everything for you, but you were the one who got cold feet.'

'You *what*? Say that again.' Nick looked like a cartoon

357

character nanoseconds before an anvil dropped on his head. 'You never said *anything*. When you gave me that out, I took it because I thought that was what *you* wanted. I was doing the honourable thing for once. And now you're saying – what? That we could have been doing what we've spent the last three days doing back then?'

'This is all about the sex for you, isn't it?' Jenny sighed with resignation because this was what Nick was like and she knew that better than anyone. 'I would have walked out on Michael and the life we'd built together, chucked all that away on something that only ever existed in my head.'

This time when Nick took her hand, Jenny let him. 'But I love you. You're amazing. You're funny, you're clever, you're beautiful, you get me like no one else does, and yes, the sex was fucking amazing . . .' Nick tried to smile but it slid off his face immediately. 'I know I don't have the best track record when it comes to relationships so, come on, let's just live in the moment, see where this takes us.'

But Jen was thirty-one now, and though her biological clock wasn't ticking, thirty-one was too old for living in the moment, lost weekends and friends who sometimes ended up fucking each other. Nick might believe that he loved her but he was never going to give her any more than that. He always thought that by touting his unreliability, it absolved him from all responsibility when he inevitably fucked things up.

'You know what? I wish that we'd had bad, clumsy sex when we were teenagers and then decided to avoid each other for the rest of our lives instead of kidding ourselves that we had this special cosmic bond and we'd be together if only the circumstances were right.' She looked heavenwards again. 'It's bullshit. We've been kidding ourselves.'

There was a part of Jenny, even if it was a tiny part, buried deep, deep down, that had imagined that one day she and

Nick might be together. Even when she'd been happy with Gethin, even when she'd felt so safe and settled with Michael, Nick had always been her *what if* and Jenny now understood that the three days that they'd just spent being naked and open with each other, in ways that had nothing to do with sex, was the death knell on their friendship.

There was no going back to being friends now.

'Michael is a great guy, but he's stifling you, Jen.'

'He's not,' Jenny insisted, though she and Michael were also at an impasse. And Michael did have a membership to *Which*, which yes, came in very handy whenever they needed to replace one of their white goods. Just thinking about Michael made Jenny feel nauseous, then sad that she felt that way, then guilty. 'I don't want to talk about Michael.'

'Jen, we belong together,' Nick said as Jenny twisted herself around so she wouldn't have to look at him and the pleading expression on his stupid, beautiful face. 'We always did. I regret that we cheated on our significant others but I'm never going to regret these last few days.'

Maybe it was because she'd come so close to death, but Jenny could see things clearly now. She would never be happy with Nick. These last stolen days hadn't made her happy and neither had the long, fractious years of their friendship. Life was too brutally and painfully short to not be happy.

The train, at last, was pulling into West 4th Street/ Washington Square. She got to her feet, Nick rising from his seat too. 'No, stay there,' she ordered, but he ignored her and followed her off the train, like he ignored everything that challenged his narrow view of himself that really hadn't changed since he was seventeen. That he was a maverick. A loner. Someone who couldn't be pinned down.

Jenny made no move to leave the platform. She couldn't go any further with Nick.

This was where their story ended.

The last stop.

'It's over,' she said, grief and relief fighting it out so she didn't know whether to cry or to wriggle her shoulders which were suddenly lightened from the load they'd been carrying all these years. 'I'm not the girl I was . . . I've changed a lot.'

'I know that, Jen,' Nick said, confusion all over his face, etching lines into his forehead and grooves at the corners of his mouth. 'Come on, let's go and get some lunch, have a drink, chat this out.'

'You don't know that because *you* haven't changed. You are *never* going to grow up. You need to realise that I'm not that little lovestruck girl who you used to know. That's not who I am anymore. It's just too hard, Nick. I want someone who's all in, not just for the passion but for the pension plan too. We're not teenagers anymore and . . . This. You and me. It's not real. It never was.'

'We've been here before,' Nick said, hands in the pockets of his jeans, staring deep into her eyes now, like he didn't ever want to look away. 'We always find a way back to each other.'

'Not this time,' Jenny vowed. 'If you see me in a bar or queuing to get coffee or by the ticket machines at Leicester Square station, just act like you never saw me. We have to stop pretending that we're anything other than two very different people who want entirely different things.'

'So, you're not in love with me. Not even a little bit.' He stated it as a fact. Despite Gethin, despite Michael, she'd always been in love with Nick as she had been since she was sixteen, and he'd known it. But Jenny was sick and tired of loving Nick; all it did was give her false hope.

'Being in love with you doesn't make me happy,' Jenny said, making sure that she enunciated every word so it would finally sink in. Not just for Nick, but for herself too. 'And I just want to be happy.'

There was nothing else to say so she walked away, up the stairs and through the station and out into a world where the air was still thick with dust and smoke.

PART NINE

2003

27

December 24th, 2003
Mill Hill East Station

Jenny liked to think she was a skilled negotiator. Actually, she *was* a skilled negotiator. That year alone, she'd triumphed at four hotly contested auctions for new novels.

But Jenny was no match for her mother and her sister-in-law, Bethany. When she'd put up a spirited argument for being picked up from her Kentish Town front door at some not ridiculous hour on Christmas Day, they'd shot her down in flames.

'Don't you think we've got better things to do on Christmas Day, like making the bread sauce and setting the table, than to come and pick you up?' Jackie had demanded.

'Don't you want to spend Christmas Eve with your favourite niece and help her put out mince pies for Santa Claus?' Bethany had asked, her voice catching like she was devastated that Jenny was being A Very Bad Aunt.

Jenny had capitulated. But only because it was best that she was at her parents' to supervise Jackie and Dot (who'd moved in the year before once a downstairs loo and a stairlift had been installed), so they didn't go rogue. Last year, they'd put the stuffing *in* the turkey, rather than as a side dish, completely forgetting that some people didn't like stuffing and didn't want the turkey contaminated with the taste of it.

Also, Jenny was an exemplary aunt. Amelie, or Milly as she was known, was eighteen months old and almost all of the entire Richards clan was besotted with her. She was the first grandchild, after all, and was both fat and rosy of cheek, with golden ringlets and a sunny disposition. More importantly, she adored Jenny who, in turn, marvelled at every one of Milly's developmental milestones, from grabbing toys with her pudgy hands to gummily gnawing on a cucumber stick. And Tim was still childless and not interested in Milly in the slightest so Jenny was number one with a bullet.

Though Milly was still far too young to have any real concept of Christmas or Santa Claus, Jenny didn't mind spending the night before Christmas on Martin and Bethany's really uncomfortable futon in their spare room if it meant she got to spend quality time with their very own Christ child.

This was why at just after five on Christmas Eve Jenny was barrelling down Leighton Road, laden down with her overnight bag, her trusty Daunts tote, handbag and two massive John Lewis carriers stuffed full of presents.

The sky had been grey and colourless for days so Jenny felt as if she'd never see the sun again. And now it was a dark, cold, damp evening. The dampness pervaded everything, seeped into her bones, frizzed up her hair and curled the ends of the fringe that she'd decided to cut in (after years of living fringe-free). Jenny wished that she'd buttoned up her cheery red winter coat while her hands had been free, but she didn't want to stop and risk missing a Mill Hill East train.

Martin was picking her up from the station at five thirty and driving her back to the house he and Bethany had bought just up the road in Mill Hill Village, so Jenny would be able to do bath time and read Milly a story before bed.

It was ironic that of the three of them, Martin, the juvenile delinquent who'd failed most of his GCSEs, was the one who now ticked all the boxes. He was Area Sales Manager of the estate agent chain where he'd started working at seventeen and had just formed a property development company with one of his friends. He'd punched well above his weight when he'd persuaded Bethany to marry him, provided the first grandchild and had also fulfilled Jackie and Alan's dream of living in the Village.

It left Jenny vying for second place in their parents' affections with Tim, who was a food scientist for Waitrose so could get Jackie a discount at John Lewis but lived in a rented flat in Walthamstow, which he shared with his girlfriend, Gretchen, who was a humourless vegan. Gretchen had once told Jenny that she couldn't really be a feminist if she insisted on wearing red lipstick. It was like being back at Queen Mary's and actually Gretchen did remind Jenny of Demonic Dominic. Anyway 'wretchin' Gretchen' as Alan called her had knocked quite a few points off Tim's score so Jenny was pretty certain she was currently the second favourite child.

As she travelled down the escalator, through the wind tunnel that was Kentish Town station, her coat flapped in the breeze and Jenny's hair whipped around her face, guaranteeing that she'd soon look like small woodland creatures were nesting on top of her head. At least she was spared the distant rumble of a train, so she didn't have to hare down the steps.

When Jenny reached the northbound platform, there were two High Barnet trains scheduled before a Mill Hill East train arriving in eight minutes. She sat down on a bench to fuss with her hair. She should have worn a hat. Then she reapplied her lipstick, because little Milly was always transfixed by the contrast between Jenny's pale skin and bright lips, and pulled her iPod out of her coat pocket to cue up the new Belle and Sebastian album, *Dear Catastrophe Waitress*. They reminded her of her teenage years and the 'Indie Pop Ain't Noise Pollution' sign she'd pinned on her bedroom door whenever Jackie was kicking off about how loud her music was.

The two High Barnet trains came and went, disgorging huge crowds of people with weary faces, laden down with shopping bags, rolls of wrapping paper peeking out. Then there were the passengers still wearing cracker crowns and weaving unsteadily along the platform after work Christmas lunches that had clearly gone on all afternoon. It was Wednesday evening, Jenny's offices had closed the previous Friday until January 5th so Jenny had had plenty of time to do all her Christmas shopping. In fact, she felt a little smug as the Mill Hill East train arrived in a gust of air, which ruffled her fringe again, as she surveyed her bags full of beautifully wrapped presents.

Jenny let the passengers off the train first but the carriage was still quite packed and wouldn't thin out until Highgate. Still, she managed to squeeze into a seat, one carrier bag between her feet, the other perched on her lap along with her holdall, tote and handbag.

The doors shut, the train pulled away, Belle and Sebastian played in her ears and Jenny shut her eyes, lulled by the familiar rhythm of the train, the thought of spending the next two days with her family, eating more food than she'd normally eat in a week, getting buzzed on Baileys, the usual Boxing Day fight over Monopoly . . .

For most of her teens and the first half of her twenties, Jenny had been focussed on pulling away from her family, from the ties that held her down, so she could be her own person with her own fabulous life. Now that she was in her thirties, those family ties no longer chafed. Increasingly, it felt like all she wanted were more family ties: a partner, children, she definitely wanted children now and oh God, with children came a house in a good catchment area, though no way was she moving back to Mill Hill, no matter how many heavy-handed hints Jackie and Dot dropped.

Dating wasn't at all like it used to be. It was almost impossible to meet anyone in the wild anymore, apart from the woolly academics that Kirsty and Erik occasionally threw Jenny's way. Though since the calamitous break-up with Michael, who'd subsequently left London and bought a watermill in Shropshire that he planned to restore, they weren't quite so keen to set Jenny up. 'Why do all your exes leave London? What do you do to them?' Kirsty had asked, only half-joking, though Jenny hadn't gone into specifics with her.

The general consensus was that being in New York for 9/11 had broken something in Jenny and when she'd come home, she was altered. Which was the truth but it was also the truth that she'd cheated on Michael and could hardly look at him, had even flinched on a couple of occasions from his lightest, most incidental touches. And so they'd split up and it was only when they were in the midst of separating their lives, that she'd told him the truth. That she'd slept with someone else while she was away. Not who. It was enough that Michael was coldly furious with her and hadn't spoken to her since she'd left her door keys on the hall table in his loft overlooking the Regent's Canal. Jenny knew that she deserved his anger but even now, nearly two years later, she still missed Michael, his solidity, his dry humour, the way he's always made her feel safe.

Jenny had tried to fling herself into the task of online dating with enthusiasm, but it was brutal out there. Jenny cast her mind back to her last internet date, a graphic designer from Fulham, who insisted they go for tapas, talked about himself for a full two hours, and ordered a hundred small plates of stuff that Jenny wasn't going to eat but she still had to split the bill with him.

As the train approached Tufnell Park, she had a minor panic that she hadn't packed the stollen and the box of petits fours she'd bought from Fortnum & Mason. Dot said that the ones from Marks & Sparks were just as nice, but she also loved that Jenny made a special trip to Fortnum's every Christmas to buy her the vile marzipan treats. 'The Queen shops there!' she always said, without fail. 'She might be eating the same petit fours at this exact moment.'

The Fortnum & Mason's bag was wedged at the bottom of the John Lewis bag on her lap. Jenny subsided with a relieved sigh as more people got out and there was a little more room. She glanced down the length of the carriage and . . . and . . . her heart hitched in her chest.

It was a familiar feeling. There were a thousand, *thousands*, of dark-haired men in London; tall, rangy, dark-haired men. Men who had a certain way of carrying themselves. Maybe one might even have a navy Manhattan Portage bag slung over his shoulder. She'd once walked behind someone of the right height and build and hair colour, a Carhartt label on the back of his jeans, her entire body clenched in anticipation, but it wasn't him. It was never Nick.

Then there had been the time when Jenny had been reading the *Guardian*'s Monday media section, turned the page and saw his face staring out at her to accompany a news story about him quitting his job as editor of a Sunday supplement to go back to his journalistic roots and helm the launch of a new music magazine and website.

Or that Sunday afternoon not so long ago when Jenny had been repainting her bedroom. She'd been listening to Radio Four because she was now the kind of person who listened to Radio Four, when she'd suddenly heard his voice leaking from her Roberts radio as he talked about the death of Johnny Cash and the legacy he'd left behind. She'd had to completely redo one section of skirting board where she'd splashed grey eggshell paint all over it.

So many times over the last two years there had been these moments and Jenny's heart wouldn't know how to behave itself. But then it would go back to beating like it normally did, just as it was doing now.

She adjusted the volume on her iPod, checked her coat pocket to make sure her Oyster card holder was still there.

Then Jenny couldn't help but look again, as they pulled into Archway and she was safely obscured by the people getting off the train.

Oh God. It *was* him. It was Nick. Sitting in the next section of the carriage with his own share of carrier bags and a leather holdall on his lap. Obviously on his way home for Christmas too. Her heart didn't just hitch but did a weird skippy, flippy thing as Jenny shrank back in her seat.

She'd come to terms with the fact that, though not seeing him, not getting sucked in again, was the right thing to do, she'd always be a little bit in love with Nick Levene. But she hadn't planned on being on the same Northern Line train as him, destination Mill Hill East.

For one moment, Jenny was seized with hope that maybe Nick wasn't going home for Christmas, the Levenes were Jewish anyway, and maybe he'd moved from Stoke Newington after he split up with Honey. It had been about six months after they'd moved into that big house with its many bedrooms. Jenny was foggy on the details; by then she'd left Lyttons so she was no longer Honey's editor (a fact, which might have played into her decision to move to one of the Big Five publishers though she'd talked a good game that the only way she could advance any further at Lyttons was to marry into the family. 'And the only eligible one is Charlie Lytton and he's not even seventeen!'). It wasn't a stretch to imagine Nick living in fashionable Crouch End or Muswell Hill, which weren't even on the tube but were reachable from Highgate.

Jenny forced herself not to glance to her left again but as the train approached Highgate, she was in an agony of expectation.

Another fleeting sideways glance but he still wasn't budging as the 1930s cream and mint tiles of Highgate station came into view.

Nick wasn't the type of person to live in East Finchley, too suburban. Or Finchley Central, even more suburban. So, Nick had to be going to Mill Hill East, the tiny off-branch of the Northern Line, where there was only one platform and a short flight of stairs leading to the tiny ticket hall and it was impossible to avoid someone that you really didn't want to see.

The majority of the passengers alighted at Highgate, the carriage almost emptying out. Jenny kept her eyes fixed in front of her, staring at her own tense reflection in the window as the train started up. She half-hoped, half-dreaded that Nick might see her and despite the decree she'd given him the last time they'd been together (to 'walk on by' like the Dionne Warwick song), he'd suddenly sit down opposite her and strike up a conversation.

He didn't though and when they reached East Finchley, (where he might get off because a lot could happen in two years. He might have got married, started a family and moved to a popular North London suburb with its own independent cinema), she felt compelled to glance in his direction again.

Nick was looking right at her and as her heart hitched and skipped and flipped, her face flaming, he nodded once.

I see you.

Then he looked away.

Now the train pulled into Finchley Central, bringing Jenny closer and closer to an awkward collision with destiny. Or rather, Nick Levene. She thought about getting out and waiting for the next Mill Hill East train but that could be at least fifteen minutes and besides, she was a grown woman and she could handle briefly bumping into Nick.

The rest was inevitable. The short journey to Mill Hill East. The train pulling into the station. She didn't know whether it was best to rush or go slow. Jenny gathered up her bags, tried to gather herself too and stepped off the train at the same time as Nick exited through the doors at the other end of the carriage.

She was some distance from the way out and quickened her pace only to get stuck in a bottleneck of people waiting to go down the stairs. Jenny wasn't looking behind her, but she knew the moment that Nick caught up with her. Could feel it in every single one of the inestimable atoms and molecules that she contained. She'd swear that she could feel his breath on her neck, his body move through her coat.

Then she was picking her way down the stairs, across the entrance, buffeted by the people behind her as not one bus, but two buses pulled up outside. There was a small but polite melee as people split off towards either the 221 or the 240 but Nick wasn't one of them, though either bus would take him within a three-minute walk of the big Arts and Crafts house where she imagined that his parents still lived. No, Nick was standing beside her at the station entrance as Jenny looked in vain for Martin's car.

He was still beside her as she sat down in the bus shelter, sitting next to her. Jenny felt dwarfed by his presence, even as she longed for him to turn to her, to say some magic combination of words that would change everything, though she still had her earbuds in, was still playing the Belle and Sebastian album though it might just as well have been whale music for all the notice that she took of it.

But they weren't talking to each other anymore. That had been the agreement. Though it was in direct contravention of that agreement when Nick put his hand on her knee.

Jenny looked down at his long fingers, his touch scorching her through her jeans and the thick wool of her coat. She could have knocked his hand away but instead she placed her hand on top of his, skin to skin, because time and distance and angry words and them never managing to be in the right place at the right time couldn't stop her from loving him.

How long they sat like that, Jenny couldn't say. Just as she knew that she'd always be a little bit in love with Nick, she'd always measured how happy she was, how well she was doing with her life, with whether she could bear to see him again. Would it destroy her? Or would she be able to brush off their encounter like it wasn't important.

The truth, the reality, as usual, wasn't so defined, but she was glad to be with him again, touching, until she heard a triumphant volley of toots and a silver car pulled into the station forecourt.

She tightened her fingers for one infinitesimal moment then took her hand away and stood up as Martin pulled up alongside her. He leaned across to open the passenger door and a blast of heated air hit her. Jenny opened the back door to dump her bags on the seat then pulled out her earbuds and as she climbed into the car, Martin telling her to hurry up, she was sure she heard Nick say something that almost got lost to the sharp wind that made her slam the door shut in a hurry.

Something that sounded like 'I miss you.'

PART TEN

2005

28

July 7th, 2005
~~Kentish Town Station~~

When Jenny got to Kentish Town station that morning, the Northern Line was down. This was annoying, beyond annoying, but not unprecedented. Later, she'd find out that there was nothing sinister about the Northern Line being down on that particular Thursday morning. Just that the Northern Line was old, cantankerous and prone to giving up – there was a good reason why Londoners called it the Misery Line.

Jenny did think about getting the Thameslink overground train to King's Cross then changing back to the tube but the changeover always took so long that she decided against it. After a few false tries, buses coming from further down the route already full to capacity, she managed to squeeze onto a 134, which would take her to New Oxford Street. Then it was a five-minute walk to her offices on the edge of Covent Garden.

She'd changed jobs again. Lured by a promotion from Publisher to Publishing Director and the chance to have her own list *and* full editorial control of a reissues imprint, which she'd named Athena, after the goddess of wisdom. Athena's remit was to find and republish out of print books from women writers, who had fallen out of favour through no fault of their own. Her first two titles were a Victorian erotic memoir written by a courtesan rumoured to have slept with the Prince of Wales and a fictional account of life in a small English village during the thirties from the point of view of the vicar's wife. It was Jenny's passion project and while the happiest time of her career had been working at Cavanagh Morton, this came a close second. Besides, Jenny had become accustomed to a standard of living that she'd never be able to achieve on a bookseller's salary.

As the bus crawled along Kentish Town Road, Jenny tried to read the yellow-paged hardback that Hetty Cavanagh had loaned her when they'd had lunch together a couple of weeks ago, which she thought might be a possible contender for Athena. She was wedged between a pushchair and the stairwell, hoping that people would get off at Camden Town, which they did, so Jenny finally managed to get a seat.

The traffic was almost at a standstill. She sighed, exchanged a pained smile with the woman sitting next to her and went back to her book, the vanity-published diary of a debutante who'd been an ambulance driver in Chelsea during the Second World War. It was quite riveting but not so riveting that it could take Jenny's mind off the fact that she was sitting in gridlocked traffic, horns beeping, sirens shrieking, the minutes ticking by. She had an acquisitions board meeting at ten and it was nearly nine thirty now. Normally, she'd have been at her desk by nine.

They slowly inched past University College Hospital where there were many, many ambulances backed up and waiting to enter the A&E bay.

'Do you think there's been a road accident?' The woman sitting next to Jenny had broken the cardinal rule of commuting and actually spoken to her.

'Maybe. It would explain why the traffic is so bad and the constant sirens.' Jenny sighed again. 'This is ridiculous. It would be quicker to walk.'

When the bus reached the next stop she disembarked and set off along Gower Street. Gower Street was one of her favourite London streets. Jenny was pretty certain that it had more English Heritage blue plaques than any other London Street. The Pre-Raphaelite Brotherhood, Charles Darwin, Dame Millicent Garrett Fawcett (Jenny usually saluted this heroine of women's suffrage as she walked past), and Lady Ottoline Merrill, literary hostess, were just some of the greats. Jenny loved to imagine them bumping into each other and exchanging pleasantries about the weather, maybe complaining about all the goings-on at the Pre-Raphaelite Brotherhood's digs but today there wasn't time for daydreaming. She hurried down the street, trying not to breathe in the exhaust fumes, motors chugging, horns still sounding impatiently.

Although she was now late, very late, Jenny nipped into the New Era café on the corner for her regular cappuccino and granary toast with peanut butter. Then she hurried into the offices via the loading bay at the back, running the gamut of those who'd already popped out for their first cigarette of the day. Jenny had managed just over five years without a cigarette by now and she couldn't help but give the assembled puffers a reproachful look.

She got into the lift at quarter to ten with two assistants from the publicity department, who said there'd been a power cut on the Piccadilly Line and that they'd had to walk from Green Park.

'How weird,' Jenny said with a frown. 'The Northern Line was down too and I think there's been a big traffic accident around Euston. Getting in by bus was a nightmare.'

They nodded respectfully because Jenny was, as well as being a proper grown-up, one of the senior members of staff.

'So, we won't be in trouble for being late?'

As Rosie, the Head of Publicity was a hard-living, hard-partying woman who could drink anyone under the table and never put in an appearance before ten thirty, Jenny thought they'd be all right.

'And, Cara, I loved the idea you had for the proof mail-out for my big autumn crime novel. I hope marketing manage to source personalised ketchup sachets,' Jenny said, as they came out of the lift on the fourth floor. 'Right, let's see how many people we're down.'

They turned left towards publicity and marketing and Jenny turned right to the editorial department, which looked sparsely populated. She hurried to the boardroom but it was empty so she hoped that the acquisitions board had been put back rather than getting all their business done in twenty minutes flat. Which would have been unprecedented. Someone would have to contact the *Guinness Book of World Records*.

She ended up on one of the sofas in the 'break out' area (which did indeed break up the unrelentingly open-plan-ness of their offices) with Ekow, her assistant, and Gauri, one of the commissioning editors, so they could swap war stories about their journey in.

'. . . then I decided it would be best to walk,' Jenny recalled as Alison, the MD's PA, scurried through the empty office towards them.

'Daniel's not in,' she said of their boss. 'He phoned. Says there's been an explosion at Liverpool Street and the station's been evacuated. They think it's a gas main.'

'What is going on today?' Jenny asked. The others shrugged but already she had a sense of déjà vu, which made her shove away her toast and peanut butter because it was leaving a claggy residue in a mouth that had suddenly gone dry. 'We should try and catch the news.'

She led the way back to the boardroom where there was a wall-mounted television. The day before the entire company had gathered there to watch the Olympic bid ceremony and when

London had been declared the hosts for the 2012 Olympics, they'd all cheered and toasted with lukewarm prosecco.

Now they were hugely depleted in number as Ekow wrestled with the remote control and finally the TV burst into life with a 'Breaking News' bulletin from the BBC showing a chaotic street scene: dazed commuters, ambulances, police and people in high vis jackets milling about.

'Police said that a power surge caused the incidents some of which caused explosions,' explained the crisp voice of the female newscaster.

'Incidents? Incidents plural?' Gupta queried. 'I hope my husband's all right. He has to travel through Liverpool Street.'

'I'm sure he's fine but you should probably phone him,' Jenny insisted, wrapping her arms round her body because she was icy cold. She didn't know what had happened but she knew that it wasn't a power surge. She'd been here before.

The camera had now switched to two men racing an empty stretcher down a London street, behind them hospital porters wheeling boxes of supplies, as the muffled voice of an on the scene reporter could be heard. 'There was a very loud bang. The train derailed. There was smoke everywhere. There's a lot of serious injuries down there. A lot of head injuries.

'There are two trains stuck in tunnels at Edgware Road and it's not known if they collided or if passengers remain on board.'

Jenny remembered now what it had been like on that other day, though she tried hard not to think about. The same gasps, the same muffled crying. She wanted to crawl under the table and stay there, but she couldn't do that.

With Daniel, the MD, absent and none of the other department heads in yet, it seemed as if she was in charge.

Jenny clapped her hands to get people's attention, to bring them back from the dark places they'd gone to. 'I think we all need to phone home. Let your partners and parents know you're all right. Alison, can you make a list of anyone who isn't in yet and we'll split the list between us, start making calls?'

There were murmurs of assent but there was still worse to come.

'We're now hearing reports that a bus has been ripped apart in an explosion in Central London.'

Jenny felt as if something in her had been ripped apart too as they now saw footage of a big red London bus, as synonymous with London as red telephone boxes and black taxi cabs and the Changing of the Guard, with its roof and sides torn off.

She went to her office, tears temporarily blinding her, and, though she longed to close it kept the door open. Jenny's phone was flashing with voicemail messages and oh, the relief of hearing from colleagues who'd given up on trying to get in to work and had gone home. There were also panicked messages from all sorts of people keen to know Jenny's movements that day.

'Mum, I'm fine. I'm absolutely fine,' Jenny said as soon as she heard her mother's shrill, 'Jenny? Is that you?'. 'Is everyone fine your end? Yes? Great. I have to go. I need to check up on my people here, but I'm good.'

'You said you were good the other time when you weren't good at all,' Jackie reminded her. Jenny had planned on never telling her parents what she'd seen on that other day. But it had taken precisely five minutes the first time she'd seen Jackie and Alan after getting back from New York, to burst into tears and tell them everything. Well, maybe not *everything*.

'I haven't been on the tube today. Had to get the bus in and then walk. There's not a mark on me,' Jenny said. Then because she didn't have time for ten minutes of 'Well, I won't keep you, but . . .' she added, 'Can you let everyone know I'm OK?

Dad, Gran, Bethany . . . oh my God, you won't believe it but even Gretchen's left a message.'

'That's not like her,' Jackie muttered darkly but before she could enlarge on all the things that *were* like Gretchen, Jenny rang off.

It was a horrible, disjointed day. Thankfully, finally, they accounted for all the absent members of staff. The people who had made it into the office, drifted about unable to settle to anything. Jenny found herself fielding emails and calls from people she hadn't spoken to in months, all checking to see that she was all right. There was a brief but heartfelt text from Michael, who she hadn't heard from in years. Even Gethin emailed from Swansea, where he was Head of Art at a comprehensive school.

That was the thing about tragedy, a fucking awful tragedy that appeared out of nowhere and made something as prosaic and ordinary as the morning commute, something that millions of Londoners did every day, into something terrifying and fatal. It shone a light on what truly mattered. All those rows, break-ups, relationships and friendships left in the dust, were no longer important. What was important was that the people you'd once worked with, lived with, liked, even loved, were OK. Not even OK. Just alive would be good.

And as Jenny finished speaking to Phil Gill of all fucking people, her mind wasn't on her erstwhile boss who had the nerve to say, 'I always knew that you'd do well for yourself, Jennifer, and I like to think that it's in no small part due to my expert tutelage,' but on Nick.

Of course it was. Did he still live in Stoke Newington? Did he work in town? Would he have taken the tube that morning? Was he all right? Please, let him be all right. Jenny couldn't imagine being in a world without Nick in it. That the chance, the possibility, of seeing him on a crowded train or across a station platform would be gone forever. It was too awful, too fucking heart-shattering to contemplate.

She thought about emailing George again, whose email she'd replied to not half an hour before, to ask him if Nick had checked in. But then she decided that what had passed between them, the distance, didn't matter today.

Even though Jenny had blocked his number and deleted his email address, she still knew both of them off by heart. It was a simple thing to email, then text him the same brief message: *I hope you're all right. J x*

By three in the afternoon when he hadn't replied, she could feel hysteria rising in her like mercury in a barometer on a hot summer's day. Of course, now her phone was suddenly, tauntingly silent and it didn't matter how many times she refreshed her email, there was still no message from Nick to say, 'Don't be a twat, Jen, of course I'm fine,' nestling in her inbox. Jenny emailed George again to ask if he'd heard from Nick, gave it ten minutes without hearing back and then rung George only to be told by his assistant that he'd just gone into a meeting for the rest of the day.

By now, it was clear that Jenny (and the rest of the staff) were getting absolutely no work done. After a brief discussion with Daniel who *was* answering his phone, Jenny told the staff to go home and not come back to the office until Monday.

The entire transport system in Central London had been shut down, tubes and buses, so the workers of London had to walk home, which was a daunting prospect, especially if you lived in Zone Six. A large contingent of Jenny's younger colleagues were heading to Ekow's houseshare in Great Titchfield Street, via the off-license.

Jenny was the last to leave. It took her ten seconds on Yahoo to find the right address then she stepped through the revolving doors out onto Shaftesbury Avenue.

It was a five-minute walk. They were a five-minute walk apart and yet she'd never once bumped into him or spotted him from afar when she was in Borders on Charing Cross Road or in the big Boots and the littler Sainsburys at the top of Tottenham Court Road. Or, as per their usual MO, queuing at the ticket machines, travelling the escalators or on the same tube train.

But they hadn't crossed paths. So now Jenny was hurrying to Hanway Street, the tiny little road curled behind the corner of Oxford Street and Tottenham Court Road. It was one of their old haunts. As teenagers they'd come to Hanway Street for its record shops, tiny spaces crammed full of vinyl and during their wild twenties, they'd come to Hanway Street to drink themselves senseless after hours at Bradley's Spanish Bar, which always had a late licence. Jenny even had the dimmest recollection of knocking at an anonymous door somewhere along the street, after chucking-out time at Bradley's, to be let into an illegal drinking den, which seemed to be someone's front room.

Her liver twinged with the memory, but then all her internal organs seemed to be tied up in knots as she counted door numbers. Fear that he wouldn't be here or fear that he was and it would be difficult, painful . . . but Jenny could handle difficult and painful as long as Nick was all right.

Then a door opened further along the street, just where it curved, and a motley collection of ten or so people spilled out onto the pavement, Nick bringing up the rear.

Jenny actually sighed with relief, even as her heart thudded out a warning tattoo.

He was fine. Nick was still here and all was right in her world so Jenny could be on her way. Nothing to see here. There was no need to linger in the spot where almost twenty years before they'd shopped for obscure indie seven inches.

Jenny didn't move, but watched as Nick chivvied the people he was with.

Most of them looked like they were still in their teens and he was speaking to them in a patient, almost avuncular, manner, which was an entirely new look for him. 'So, you all know where you're going, right? Charlie, you've got the A to Z?'

'Yes, Dad,' called out a particularly youthful specimen who couldn't have been more than twelve.

'I reckon that once you clear Vauxhall, you'll find that the buses are running.' Nick shrugged then grinned. 'Or a pub.'

'You won't come with us?' asked one of the girls and now it felt as if Jenny's heart had stopped, at the thought that Nick might be seeing one of these ridiculously young *children*.

Nick shook his head. 'Go south of the river?' he asked incredulously, then held his fist aloft. 'North London 'til I die!'

His friends, colleagues, school tour, whatever, ambled off with some good-natured grousing, leaving Nick behind. He looked down at his phone then looked up and caught sight of Jenny still standing there like one o'clock, half struck.

29

July 7th, 2005
Tottenham Court Road Station

Jenny had often thought about what would happen when they inevitably saw each other again, especially after their encounter at Mill Hill East. Imagined that it would be fair to middling hideous but today wasn't an ordinary day. Today, Jenny couldn't help but walk straight into Nick's open arms, which closed around her tightly. She was happy to hug Nick back, much tighter than was strictly necessary, her face buried against his shoulder. He smelt different; he must have stopped smoking and changed his aftershave but he still felt the same: a bit bony, a bit like he was going to squirm away at any second.

But he didn't. Instead, he kissed the top of her head and said, 'Here you are.'

'And here *you* are!' Jenny hugged him even harder. 'Oh, Nick, I've been worried about you. I'm so glad you're all right.'

'I am all right, but you keep squeezing me like that and I'm going to have a couple of broken ribs,' Nick said, his voice laced with amusement as Jenny reluctantly let him go.

'I thought you were dead, you dick,' she snapped and thumped him hard on the arm. 'You could have texted me back!'

'Ow! And ow!' Nick made a big show of rubbing his arm. 'Also, so odd, bumping into you like this.'

'It was on my way home, I always cut through Hanway Street to avoid the crowds,' Jenny lied.

'Anyway, only just seen your text.' Nick held up his phone. His hair was ruthlessly short, practically a buzzcut, which made his face look thinner, hungrier. He was wearing his regulation media uniform of Adidas shelltoe trainers, Carhartt jeans and a retro T-shirt; this one featured the Trojan Records logo. 'It's been a day. We couldn't account for one of the team. Spent hours ringing round anyone who knew him and then the hospitals.'

'Oh my God,' Jenny muttered, because she'd made Nick's radio silence all about her when he'd been dealing with something truly terrible. 'I hope he's all right.'

'He's fine. The stupid sod couldn't get in to work so he went home, turned off his phone and went back to bed.' Nick rolled his eyes. 'What is it with kids today and their hatred of speaking to people on the phone?'

'I know,' Jenny agreed with feeling. 'To this day, I can't *not* pick up a ringing phone.'

'And I'm sure we weren't so helpless when we were in our twenties. My team are great, enthusiastic, but they lack basic life skills. It's like herding cats.'

Jenny nodded. 'My reports are very chippy. I told my assistant that I had to work three jobs when I was his age, all of them crappy ones, when he expected a pay rise after his probation was over and he just said, "Yeah, yeah, Grandma."' They both smiled nervously. Jenny gestured at the doorway, which Nick had emerged from. 'I read about your start-up. I thought your offices would be swankier, an industrial loft somewhere in Shoreditch.'

Nick looked back at the door too. Once upon a time it might have been painted white but now it was a grubby, grey colour adorned with a couple of half-hearted graffiti tags. 'I decided to use our investment money on hiring really talented people and paying them a decent wage rather than on a fancy, serviced office with a ping-pong table and high-concept pods, which are meant to facilitate brainstorms.'

'We have this space called the bird's nest, which you can only reach by ladder, which is meant to encourage blue sky thinking,' Jenny shared. 'I have never once been up that ladder.'

Nick was now giving Jenny the old up and down too. Taking in the hair that she'd been tugging at all day; the fringe she was growing out, pinned back. She'd left her house with a full face of make-up but it was long gone. Even Jenny's indelible MAC Ruby Woo lipstick (her beloved Clinique 100% Red had been discontinued on a very dark day a few years before) had been chewed off. Her vintage puff-sleeved, cherry-adorned white blouse and A-line, knee-length denim skirt with big red buttons and red top-stitched pockets were crumpled. Like every other woman under the age of forty who worked in her building, she was wearing white one-strap Birkenstocks bought from the shop on Neal Street.

'Always so laden down,' he said, relieving Jenny of her ubiquitous and bulging Daunts Books tote bag, which was full of proofs and manuscripts. 'Are you walking home? Still in Kentish Town?'

'Yes and yes.'

'Want some company?' he asked tentatively as if he wasn't at all sure of her answer, that she'd ceased to be the most predictable person he knew.

Jenny had told Nick that he was to walk past her if he ever saw her. But she'd been the one to seek him out because today was extraordinary just like that other day, which had briefly brought them together. The memories of that day, that night, the fall-out afterwards, should have been a warning . . .

Jenny shrugged. 'Why not? I'm basically walking in a straight line from Tottenham Court Road until I get home but are you still in Stoke Newington? You need to walk down to Theobalds Road then head towards Islington.'

It was Nick's turn to shrug. 'I know how to get home, Jen. Let's walk together for a while.' He hefted up her tote bag. 'Christ, this thing weighs a ton. It's a miracle that you haven't worn a groove into one of your shoulders.'

He was already a few steps past Jenny with two exclusive 'first look' manuscripts as hostage. She quickly caught up with him. 'Now that you mention it, I have been to see an osteopath. He suggested that I get a backpack.'

'You're really not a backpack kind of person,' Nick said as they walked back along Hanway Street.

'I really am not,' Jenny agreed and if this was how it was going to be, falling back into the light banter of older, happier times, then that was fine. In fact, it was just what she needed.

Jenny thought she knew London, her London. She'd seen the city in so many different iterations. In the early morning, when the sun was still edging up over the gasometers at Mill Hill East, and she felt like the only person awake. Late at night, Piccadilly Circus, waiting for a night bus that wouldn't come and shivering in silly, skimpy dresses while cadging fags off the rent boys who used to congregate there. She'd marched down Whitehall with placards protesting Clause 28, the Poll Tax, apartheid in South Africa. She'd stood outside Soho pubs on warm summer evenings with a glass of white wine clutched in a sweaty hand. She'd danced in Finsbury Park to that most London of bands, Madness. She'd cried, laughed and kissed on corners the length and breadth of the city; she knew these streets as well as the cluster of veins on the underside of her wrists but she'd never seen a London like the London she saw on this July afternoon.

There were no buses. Barely any cars. Just people. Hundreds of Londoners walking on the pavements, walking in the road, their faces resigned to the long trudge home, but also determined, resolute that what had happened that morning didn't define London, their home, their story.

What defined you wasn't the thing that had made you falter and fall. What defined you was the way you got back up, put one foot in front of the other and kept on walking.

So Jenny and Nick joined the throng walking down Tottenham Court Road and caught up with each other's lives, steering clear of anything more personal than career and property. Nick was much more fulfilled at the helm of the music magazine and website he'd launched than the high luxury, high stress world of broadsheet newspapers. 'On the Sunday supplement, I spent half my time being screamed at by the owner for not featuring the houses and gardens of his plutocrat friends and the other half of my time sucking up to advertisers.'

'But you did also get to suck up to models,' Jenny reminded him drily because the unspoken rules of this strange *entente cordiale* meant that she could still gently rib him.

'Not as much as I would have liked,' he said, with a sideways rueful grin that made her nudge him with her elbow. 'You know, I remember you saying that after 9/11, you had to prioritise your happiness and that stuck with me . . .'

Entente cordiale be damned. There was so much history and bad blood between them. Also, guilt. 'I said a lot of things that day. I should have been kinder and it wasn't just about you and I . . .'

'No, Jen, I'm not angry,' Nick said earnestly, which was so unlike him to be earnest and sincere without a glint in his eye and a smirk to show that he was just playing. 'You were right. About everything, really.'

'But I wasn't just angry with you. I can see now that up until then, I'd been living my life in a very selfish way. Making bad decisions, bad choices.' Jenny shook her head.

'Was I one of your bad decisions?' Nick asked, coming to a

stop as they waited for the lights to change so they could cross over Euston Road. It was chaos at University College Hospital, ambulances still queued up outside, a heavy police presence, everyone grim-faced and ashen.

The lights changed and the beep sounded. Jenny turned her attention back to Nick as they walked across the road, forcing herself not to look to the right where, just around the corner, that smashed bus might still be sitting with its innards exposed; people's belongings, their personal items, even remnants of the clothes they were wearing, still strewn about the road, the pavement . . .

'Jesus . . .' she muttered under her breath and Nick put his hand under her elbow. She was perfectly capable of crossing the road by herself and she wasn't about to have a fit of the vapours either but his touch soothed her, anchored her and she was glad of it. She remembered what he'd asked her. 'Not a bad decision, Nick, but I never knew exactly what we were, how to define our relationship, the whole time that we were in each other's lives. That was the problem.'

'I know,' he said softly as he adjusted to Jenny's slower pace. 'Anyway, how about you? I still see your pieces in the *Guardian* and Aaron told me about your swanky new job. Are you drunk on the power?'

'It's very corporate, so many meetings, but I have my own reissues imprint . . .' They covered her new job, the slow redecoration of her flat, Nick's stressful purchase of his own flat in Stoke Newington and the new roof that it had needed, which took them to Camden Town. Rather than walking along the High Street, scene of so many of their younger, Bacchanalian nights out, they nipped down Bayham Street, which ran parallel.

'I now know what flaunching is,' Nick said as he told Jenny about his formerly leaking roof, which, to be honest, wasn't that interesting. 'It's knowledge that I never wanted and, quite frankly, I resent it.'

Jenny was just about to ask him what flaunching was, to show willing, when they were waylaid by an elderly women standing outside the front door of one of the short, squat council blocks, which lined a section of the street.

'Here you are, my loves!' she called out, beckoning with a clawed, arthritic hand as they drew level. 'Can you help me?'

'What's the matter?' Jenny asked, moving close enough that she could see the woman's skin was tinged yellow, like an old book, her chin all whiskers, her grey hair matted to her head. She was wearing a thin housedress, which had seen better days, better years, with ulcerated legs poking out of the bottom. 'Are you feeling all right?'

'You look like nice people, can you pop across the road for me?'

'What do you need?' Nick asked and the woman thrust her hand nearer, so that Jenny could see she was clutching a five-pound note.

'Can you get me twenty Rothman and a packet of bourbons?' came the request and, as a fervent ex-smoker, 'poacher turned gamekeeper', Kirsty always said, Jenny didn't really feel like she should enable someone else's nicotine habit but then again, she didn't really feel like she could say no either. Or make this woman get her own cigarettes on her own painful-looking legs.

'I'll go,' Nick said, dropping Jenny's tote bag with evident relief and holding up his hand when the woman tried to thrust the fiver at him. 'No, I'll get it. My treat.'

'What a nice young man,' the woman said, as they both watched Nick dart across the road. 'You married?'

'Old friends,' Jenny said automatically and when Nick got back she'd tell him that it was silly to walk her all the way to

Kentish Town when he had his own long walk home to do. That it had been wonderful to see him but they'd had an agreement and . . .

'So, what's been going on today, then? I've never heard so many sirens. Something happened, has it?'

Jenny turned to the woman, her face incredulous. They were less than a mile away from where a suicide bomber had blown up a bus with everyone on it. 'You haven't seen the news?'

'I only watch my soaps.' The woman had small currant eyes, which were peering myopically at Jenny. 'What's happened then?'

Nick came back with cigarettes and biscuits as Jenny was getting to the end of her bleak news bulletin, punctuated by a Greek chorus of 'well I never' and 'bleeding hell'.

'. . . and so that's why we're walking home,' Jenny concluded, as the woman snatched a cigarette out of the packet and fumbled in the pocket of her dress for her lighter. 'It's awful. Just awful.'

She'd held it together all day. Had to. But now she sniffed and opened her eyes extra wide in a futile attempt to stop the inevitable.

'Oh my God,' the woman said, breathing out a plume of smoke like a fierce little dragon. 'That Al Qaeda, he wants shooting, he does.'

Instead of a sob, a shocked giggle leaked out of Jenny's mouth. Then another and another, until she was bent over double, laughing.

'It's been a very emotional day,' she heard Nick say. 'I feel like crying myself.'

'I'm not crying, I'm laughing,' Jenny wanted to say but then she realised that she was crying. Weeping, really, holding her ribs like they hurt as tears streamed down her face.

'How could they? Here? In London, *our* city. All those people, those poor, poor people . . .'

She was gathered up by the old lady in a ripe, Rothman-scented hug. 'Oh my darling, we'll be all right. We've got grit in us. We've been blown up before and it was by a better class of bastard than this.'

Jenny was still crying when Nick led her away, his hand in hers. 'She's right, you know,' he said. 'We've survived worse.'

'I didn't think my heart could break again.' She stopped dead in the middle of the pavement. This had been nice. It had been lovely. To see Nick again. To be with him. But it wasn't real. It was never real. But while it lasted . . . 'I don't think . . .'

'What were you doing there, Jen? Outside my office? Was it just a coincidence?'

'It was a coincidence in that I looked up your address and once I'd checked you were still alive, I was going to be on my way,' Jenny admitted, her smile weak, her eyes still teary. 'You didn't reply to my messages. I had to know you were okay.'

Nick's expression was . . . quite forbidding, his eyes wary like he didn't trust what she was saying. Then he shook his head as if he were clearing away the cobwebs. 'Let's sit down.'

30

July 7th, 2005
Camden Town Station

Nick took Jenny's elbow again to guide her across Camden Road to Camden Town station. Its metal grilles were closed and locked tight and so Jenny could sit, or collapse really, on the steps that would normally be teeming with people coming and going.

'I know I was pretty clear last time we spoke that we should just call it quits . . .' Her voice was nasal with tears, her heart not so broken that it couldn't beat out a frantic rhythm. 'But I've been worried about you all day.'

'This morning, before it all kicked off with our missing software guy, I was going spare not knowing what had happened to you,' Nick said, sitting down next to Jenny so he could take her hand and turn it palm side up to trace her life line. 'I couldn't get through on your mobile and I didn't have your work email. I even thought about calling your parents.'

'Like you could even remember the number,' Jenny sniffed.

'Nine five nine six three one four,' Nick reeled off. 'I can only remember four numbers off by heart. My parents' number, my phone number, my local Chinese and your parents' number because I rang it so many times when we were at college. Jen, I can't even remember my own mobile number.'

'And then I texted you . . .' Jenny said slowly.

397

'Emailed me too, it turns out, like you really did care about me.'

'Of course I care about you! I wanted to know that you weren't, like, *dead*. I'm not a monster . . .'

'And when I found you waiting outside my offices, you smiled and walked straight into my arms. Like you were pleased to see me and didn't have any immediate plans to shoot me down and break my heart again.'

'What do you mean *again*?'

'I can't believe that you've forgotten about the time you broke my heart on a subway platform in New York,' Nick said and Jenny sucked in a breath because it had been her heart that was broken, but Nick wasn't finished. 'I was lying before when I said I wasn't angry with you. Because, actually, I'm fucking furious with you. Have been for a couple of years now.'

He lowered his head to press a kiss to the underside of Jenny's wrist where her pulse was thundering away like a jack-hammer. It was a soft, tender gesture so at odds with what he'd just said.

'Why are you furious with me?' Jenny asked with a dread that interrupted her selfish hoarding of the minutes that they were spending together. 'I haven't done anything!'

'Precisely. You haven't done anything. That Christmas Eve at Mill Hill East, you cracked open a window, Jen. It gave me just enough hope,' Nick said softly, 'to see you that day, to sit with you . . . but then nothing. You slammed the door shut in my face again.'

'I thought it was for the best,' Jenny muttered, because four years ago in New York she'd been convinced she could be someone else. A someone else who might one day be able to stop loving him. 'I thought we needed to get on with our separate lives, without always complicating things for each other. It was never the right time for us. Other things, other people, even our own selves always got in the way.'

'Which is why I've spent the last four years getting my house in order. Quite literally. I've explained about the flaunching, haven't I?'

Jen nodded, but she didn't dare speak, so desperate was she to hear the next words out of his mouth.

'I quit smoking. I even got a pension plan that I don't actually understand.'

'You got a pension plan?'

'I did,' Nick confirmed but he didn't seem that happy about it. 'I did all these things because you telling me that I needed to grow up finally knocked some sense into me.'

'I wanted you to be happy, Nick,' Jenny said, her fingers entwining with his because it felt so good to touch him once again. 'I will always want you to be happy and well . . .'

'I did all these things to make myself worthy of you and that Christmas Eve came and then you merrily carried on without me,' he said bitterly and he tried to pull his hand away but Jenny clung on tightly.

'I didn't do that to be cruel. I really thought we'd be better off without each other,' she tried to explain but putting it into words, sounding them out loud, on this particular day, made her realise that her actions could have been interpreted as petty, even childish.

'I realised then I was chasing a phantom. Pinning all my happiness, my future, on a woman who I've known for over half my life who's never once told me that she loved me,' Nick said softly as Jenny stared at him aghast, a fresh wave of tears about to start their journey down her face.

'Don't be ridiculous,' she said, because she'd been in love with him for nearly twenty years, often against her better judgement. 'Of course I have.'

'Not once,' Nick repeated.

'That New Year's Eve at Chalk Farm!'

'No, I told you that I loved you and you insisted that I didn't.'

That wasn't how Jenny remembered it. 'What about New York? I definitely said it in New York.'

'The closest you came was saying that you loved it when I put you on your hands and knees . . .'

'I'm sure I said it back then,' Jenny insisted, her face burning up not just from Nick's relentless gaze and recall of all the times when she was *absolutely positive* that she'd confessed her love, but because she was suddenly assaulted by the memory of the exact moment that Nick had been referring to.

'What about that time on the Circle Line . . . ?' Jenny asked hopefully though actually she was pretty sure that she *hadn't* said it then. And now that she thought about it, really thought about it, had she ever told the man who she always thought of as not just the one who got away, but the love of her life, that he *was* the love of her life?

'Not then,' Nick confirmed. He finally looked away. 'You still can't say it, can you?'

Suddenly it was the easiest thing in the world to blurt out in a voice croaky with tears, 'But I do love you, I always have. I came to you today . . .'

'It's not enough, Jen. It's too little, too late,' Nick said sadly. 'That's the thing about growing up, you realise when something, someone, is a lost cause.'

Then Jenny couldn't say anything because she was crying too hard to speak. Her vision was blurred, but she heard Nick sniff and wondered if he was crying too.

It couldn't be too late. There had to have been an instance when she'd said it. Jenny looked up at the familiar station façade and wondered why it was always Camden Town that was destined to be the scene of her greatest humiliations. Like her eighteenth birthday when they'd had that awful row just a few metres from where they were now sitting.

Had she said it then? No, she'd confessed, under duress, that she fancied him, which at eighteen amounted to telling someone that you loved them. She wondered if that might count, but then she remembered something else that had happened that night.

Jenny reached into her bag and pulled out her purse.

Nick sighed. 'Look, I'm sorry, Jen, but . . .'

'No . . . don't say anything. Just wait.' They were there, nestling next to a few dollar bills and euro notes, because she still kept them in her foreign money compartment. Jenny pulled out the strip of photos they'd taken at Mill Hill East station. 'I might not have said it, but I've carried these around with me for the last seventeen years. One time, my purse got nicked in a pub and I went back later that night and I searched every fucking bin until I found the purse, minus my credit cards, because these photos, they are the most precious thing I own . . .' Her voice cracked again.

Nick took them from her and let out a breath. 'Wow! I'd forgotten all about these. I don't think you ever let me see the finished results.'

Jenny put a shaky finger on the bottom photo of the strip. Nineteen-year-old Nick kissing eighteen-year-old Jen on the cheek, her eyes cast to the heavens, joy radiating from her every open pore. 'Look at that then tell me that I don't love you, that I've never loved you. Can't you see that it's written all over my face? I loved you then and I loved you in between and I still love you now.'

His face was impassive as he stared down at the photos. Jenny waited for him to say something but he was silent for long enough that it crushed what was left of her hopes and dreams. She cringed at what she had to ask. 'Do you still love me?'

For a moment, he didn't move but then he leaned forward to kiss her. It wasn't like their usual forceful, frenetic first kisses. Nick's mouth was moving on hers slowly, gently, and Jenny kissed him back, even though it felt like goodbye. *I can live without Nick Levene*, she decided, because she always lied to herself when he kissed her. She wanted one more kiss to keep in her memory box. A kiss that she'd carefully unwrap on those dark days when she was paralysed by the past and needed to bask in the warmth of better times.

When Nick let her go, or rather he had to push her back because she didn't want to lose the feeling of his lips caressing her, Jenny moaned in protest. A tiny whimper, which she knew she'd be mortified by when she played this back.

'You don't love me then?' She wished the words back as soon as she said them because she didn't want to know the answer.

Nick was still silent but he brought her hand to his mouth and peppered her taut knuckles with kisses, his eyes fixed on her tear-stained face.

'Just say that you don't love me,' she said, turning her head away so she wouldn't have to see his pitying expression.

'Will you look at me? Jen!'

She never could resist that dark, commanding tone that he'd get. She looked at him and he'd never looked at her like that before; his face was stripped back, pared back, his eyes full of longing but uncertainty too.

'Why are you torturing me? Just tell me!' She didn't have the energy for this. Even if he said that he did still love her, what would it actually amount to? A few weeks, maybe months, of fucking each other and then they would implode like they always did and she couldn't keep putting herself back together.

'Of course I still love you. I don't know how to stop,' Nick said, but he didn't sound very happy about it. 'I love your good bits and the filthy X-rated bits and the messy bits and the bit of you that is so ridiculously, unnecessarily picky that I used to fucking dread going to a restaurant with you.' Nick held his hands wide so Jenny could see that this wasn't a sleight of hand, he wasn't hiding anything, or even crossing his fingers behind his back. 'It wasn't until I didn't have you at all, that I knew I needed all of you.'

'So, can we finally have that affair we've been almost having for the last twenty years?' Jenny asked, because every part of her, apart from her stupid, logical head, would love to have an affair with him. Even when it ended. Even when he broke *her* heart all over again.

'I don't want to have an affair with you,' Nick said sharply.

'Then what? Friends again? Friends with benefits?'

'You just don't get it, Jen. Christ, you have two degrees and you still don't get it.'

'Get what?' Jenny asked in exasperation.

Nick glared at her. 'I don't want to be your friend.' His features softened. 'I want to be your everything.'

And just like that, Jenny went from despair to getting the whole world handed to her. 'You want everything?' she repeated and who could blame her for sounding so sceptical, but nineteen years of loving someone in secret would do that to a girl.

Nick nodded. 'Everything. I'm in. I'm all in. Do I need to have it tattooed across my chest?'

'I don't think that will be necessary ... Oh, Nick ...' She was close to tears again, beyond words; Nick too, because they sat there for long moments, fingers entwined, foreheads pressed together. It seemed to Jenny that even their ragged breaths were in perfect time.

The mood was temporarily broken by the jangle of keys and they broke apart to look behind them and see a TfL worker peering out through the locked grille at them. 'We're not opening today,' he said. 'No matter how long you sit there.'

'Sorry. Just taking a breather,' Jenny said. 'We'll be gone in a minute.'

'Actually we're declaring our undying love for each other so we might be here a while,' Nick countered and Jenny couldn't help but lean in for another kiss.

'As you were,' the man said and with one more jangle of his keys, he was gone and Jenny was free to stroke the back of her hand down Nick's cheek, because she could do that now.

'You're really all in?' she checked again. 'We're really going to do this?'

'We *have* to do this,' Nick confirmed, pressing a kiss to her palm.

'I've thought about this a lot,' Jenny admitted. 'Even when it seemed impossible that we'd even be in the same room together again. We've come so far, been through so much, behaved like such a pair of idiots that we have to agree that we're not going to throw in the towel the first time we have a fight.'

'We will fight,' Nick agreed. 'We love a good row, don't we?'

'We live for it, but if we're going to do this, then we have to make a pact that we're not going to fall apart after we argue about . . . I don't know, pizza toppings or . . .'

'Or you buying yet another copy of a book you already own . . .'

'Or you playing Lou Reed's *Metal Machine Music* on a loop like you did that one summer . . .'

'Or being unable to agree on which school we're going to send the kids to.'

'Kids?' Jenny choked on the word because she was

unequivocally yes on having children now, but she'd never expected . . . with Nick. 'You want to have a family with me?'

He nodded. 'I told you I want everything, Jen. I'm all in. How about you?'

She could feel hope battering down the last section of wall that she'd built around her heart. 'I'm so in. Completely and utterly in.'

Nick smiled. 'OK, then.'

Jenny folded her arms and smiled too. 'OK.' She leaned in for yet another kiss, though it wouldn't be a last kiss this time. There were going to be so many more kisses to come. 'Let's do this.'

EPILOGUE

A Saturday in summer, 2021
Northern Line (Edgware Branch)

She hadn't been on a tube train for over a year. Which seemed unthinkable but there had been so many unthinkable things that had happened over the last eighteen months and she'd somehow got used to thinking about them. Trying her best just to get through them.

It had been the twenty-first of March, last year, a Saturday evening. They'd known they were going into full lockdown on the Monday so she and Kirsty had decided to have one last hurrah. Meeting up at their favourite Italian restaurant in Clapham, which was roughly equidistant between their two homes, because Kirsty and Erik still wouldn't see reason and still lived in New Cross.

They'd sat close together, water droplets flying; nobody knew it was an airborne virus then, as they chatted and laughed but they hadn't hugged goodbye, just bumped elbows.

'Don't forget to wash your hands when you get home!' Kirsty had shouted when they parted ways at the bottom of the escalator. Now, Kirsty had done what she'd been threatening to do for years and moved back north. She and Erik and their miraculous, precious eleven-year-old Freja had swapped a cramped, terraced two up and two down in New Cross for a huge, mortgage-free, 1920s detached house in Lytham St Annes with sea views and one and a half acres of garden. With a pantry. There were few things in life that she coveted more than that pantry.

Still, she loved her own very much mortgaged, tall, skinny house in King's Cross, in a Grade 2 listed cobblestoned terrace at the southernmost tip of the Caledonian Road. 'Just off the Cally,' was how her neighbours described their location but she would always say, a little proudly, 'We *literally* live next door to King's Cross.' They'd bought it for a song, because it needed a complete renovation and who the hell wanted to live in King's Cross in 2007?

'You'll have prostitutes on your doorstep,' Jackie had warned repeatedly. 'Prostitutes and pimps and drug dealers.'

But the rehabilitation of King's Cross had already been underway, ever up since the Eurostar terminal had opened and in the subsequent years, King's Cross had continued to come up in the world. It was fancy. Before the pandemic, friends had called round so they could spend an afternoon browsing the shops at St Pancras. Then it was the shortest stroll over to Granary Square and Coal Drops Yard with its trendy restaurants and minimalist shops. The *Guardian* was there, Central St Martins had moved from Soho and, even better, there was a very large Waitrose. Everything was on their doorstep.

She looked down at the ubiquitous, bulging tote bag on her lap. Not from Daunts but from her very own bookshop in Bloomsbury. It was a twenty-minute walk from her front door to Austen & Company (named in tribute to the famous English language bookshop in Paris, Shakespeare and Company), where she sold new books but had a backroom dedicated solely to second-hand Penguin Classics. In the office behind that was the nerve centre of Austen & Company's publishing arm, which reissued one out of print book every month in a beautifully designed clothbound cover.

That shop in Lamb's Conduit Street and all it contained was one of her proudest achievements.

'Jen, should we tell them to stop behaving like savages?' asked Nick, nudging her arm, as they sat side by side in the almost empty tube carriage.

Jenny looked past him to where her two actual proudest achievements were trying to do pull-ups on the metal bar in front of the doors. 'Let's pretend they're not with us,' she decided.

'Sounds like a plan. In fact, we could duck out at Colindale and leave them to fend for themselves.'

'I'm not skipping out on our cake supplier,' Jenny said, tapping her tote bag, which contained several large Tupperware containers full of brownies, traybakes and biscuits, courtesy of Stan who'd been born exactly two minutes before his younger brother, Louis. Named for their respective maternal grandfathers, (though Jenny suspected that Louis was also named after Lou Reed from The Velvet Underground). Stan had coped with the pandemic by learning to bake and Louis had coped by filming the bakes and uploading them to TikTok. Nick had also taught Stan how to mix the perfect gin and tonic, but Jen had forbidden Louis from uploading any of that footage, in case Social Services got involved.

Ordinarily, they'd have been less indulgent of their sons' antics. But today was the day that everything went back to normal. London, and the suburbs, the high streets, the green spaces beyond, picked itself up, dusted down its skirts. Its habitants no longer needed to bubble, obey the rule of six, keep two metres apart from the people they loved or only see their faces on a screen. Besides, the tube was practically deserted so who cared if the boys were a little over-exuberant? If she'd had any upper body strength, Jenny would have been hanging from the bar herself.

They were on their way to the little 'Tudorbethan' house where Jenny had grown up. To reunite with her brothers, her sisters-in-law, Stan and Louis's adored cousins whom they hadn't seen for months. And they were finally allowed to see Dot, who was pushing ninety-five and a 'little doddery on the pins but I've still got all my marbles, thank you very much.' Not even the Queen had been as cosseted, shielded and protected as Jenny's grandmother. As it was, everyone in the family had been double-jabbed and Jenny had made the four of them take lateral flow Covid tests every day for the last two weeks. En masse, the Richards clan were going to celebrate every birthday (including Jenny's fiftieth, though some days she still felt seventeen and other days she felt like she was pushing ninety), every anniversary, the Christmas and the two Easters that they'd missed.

Just thinking of seeing her parents, of finally being able to *hug* them, the happy little sound that Jackie always made when Jenny's arms closed tight around her, was enough to make Jenny's eyes smart . . .

'You're not crying already, are you?'

'I'm *not* crying,' Jenny insisted. 'I'm just contemplating the tears I *might* shed. I haven't hugged anyone but you for over a year.'

The boys wouldn't let her hug them anymore. They were thirteen after all. Occasionally, they'd lean *on* her, in much the same way as Hector, George's grumpy pug, used to, but that was hardly the same.

'It won't be the hugging that will make you cry. What will make you cry is when Alan clocks you in your very on-trend jumpsuit and asks if you've come to service the boiler. Then you'll cry,' Nick said because he knew her better than anyone. 'My dad jokes don't even come close.'

'Although your dad jokes are pretty bad,' Jenny reminded him because in the biggest plot twist of all, Nick Levene, pretentious, unreliable, wicked Nick Levene, had turned out to be an exemplary dad. The king of all the dads. But before the twins had changed everything, she and Nick had had so much lost time to make up.

Their first year together had been the happiest year of Jenny's life. Apart from when they were at work, she and Nick had spent every waking moment together. It was like being teenagers again except now they had disposable income, no parental supervision and could have as much sex as they liked.

Within a year, they'd sold both their flats and bought the house in King's Cross. Six months after that, they'd tied the knot at Camden Registry Office then honeymooned in Brighton. And a year after that when the house was as done up as they could afford and they *at last* had hot water, they'd agreed that Jenny would stop taking the pill just to see what might happen.

What happened was that she was pregnant with twins within two months. Which had been shocking because they'd both conveniently forgotten that twins ran on both sides of their families. And it had caused a rift with Kirsty who'd been on her fifth unsuccessful round of IVF. But it was Kirsty who walked behind with Nick as Jenny waddled slowly up the Euston Road to University College Hospital for her planned C-section because she was an 'elderly primigravida' whose in utero twins hadn't got the memo that they were both meant to be on the small side.

If their first year together had been happy, then the first year with the twins had been exhilarating, exhausting and also, as she later admitted to Nick, so tedious that there were times she wanted to start screaming and never stop. Jenny loved the boys with a fierceness that felt like it had been forged from the depths of her soul but she also felt as if she'd lost herself. She'd taken a full year of maternity leave but wasn't sure how she could go back to work now they had to find the money for two lots of childcare or a full-time nanny, when Nick stepped up.

'You've done a year, now I'll do a year,' he told Jenny, when Susan offered to step into the breach, though she was still recovering from her first bout of breast cancer. 'I'll go freelance.'

Jenny had pointed out that he wasn't going to get much freelance work done in between twin-wrangling but Nick had taken to full-time parenting much better than Jenny had. He was all in again. Happy to chase after two rambunctious little boys who were into everything once they started walking. When Nick's year was up, he established a potted, portfolio career around nap time, Tuneful Tots, Baby Gymboree and the two days a week they had a nanny share. And on Wednesday mornings, accompanied by George who'd moved back from New York, they'd go to baby swim classes at the YMCA in Great Russell Street, which was a wholesome change from what the pair of them used to get up to when they were last both living in London.

Jenny hoped that she was a better, happier mother for going back to work, where she was creatively fulfilled so that when she came home, she could be present. It wasn't until Stan and Louis were ready to start primary school, that she and Nick swapped again. He'd pitched a documentary series to a TV production company on the history of indie music, never expecting it to be greenlighted. Then he spent the next year travelling from Glasgow to New York to Manchester to Seattle and all points in between.

It was Jenny's turn to go freelance, and there was no shortage of work, but one day after dropping off the twins at school in Bloomsbury, she'd popped into a local bookshop and got chatting to the owner, who was retiring and wanted someone to take over the lease. 'It's a silly idea,' she'd said to Nick who was working on his production notes in a hotel room in Boston, where he was interviewing Black Francis from Pixies the next day. 'But I loved being a bookseller and I've been working in publishing so long . . . there's not many new challenges left. We'd have to break into our savings . . .'

'Do you really want to do this, Jen?' Nick asked and after Jenny had spent the next ten minutes explaining how the bookshop was currently very badly run and just how she'd improve it, he said, 'Well, if you're in, then I'm in.'

Back when they were at college, Jenny had the notion that her career would mean going to an office every day between the hours of nine and six, for the rest of her working life. That was what Alan did. But the world of work was changing. Nick's industry had been absolutely decimated by the internet, there were no new magazines launching and the ones that were still around were on life support. It made sense that Nick would have to diversify, which is why on his Twitter bio, it now said, 'Writer, broadcaster, podcaster, producer. Having pretentious opinions since 1986.' While Jenny described herself as a 'bookseller, publisher, editorial consultant, arts journalist and possessor of many books, approximately 47 per cent of them currently unread' on Austen & Company's website.

In between times, they raised the boys in their tall, skinny house, which was stuffed full of books and records and interesting people always popping around. Jenny would have loved to have grown up in such bohemian surroundings but Stan and Louis were both largely unimpressed that Johnny Marr might be in their kitchen recording a podcast with Nick or that Jilly Cooper was coming round for tea. 'They'd better not eat all the nice biscuits,' was their usual complaint.

Then Covid had happened and everything stopped. It felt to Jenny as if she and Nick had been in a frenetic, forward motion ever since that moment when they'd sat on the steps of Camden Town station. Now, they had to pause, were forced to take stock, and spend day after day, hour after hour, the four of them in a narrow house in central London with no back garden, just a strip of paved terrace. When Jenny had taken the boys on a walk to the nearest park, Coram Fields, they'd been stopped by an over-zealous policeman and asked if their journey was strictly necessary.

Jenny had thought that she'd already seen London at her most glorious, and also London at her most wretched, but this past year, she'd seen a London completely unlike the city she'd lived in for her entire life.

Euston Road, that choked artery running from Marylebone to King's Cross, silent, still and devoid of traffic. The museums, art galleries, theatres and, even more devastatingly, the bookshops and libraries where she always found solace and new friends, all shuttered. The days punctuated by the constant shriek of sirens. It was like the city's beating heart had slowed to a barely discernible rhythm.

It had been a tough year and a bit. Jenny had been desperately trying to save the shop and her staff's jobs, supervise the boys' homeschooling and spend hours on the Ocado website trying to book her parents a weekly slot. It had been tougher still for Nick. They'd lost Susan to cancer at the start of the first lock-down and his father to Covid a few months after that. He'd always had a difficult, diffident relationship with his parents, though they'd been the most doting and indulgent of grand-parents, and he'd grieved quietly, almost as if he felt that he didn't have the right to grieve them at all.

Their house had felt too small, unable to contain Jenny's panic, Nick's sadness, the boys' constant and combative arguments with no space even to kick a ball around or burn off the big, ugly feelings that they didn't know how to handle.

And underpinning it all, a dread that increased exponentially with every day, as Jenny doomscrolled and watched in horror the news reports from swathed hospital wards, beds full of people gasping for each breath.

Instead of coming together, they'd all retreated. Stan to the kitchen with a truly alarming sourdough starter, which needed almost full-time care. Louis to his room to play Fortnite, his face permanently illuminated by a glowing screen. Nick to his office at the top of the house, and Jenny to their bedroom with a large gin and tonic. Sometimes she'd lie on the floor and cry silently, hopelessly, because her precious family was changing shape into something twisted and gnarled and she was scared that it would stay that way permanently.

It hadn't. Nothing to do with an easing of restrictions or coming out of lockdown, though she and Nick had gone out for a champagne brunch to celebrate the day the boys went back to school. But before that, at the tail-end of the second, mini-lockdown, one afternoon while decluttering, because what else was there to do, in an old handbag Jenny had found the strip of photos taken on her eighteenth birthday at the photo booth in Mill Hill East station.

She'd climbed up the stairs to Nick's office. When the door was shut, it meant that he wasn't to be disturbed, but she'd knocked gently and pushed the door open without waiting to be granted admittance.

He was hunched over his desk, his laptop screen, and didn't even look around. Didn't even snap at her to get out like he'd used to do. Jenny had come up behind him and placed the strip of photos on the desk in front of him. Had tried to ignore the hurt that pierced through her when she placed a hand on his shoulder and he flinched at her touch.

'I've known you thirty-three years, Nick. That's two thirds of my life. I'm your family, I love you and I know that you're sad,

I know that you're mourning, but don't shut me out because I really, really miss you,' she'd said. 'I'm still all in. Are you?'

She'd thought that maybe she needed to say more than that, but he'd shifted his chair, pulled her onto his lap and buried his face in her neck, damping her skin with his tears. 'Always.'

After that, there had still been rows about screen time and playing Roblox instead of completing their maths assignments, but they sat down together to eat dinner every night and Nick had made them spend the evenings, the four of them, watching boxed sets and playing board games. He'd led the way back to some semblance of how they used to be, because it was Nick who would always be the heart of their family.

For her birthday that year, the big five-o, he'd had that strip of photos expertly restored, blown up and framed. It now hung in the hall just outside their bedroom door.

Now, the train came hurtling out of the tunnel just before Colindale station. Hendon Police College had been completely refurbished and rebuilt. The assault course was no more and there was no chance of seeing plucky police cadets scrambling up walls and through netting. Another thing that Jenny missed.

She sighed and turned to look at her sons who had abandoned the pull-ups in favour of sitting. Somehow, more by accident than design, she and Nick had managed to raise two sons who were kind, open-hearted, accepting, passionate about the things they loved and also had what they called 'good bants'. They'd inherited a lot of the Levene genes, apart from their blue eyes, hatred of vegetables and fondness for stomping upstairs and slamming doors, which was all Jenny's DNA. They both had dark, curly hair, long legs sprawled out, their already enormous feet clad in boxy fluorescent trainers, which they'd probably outgrow by the end of next week. Though they weren't identical, they both wore the same smile, Nick's smile, as they looked at something on Stan's phone, voices low, their faces just a bare suggestion of the people they'd become.

As if they were aware of her scrutiny, they both turned to look at her, with plaintive expressions. 'Mum?' How was it they could make that three-letter word sound like it contained several syllables? 'Can we get an Uber from the station?'

Jenny stared Stan down, because he was the official spokesperson for the pair of them, while Louis was the ideas man, and even though half her face was obscured by her mask, he knew what that look in her eyes meant. 'Yeah, nice try. You know we're getting the bus.'

'Or we can walk,' Nick added. 'It's your choice.'

If there'd been anyone else in the carriage with them, they'd have witnessed this exchange, looked at Jenny in her Boden denim jumpsuit and Dunlop Green Flashes with her bookshop tote, and Nick with his greying mop of hair and his Paul Smith dinosaur T-shirt and man bag and imagine that they were the worst kind of smug, middle-aged, middle-class parents.

Maybe they were. But she and Nick, they also contained multitudes.

Jenny turned to look at Nick. Though half his face was obscured by his mask, she could see the lines and furrows carved into his face that never used to be there. He still had that glorious tumble of hair but it was streaked through with huge swathes of grey now. She'd always be able to see echoes of that seventeen-year-old boy though who'd danced with her at the last ever Smiths concert.

'This takes me back. You and me on an Edgware-bound train,' Nick said as if he could read her mind, a glint in his eyes. 'I feel like we're travelling backwards in time and when we get to Edgware, my dad'll be waiting to give us a lift in his top of the range Volvo Estate.'

'Darling . . .' Jenny put her hand on his arm.

'No, I'm not sad, I'm just thinking about that night . . . the last Smiths gig at Brixton Academy.' She could tell he was grinning. 'Technically, our first date.'

'I appreciate the sentiment but it was really not our first date. You didn't even buy me a drink!'

'I would have if I'd known that the sulky, melodramatic girl I'd got stuck with would end up being the beat of my heart,' Nick said softly and even though it was an almost unbeliev-able thirty-five years since *technically* their first date, he could still melt Jenny with just one sentence. She felt giddy and sixteen again even though somehow she was fifty and had a Tupperware drawer and a pair of reading glasses that she kept on a chain around her neck so she didn't lose them.

'And if only I'd known that the pretentious, up-himself boy who acted like I was a major pain in his arse would end up being my one true love . . .' she tailed off because on some level, even at sixteen, there was a part of her that had known that they were meant only for each other.

'Do you wish that we had got together then and stayed together?' Nick asked, taking Jenny's hand and rubbing his thumb against the platinum band that she'd only ever taken off when she was pregnant with the twins and had swelled up like the Michelin Man.

Jenny thought back to their teen selves. Thought about all the very specific ways they'd hurt each other. About the other men she'd loved. The different versions of herself she'd been and finally, she glanced again at Stan and Louis who were still riveted by their phone screens. 'No,' she said firmly. 'Because if we'd got together then we wouldn't have this exact life that we have now.'

'Do you love the exact life we have now then?' He threaded his fingers through hers.

'This exact life of ours is more than I dared to imagine,' Jenny said gently, just as the train pulled into Burnt Oak station and the doors opened allowing fresh air to circulate through the carriage so that Nick could pull down their masks.

After so many years together, he knew how to devastate her with a kiss that wouldn't smudge her red lipstick.

'Oh my God, those two are *so* cringe,' she heard Louis mutter as the doors closed.

Jenny nuzzled into Nick just long enough to whisper, 'I love you,' in his ear and for him to tighten his fingers around hers before they pulled their masks up again.

They held hands until the end of the line.

Acknowledgements

Thanks to Rebecca Ritchie, the most encouraging, unflappable and diplomatic agent any writer could ever want. Also, Alexandra McNicoll, Vickie Dillon, Prema Raj, Mairi Friesen-Escandell and all at AM Heath.

To Kimberley Atkins for falling in love with my hero even more than I did and making this book ten times better than it was, Amy Batley who handheld me through a traumatic editing process, Katy Blott, Swati Gamble and all at Hodder.

To Kirsty Connor who has been such a long-time supporter of my books, so much so that I'm always half-dreading Kirsty's reaction to a new novel in case I've failed to delight her. This is why I was thrilled that Kirsty provided the winning bid to have a character named after her in the Books To Nourish auction, which raised money for FareShare, the UK's longest running food redistribution charity. Kirsty, I really hope fictional Kirsty doesn't disappoint.

To my doorstep drive-by friends, Sarah Bailey, Cari Rosen and Eileen Coulter who fed my soul and also fed me cake and chocolate.

To my writer friends who kept me going through shielding, doomscrolling and ALL the lockdowns with Zooms, Tom

Hiddleston gifs and the constant ping of WhatsApp messages: Jenny Ashcroft, Kate Reardon, Katherine Webb, Cesca Major, Claire McGlasson, Lucy Foley, Iona Grey, Harriet Evans, Jane Casey and Anna Carey.

And to Jacqui Johnson and Kate Hodges, who I used to behave very badly with during our wilder, younger years.

Reading Group Questions

1. The book begins with a quote from Virginia Woolf about London:

   'The streets of London have their map, but our passions are uncharted. What are you going to meet if you turn this corner?'

   What role does London play in the lives of Jennifer and Nick? What is the significance of the city and what does it come to represent for them?

2. Both Jennifer and Nick have relationships with other people throughout the book – do any of these people stand out to you and why? Might any of them have been better suited to our main characters?

3. The novel spans 35 years – how are the changes in society and culture during this period of time captured in the story?

4. Throughout the novel, Jennifer is known by different versions of her name (Jennifer/Jen/Jenny). What do you think she hopes to achieve by this and is she successful? How does her choice of name affect her identity?

5. Throughout the novel both Jennifer and Nick are guilty of supressing their feelings (not just regarding one another) – do you think one of them is more guilty than the other of doing this? And what are the consequences?

6. Several real-world events are covered in the story (including Princess Diana's death, the new millennium and 9/11). Discuss the portrayal of these events in the novel and the impact they have on Jennifer and Nick.

7. 'Do you wish that we had got together then and stayed together?'

   This is the question Nick asks Jennifer at the end of the novel, referring to the night of The Smiths concert when they were sixteen. She responds: 'No . . . Because if we'd got together then we wouldn't have this exact life that we have now.'

   Do you believe this answer? How did you feel about the ending?

8. Discuss how the concept of fate is presented in the novel. Are Jennifer and Nick in charge of their own decisions, or does it feel as though their paths were predestined from the start?